THE CARDINAL VIRTUES

ANDREW M. GREELEY

THE
CARDINAL
VIRTUES

A TOM DOHERTY ASSOCIATES BOOK
New York

THE CARDINAL VIRTUES

Copyright © 1990 by Andrew M. Greeley Enterprises, Ltd.

Originally published by Warner Books

Map by Heidi Hornaday

A Forge Book
Published by Tom Doherty Associates, LLC
175 Fifth Avenue
New York, NY 10010

www.tor-forge.com

Forge® is a registered trademark of Tom Doherty Associates, LLC.

ISBN 978-0-7653-2442-9

First Forge Edition: June 2010

Printed in the United States of America

0 9 8 7 6 5 4 3 2 1

For Father Leo Thomas Mahon,
not exactly Father Lar but
not totally different from him, either

While this story is located in the culture of the archdiocese of Chicago at the present time (1988), none of the characters in the story are based on real men and women. Nor is there any real counterpart of either Saint Finian's parish or the West Side suburb of Forest Springs.

None of the institutions or events of the story are modeled on institutions that actually exist or events that have actually happened. The Society of Corpus Christi exists only in my imagination, though there are real organizations that have as much power and are very little better.

Are there "New Priests" like Jamie Keenan in the Catholic Church today? Sure there are. Not very many perhaps, but as Father Lar says in this story, you don't need more than a few such priests.

Must Christ be crucified in every generation by those with no imagination?

—George Bernard Shaw
Saint Joan

No merely human institution governed by such knavish imbecility would have survived a fortnight.

—Hilaire Belloc

Faith, the Bark of Peter must be divine; otherwise, we boys would have kicked the bottom out long ago.

—Elderly Irish Monsignor

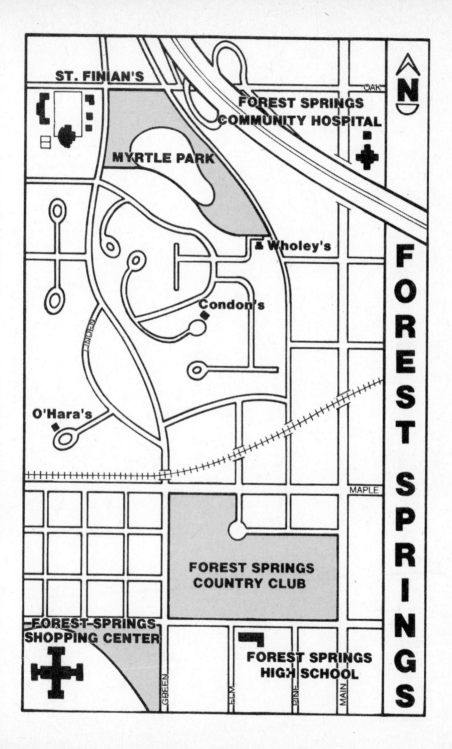

CHAPTER

1

"Father Lar," Jackie shrieked into the phone. "Father New Priest is here!"

With those words, the crisis in my priesthood, already serious, entered its acute phase. Even at that moment I was dimly aware of its onset. I was losing faith in myself, in my parish, in my priesthood, and in God.

"Is Father Keenan cute?" I tried to laugh away my unease. Must not let the troops know I had my doubts about the new priest.

"Awesomely," the red-haired teenage receptionist giggled. "He's fixing the computer!"

"No one can fix the computer." I hung up the phone gently.

Or anything else that is broken in Saint Finian's parish. For us the new technology never works.

I had become a priest to save the world. Now I wanted only to save the people of the world writ small that was my parish. What would happen to me when I lost even that dream?

It's hard to sustain a spiritual dream when so much of your time is devoted to fixing busted machinery.

I sighed, almost as loudly as our West-of-Ireland Cook when none of us had finished our immense helpings of her latest culinary masterpiece. I had been a New Priest once, not awesomely cute perhaps but still filled with enthusiasm and energy and youthful zeal. Now I would need all of the four cardinal virtues—justice, temperance, fortitude, and prudence—to cope with my new associate.

A long time ago I had lots of those four virtues, too.

Well, I had always been a little short on prudence.

"McAuliffe!" shouted the seminary's Prefect of Discipline (in a more modern Church now called the Dean of Men), "you're imprudent!"

"Imprudent or impudent, Father?"

"Both! And that question proves it!"

My hand rested on the phone as I searched for the physical energy to walk down the stairs to greet the New Priest. Long ago I had been a bomb-throwing radical. Then I had become a liberal enthusiast. Now I was a worn-out, angry, disillusioned Old Priest. I was quite incapable of responding to the vitality and zest of someone fresh out of the seminary.

Color me *Mass Appeal.* Well, I wasn't a drunk like the pastor in that play. Not yet, anyway.

Moreover, I could still banter with teenagers like Jackie, I thought as I forced myself out of my chair. That, however, was a genetic trait. I had inherited it from a parent who, before he became a captain, was your all-time all-American genial cop on the beat.

A new priest and the Condon crisis on the same day. Probably a fight with Jeanne Flavin. It never stops. Maybe I could assign him the Condon case. What else are associate pastors for if they don't take your worst problems for you?

Maybe he could cope with my self-defined Stalinist director of religious education. She had already defined him as a rival, a class enemy. Poor woman. A lovely, wounded Stalinist, so pretty and so haunted that she'll break your heart.

I had not wanted a new associate pastor. After twenty-eight years in the priesthood and six years at Saint Finian's, I was confident that I could respond to the religious needs of the People of God (as we call the Church these days) in Forest Springs without an associate pastor.

"No," I said firmly to the chairman of the personnel board when he phoned.

"But, Lar—"

"No," I repeated. "I don't want one and I won't take one. The two residents and I can cope."

"But, Lar—"

The personnel board is not interested in making good appointments. It gave that up long ago. Now it fills slots. Better the old days when the Vice Chancellor was alleged to throw darts at the list of priests to make appointments.

"I said no." I then hung up on him. No more Father Nice Guy. I was tired, and especially tired of new priests.

That was not the end of it. Joe Simon, the Vicar General, called me the next day.

"Lar, what's this I hear about you not taking an associate?"

Joe remembers the days when the VG was the Fourth Person of the Trinity, and tries to talk tough like some of his predecessors did twenty years ago. It doesn't always work, mostly because Joe is an overweight North Side German who oozes political sleaze. He scares quite a few of the older generation of pastors, however.

"You heard right."

"Why?" he snarled, now moving into his supertough mode.

"I've had three associate pastors since I've been here, right?"

"Right."

"Who were they?" I demanded.

"First, there was Tim Kelly," he mumbled.

"Who made passes at all the women on the staff and half the women in the parish, carried on at least three love affairs, and then resigned because there was no future in the priesthood."

"We won't send you another of those." He was on the defensive, unprepared for Father Nice Guy playing hardball.

"Then there was Ron Lane, né Lesniak, a gifted musician and artist. He's still recovering from the nervous breakdown that the Corpus Christi crowd gave him."

"Corpus Christi" is not a city in Texas or a feast in the pre–Vatican Council calendar. Rather, it is the moniker of a "secular institute." It was founded in France after the War and spread to Spain during the declining years of Franco and the Falange. Their membership, lay and clerical, are notably to the right of Pope Innocent III.

And right of Caesar Augustus, too, as far as that goes.

They are now trying to repeal the Second Vatican Council and restore the glorious Church of the thirteenth century. They have amassed so much power in Rome that they might be able to do just that. If they succeed, Catholics can prepare to have their lives ordered by folks that think daily self-flagellation should be a staple of the devout life.

"You have to defend your people and priest against them," he said piously.

"When you and the Cardinal get them out of power in the Vatican, I'll throw them out of the parish. . . . Then came Terry Howard, a genial conversationalist who turned on his TV for Kathleen Sullivan in the morning and didn't turn it off till David Letterman at night."

"He is a bit lazy."

"So lazy that even the laity noticed it. Look, Joe, you and I both know that the priesthood is in trouble. Things are going to get a lot worse before they get any better. I'm too old to play nursemaid to the misfits you guys ordain these days. Just leave us alone out here in Forest Springs."

"I'll talk to the Boss."

"You do that."

There was silence at the other end of the line for a moment,

Joe Simon thinking. I strained to hear the sound of the gears meshing.

"You think you're pretty smart, don't you, Lar?"

"Smart enough to know what you are."

"I'm a guy that's doing a tough, rotten job. I'm serving the Church and the Boss in tough times. I'm giving him the best I have for the good of the Church. You're just a smart-ass who sits out there and takes potshots at us."

"Wonderful metaphors, Joe. Highly original."

"Someday you'll go too far and we'll get you. I'll love every minute of it."

"Be my guest." I hung up on him.

I leaned back in my desk chair feeling considerable satisfaction. No more Father Nice Guy.

Then I felt sorry for Joe Simon. No doubt he believed his self-justification. It was indeed a rotten job. I wouldn't mind, if Joe didn't so obviously enjoy the power that came with it.

The Cardinal cornered me at the funeral of Red Murphy, who had once been my pastor and for whose departure from this world I could mourn only with some difficulty. The Cardinal's public persona is that of a shy, vulnerable man, almost like a hobo asking for a quarter to buy a cup of coffee.

Joe Simon had to point me out because the Cardinal doesn't remember names too well.

"Larry." He clapped me on the back and beamed, one of the most astute Polish diplomats in recent history, until you figured him out—and 90 percent of us had figured him out.

"Your Eminence."

"I don't have enough skilled pastors as it is. Who will train the young men if priests like you don't?"

"You want my resignation, you can have it."

The Boss recoiled as if I had slugged him—the public persona is not entirely an act. The word had not reached him that Laurence O'Toole McAuliffe was no longer a nice guy.

"That's not the issue, Larry."

"Cardinal, no one calls me Larry. It's been Lar for forty years at least."

I walked away.

My family calls me Laurence, not that it matters.

I suspect that the Boss, who is given to worrying and then praying about his worries, didn't sleep that night. Good enough for him.

So here I was, working up the energy to walk down the spiral staircase to the office to welcome Father New Priest. How come?

I don't know. I guess the nice guy won after all.

Damn him.

He was taken in by the Cardinal, for whom the nice-guy role fits easily if deceptively.

The Cardinal had stopped by the rectory one morning during the summer on the way to his one-week vacation at some fishing stream in Arkansas. Dressed in old black trousers, a worn black sweater, and a collarless shirt with a stud in it (his version of sport clothes), he soft-soaped me while drinking a Diet Pepsi.

"Larry, I have a newly ordained priest who has a great future in the Church. He is someone special. They tell me that no one can train him as you can. Please do this for me and for the Church."

I knew even then that the New Priest was less important than the Cardinal's need to be liked. He delayed his vacation by a couple of hours to win me over.

How can anyone turn down someone who looks like a bushy-haired French farmer in a 1940 film and drives a dirty, four-year-old gray Pontiac?

So this "Father New Priest" of Jackie's was so special that a Cardinal would personally worry about his assignment?

Well, we'd see about that!

On my first assignment I had to wait three days to get an

appointment to see the Monsignor Red Murphy (who was egg bald even then). Early on he decided that my first name was Marty, which is what I was called by the other curates for my full term at the parish. The pastor was always right, by definition. Some things do change, you see.

Red Murphy did not need a conscience. I was plagued by one, usually after the fact.

My conscience bothered me about Ron Lane more than about the other two new priests. I tried to protect him from the Corpus Christi complaints to the Chancery and to Rome about his modern art exhibit and from the hostile articles in *The Drover* and *The National Catholic Review* that made fun of the show. Dolph Santini, the Vicar for Liturgy in the archdiocese, appeared at the rectory, under pressure of a formal Roman complaint, to inspect the exhibit. (We don't have a Vicar for Art because art isn't important to the Church anymore.)

After much shaking of his head and sighing, Dolph (of whom it is said that he not only never had been inside the Art Institute but was unaware of its existence) advised Ron to be more "prudent."

Ron thereupon retreated to his room, locked the door, and brooded. Poor, sweet, innocent young man that he was, he expected the institutional Church to protect him from the crazies.

When the crazies started to harass his parents on the phone with promises of prayers for the "conversion" of their only son, poor Ron went round the bend.

I wondered whether I could have done more to protect him, as Joe Simon (who had sent Santini out with his verdict formulated before Dolph had seen the art show) had argued.

As I walked down the spiral staircase, I consoled myself with the thought that George Wholey and his Corpus Christi bunch would have a harder time with this New Priest than they did with poor Ron. The Keenans were not people to mess with.

That's right: I did say spiral staircase. Saint Finian's boasted the standard suburban Catholic white brick modern church (it could serve as a zeppelin hangar in an emergency), school, convent, ministry center, and parish hall. But the rectory was a vast old Gothic home that the founding pastor had bought and next to which he built the rest of the parish plant. It does not seem to be haunted, but in its nooks and crannies and turrets and battlements, there ought to have been scores of ghosts—clerical and lay.

"Hey"—the New Priest looked down at the recalcitrant word processor, which had not worked properly since the day we bought it—"I think we have this creep shaped up. Hold your breath, Jackie, and pray."

He slammed the top of the three-thousand-dollar machine with his massive paw. It jumped like someone had stuck a needle into it.

And the monitor obediently lit up in the appropriate color of amber.

Outside, Forest Springs was washed in the blue and gold of a perfect September afternoon.

"Hooray for Father New Priest," Jackie shouted.

Jackie had not exaggerated his good looks. In his clerical shirt, with the white Roman collar tucked in the breast pocket (I was wearing a sport shirt and gray slacks, by the way), my new curate had Robert Redford good looks. He was over six feet, though not quite as tall as I am. In every other respect, however, I would be the clear loser if I were vain enough—and dumb enough—at my age in life to make comparisons. Blond hair, long and slightly curly, dancing blue eyes, dimpled chin, an engaging smile, strong, broad shoulders, thick arm muscles, flat stomach, James Keenan looked like he could hit a golf ball 250 yards dead straight down the middle of the fairway and model golf clothes at the same time.

In this respect I made an error. Two hundred and eighty-five yards would be a more accurate estimate. His handicap, as he would later admit under some pressure from Cook (her self-designation) at the supper table was three.

Special, huh?

"I can fix anything, Father." He grinned boyishly. "Pipe organs, word processors, golf carts, volleyball nets, difficult head ushers, leaky roofs, Mothers Superior—should there be such on the premise, as seems improbable—walls that need tuck-pointing, rebellious teenage doorbell answerers like this young person here . . . you name it, I'll fix it."

"Ah," I replied with what I hope was notable lack of enthusiasm, and thought, Omigod!

"The Big Boss, His Eminence, Jackie," he took no note of my notable lack of enthusiasm, "the Boss said, 'Jamie, you go out there and help my friend Father McAuliffe for the next six years. Fix everything that needs to be fixed. And, Jamie,' the Cardinal says in a whisper so the VG—that's the Vicar General, Jackie, Father Simon—can't hear him, 'just between the two of us, there's a hell of a lot that needs fixing out there.'"

"Ms. Flavin is going to LOVE you, Father Jamie," Jackie said with that instinct for the political jugular with which Irish women are born and too many, alas, lose after their teens.

"Porteress," I said, whispering a prayer to a number of Irish martyrs, like my patron, Saint Laurence O'Toole, to protect me from their fate.

"I beg pardon, Father?" My new curate grinned cheerfully.

I must explain the presence of Jackie in the rectory on a late afternoon of a school day. There are two approaches to gatekeeping at a Roman Catholic rectory. The first is the old way: the doorbell is assigned to the housekeeper, who often doesn't hear it. When she does, she requires five minutes to answer it. If the waiting lay person has not already departed in anger or despair, then the housekeeper's routine response is "Father isn't home."

The experience is likely to discourage further visits.

It's an effective technique for protecting rectory peace; in this day and age, however, it leads to angry letters to the Chancery office and angry phone calls from Joe Simon.

I hasten to add that such would not be the problem with Brigid, our cook and housekeeper. On the contrary, given half a chance, Brideheen (to use one of the many nicknames we Irish have for the goddess, later the patron saint of spring) would spend the whole day in the rectory offices, gossiping with parishioners.

The other approach is to hire teenage women (note I do not call them girls) to guard the doorbell after school and in the evening. They bring vitality, charm, and empathy to the gatekeeping role. It's hard for the most angry Lay Person of God to sustain his or her wrath in the face of Jackie's defiant red hair, sturdy young body, and happy grin. On a good day the porteresses will remember to write down half of the telephone messages they take, which is better than average for a rectory.

The downside is that teenage women tend to be bossy, especially if their ethnic background happens to be Irish. Given half a chance, they will take over the rectory completely. It is better for the People of God that their parish house be dominated by a teenage porter than by a housekeeper. In the case of the former, the charm is so subtle that you almost don't realize that someone like Jackie is running the parish.

"Jackie is a porteress."

"I see. You mean a porter person, obviously. . . . Father James Stephen Michael Finbar Keenan at your service." He bowed, first to me, then to the already adoring sixteen-year-old porter person. "We aim not only to please but to fix. Now about that director of religious education you need to fix, Father—"

"How do you know that we have a DRE who needs fixing?" Was the Cardinal that well informed about our parish?

Perhaps I should note here that I have been accused by my

colleagues in the priesthood of surrounding myself with beautiful women. I can't deny the fact. Jackie herself in a prom dress (in which she must come to the rectory to demand pastoral praise) would make any man wish he was eighteen again. Brigid the cook, only a few years older than Jackie, is a lithe blond Viking, even if some have suggested that her West-of-Ireland accent requires English subtitles. Linda Meehan, the youth minister, is not so striking; her intensity, however, exudes subtle but powerful erotic appeal. And Jeanne Flavin . . . well, that's a story in itself.

I could reply that the composition of the staff was an accident. Or I could be a chauvinist and cite Sister Cunnegunda, the school principal, as contrary evidence. However, I usually content myself with wide eyes, pursed lips, and the remark that I hadn't noticed.

"Doesn't everyone have a DRE who needs fixing?" My new curate spread his hands soothingly. "Don't worry, Father, don't give it another anxious second. . . . Is it working, porter person?"

He'd been pulling my leg about fixing the DRE. He's been in the rectory only a few minutes and already pulling the pastor's leg.

"Perfectly," the redhead chirped. "Now I can do my term paper tonight!"

"That's why we have word processors in rectories these days," I observed with a sigh of resignation.

"The next tactic, Jacqueline mavourneen, which I will save for phase two, is to kick the thing. You'd be surprised how well that model responds to being kicked. Now, Father" —turning to me—"I suppose you're about to ask me up to your room for a drink?"

"Well, that's the ritual these days. I hope you don't mind Bushmills Black Label?"

Father James Michael Whatever Keenan reached into the

Gucci overnight bag he was carrying and produced a three-pack carton of Black Bush. "Your wish, Honored Pastor, is my command. You can't have any, Jackie; porter persons are not nearly important enough to sip this ambrosia of the Ulster goddesses—triune of course, as are all Irish goddesses."

"You come well-equipped, Jim." I was prepared to give the young man some points for thoughtfulness if not for maturity.

"Most people call me Jamie, Father."

"My name is Larry, uh, Lar."

"Yes, Father."

Thus came my new curate. Except they are not curates anymore but associate pastors. A rose is a rose, you say?

A curate in the old days would never turn up with three bottles of the pastor's favorite substitute for marriage.

And if their name was Jamie, they wouldn't insist on calling you "Father."

I wasn't sure I was young enough for Jamie Whatever Keenan.

A prophetic insight if I ever had one.

Most stories about Catholic parishes, from the *Luke Delmege* of Canon Sheehan of Doneraile to the *Mass Appeal* of James Davis, start with the coming of the New Curate (one of Sheehan's novels is called *My New Curate*).

With the coming of "Father New Priest," something dies and something is born in the life of a parish. When he walks into the rectory (in the past hardly with Gucci luggage), the New Priest represents both the continuity and the change that is typical of the Catholic parish. (And as a laywoman remarked to me, it is one more occasion for the indomitable and usually futile hope of the good parishioner: "Maybe this one can preach!")

Moreover, in the relationship between pastor and curate, between old priest and new priest, one has the classic struggle between the generations—idealism versus wisdom, zeal versus experience, rigidity versus understanding, freshness versus disillusion: choose your own ideological clichés.

At the end of his first year, my last associate pastor—the Kathleen Sullivan–David Letterman fan—and I did some "discerning of the spirits" and agreed that he would be happier elsewhere. I must say he was a perfect gentleman about it; he even told me so the day before he left on his summer vacation in May.

Normally these days, pastor and potential associate negotiate—like Baghdad merchants—about the terms of employment, an exercise that is about as useful as man and woman trying to bargain about the responsibilities of their common life in a prenuptial contract. The personnel board, however, sorts out the precious newly ordained and sends them to pastors who are supposed to be good teachers, a category into which I apparently fall.

Or fell.

The process is accompanied by the Cardinal's normal sigh-of-relief consent to anything that will diminish the number of decisions he has to make.

So after the Cardinal's impromptu visit to Saint Finian's, I received another call from the chairman of the personnel board, who was much more officious than the vice chancellors used to be when they made appointments by throwing darts at names on a wall. "We're sending you Jim Keenan, Larry. Packy Keenan's nephew. He's one of the finest in the class. We hope you will do your best to get along with him."

"Where was he a deacon?"

"Saint Symphorosa and her Seven Sons in Greenville."

As soon as this democratically elected bureaucrat hung up, I phoned my classmate Tim Aherne at Saint Simp's and the Seven Wimps. He was greatly amused.

"You got Keenan! Wow! That'll be a show and a half."

"Does he work?"

"Hardest-working young man in the archdiocese."

"Can he preach?" I thought of the woman and her indomitable hope.

"A modern Fulton Sheen."

"Is he contemptuous of us?"

"A paragon of respect."

"What's wrong with him? Gay?"

My classmate laughed for almost a solid minute. "Not likely," he finally managed.

"Well what *is* wrong with him?"

"Nothing, absolutely nothing. He's the perfect young priest. A modern pastor's Christmas request to Santa Claus." He was carried off by a new fit of laughter.

"Then what's so funny?"

"You'll see, Larry, you'll see. The whole archdiocese will be watching you two."

I hung up the phone, exhausted. Monsignor Patrick "Packy" Keenan is a half-dozen years older than I am and a man of boundless energies and enthusiasms. If this young priest was a chip off the family block, I was in for trouble.

For the first time I wondered whether it might not be worse to have an energetic associate pastor than a lazy one.

In my room that September afternoon, he poured two rather large shots of the precious Black Bush into my old tumblers, remarked, "No Waterford? A pastor should have Waterford, he's entitled, I'll have to pick up some for you," and proposed a toast: "Let's have lots of fun, Father, that's what religion is all about, right?"

"I guess." I returned the toast. "And my name is Lar."

He shook the non-Waterford tumbler at me. "After I get to know you, maybe Father Laurence, but pastors are entitled to respect. The role has a critically important symbolic function in the Church and its inherent dignity must be preserved. Anyway, you don't have to establish that you're a democrat. *Everyone* knows that."

"It's good to have you," I said, meaning, I think, that I didn't expect the next few years to be dull.

"Good to be here. Now tell me about this Marxist DRE you have."

So he did know. Packy must have told him. Packy and Jeanne Flavin had tangled at a couple of meetings. He had enjoyed the fight as he always does. Jeanne had been furious at him—"a pseudoliberal bourgeois reactionary."

"Actually, a cynical opportunist." I knew a few Marxist terms from my own bomb-throwing days.

"I am *serious*, Lar." She pounded my desk with her fist.

"Stalinist," I said to the New Priest. The thought of that subject made another small shot of Bush imperative. Jamie politely declined. And, I noticed, nursed his drink slowly. Of course, the perfect associate pastor doesn't drink too much.

"Jeanne Flavin—J-e-a-n-n-e, and be sure you get the spelling right."

"The kind of name you would expect from a Stalinist. Probably a left-wing deviationist. Well, better that than a right-wing revisionist." He stretched his legs. "Sounds like fun."

"Huh?"

"Marxist heresies. Have you read Marx, Father, or Lenin?"

"Uh, no."

"You should, you know. They're quite wonderful." He sipped judiciously from his non-Waterford goblet. "I mean for putting down clerical Marxists who would have never even held *Das Kapital* in their hands."

"I see. . . . Uh, Jamie, about Jeanne, she had a hard time out in the Philippines. Go easy on her."

"No problem." He waved an airy hand. "I said fix, not do in. Well, I'd better unload the truck outside. You pick up more junk when you wander around."

"There's no TV in your room. You can have one of course, if you want us to buy it. But there's a big-screen in the community room—"

"TV?" He seemed genuinely shocked. "I only watch it when the Bears are out of town. By the way, if we can both get off early enough, I'd like to invite you to the season home opener, Father. I've had tickets for a long time. They're not perfect, forty yard line, but they're in the east stands at Soldier Field, so you are protected from the wind off the lake."

"That sounds fine. Let's see what happens."

Who knows—I might be in a mental institution by then or up at Guest House, drying out.

At the door of the pastor's suite, whose color scheme I suspected offended Jamie Keenan, my new curate turned for his parting shot. "You know why Jesus went out into the desert by himself?"

"The Bible says to pray."

"Nah," he said, dismissing the Bible's version with a wave of his hand to which I was becoming accustomed, "to laugh. He found our seriousness and solemnity hilariously funny. He had to laugh, and he didn't want to hurt our feelings by laughing in our faces."

"G. K. Chesterton."

"Right! You like him, too? This is gonna be a great assignment!"

Thus did my new curate, Father Jamie Whatever Whatever Keenan, arrive at the parish. I dug out Canon Sheehan on the subject. Jamie Keenan would have been inconceivable in those days.

Hell, he was still inconceivable.

But just the same, there he was carrying his vast array of Gucci matched luggage up the stairs of the rectory.

Jeanne Flavin would love him about the same way she loved American capitalism. As the Irish say, the Lord made them and the divil matched them.

CHAPTER

2

"I won't work for a spoiled brat."

"You'll be working with him, Jeanne, not for him." I suppressed an impatient sigh.

"He's a man and a priest." She twisted her face into an expression of hatred. "By definition, he's a member of the oppressor class."

"So then am I."

"You're different." She waved a hand, dismissing my argument. "You . . . you're reasonably enlightened for a white male priest."

"Over fifty."

She tried not to grin. "Don't distract me from critique."

"Dialectical critique."

"Stop it, *Lar*! I'm being serious. You *will* not turn me away with your goddamn Irish wit."

"Yes, ma'am."

I was sitting on the edge of the desk in her small office in the ministry center, a collection of offices and meeting rooms which the Founding Pastor had added to the parish hall a couple of years before my arrival. Like the gym, they were intended to be seen and admired but not used.

"I want to be a pastoral associate." She recaptured her irate frown. "I insist on dealing with him from a position of relative equality."

She is a tall, slender, handsome woman, about forty, with coal black hair tinged now with silver, a thin, haunted face, explosive dark blue eyes, and a trimly shaped . . . well, mildly voluptuous . . . figure of which she seems unaware and of which every man in the parish is well aware. Jeans, T-shirt, or sweat-shirt, and worn black down jacket in winter constitute her rev-olutionary uniform, a kind of punk-age nunnish habit.

Back in the days when she was a debutante in one of the early presentation balls, she must have been sent to ballet school, be-cause she walks and stands and sits like an archduchess instead of a revolutionary. You realize as you look at the happy, hope-ful young woman in the pres ball photo, that she is more beau-tiful now than she was then, but that the happiness and hope are gone.

In another era she would have been a mother abbess about whose tragic past novices would gossip in whispers.

You almost forget the "beautiful" adjective soon after you've met Jeanne, because it is clear that she despises physical attrac-tiveness and has chosen not only celibacy but sexlessness. A per-son can't make that choice, of course. Hormones won't let you.

"I've told you, Jeanne, that I'm perfectly willing to make you a pastoral associate if you'll accept a three-year contract."

"Three years working with Monsignor Patrick Keenan's nephew? Don't be absurd." She shifted fretfully in her chair, revealing hints of a glorious figure, which baggy clothes could not obscure.

I would have struggled to salvage anyone in Jeanne's predica-ment. I only fall half in love with the pretty ones.

"Everyone calls him Packy. . . . I can't commit the parish to a pastoral associate's salary without the usual three-year con-tract, Jeanne."

A pastoral associate is a person who is hired to do every-thing the priest does except administer the sacraments. It's a job title that enables the American Church to push toward having women priests and married priests without going into open revolt against the Vatican. I'm sure there're parishes in America where the Pastoral Associates say Mass.

"It's a meaningless title for a woman," she fired back at me. "Why should I be held to a three-year contract?"

I wouldn't have fallen half in love with her merely because she was physically attractive. Her appeal for me was the result of a combination of her fragility and beauty. Jeanne was a tormented and unhappy woman who in three years at Saint Finian's had begun to emerge from her cocoon of bitterness and fear. Despite her politics, the people in the parish had begun to like her. Some of the time she permitted herself to respond to their warmth, especially with kids like Jackie, with whom, on occasion, she could be thick as thieves—two giggling thieves when the pastor would appear, as if her career had taken a different path and she was student adviser in a Catholic college.

"Quiet, Dr. Flavin! Himself is here!"

"We weren't saying anything wrong, Jackie!"

"Let him think we were."

I assumed credit for this transformation, probably without reason. If we could keep her around for three more years, we might change her life.

Three years was her longest time in any parish, and she always left after a bitter fight.

I stood up. "Jeanne, I don't want you to prejudge the New Priest. Give him a chance."

"I'm sure he's a miserable, oppressive male chauvinist pig. I will not work with him. If you want to fire me, go ahead." She rose too. "I won't demand mediation because you violated my contract."

It's hard to fight with a woman when your unruly celibate imagination is pulling off her black sweatshirt. Nonetheless, I tried.

"I will not fire you, Jeanne, and you will cooperate with the New Priest."

"You're a male bastard like all the others," she shouted at me.

"I don't mind your ideology," I chose my words carefully.

"As I've said before, radicalism is a useful perspective. Nonetheless, as long as you work in Saint Finian's, I will not tolerate a confusion of ideology and your professional responsibility to the parish. Is that clear?"

The appeal to professional responsibility usually worked with her.

"Get out of my office," she screamed.

What would a man married to a woman like her do?

Probably what I did: leave the office.

Trying to concentrate on the red and gold colors that were emerging on the trees of Forest Springs, I walked back to the rectory. Jeanne was reverting to type. The New Priest would be a bad influence on her.

How would she affect him?

CHAPTER

3

Pederasty was the subject at the rectory dinner table that night. It is a subject in the archdiocese second in popularity only to conversation about the Cardinal.

It took my mind off the argument with Jeanne and the coming confrontation with the Condons and gave me a chance to watch Father New Priest react to the other two priests who shared our haunted rectory with us.

"It's like the Gestapo," said Father Tom "Turk" Nelligan. "The Vicar for the Clergy shows up in the middle of the night with another priest. They take you off to a rectory on the other side of town, tell you they've hired a good lawyer for you, and try to send you off to one of the funny farms for clergy that are so busy these days."

Our dining room is oak paneled with high ceilings. Impossible to keep cool in summer or warm in winter, it would be perfect as a boardroom for a team of vampires.

"On the whole they treat us drunks better," responded Father Mike Quinlan. "They don't disown us."

"Given all the suits, and the threat to jail bishops for being accessories to buggery," Jamie said as he munched contentedly on his Caesar salad, "you can understand their concern."

Brigid had produced the salad proudly with the announcement—in the tone of voice she might have used if she were in front of the GPO on Easter Monday 1916 proclaiming the Irish Republic—"Father Keenan himself made the Caesar salad."

Another conquest for Jamie Keenan.

We were all wearing sport shirts. Jamie, however, was still wearing his Roman collar, though without a jacket.

"Yeah, but they treat you like you're guilty until you're proven innocent," Turk protested, "and even if you're proven innocent—as two guys have been in the last six months—you're still guilty."

"So what else is new?" Mike grinned merrily. "Great salad, Jamie. Don't threaten Cook's job, though—her boyfriends are all IRA gunmen on the run. . . . Where was I? Oh, yes. I was saying that in the minds of authority in the Catholic Church, you're always guilty once an accusation is brought, regardless of incontrovertible proof of your innocence."

"Unless you're on the Cardinal's staff," Turk replied. "Then you're always innocent even if you're proven guilty."

Both Turk and Mike are of my generation—a quarter century older and more than the New Priest. Turk, a lean little man with a tuft of brown hair around the edge of his head and an eternal frown etched on his narrow face, has worked at Catholic Charities for twenty-five grueling years. No one in the state is better at administering adoption and foster-care programs

than he is. He works hard all day, every day, goes to every wake
in the parish, and visits hospitals on Saturday. He hasn't taken
a day off or a vacation in twenty years. He works hard on his
sermons, which are dry but intelligent, and does his best to
smile at people in the back of church after Mass. He is profoundly cynical about the Ecclesiastical Institution and has
been running on empty, or so it seems to me, for at least a de-
cade.

Mike is one of the most brilliant and gifted priests in the
archdiocese—tall, handsome, white haired, eloquent. He was
merely a heavy drinker when he was an associate pastor. When
he was assigned to a "place of his own" in a brand-new suburb,
the strain of doing all the work by himself was too much. He
eased over the line that is the boundary between social drinker
and problem drinker without anyone noticing it—until he
preached at all the Masses one Sunday roaring drunk. Since
then he has been in and out of Guest House, a treatment center for clerical alcoholics, five or six times.

When he asked me if he could live at our place, I was hesitant. He was a great preacher, but it was at the time the Corpus
Christi folk were pushing Ron Lane round the bend, and I
wasn't sure I wanted to turn Saint Finian's into a psychiatric
home. As it turned out, Mike was a great help to poor Ron and
to me. He's been on the wagon now for almost three years,
though as he says, it doesn't make any difference—three years
or one day.

Both men were too good to deliberately test Jamie's supper
table reflexes. They were simply playing the roles Providence
had assigned them.

"I don't see how the Boss gets away with it," Turk continued. "He has those kind all around him. I don't mean just gays,
I mean the kind that play with little boys. And he warns the
rest of us to stay out of gay bars and to report any charge of
sexual molestation."

"He inherited most of them from his predecessor." I don't like the Boss particularly—he's too cute by half, as the Irish say—but fair is fair.

"And when he finally has to get rid of them, he makes them pastors of big parishes. Ordinary guys they lock up in the funny farm, his staff they make pastors."

"I wish," Mike Quinlan added with a sigh, "they were as easy on us straights. Like in the old days when it was sort of expected that you'd have a mistress. What about it, Jamie? Wouldn't you like to have an officially sanctioned mistress?"

"I'm told by those who know better than I"—his blue eyes twinkled—"that wives are difficult enough to keep happy, let alone a mistress."

"In Ireland till the sixteenth century," Mike said, grinning happily, "bishops could have four wives."

"Brehon laws," Jamie said as he refilled his salad plate. "Poor men, even if their wives were all as lovely as Cook." He nodded at Biddy, who had arrived with the meat. "Four wives would have been too much of a responsibility altogether."

"Go 'long with you," Biddy replied, her fair skin turning crimson. "'Tis the Irish women who have all the responsibility."

Mike raised an eyebrow in my direction when Jamie mentioned the Brehon laws. That made two priests in the archdiocese who knew about them and both at my dinner table.

"It frosts me"—I jabbed at the roast beef, which was steeped in some marvelous sauce that Brigid may well have invented—"like you said, Mike, that gay priests can get away with it but straight priests can't. The Chancery turns the other way when they take lovers, but if I found a woman who would let me into her bed, I'd last about a week before I was dispatched to a monastery or a funny farm."

"That'll be the day." Mike chuckled.

I was growing more grouchy by the minute. "Moreover, if I

should bring such a lover into the rectory, we would survive for about as long as it takes Joe Simon to pick up his phone. But there are lavender rectories in the archdiocese, and the Boss pretends to himself that they don't exist!"

Mike grinned genially. "That's because women are still Satan's traps for men according to the unconscious of our leaders. Remember what the rector in the seminary told us? Every woman is a womb waiting to be fecundated!"

"Actually"—Jamie scooped another huge slab of Brideheen's roast beef on to his plate—"they're afraid of women, as well they might be. In another generation, they'll take over the Church and run it properly for the first time in two thousand years."

He said it with a perfectly straight face.

Brigid had reappeared with a bottle of Beaulieu cabernet sauvignon.

"High time," she agreed with the New Priest. "And won't they be doing a much better job, especially if they're Irish?"

"And won't you be after spilling the wine if you pour it that way?"

"Ah, sure, and wasn't I after forgetting that the wine is a present from Father Keenan's mother?"

"Save some for yourself, Cook," Jamie instructed her.

"What do you young priests think about the rumors," Turk plugged on doggedly after Cook had slipped away, "concerning some of the men around the Cardinal and even the Boss himself?"

Jamie scooped up a huge hunk of mashed potatoes, more than I would dare eat in a week. "We feel that it's their affair and not ours."

None of us reacted to the pun. Was it intended or not? That night I was sure it wasn't. Later I wasn't so sure.

"I'm sure the Boss is straight," I said quickly. "And celibate, too."

"Which would be better, Jamie?" Mike lifted a fork. "An able bishop who kept lovers—of either sex—or an inept one who was chaste?"

"Same answer as Saint Teresa, Father." He plowed into the potatoes.

The good Hispanic saint had said that she would prefer a wise confessor to a holy one.

"Do you think we ought to be ordaining gays?" Turk demanded.

"My mother"—he beamed proudly at the mention of his parent—"says that gender is a continuum rather than a polarity."

"Your mother?"

"Dr. Margaret Mary Keenan," I interjected hastily.

"Margaret Mary *Ward* Keenan, past president of the American Psychological Association," Mike added.

There may have been four or five priests in the archdiocese who did not know that Packy Keenan's adored sister-in-law was the president-elect of the APA, but such ignorance, God knows, was not Packy's fault. Turk's ears must have been plugged.

"Don't forget the Ward," Jamie said, blushing happily. "Dr. Margaret Mary Ward Keenan. Mama Maggie to us. I'm sorry, Fathers. I'll try not to quote her more than once a day."

His father, Jerry Keenan, was a retired federal judge (retired at sixty) and a novelist. A couple of years ago he had written a charming fictionalized biography of his courting of Maggie Ward.

"I'm sure she's worth quoting, Jamie," I observed judiciously.

"What's it like to grow up in a psychologist's family," Turk demanded—with insensitivity extraordinary even for him.

"It was never dull, Father." Jamie smiled benignly. "You weren't sure whether you were going to turn up in a scholarly article or a best-selling novel."

Set and match to the New Priest.

"But what about ordaining queers? What does your mother say about that?"

Turk never knew when he'd lost.

"She says we should have good priests and chaste priests." Jamie smiled mildly. "I agree."

Turk finally quit.

Mike stuck his head in the door of my study after supper. "A Billy Budd, Lar, a Billy Budd."

I looked up from the financial records over which I had been puzzling.

"Jamie?"

"Hey, he grows up in an adoring and happy family, loved by his mother and father and his older brothers and sisters and his Uncle Packy. He's never experienced the hatreds and the resentments and the envies that are part of the human condition. He's going to get killed."

"You're exaggerating, Mike," I said uneasily, closing the account book.

"Jamie's an innocent."

"Like Ron was?"

"No, not like Ron was. There are different kinds of innocence. His kind they hang real high."

"I think he can take care of himself."

"Remember what happened to Billy Budd? He was an innocent, too, and what did they do to him?"

"They hanged him."

"Unjustly?"

"Yeah."

"Same thing is going to happen to your new priest."

"The Corpus Christi gang? I don't think so. The Keenans are powerful people themselves."

"The Church will hang him, one way or another. Mark my words. You know Shaw? 'Jesus must be crucified in every generation by those without imagination.' That's Pierre Cauchon, the Count Bishop of Beauvais, on the subject of Joan of Arc. Lar, you have a fucking Joan of Arc on your hands."

"Come on, Mike."

"Mark my words!"

After he left, I tried to laugh him off.

Jamie Keenan was not Joan of Arc.

And I wasn't the Count Bishop of Beauvais.

Or the Dauphin of France.

No way.

CHAPTER

4

Our intense young youth minister, Linda Meehan, was the latest victim of Martina Condon, a woman who needed periodic fixes of hate the way a vampire needs blood.

"It isn't fair, Father. I'm innocent," the victim pleaded a couple of hours before my New Priest showed up. "I didn't do it."

The argument was about a tempest in a teapot—whether Linda had interfered in a High Club election in which Coady Anne Condon was a candidate.

A trivial issue? Sure, but important to all those involved. A pastor has to learn early in the game that he takes seriously any problem that his parishioners take seriously.

"Joe Condon says they will be forced to pull Coady Anne out of Mother Mary High School and send her away to boarding school for her senior year. Your remarks on her sex life make it impossible, Joe says, for the poor kid to show her face either at school or here in the neighborhood."

"It isn't true," Linda sobbed. "I never said a word."

Ah, but she did, you see: there was no appeal from Martina's guilty verdict. She controlled her children by hating those who allegedly persecuted them.

I had to put the charge on the record. I would have to face the Condons later in the day. I wanted Linda's explicit denial of the allegation that she had conspired to prevent Coady Anne Condon from becoming president of the parish teen club.

It all sounded vaguely like an FBI scam: "allegation," "conspire." Such is the atmosphere of the Catholic Church as the twentieth century lurches toward an uncertain conclusion.

Linda Meehan, our youth minister, was an intense, stringy, generous young woman in her middle twenties. She would have been an intense, stringy young nun thirty years ago. In these days, dedicated young people calculate, reasonably enough, that the Church can lay valid claim to only part of their lives. Linda was by no means unattractive, as I have already suggested, and doubtless would leave us in another year or two to begin the process of creating future teenagers who would harass another generation of youth ministers. On the whole, that was a much better outcome for the Church than that she should stay in a religious order all her life, a bitter woman who had burned out in the teenage ministry at twenty-seven.

"Even if you had conspired to keep Coady Anne Condon from being elected president of the teen club, it would not have necessarily been wrong. Why, I remember—" I cut short my recollections of rigged parish elections in ages past. First of all, pastors ought not to indulge in too much reminiscing, or they will be thought on the high road to senility. Second, in the new, nonclericalist, democratic Church of the era after the Vatican Council, one did not rig parish elections.

Or one did not admit it, not even, as the scripture says, in the quiet of the closet.

"I would have been perfectly happy to work with her. She's a sweet girl. There never was much chance of her winning. Even if I didn't want her as president, I would not have had to say a word against her. I certainly wouldn't have raised any questions about her . . . her sexual behavior. There isn't any, Father, I'm certain of that."

"So her mother tells me," I replied dryly.

The issue wasn't Linda or the election, anyway. Martina Condon was the wagonmaster leading her family through hostile territory toward the promised land. Periodically she needed to circle the wagons and impose the discipline of a caravan under siege to control the family. In the absence of any real savages on the attack, Martina conjured them into existence. Linda was the current Chief Crazy Horse.

"What did I do wrong, Father?" She dabbed at her eyes with a crumpled tissue. "Martina and I were such good friends. How could she possibly suspect I would conspire against poor Coady Anne?"

Somewhere far beyond the boundaries of the parish and beyond the knowledge but not the curiosity of the members of the teen club, there was a boy whom Linda allegedly dated with some regularity. (Arthur, by name, if you were to believe the teen club gossip.) Linda was not slaking all her needs to love and be loved with the parish adolescents.

"I'm afraid that was your mistake," I said as gently as I could.

"Martina didn't seem to make any demands."

"That's part of her game."

It might not seem like an important game. Is there a church in the country without mothers who push their children beyond the kids' competence or popularity? All right, there were some special twists to Martina's game. After one term as a pastor in a modern Catholic suburban parish, the demitasse tempest of *l'affaire* Coady Anne Condon should be no challenge to me.

True enough, if I were willing to offer Martina the head of our youth minister on a silver platter.

Penny ante? Especially since Linda was not likely to want to renew her contract a year from now? Couldn't the pastor have a nice little talk with her and suggest that she might want to take a sabbatical after Christmas—with pay, of course?

Sure it would be easy—if the pastor had no character at all (like a bishop). But while I can compromise with people till the day before the last judgment, I was not about to let Tina Condon win this one.

"Her husband"—Linda dabbed at her red eyes—"always agrees with her."

"Tell me about it. What kind of a father is it who won't stand up for the rights of his children?"

"He's such a nice man."

"Nice men are especially likely to believe their wives. . . . Linda"—I don't think I sighed too loudly—"have you become good friends with another couple in the parish lately? Not that there's anything wrong with that."

In the old days when I was a curate (*not* an associate), only the pastor was permitted to have friends in the parish.

"No, Father, not that I can . . . Well, there's the O'Learys, but Tina introduced me to them."

"That figures." I did not want to sound like a cleric whose degree in counseling from Loyola makes him think he's as qualified as Freud. "You see, the O'Learys were a test. If you liked them more than the Condons, you were already on the way to disloyalty."

In Martina Condon's mythology, Crazy Horse always had to be the friendly guide turned enemy. Not only was the wagon train under assault, it had been betrayed.

"But I don't—"

"You don't understand the game, Linda. You were certain to like them more, no matter what you did."

"I couldn't win?"

"You've got it. . . . Is that boy we never see really called Arthur?"

"No." She flushed an appealing shade of crimson, which persuaded me that Arthur, or whatever his name might be, was a lucky young man. "That's the kids' name for him. I won't tell them his real name. It protects a part of me from their curiosity. His real name is—"

"Consider me one of the kids. Call him and tell him he owes you a supper tonight. OK?"

"Sure." She continued her appealing crimson blush. "No problem."

"I'll worry about it for a while. We're not going to feed you to the wolves, Linda."

When I had come as a new pastor, I was not well received by some of the old-timers, who resented the fact that I had replaced the Founder (of whom it was said, with only a little irony, that he was one of the better prelates of the middle-nineteenth century). I was also an uncertain quantity to most everyone else. Martina Condon quickly made her move to "adopt" me. Since she was intelligent and generous with her energy and her concern, and her husband was likable and fun to argue with, I was tempted. Some residual instincts of Irish political sophistication that I had inherited on both sides of the family made me hold back from the obvious offer of support, consolation, and admiration.

"Wait and see" was my mother's favorite expression. I waited, I saw, and I decided that I would get along much better with the Condons if I kept a wary distance from them. It was a wise choice. I had not quite made it sufficiently into her orbit to be accused later of disloyalty when she drew the wagons in a circle.

Her hates were not ideological but maternal. Her mother love was a ticking bomb. She did not feel that she was a good mother unless she were hacking with her broadsword those

who were seeking to assault her children. Since she had elected
to define motherhood as a career and the source of her worth as
a person, it was necessary to swing the broadsword—early and
often, as we used to say in Chicago politics. It was also necessary to dominate her children's lives.

So while I was the boss (which along with a dollar will get
you a ride on Mayor Rich's subway) and held the cards, and
while I would not sacrifice poor Linda, who had more than
earned her keep, I looked forward to a battle with Martina Condon much as I would to combat with a saber-toothed tiger whose
cubs I had carried off.

Before the New Priest arrived, I thought I'd do a little investigation. Some of the junior boys were at the parish basketball
court, a place on which they could be found during the autumn
months at any hour of the day or night. I offered to engage
them in a game of twenty-one. They dared not refuse. After all,
I *am* the pastor, and as I told them, if I couldn't play, I'd take
up my court and go home.

You have to be either dedicated or unbalanced to enjoy
teenagers, especially junior boys, after your thirtieth birthday.
Whether I am either or whether it is merely flattering to my
morale to rout them at twenty-one (standing six feet three
helps) is a matter that need not detain us at the moment. I was
on an intelligence mission.

"I hear the High Club election is disputed," I said, as I missed
a jump shot that ten, well, no, twenty years ago would have been
little more than a lay-up.

"Goofy Mrs. Condon," said one of the animals, hitting a
shot which was deliberately fired from the same spot where I
had missed.

"Is Arthur a nice guy, Father?" The second animal fed the ball
for a lay-up to his fellow. "I mean, poor Linda, she doesn't need
a geek boyfriend when she has to put up with Mrs. Condon

and"—his voice turned into a fair imitation of Tina—"poor sweet little Coady Anne."

"Arthur," I said firmly, tossing the rebound to the second animal, "is no geek."

Their blood drenched with reproductive juices, these animals were normally capable of considering a girl only in the most explicitly clinical aspects of her body. Their concern for Linda Meehan demonstrated that *(a)* emotional maturity was catching up with the reproductive juices in this collection of barely domesticated beasts and *(b)* Linda had succeeded in her mission with them.

"Mrs. Condon," continued the other, "is an airhead."

"Coady Anne had the same right to run as anyone else."

"Poor sweet little Coady Anne"—he sank his third jump shot—"couldn't attract freshmen to a strip show."

"Really major," agreed the other.

"I mean she's all right, kinda cute, if you like them little, but no way she's going to win a High Club election."

"The sophomore animals would run all over her, poor kid."

"So why should Linda bother? Everyone thought it was a joke, like Mrs. Condon pushing poor sweet little Coady Anne into running when she's going to get creamed. Right? Patti O'Hara would win by tons of votes if she was running against Miss America. Right?"

Right, indeed.

Patti O'Hara would cream the archangel Raphael in an election.

They would have denied an anti-Coady fix in any event. Linda was one of their own, and like Mafia dons, priests, and surgeons, teenagers stood by their own. A solemn high and serious denial would have confirmed Tina's charge. The denial I heard, touched with ridicule and cruelty, supported Linda's story, as I had expected. Did Linda with maybe a twitch of her lips (perhaps at the thought of poor sweet Coady Anne confronting our sophomore animals, who were especially animalistic this year) at the mention of Coady's candidacy give perhaps a basis, as thin as angel-hair pasta, for the charge?

Maybe. But finally, so what? In Tina Condon's world Coady Anne would be cute as teen club president, just as she was cute in the designer clothes that she wore when she was ten. In the world of the electorate only a space cadet would think that Coady had a chance to win. Her candidacy deserved to be treated respectfully but not seriously. No one can be held responsible for an occasional twist of the lips or a functional equivalent thereof.

Back in the store—that is, the rectory—I turned on the four-thirty news. There were problems in South Africa, Lebanon, Yemen, and city hall. And I was barely restraining the forces of chaos in my neighborhood over a teen club election.

There is no proportion, a wise person (tell you the truth, I don't remember who it was) once remarked, between the importance of a prize and the passion with which it is sought.

I had a faint hope that maybe I could save Coady Anne from her mother. None of her older brothers or sisters were married, all of them still firmly tied to their mother's apron strings even if they had apartments of their own. Coady Anne, the youngest child, was more rigidly controlled than all the rest. Saving her from her mother would be more difficult than bringing peace to Ulster.

Then the New Priest came to distract me from my worries over the Condons.

When Joe Condon had phoned me before my conversation with the youth minister, his tone was sad and troubled—not angry or reproachful. Indeed, his posture was that it was all over and the die had been cast.

"We've decided that the best thing to do, Father, is to pull poor Coady Anne out of Mother Mary High School and send her for her senior year to a boarding school in California. I've spoken to the nuns out there, and they tell me she should have no trouble catching up with the work."

The call was my first hint of the controversy. But by assuming that I am well informed, Joe was indicating that he took for granted my acquiescence in the injustice and calumny. He was demonstrating that he and Tina were prepared to be good sports about it all, even though their hearts were breaking.

"Well, after what Linda Meehan did, it seems to be the best choice for everyone, little Coady Anne, Linda, you, everybody else. We certainly don't want to be a parish problem all year long."

You betcha.

I had been through annual sessions with the Condons and knew the scenario by heart.

The first time it had been the Crawfords. Joe and Tina appeared at the rectory door—a solemn, if mismatched, couple: Joe, tall and lean, in sport clothes perhaps more suitable for spring than for mid-September; Tina, as slight as an injured sparrow, in subdued colors appropriate for a sparrow.

Tina was well named, a little woman with small body and small bones, doubtless cute when she was young, like her daughter, and hardly ugly now—a kind of well-groomed, well-turned mouse at first impression.

OK, as the animals had said on the court, if you like them small, which, to be honest, I didn't. My imagination was never unruly when Tina was in the office.

The conversation about the Crawfords was not hard to remember, because I had heard it several more times, with minor variations, since the first episode.

Joe: "We're worried about the Crawford children, Father. There's nothing much we can do about it, since we're not friends with them anymore, but maybe you can have a talk with them about the kids."

Me, knowing the Crawfords had been good friends of the Condons, maybe even gone on a vacation with them: "Oh?"

Ever tried something like that? It's not either easy or fun.

Joe: "I don't understand much about such things—I didn't graduate from college, you understand—but when kids grow up in an atmosphere of constant deceit, you have to worry about whether there's any chance for the kids to achieve full maturity. . . ."

Me: "Oh?"

Tina: "What does an atmosphere of deception do to children, Father?"

I went along with the game, explaining about psychopathic personalities and their impact on children. It was a mistake. I had permitted myself to be dragged down a long, intricate and convoluted path, at the end of which it was assumed that I had accepted their diagnosis of the Crawford family problem. Mrs. Crawford was a psychopathic personality, and her husband was afraid of her.

I was never told exactly what the Crawfords had done. It was somehow assumed that I knew the whole story before Tina and Joe showed up at the rectory, and thus it was unnecessary to provide me with the details.

"What exactly did they say about your boy?"

"We wouldn't want to repeat it, Father." Tina was always calm, cool, rational—the utterly self-possessed mother dealing sadly but realistically with betrayal and attack.

What was I supposed to do?

Their explicit agenda was to suggest that I have a talk with the Crawfords about the dangers of deceit, described always in the abstract, to their children.

"They can do so much harm, Father, to their own children too without even realizing it, can't they?"

Having thus transferred the burden of their terrible knowledge about the Crawfords to their pastor's shoulders, Joe and Tina could return home with clear if still worried consciences.

Then there were the Murrays, who were guilty of some sort

of terrible public discussion of sexual intercourse in front of the children, and the Ryans, who had turned all the other children against the Condon children.

I carefully checked out the stories each time. There was never any basis in fact. "Father, it all exists in her head, poor woman," Jean Ryan said with a sigh. "And she's such a nice friend until she goes haywire. You know it's happened to others, but you can't believe that it's going to happen to you."

"*Catch-22*, Kafka's *Trial*," Steve Ryan, a professor of literature at Chicago Circle, added, "and *Wonderland* all rolled into one. Out of sight. It's obviously a trick to manipulate her kids. Yet you still can't believe it's happening to you."

So when I opened the door and admitted Joe and Tina to the rectory, I knew the general story line that was to be played out. I wasn't sure, however, what nuances would be added. I was, to some extent, responsible for the assault on poor sweet little Coady Anne.

I resolved that, however difficult it might be, I had to stand for reality. Linda had not conspired against little Coady Anne. The latter had lost the election. She had finished fifth among five candidates because, as Richard Daley observed of Hubert Humphrey, she didn't have the votes. No way, José—as the animals would say—was Linda to be replaced.

Brave words. None of which would help Coady Anne; nothing would help her.

※

They were both tense, solemn, preoccupied—like the people you see in the waiting rooms outside of surgery in the hospitals. Tina's eyes were red from weeping.

I clenched my fists and told myself that I was sane and that this couple was just a little bit mad. I also insisted that they were my parishioners and that they were hurting badly. Therefore I must both stand for reality and try to heal them.

"It looks like we're going to have to move, Father," Joe began, his thin, black-Irish face knotted in a fierce scowl. "If you think that's what's best, just say the word, and we'll put the house on the market tomorrow. Change every fifteen years is good for a family anyway."

"I've investigated the matter," I said, sounding a bit like the United States Attorney at the daily press conference in which he confirms the leaks from the day before by apparently denying them, "and there is no evidence that Ms. Meehan ever spoke a word against Coady Anne. If you could tell me what it was exactly that she is supposed to have said, I'll be happy to look into it further. . . ."

You'll note I did not say "alleged." Pastor, not United States Attorney.

"I feel so sorry for the poor girl." As always and despite her red eyes, Tina was cool, self-possessed, and reasonable. "What will it do to her own children? I mean how can you grow up to be normal and healthy if your mother feels that popularity is better than integrity? And makes up stories about another person's sex life just so she can be popular? What are the effects of that kind of home environment, Father?"

Tina was wearing a simple, and expensive, navy-blue tailored suit: the mother as professional woman.

"As best as I can determine," I continued on my truth-telling tack, "Patti O'Hara would not have lost to the Blessed Mother, should she have been a candidate. Patti received three times as many votes as all the other candidates put together. There's no need to rig an election in favor of such an accomplished politician, and certainly no disgrace in losing to her."

Truth to tell, if Patti O'Hara was set down in Rome two weeks before the Cardinals went into conclave, she would be elected Pope. By about the same margin. On the first ballot.

"She's been good with the kids. We were all fond of her,"

Joe plowed on, his left eyelid twitching nervously, "and we understand that she's close to getting engaged to Arthur. . . ."

"His name is not Arthur."

"You have to worry about a girl with that kind of character defect, don't you, Father?"

"There are different talents given to different people. Patti is a great politician, but she can't sing a note or play the piano. Coady has the makings of a concert soprano, I am told."

"And there is the problem," Tina went on, resolutely thoughtful, objective, dispassionate, "of the influence such an anti-social character defect might have on the young people with whom she is working today, not that it's our responsibility to worry about that."

"I have complete confidence in Linda."

"We are concerned about her, Father." Joe shifted uneasily on the hard chairs we keep in rectory parlors, even in the post-conciliar era, because they discourage parishioners from staying too long. "Maybe if she spent some time in an institution, a few weeks, anyway, it would help." He grinned. "I kind of feel sorry for poor Arthur."

"His name is not Arthur!"

Tina leaned forward, fingertips under her tiny firm chin, a whiff of expensive scent easing its way discreetly across the parlor. "I suppose that there's no way—is there, Father?—that you can screen for those character defects before you hire a youth minister? I know they screen young men in the seminary."

"When her contract expires, Linda tells me that she may go back to school for her doctorate, but I would have no problem renewing it."

Well, that should have made things clear enough, shouldn't it?

"The whole thing is unfortunate." Joe was now playing with his Cadillac key chain as his eyelid twitched violently. "Mind you, it's not your fault, Father. Everyone says you're doing a great job here under the circumstances."

"Poor sweet little Coady Anne didn't want to run." Martina shook her head, baffled over an insoluble puzzle. "But all her little friends insisted. And Linda encouraged her, which was her business, she certainly didn't have to do it. And I said to her, I said, 'Coady Anne, Patricia O'Hara is a formidable candidate.' And she said, poor little tyke, 'I don't have to win, Mummy; I only want to see what it's like to run.' That's why the outcome is so unfortunate."

"What outcome?" I shouted, angry at myself that I was angry and angry that again I had been pulled into their Wonderland scenario.

"We'll do whatever you think best, Padre." Joe put the Caddy keys into his blue sport coat (ideal for dinner at the country club after golf). "We understand that we've become something of a parish problem. We're sorry, but we feel we have to stand by our kids, especially when there are sexual innuendos. What else"—slight choke in his voice—"do you have if you don't have your kids, right? And if you don't stand by them, who will you stand by?"

"So," Tina took over for him, as if rescuing him from the incoherence his strong emotions had created. "If you think it would be better for us to move, we'll do it, without any ill feelings."

"I don't think you ought to move," I exploded. "There's no reason for that."

"It'll be hard." Joe had actually pulled out his handkerchief and was wiping his eyes. "We've always thought of this parish as home."

"For the love of heaven, what do you want me to do?" I shouted so loud that the new associate pastor told me later he could hear me.

"Poor sweet Coady will be all right, of course. She has a

family to stand by her. She feels fine, actually." Tina arranged the folds of her skirt. "It's Linda we're concerned about, Father. Her parents are both dead, you know."

"Will you both shut up and listen!" I rose to my full six feet three inches of slightly moth-eaten, silver-haired, blue-eyed dignity. "I don't want you to leave the parish. There is no reason to do so. Linda did not interfere in the election against Coady. There is no conspiracy against you. This whole crisis is a product of your imaginations."

I promised myself a double shot of Bushmills Black Label. Protestant ministers have wives on whom to dump this sort of crap. Black Bush is a harmless substitute, not so pleasurable but not so demanding, either.

"Maybe you could have a talk with her, Father," Tina murmured softly.

"Coady?" I was girding my loins for a full-scale attack on Martina's game—demolish the whole thing in one fell pastoral swoop. Act like a monsignor even though they were an extinct species.

"Oh, no, she's fine. I mean Linda. Maybe if she went into therapy before she was married—"

"I'll think about it," I muttered, wanting them to walk out the front door before I was trapped in Wonderland with them.

Those magic, if quite dishonest, words were enough. They had discharged their responsibility.

We shook hands, they thanked me and assured me that everyone thought I was doing a great job "under the circumstances." Then they left the rectory and walked briskly down the steps into the warm, caressing Indian summer night—brave, mature Christians, coping well with intense personal pain.

My heart unaccountably heavy despite my victory, I went to the office instead of the parlor. Paying no attention to the red-haired sixteen-year-old porteress who was dying for information, I glanced out the window.

Joe had his arm around Martina, a protective, reassuring husband standing by his wife in her grief. She was sobbing hysterically, her body shaking like that of widow at a graveside.

"Is Coady Anne REALLY going away for the rest of her senior year?" The redhead's curiosity finally tore its bonds asunder. An Irish biddy in training.

"I don't know, Jackie." I turned away from the window. "Maybe."

"Poor kid. Everyone likes her. She has tons of friends. Really."

"I know."

"They chill me out, but I feel sorry for Mr. and Mrs. Condon, too."

Also a gentle Irish mother in the making.

"I feel sorry for everyone, Jackie."

"Yes, Father."

You give up a family of your own and you dedicate yourself to a life of compassion for the least of the brothers and sisters. Fine. But my compassion reared its hesitant head only after Joe and Tina Condon left the rectory. It probably would not have healed their pain, but how did I know that? What sort of compassion is it that excludes those who are strangling on their own hate?

The saints would judge Linda innocent of betrayal. As I sipped my Bushmills, what would they think of me?

What would New Priest think if I told him the story?

CHAPTER

5

"You want to show me how to do those records, Father?" Jamie's broad shoulders appeared in the main office on the first floor of the rectory. "You shouldn't have to do all the work yourself."

He was, need I say, still wearing his Roman collar.

It was after eleven. I was catching up on the wedding and baptismal books because I did not want to try to sleep and be forced to dream of the Condons—and the three marriage preparations that had followed them.

The first-floor office, where the parish secretary defended the fort during the day, suited my mood perfectly: not only did it have the usual weary oak walls and high ceilings, it was actually one of the turrets of the old house. It would have done nicely as the reception room in a Victorian funeral parlor.

I had left up the pictures of the five Popes with which the Founding Pastor had decorated the room. I added Pope John whom he had banished, thus depriving the Founding Pastor of some of the happiness of his heaven if he knew about the new painting.

"I'm used to doing them." I leaned over the books defensively.

In truth I didn't want to give them up. The first two associates had made a mess out of the parish records, and I had decided reluctantly that the old rules no longer applied: you could not demand that associates do the record keeping. Cursing the fact that I had been born between generations and had in my decline to do the work I was obliged to do in my salad days, I took over the records myself.

Now it was a pastoral prerogative, a part of parish life over which I still had control. Dear God, I was getting not only old, but fussy.

"Yeah, but it's an associate's work." Jamie deftly slid the wedding book away from me. "You have enough other things to do."

I pushed a stack of marriage envelopes across the desk. "We're not going to have associates much longer, Jamie. Not with the vocation shortage."

"If priests were happier"—he was inscribing the records in clear and elegant calligraphy—"there wouldn't be a shortage."

"I hear the Cardinal is praying for vocations. He figures that there's nothing else he can do. If the Cardinal is praying for everything he says he's praying for, however, he must be on his knees all night."

"Not a bad place for the Cardinal to be, is it, Father?" He turned a page. "Were those wedding preparations tonight?"

"The last three were. One of them was a couple that was already living together. Those take more time."

"Oh?" He put down the pen and looked up at me. "What do you say?"

"Well, you can't give them the old line that the Church disapproves. They know that and they couldn't care less. So you take them out for supper early in the marriage preparations and ask them why they have decided to get married and what difference it makes. They usually have pretty good answers, although some of my classmates who've never asked the questions don't believe that. Then I use their answers as a basis for further discussion about what public and permanent commitment means. It's a lot of extra work, but maybe there's a payoff. You can never tell in this business."

"You always take engaged couples out for supper, Father?"

"Sure. At least once in the preparation; it's a much better

context than the rectory office. Dinner with a priest is still a memorable event for lay people, God knows why."

"Most of them are afraid of marriage, I think." He was back at the records. "Cohabitation may not be an effective way of finding out whether you're compatible. They're so scared that they'll do anything to reassure themselves—especially if they are from broken homes themselves."

"In this case the bride's father ran out on them when she was thirteen. . . . The voice in that observation was Father Jamie, but the words sound like they may be Mother Maggie."

He blushed, quite pleased with being discovered. "You can always assume that when I say something that sounds intelligent, it's Mama Maggie talking. . . . All marriage cases tonight?"

"The first one wasn't."

"Sounds like it was rough."

He had picked up his mother's counseling-room style, too.

"Crazy more than rough."

So I told him about the Condons. His "nondirective" attention was so sympathetic I even told him about my reaction as they left the rectory.

"Maybe you're being too hard on yourself, Father," he observed when I had finished. "Mom says that those of us in the caring professions must leave people free not to be cared for when they don't want to be cared for."

So what do you say to that?

"What about the kid? Martina will destroy her."

"My mother also says that we should leave some room for the Holy Spirit to do Her work."

"This Mama Maggie I have to meet."

"Oh, you can count on that." He laughed ruefully. "She'll be around one of these days to inspect the premises. She'll love this place. She's into houses that might be haunted."

"I'll sell it to her cheap!"

We both laughed, and he returned to work.

I thought I'd be a gracious loser. "I think I'll turn in."

"I'll finish these and get them out of the way. . . . Oh, Father, do you mind if I visit the school tomorrow?"

"Certainly not. The kids will be astonished that an associate pastor knows where it is. Pay a courtesy call on Sister Cunnegunda first—to ask her if it's all right. She thinks it's 1935."

The parents of Saint Finian's loved "Cunny" because they believed that the great merit of Catholic schools was discipline; Cunny ran the tightest of tight ships. However, so long as there was silence in the corridor and order in the "ranks" coming in from the school yard after the bell had rung (and induced a graveyard silence) Cunny was content to leave the actual teaching to a bright young faculty.

She would, I thought, not be particularly pleased with the New Priest.

"Nineteen thirty-five was not a totally bad time," he said to me.

"Just be sure you don't talk in the corridor."

As I was leaving the room, he looked up at me. "Hey, Father, do you think the Condons will move?"

"Even money." I moved my hand in balancing gesture. "Maybe they'll decide to stay because they think I agreed with them tonight. It's off and away for poor Coady Anne."

"What if I talk to Jackie, and she and this legendary Patti O'Hara bring over a crowd of kids to plead with the Condons to let Coady stay?"

I swallowed and decided—as I would often in the months ahead—that Jamie Keenan was not an innocent after all.

"It would probably work."

"Do you mind?"

"Hell, no, Jamie. It's a great idea!"

One, I told myself as I wrestled later with sleeplessness, that I should have had.

CHAPTER

6

The phone rang a few moments after I had fallen asleep. I fumbled for it in the dark.

"Hi there, good buddy, you shouldn't be up at this hour of the night."

"I was sleeping," I muttered through clenched teeth. The caller was a drunk who phoned maybe once every two months when he was halfway along on the trip to bouncing his face off a barroom floor.

He wouldn't tell me his name. I suspected he was a parishioner. He needed help badly.

"Hey, good for you. Guy like you works so hard he should get a good night sleep."

"I won't now."

"I'll only keep you for a few minutes. Hey, is it true that your white-haired priest is a drunk, like me?"

"No," I rolled over so I would be closer to the phone. "He's not like you. He hasn't had a drink for almost three years. He goes to a lot of AA meetings every week, as you should. He doesn't wake people up in the middle of the night. He's a reformed drunk. You're just a drunk."

"Good for him! Someday I'll be a reformed drunk, too. Now I'm a plain, old-fashioned drunk."

"You'd better believe it."

So it went for a quarter hour or so. Maybe I should have hung up on him. Listening to his inebriated babble probably didn't do him any harm. Hanging up on him, however, might have discouraged him. So I listened.

When he finally said good-bye, in the midst of an outburst of alcoholic tears, I wondered what Mama Maggie would have said. Most likely told me that I was indulging him and my own need for omnipotence.

Now that I had a real live associate pastor, I'd work out a schedule in which the phone would ring in his room half the nights. Maybe he could respond effectively to my nameless friend.

I had settled down and begun to drift back to sleep; the phone rang again.

"Don't ever call again at this time of night," I yelled into it. "You're a drunken bum!"

Reality therapy, tough love. Right?

"Lar?"

"Jeanne?"

"I'm sorry if I woke you. . . ."

"And you're not drunk. That was the last caller."

"If I had any brandy in my apartment, I might be."

She sounded like she had been crying. Tearful drunks, tearful Stalinists.

I waited.

"I'm sorry about this afternoon. I . . . was dreadfully unprofessional."

"You sure were," I responded irritably.

"It's unprofessional to call you this late. . . ."

"It is."

No more Father Nice Guy. I mean, REALLY!

"So I'll call back tomorrow."

"No, you won't. You'll say what you want to say now."

"Yes, Father." She had the nerve to giggle.

"Go on."

"I apologize for acting like a child. I may not like your New Priest, but I'll work with him and honor the terms of my contract. Please forgive me."

Jeanne had never apologized. We were making progress.

Now I had to say something professional and tender.

"I wasn't asleep Jeanne. If I were, it would have been worth waking up to hear those words."

More tender than professional, I guess. What the hell.

"Thank you, Lar." She was surely crying now. "I like it at Saint Finian's even if it is a reactionary bourgeois community. I'm happier here than I have been for a long time. You've been very patient with me."

"It's not hard to be patient with you, Jeanne." Too tender. So I added, "You're good at what you do. Ideology or not, the people like you."

Her usual answer would have been that she didn't care whether they liked her or not.

"I know they do. . . . I don't—Thank you, Lar. Sorry for waking you."

"Anytime," I lied.

Jeanne Flavin simply did not apologize. Much less admit that she knew that the parish liked her, despite her radicalism and her anger.

We were making progress.

I hoped the New Priest and she would not fight too much.

I slept peacefully the rest of the night.

CHAPTER

7

The New Priest cornered me after my Mass, uh, Eucharistic Celebration, the next morning.

"I don't want to alarm you, Father, but the bell tower is in bad shape."

"I know." I usually sound irritable before breakfast.

"It's not the electronic chimes—"

"They haven't worked in fifteen years."

"No problem"—the now-expected wave of the hand—"I'll have them playing the Angelus by suppertime. It's the walls of the bell tower. They need tuck-pointing as soon as possible or you'll have a major problem. I can't be responsible," he added, shaking his head sadly, "for what happens even next month if we don't do something now."

I am the pastor. I'm the one who is responsible if the bricks start falling out of the bell tower. That's what I thought. What I said was: "The finance subcommittee of the parish council didn't see how we could fit it into this year's budget."

"No problem, Father. I can get it done free. I'll have the tuck-pointers here this afternoon."

"I think we ought to be able to pay our own way, Jamie."

"With the budget you're carrying, Father? Anyone who is providing quality private education for his people at such low cost is entitled to a little community service help now and then. Don't give it another thought. It's on the house."

I didn't ask which house. I didn't want to know.

"Come on," I said, "let's take a hike around the parish."

"Great idea! Tell me about the people!"

A light Indian summer haze touched the carefully manicured lawns and old oak trees of Forest Springs, hinting at the gentleness of a lover's hand. It would be one more of those kind of days—golden, nostalgic, infinitely sad.

"They're not bad as people go." Jamie Keenan was the first associate who did not have to race to keep up with me. "In fact, they're a lot better than their priests, present company tentatively excepted."

He chortled at that. Kid didn't miss much.

"Hell, religion is retail, not wholesale."

"It exists at its best in the parish and not in the Chancery or the seminary or the Vatican."

"You don't understand, Father New Priest. You're supposed to ask me what my epigrams mean."

"Yes, Father Old Priest."

"Anyway"—I retreated from that defeat—"they're generous according to their lights, dedicated to the parish and the faith as they see it, and totally loyal to the Church—on their own terms. Naturally."

"Naturally."

"There's nothing left that we priests could do that we have not done to drive them out."

"Not for want of trying."

"They'll complain and bitch and offer stupid suggestions, but if something goes wrong, they rally round one another with a fervor that you might find in the Acts of the Apostles."

"Peasant village."

"Take that house over there at the end of Oak Street across from Myrtle Park. Kate Daly lives there. Well, so do her husband and kids, too. However, it's always Kate Daly's house. Her only fault that I know of is that she's a Republican, a precinct captain as a matter of fact."

"Redemption is yet possible."

"Barely. She may be the most generous human being I've ever known. There is not a tear to be wiped away in this parish to which she is not attentive—with a pot roast and potato salad and a powderless chocolate cake thrown in for good measure. You may not want to be adopted by Kate if you're hurting, but you don't have much choice in the matter. I doubt that there's a priest in the archdiocese that is as good a Christian as Kate."

"And herself a Republican, too!"

"No one is perfect. If, as seems unlikely given your youth, you should fall sick in the winter, you will not only have to eat Cook's marvels, you'll have to dispose of every last crumb of Kate's daily offering."

"I'll look forward to it."

"The typical suburban Catholic parish," I began my lecture, "despite J. F. Powers's new novel, is a mix of 'Hill Street Blues' and 'Cheers,' of 'Miami Vice' and 'All in the Family.' You move from comedy to tragedy, from meanness to generosity, from the mystical to the trivial without warning and without time to adjust."

"I didn't know you watched television so much, Father," he said solemnly.

I searched his handsome young face for a trace of irony. It was bland, innocent, definitely Billy Budd–ish. Then his lips moved impishly as he failed to hide his big grin.

"I heard about it from one of your predecessors."

"I know. He began with Kathleen Sullivan and ended with David Letterman. Good taste in women anyway."

"My quotes get around," I said, searching for some pastoral dignity.

"I do take your point." He laughed. "And the priest must be a mixture of Daniel J. Travanti, Don Johnson, Bill Cosby, and George Wendt?"

I laughed with him. "Something like that. . . . And before this is over, I may want the TV-watching associate back!"

"He won't bring Bushmills!" The New Priest laughed again.

I wondered, as I often would—as I still do—whether he was Billy Budd or Puck or some wild West Side Irish mixture of the two.

So we loped through the parish, the worn-out old stallion and the frisky colt preparing for the Derby. I pointed out the homes and told him about the people.

"You know every family in the parish and everything about them, Father?" he asked with a certain tone of awe. I was now to be revered instead of gently ridiculed.

"It's not all that big, and I probably miss on some of our Christmas and Easter folk."

That afternoon the tuck-pointers, as promised, arrived. Fifteen minutes after they began to work, Mel Maguire was on the phone. "I noticed that you're tuck-pointing the bell tower, Father."

Mel, who is the chairman of our finance committee, watches me like the *Washington Post* watches the defense department.

"From your office in the Loop? Have you moved to Sears Tower?"

Small laugh. "Actually Sue called me."

"Donation."

"Really?"

"Father Keenan arranged it. The New Priest." Then, because I was in a contentious mood, I added, "He says the bells will be working by suppertime."

"You know that they haven't worked in sixteen years, Father. And it would cost at least eight thousand dollars to fix them. I don't have to tell you that we don't have that kind of money in our budget, do I?"

"Father Keenan has undertaken to fix them himself. He assures me that they are 'no problem.'"

"Does this New Priest walk on water?"

"I shouldn't be the least surprised."

The finance committee does not, strictly speaking, have the right to veto my decisions. But I've found through the years that a pastor is smart if he gives the laity a share of the action.

I'm not a bomb-throwing radical—not anymore, that is. I guess I am your certified Catholic liberal. I'm against apartheid and for the ordination of women, for the merit selection of judges and against nuclear weapons, for the poor and against the rich (more or less). So naturally I'm for lay participation in parish decision-making. It takes a lot more time in the short run but makes things easier in the long run.

Or so I tell myself.

Everyone knows that I'm the boss if push comes to shove, but we manage usually to avoid both pushing and shoving.

Mel Maguire is the kind of guy I'd like to shove.

I'm not sure how liberal I am anymore. It's hard to keep up. I heard someone at a Priest Senate meeting describe me as a "moderate." And my last associate pastor told me that I was in fact a "new conservative."

I didn't throw bombs when I was young, you say?

Ah, but I did!

It was back in the sixties. I'd been ordained a couple of years and had finally been liberated from Red Murphy's tyranny. I had been assigned to a "changing" neighborhood on the West Side. The community was mostly apartment buildings and two-flats, with a sprinkling of single-family units. The panic peddlers—"blockbusters" we called them—concentrated on the single-family places. If they could create terror among the owners of such homes, they could buy them cheap. Then on May 1, moving day, the apartments would be emptied out, and an all-white neighborhood would have become over-night all black.

The home owners would have lost much of their invest-ment. The blockbusters would have made millions of dollars. And re-segregation would have claimed yet another commu-nity.

Racial prejudice and fear were part of the terror. They were, however, aggravated by fright at losing one's equity in one's home. Looking back on it, the housing stock in the neighborhood was not all that good; the community would have eventually dete-riorated anyway. The blockbusters, nonetheless, hastened the deterioration and grew rich out of racial distrust that they themselves had made worse.

In those days, they looked like evil men. Hell, even today they look like evil men.

Another young priest and I decided that Mile Hi Realty

(I never did learn where the name came from—maybe they were Denver Bronco fans!) was the enemy. We confronted the owners—two genial Irishmen who were both ushers in their parishes out in the suburbs—and told them that they were enemies of the people. (It was, you will remember, the 1960s.) They replied that they were good Catholics.

We formed a community organization to fight them, but it was too late. You can take it as axiomatic that by the time the Church wakes up to a social problem and tries to do something about it, the battle has already been lost.

We were no match for their ruthless greed and political clout. We picketed City Hall in vain. We went on TV and were warned by the Chancery that the Cardinal was displeased with us.

We knew we were losing the battle, and like the laity of our generation, we could not accept defeat as part of the human condition.

So my friend and I decided that the time had come for "direct revolutionary action." Mile Hi was a legitimate target for the anger of the People.

We were, naturally, the People.

So we determined to send Mile Hi a mile high.

We "liberated" some explosive from a demolition company about which my friend knew. On a cold November night in the drizzle and fog, I blackened the license plates on my car with mud, donned a ski mask like they did in the movies, and drove slowly over to the dimly lighted street where the enemy lurked. I think I even wore a black turtleneck and black jeans—if I were a few years older, I might have donned a trench coat à la Bulldog Drummond. With the mixture of caution and frivolity that amateur revolutionaries affect, we carefully laid the charges around the storefront Mile Hi occupied (the other stores in the building and the apartments being vacant). With a nice flair for the dramatic (stolen from the astronaut launches), we counted down from ten. I pushed the plunger on the mechanism, which was supposed to ignite the explosive.

I felt like I was in Leningrad and it was October 1917. All I needed was a Trotsky cap (I was bearded in those days).

We waited. Nothing happened.

We continued to wait.

No explosion.

Bombs went off more efficiently in October 1917.

We knew almost nothing about explosives. I assumed that somehow we had bungled our direct revolutionary action. I had begun to walk toward the storefront to see where we had made our mistake; then the whole building went up in a blinding puff. I was transported some ten feet backward and dumped unceremoniously on my rear end.

Mile Hi had gone a mile high all right. So had the rest of the building, a traffic light, several street lights, and an empty two-flat around the corner.

The explosive was a lot more powerful than we had thought it would be.

It was probably the single most effective direct revolutionary action in Chicago in the late 1960s.

We were fortunate that we didn't go a mile high, too.

Instead, we slipped away into the night, feeling that we were the highly successful vanguard of the People.

Naturally we didn't have enough sense to keep quiet about our accomplishments.

For some reason the forces of justice, reaction, and law and order never caught up with us.

The Mile Hi parish ushers suspected us but couldn't prove it. The cops were pretty sure we had done it, but they didn't like Mile Hi and, in the absence of anything more than rumors, were content to laugh at us. The Cardinal who, as you will doubtless remember, was nuttier than a fruitcake, dismissed the rumors as ridiculous.

Years after the statute of limitations had expired, a prominent person in the criminal justice system commented to me, "You two punks were lucky you didn't kill yourselves that November night."

"What November night?"

"The night Mile Hi went a mile high."

"Do I look like a radical bomb thrower?"

"You don't, that's just the trouble."

I cope with that episode by trying to persuade myself that it was someone else. Laurence McAuliffe is an enlightened liberal, a *Commonweal, America, National Catholic Reporter* moderate. The kid that pushed the plunger on Mile Hi was a young nut—even if he was almost thirty years old. It was a miracle that the idiot didn't kill himself.

And, I think with a shiver, other people, too.

Worst of all, Mile Hi was open for business at another storefront two days later.

What was Jamie Keenan? A radical? A liberal? A conservative? Or didn't those terms mean anything anymore?

My reverie about Mile Hi was interrupted by the house phone: Sister Cunnegunda from the school. In high dudgeon.

"Your associate pastor is disrupting my school."

It wasn't her school. It was Saint Finian's school. I was the pastor, the supreme authority over the school.

Right?

However I am a modern, permissive pastor. And I'm still afraid of fierce, elderly nuns.

"Didn't he ask permission to visit the classrooms?"

"Certainly," she huffed. "My teachers would not admit him to the classrooms unless he had my permission. But I did not give him permission to make the children laugh."

"Laugh?"

"We do not have laughter in this school, Father McAuliffe. Not while I'm principal."

Then I'll get a new principal.

"I don't think I can censor my associate pastor's classroom behavior, Sister."

"Then I will forbid him to return to the classrooms. I will not have my teachers' work disrupted."

"No, you won't, Sister, not unless I have proof of disruption."

Plunge the charger again!

"I beg your pardon, Father?"

Here comes the ice truck.

"I think we all agree, Sister, that one of the great advantages of Catholic education is the contact established between children and parish priests. Father Jamie, um, Father Keenan is the first associate pastor in years who has been interested in the kids. He will continue to visit the classes, in consultation with the teachers so as not to interfere with their work. Should I be presented with evidence of such interference, I will ask him to modify his behavior. Is that clear, Sister?"

"Yes, Father."

"Good."

When dealing with a 1935 nun, you simply act like a 1935 pastor, right?

I wandered into the school yard as the kids were coming out.

"You know what, Father Lar?"

"No, what, Melissa?"

Blond, ponytail, fifth grade.

"Father Jamie told us a story about raspberries."

"And dandelions!"

"Really, Jeremy!"

"And Rory the storyteller!"

"And the peddler of Ballybagadeen!"

"Know what, Father Lar?"

"No, what, Matthew?"

"Father Jamie is the greatest storyteller in all the world."

"I believe it, Matthew. . . . What do you think, Ms. Grady?"

Brown hair, short, twenty-four, lovely.

"He saved the day, Father Lar. On warm Indian summer af-
ternoons we all fall asleep—teachers, too. Father Jamie's stories
woke us up—and we'll spend religion class the rest of the week
on them."

"Great!"

"You'll keep coming, too, won't you, Father?"

Ms. Grady wanted to spare my feelings.

And made it worse.

"If Father Jamie tells me some of his stories."

Laughter all around.

So much for Sister Cunnegunda.

And for a bomb-throwing pastor.

That night at supper the chimes rang on schedule, for the
first time in the memory of humankind. "Would you lead us in
the Angelus, Father?" Jamie Keenan asked me.

After I had finished the prayer, Cook, her long blond hair
trailing behind her like Queen Maeve herself, swarmed into the
dining room with a platter of rolls carried in one hand like
pirate booty! "Father Keenan himself has made the cinnamon
buns."

"And does your man make good cinnamon buns, Biddy?" I
asked.

"Och," she said as she swept out under full sail, "would I be
after serving them to Your Reverence if they weren't the best?"

They may not have been the best, but they were better than
any we'd eaten at Saint Finian's rectory in a long time.

Come to think of it, I couldn't remember when we'd had
cinnamon rolls for supper.

The chimes turned to "Adeste Fideles."

"Out of season, Jamie," Turk observed, not displeased to
have caught the unflappable Jamie in a mistake.

"I'll get the seasonal cycle running before Mass tomorrow morning." Jamie waved his hand. "No problem."

In the next five days, a new layer of asphalt was laid on the parking lot, and the lines were redrawn "for greater efficiency in parking the cars." New backboards were installed in the courts; the volleyball nets were replaced; the leak in the large conference room of the ministry center was fixed; and new carpet appeared in the sacristy. None of these improvements cost the parish budget a penny. I don't wish to suggest that Jamie was bumptious or disrespectful about these "fixings" as he called them. I was consulted at every step. My doubts and hesitations about the "improvements" as I called them were treated as agreement and approval.

And six Waterford crystal goblets—Lismore pattern—appeared on the shelf above my small refrigerator. The New Priest, with a disarming chuckle, said that he had no idea how they got there.

Where did the money come from to pay for the quick refurbishing for our parish "plant"? Some of the work was done as a return of "favors" to Jamie or his family; others were pure donation; and yet others (like the new lines on the basketball and volleyball courts and the new "weather resistant" volleyball net) Jamie paid for himself. "As long as you have money," he assured me, "it's only a problem if you take it seriously."

Quiet inquiries revealed to me that Jamie's family had enough money to buy and sell most of the families that we thought were affluent in the parish. The Gucci luggage fit with that, though not the off-the-rack black suits (and it's hard these days to find a rack with a black suit) and the six-year-old Chevy Nova he drove.

The New Priest black hurricane continued to sweep through our parish. Jamie visited the sick and the dying, buried the dead, instructed those about to be married, played basketball with the kids (he was not quite as good as I was at his age, but

I was no longer his age), preached every morning, revitalized the dormant parish census, and prayed in church for a half hour at the end of every day.

He also introduced a new set of computer programs.

I was summoned one night to his room. On a table, crowded up against his desk in the battlement that served as his study, a toolbox affair and a video screen faced me.

"Compaq 386/20," he beamed proudly, still wearing his Roman collar. "A hundred-megabyte hard disk and ten megabytes of active memory. OS/2 compatible. VGA screen, and Laserjet II-B printer. Top of the line, state of the art."

"Impressive."

He might as well have been talking Aramaic.

"I've got a program that will do the parish accounts in a jiffy, another to update our census records, and even one that will keep the marriage and baptism books."

"Then you won't be able to use the machine yourself."

"No problem," he waved his hand, "I use OS/2. We'll do the parish stuff in background mode when I'm working on a sermon or something in foreground."

"I see."

"And we've got an Aldus desktop publishing system and an HP scanner, so we can turn out our own parish bulletin." He waved a sheet of paper at me triumphantly. "I mean, isn't this radical?"

"Astonishingly professional. Who did the sketches of the church and the rectory? I like the rectory. It looks properly comic."

"Oh." He waved a hand as if that were unimportant. "I did them."

"On that screen?"

"No, I input it with the scanner. We can input almost anything, although the laserjet has trouble with some of the grays. I don't think we're ready for color yet."

The proposed newsletter was clean, neat, and elegant. It contained all the announcements, a number of spiritual observations that were doubtless his, and a blank column headed "From the Pastor's Desk."

I was to be allowed to contribute.

No, I was expected to contribute.

"How much"—I turned the sheet of paper over—"will this newsletter cost us?"

"What four reams of pretty good quality paper cost."

"But the, uh, technology?"

"On the house." He waved his hand as if fending off a light autumn breeze. "Most of my class have these systems."

We used to worry about buying chalices. Now we worried about PC systems.

"I can't fight it, Jamie."

"And look." He pushed a couple of keys enthusiastically. "This will keep the records and"—he waved a sheet of blank checks—"print out the payroll."

"Print out the payroll!"

"Sure! Look." He touched a couple of other keys, and the screen flashed an attractive color of ocher. "You simply enter the name here, and the salary here, and then the machine prints out the check and calculates the tax and social security payments and prints them out on government forms after it does the checks."

"Diabolical!"

"Seraphic! . . . I can teach Mrs. Clarke and Jackie and Lisa and Sarah and Jennifer. They won't be bored in the office after they've finished their homework. We may have to raise their pay a little because they've become skilled workers."

"No problem." This time I waved my hand. "It will do the payroll?"

For a time we had sent out the payroll to a service that promised to do it for us professionally. I'm sure most such organizations are competent. The one that lured us did all things well except for the actual delivery of the checks on time.

The staff was, as you might imagine, intolerant of such errors. So Mrs. Clarke, our long-suffering parish secretary, wrote out all checks by hand.

"Sure. I've already talked to Mr. Maguire, and he says he can't figure out why such software didn't exist before."

"You did the software, too?"

"Of course not, Father. That takes talent."

"I understand."

"I can," he said, lowering his head shyly, "teach you how to work some of these programs."

"No way."

"It's a lot easier"—he turned away and bit his lip to suppress a grin—"than setting off dynamite charges."

"You know that story?"

"Everyone knows it." The grin was escaping the restraint of his teeth.

"Don't believe it."

"Yes, Father."

Silence.

"Jackie can work this thing."

"Oh, damn, what do I do first."

Thus did I enter the computer age.

After a brief introductory lesson—at which I was notably less than a complete success—I drifted into Mike's room and collapsed into an easy chair. He was watching something about wild animals on PBS and sipping a diet Cherry Coke.

"The kid wearing you out, Lar?" He cocked a wise brown eye in my direction.

"I was never that enthusiastic, Mike, never."

"Oh?"

"Remember what it was like? You were filled with zeal, you fell in love with the parish, you worked eighteen hours a day, you thought the new age of Catholicism had been born and you were part of it."

"And you weren't?"

"Animal spirits, Mike, animal spirits. What frosts me about Jamie is the thought he may never become old and disillusioned."

"Never run out of enthusiasm?"

"Don't play the client-centered counselor with me. . . . Yeah, something like that. It may be genetic. Look at Packy and his parents. Some people are born enthusiasts."

"You ought to know, Lar."

"Not me."

"Ha!"

"Cut it out!"

"Did I not hear you taking computer lessons?"

"If I weren't the pastor, he would have given me an F."

"Who else of our generation of clerics would try?"

"Doesn't prove anything."

I ambled back to my room. My enthusiasm had died in the summer of 1968 when Paul VI issued his birth control encyclical and extinguished the fires of hope lighted by the Vatican Council. .

Only Jeanne Flavin was unimpressed with my New Priest.

"Just as I thought. A spoiled young brat," she hissed at me in the sacristy after Saturday Mass.

"He works hard," I replied to Jeanne. "We're lucky not to have another TV addict."

"He knows nothing of life." Jeanne pursed her thin lips. "And probably will never have to suffer enough to understand what suffering is. He's not even dry behind the ears yet."

"The surest sign that we're getting old, Jeanne, is that we start to complain about the young. I've resolved never to complain about them and hence not grow old."

"That's age-group prejudice," she responded tartly.

I've said that Jeanne was a Marxist, even a Stalinist, because that is how she would describe herself, poor woman. I must explain that I did not mean that she had read Marx or Lenin or Engels or that she had seriously adopted dialectical materialism as a philosophy.

Thus when an American nun or ex-nun like Jeanne tells you she's a Stalinist, she merely means that she supports violent revolution in "Third World countries." She does not mean that she belongs to a revolutionary cell either here or abroad or that she personally would engage in violence to end oppression.

Once you understand the rhetoric, you are less likely to be offended by the combination of radical fervor and Communist language that women like Jeanne speak. While some of our parishioners are still offended that we have a self-professed "Catholic Communist" on our staff, most of them now realize that Jeanne is not dangerous and that she is not leading our young people into the Communist camp. They are content to admire her Faye Dunaway good looks, feel sorry for her, and tell you what a fine job she does with the religious education program.

Unfortunately in other countries the authorities are not likely to be so tolerant. As Jeanne had found out.

"Men like James Keenan offend me." Her habitual frown deepened. "Their poise and their lifestyle are the result of draining blood from the bodies of the poor. He cannot imagine what it would be like to be poor and will never feel any guilt for having exploited the poor."

"He works hard," I said mildly.

Her eyes blazed. "For men like him salvation will be possible only when they are prepared to expiate their guilt."

As a daughter of Lake Forest wealth, Jeanne had long ago chosen to make guilt expiation her life vocation.

"By this shall all men know that you are my disciples," I said mildly, "that you expiate your guilt to the poor."

I knew it was a mistake when I said it, and Jeanne then strove to raise my consciousness about my own responsibility to the poor.

"Don't worry, Lar," she said, relenting a little, "I'll keep my promise and work with him professionally, and"—she managed a quick smile—"I won't wake you up with a teary phone call again."

"It's *my* professional responsibility to answer night calls, Jeanne. That's one of the reasons for having priests."

She nodded and turned away quickly, probably to hide more tears.

Jeanne Flavin had not cried in my presence for two years. We were indeed making progress.

I hoped we were.

Since she was always intelligent—within the constraints of her political blinders—and since she does not listen to what the other person says when politics and economics are the subject, arguments with her are frustrating and pointless. However, one need only listen patiently while she recites her creed. Having discharged her obligation to the revolution, she becomes a sensible and creative teacher. And a fragile, fragile woman hopelessly dependent on your approval.

We'd had a big fight early on about the RCIA, Rite of Christian Initiation for Adults. It's a book liturgical scholars put together after the Vatican Council. The ritual itself is harmless. However, many of the "liturgists" and "religious educators" who afflict the Church these days want to turn it into a blueprint for "transforming the people, winning them away from their consumerism and privatism and individualism."

These folks are cultists who want power in the parish and power in the Church—power to mold others to be what they want them to be by putting them through a long, involved, convoluted, and mostly artificial process.

"All the ministry of the Church"—she thrust the book at

me—"should follow the model of the RCIA. It's *mandated* by the Vatican and the American bishops."

"So what?"

"The *Church* wants it."

"The Vatican and the American bishops say women can't be priests."

"That's different."

"Look, Mrs. Donlon wants to become a Catholic. She's finally decided to take the big step. Don't ask me why it's been so long. That's between her and God. Now she wants in. I say let her in. Now."

"But—"

"No 'but's. She has been coming to Mass with her husband and kids for fifteen years. She's the best High Club chaperone in the parish. She's been receiving Communion for five years. I will not permit you to banish her from the church after the homily and bar her from Communion, do you understand that?"

"She must go through the rite of election, the scrutinies, and the mystagogy."

Like all cultists, the RCIA folk have their own buzzwords.

(You want to know what they mean? The "rite of election" is the official approval of the candidate; the "scrutiny" is a public "exam"; and "mystagogy" is follow-up instruction. All three are empty rituals, made no less empty by the fancy buzzwords.)

"She doesn't have to go through anything. We'll admit her to the Church on Christmas Eve—catching up with something the Holy Spirit did long ago."

"Easter is the proper time for baptism!"

"The proper time is whenever is best for people. I will not exclude Edna Donlon for one more day, no matter what some goddamn ritual says."

I was, you may have noted, getting hot under the collar.

"You can find yourself a new DRE!"

"Only if you want to violate your contract and quit on us."

I then explained at some length that one must interpret all regulations and rituals according to the needs of the people and the community.

"I'm not opposed to the restoration of the Catechumenate, Jeanne. The point is that Edna has been a catechumen for fifteen years."

"She still should be dismissed after the homily for further instructions, like all other catechumens." She had backed off from her threat to quit.

"We tossed out those who were preparing to be Christians in the old days because of the Discipline of the Secret, which was supposed to protect us from spies who worked for the Roman Empire. In case you hadn't noticed it, Jeanne, the Roman Empire expired long ago."

"You're the male priest, so you have all the power," she ungraciously admitted defeat.

Then she prepared, with Edna Donlon and her family, a beautiful ceremony of "reconciliation" with the Church. I didn't much like the title, but a rose is a rose.

"Why do you keep her on the staff?" my seminary classmates ask me. "She makes trouble wherever she goes."

I reply that at least she doesn't sue every parish at which she works, like a certain church musician does. Which is no answer. Do I renew her contract every year because I feel sorry for the poor woman, as some on the Parish Council suggest?

I don't think so. The simple fact is that she is a first-rate religious educator. I'm not sure we accomplish much in our religion classes for kids who go to public schools, but if our program, like most of the others, is a waste of time and money, it's not Jeanne's fault. She had acquired a doctorate in educational administration before she left for Asia. She runs a smooth, professional operation in which the kids are exposed to solid, if contemporary, Catholic teaching and not merely romantic

Third World clichés. Her Marxist tirades, always in well-modulated, periodic sentences, are added above and beyond the regular classroom material.

"If she wasn't a little nutty on Communism," one of the more perceptive Irish lawyers on the Parish Council observed, "we wouldn't get that quality religious education at the price we're paying."

Moreover, we are a rather self-satisfied, complacent, comfortable Catholic community. It is good for all of us to hear about the poverty and misery that still afflict many of our fellow humans. I don't believe that they're poor because we're affluent—and here I dissent from Jeanne and the rest of the Catholic Marxists—but I do believe that we should be troubled by their plight and always wondering what we can do to change it. Someone, like Jeanne, who has lived through the agony of terrible poverty and suffered because of her horror of it is not a bad sign of contradiction to have around the parish.

Sure, I do feel sorry for her. She has drifted from parish to parish since she left her order, looking for a place in which she can preach her gospel of expiation (since there's no chance of her getting into a Third World country, no matter what her skills). She's kind of a Flying Dutchman of Catholic social guilt, a restless, driven woman searching for peace, which presumably she will never find.

Since she's not a problem once you understand how to deal with her, it's no great trouble to provide her with a reasonably supportive home until her restlessness drives her somewhere else.

I can't figure out exactly why, but the teenagers like her. Somehow they can discount her bad temper and her ideology and turn to her for advice.

"Do you like my prom dress, Ms. Flavin?"

"A lot of boob, Jackie."

"Too much?"

"Not quite."

"Sure?"

"What does your mother think?"

"She says it's a little too daring."

"Mothers are like that." Jeanne would laugh. "I bet she'd be disappointed if you didn't wear it."

"I think so, too."

Joint laughter—and then dead silence as they saw the pastor in the doorway.

"What do *you* think?" there would be a hint of mockery in Jeanne's eye.

"I wouldn't dare have an opinion."

Later Jeanne cornered me.

"I hope you didn't mind about me and Jackie, Lar."

"A figure like hers ought not to be hidden."

"Chauvinist! I didn't mean that."

"What did you mean?"

"Well . . . maybe I am getting too close to them, interfering in Linda's world."

"Anyone whom those kids trust has jurisdiction, as far as I'm concerned. I'm sure Linda doesn't mind."

"I. . . . I kind of enjoy them."

"Shame!"

She ignored my joke. "They remind me of what I was and of what I wanted to do, which was work with people like them."

"Don't you in the CCD classes?"

"It's different." She turned away, as though she had already revealed too much of herself.

Little vignettes like that might not happen very often, but each time I witnessed one, I figured there must be others that I didn't observe and that maybe Saint Finian's was good for Jeanne, just as she was for us.

Finally—to be perfectly honest—as I said before, I think I'm just a little bit in love with her.

A priest fall in love? Why not? We're human beings and human beings fall in love or come close to it all the time. It does not follow that such emotional reactions (of infatuation) need ever go beyond the imagination.

Nor is it ever easy, as everyone knows, celibate or not, to keep them only in the imagination.

In the caring professions, as Mama Maggie apparently calls them, you have power over other people, a power which is especially poignant and disconcerting when the other is an attractive and wounded member of the opposite sex. I was not only Jeanne Flavin's priest and confidant and intellectual mentor. I was most of her emotional support, and I literally controlled her destiny.

Such power imposes a heavy burden on a relationship but also weights it with delight. Tenderness for someone who has been hurt is the first step toward falling in love if the other is sexually attractive. And Jeanne was surely that, in my eyes anyway.

The kids seemed to agree.

The ineffable Patti O'Hara—brown hair, brown eyes, and five feet eight of womanly athletic grace—and Jackie were discussing that subject one evening in the latter's office in the rectory. Patti had come with her current set of ukases for the High Club.

"She'd be bitchin' if she took care of herself."

"She ought to work out every day. Maybe we can give her some weights for Christmas."

"You know what? Maybe we can find a man for her."

"Hey, that's a good idea. Let's make a list!"

I withdrew before I could hear more.

I am not suggesting that I was about to make a pass at Jeanne. Much less ever take her to bed. Trust should generate reverence and respect. She trusted me. For reasons of professional responsibility, if not of priestly virtue, I must reverence and respect her.

Such restraints did not make her any less appealing.

Did she respond the same way?

I had been around long enough to know that in the circumstances she surely must, almost certainly not admitting to herself any attraction toward me.

So my sessions with Jeanne Flavin were always tense, exhausting, rewarding, and delightful.

Was I helping her? I was pretty sure that I was. But I also knew that I had to be careful. No taking her in my arms as I often ached to do.

Oh, yes, the sparks would fly between her and my New Priest.

Everyone on the staff resents a young associate. He is inexperienced in our craft; he does not know the parish; he has no sense of the history of our problems or of the experiments we have made and the conflicts we have resolved. Nonetheless, because he is a priest—not a music director or a director of religious education, or a youth minister or a permanent deacon or whatever other new kind of cleric or quasi-cleric you have added to the parish budget—he enjoys more status, more power, and more respect than anyone else on the staff, the pastor alone excepted.

Under the best conditions Jamie Keenan would be less than welcome. His self-confidence, his astonishing good looks, his charm, his skills were especially offensive. To no one more offensive than to Jeanne Flavin, a woman from the same background, on whose Pietà face I had never seen the hint of a smile.

I was worried, then, about the confrontation between those two polar opposites?

God help me and forgive me for it, I was looking forward to the conflict the way I used to wait for the Notre Dame–UCLA basketball games or more recently the struggle of the titans, respectively from North Carolina and Georgetown. Or Arizona and UNLV.

"I don't want him in my RE classes," she said to me decisively in back of church that first Saturday morning at the end of September. "We are concerned about serious education, not clerical happy talk."

"That's between you and him," I said with the fine sense of decisive leadership that Roman Catholic pastors cultivate these days.

"It's my program, my responsibility," she retorted, scowling fiercely. "You promised me full control as long as I adhered to the guidelines."

"I won't go back on my promise, Jeanne, but I'd rather that you and Father Keenan work out the problem yourselves, should it arise. I think the young people in your program are entitled to have a priest in their classroom occasionally."

"We were better off," she said grimly, "when we had a curate with TV addiction."

"Associate," I corrected her. "We don't have curates anymore."

"Of course." She did not smile.

"I repeat, Jeanne, that the parish priests ought to visit your classes more frequently than I am able."

She melted as she always did when I managed to sound authoritative.

"You're right, Lar—as always. We'll work something out."

"Sound, professional decision."

"Thank you. . . . Now could you make some suggestions of how we might explain this first section of chapter ten of St. John's Gospel?" She opened the Bible she'd been carrying and pointed out the passage to me. "I'm not sure I understand it myself."

In the transition from revolutionary to teacher, Jeanne

Flavin seems always to experience a moment of frightened vulnerability, as if in the change of masks she might be for a few seconds utterly defenseless. I suppose it was those few seconds of naked terror that were my main reason for not firing her.

They were the times when I loved her most, the times when I was closest to taking her into my arms. That Saturday morning I escaped virtuous, as I always had.

As usual, I was also poignantly aware that the line between desire and lust is thin indeed.

I was not hopelessly in love with her: she was not on my mind all the time. The chemistry worked only when I talked to her—or saw her at a distance. Yet I did not kid myself: it was not a completely safe relationship.

They never are. A twist of thigh as someone walks by, a hint of breast under a sweatshirt, and you're in trouble.

It comes with being human.

I was prepared for the sparks to fly between my New Priest and my Old Communist. Despite my own half-infatuation with this tragic woman, I was not prepared that they be sparks of love.

CHAPTER

8

Like buzzards circling the body of what might be a dying beast, the Corpus Christi bunch, led by the indefatigable George Wholey, descended on my New Priest.

It was a serene Indian summer Sunday, wrapped in a light golden haze—perfect for golf, football games, walking in the woods, and a lazy afternoon nap (with or without a beloved, if you happened to have one). It was not a day for heresy hunting.

The ethos of the Corpus Christi, however, allowed little value to the beauties of nature or concern about the Chicago Bears. The New Priest was standing in back of church after his Mass and hence a perfect target.

Orthodox doctrine, taught in orthodox language, was the all-important reality.

The Society of Corpus Christi is what they call a "secular institute," a group of laity and clergy who do not live a common life but have banded together under a rule and endeavor to represent Christian values in the world in which the laity work. Nothing wrong with the idea. In practice, however, they have become right-wing authoritarian communities hungry for power in Church and society. The Opus Dei, a first cousin of Corpus Christi, was called the "white Masons" in Spain, a comparison which I think is unfair to the Masons. In recent years they have devoted considerable energy to hunting and denouncing heresy, much to the delight of their patrons in Rome.

Here it goes, I thought as George Wholey, notebook in hand and his long-suffering wife, Jill, and four other Corpus Christi couples trailing behind him, closed in on Jamie.

He can't say I didn't warn him, I thought virtuously.

Jamie had preached about Martha and Mary and contended that they were teenage friends of Jesus (obviously young because they were not married). Mary, he suggested, had a teenager's crush on an older man, which delighted Jesus, who responded to it with just the right combination of respect and restraint.

The parishioners swarmed around him after Mass to praise the homily. A bevy of teenage girls lurked in the background, imitating the example of the sisters of Lazarus. Then they rushed in to introduce themselves to "Father New Priest."

"Uh, Father," George interrupted the teenage babble. "Can I have a few words with you? It's sort of a matter of conscience."

Everything was a matter of conscience with George. He sounded like an undertaker when he was pretending to be friendly.

He was a big, bald man whose immense forehead was always contorted in a worried frown. By "big" I mean a vast balloon that you often pictured pricking to see if the hot air would rush out and he would collapse. Some of his immensity was muscle left over from the days when he was a construction worker. Much of it was layers of fat piled on after he made a success of his own construction company in the building boom of the late sixties.

George had enough money to live in the parish, not at the top of the economic pyramid but not at the bottom, either. Although he was not as smart as our M.D.s and lawyers, stockbrokers and commodity traders, business executives and real estate developers, he was a shrewd, not to say ruthless, practitioner of the skills of a construction contractor.

"You don't want to get in a bidding war with George," an architect from the parish told me. "In fact, if you're smart you don't want to have anything to do with him at all."

Shrewd, then, he was. He lacked, however, the smoothness, the polish, the appearance of flexible intelligence which was usually required to be accepted in Forest Springs.

Unlike most of the people in the community, George had been born in Forest Springs and on the wrong side of the railroad tracks at that.

Forest Springs is a railroad town, forty minutes west of the Loop by train and beyond the ring of suburbs that had been built up before the Second World War. In those days, when George Wholey was a small boy and his father a brakeman, the railroad employees and their families lived on one side of the tracks in a small cluster of frame houses; on the other side, the brokers and traders who had survived the Great Depression sought peace and quiet and, if they were Irish, relief from their hangovers along the top of a wooded hill (a lake dune tens of thousands of years old).

For many years the two rows of homes faced one another in solemn confrontation. The "hill" people ignored the "track" people, and the "track" people despised the "hill" people.

The cluster of cottages had long since been demolished, to be replaced by town houses (in which Linda and Jeanne rented tiny apartments). The string of elaborate Tudor homes, not quite mansions, on the hill still survived.

George lived in one of them but was not quite able to act like he belonged there.

In the old days a thin and brave main street between the two communities, along the fringe of the tracks, struggled to unite them—a tiny Methodist church, a town hall and fire station, and a couple of stores. Jill Wholey's parents owned the bakery.

George's father did not come home from the war. His mother died the year George graduated from Oaktown Township High School—1956. He began to work full-time for a local construction company, which built the cheapest homes in town, and married Jill five years later.

Judging from the pictures, he looked like a young Marlon Brando in those days, and Jill a high school beauty queen. What had gone wrong? Maybe he had married a little bit above his station—her mother had gone to college. Maybe the long years of taking care of his secretly alcoholic mother had worn them both down. Probably they had never quite found the right sexual codes to communicate with one another—both may have seen more sexiness in the other than either was able to practice in bed.

The worst problem, however, was that George did not like change. He had worked hard to become successful; then, just at the moment he thought he had made it—about 1968—all the rules changed in both the Catholic Church and American society. Never too confident of himself, especially with a wife "above his station," George began to strive desperately to quiet the social and religious orders that were quaking beneath his feet.

By then Saint Finian's had been founded; the town had expanded; the Interstate had wound its way past the other side of the hill, and the farmlands which separated Forest Springs from the city had filled up with new subdivisions. Unlike a lot of old/new suburbs, Forest Springs was lucky: it emerged from the building boom with just one "low-cost" subdivision (boxes on slabs with picture windows and gaping garage doors) to mar its elegant curving and tree-lined streets, most of them on either slópe of the hill.

George's company built that eyesore, although George didn't own the company then. When he finally did buy out the company in 1970, Forest Springs had expanded to its limits. He discovered other farmland on which to lay down the cement slabs that were the foundation not only of dubious "town houses" but also his fortune—a modest one by the standards of Forest Springs, indeed more modest than George realized.

How can I describe George Wholey?

He was not a conservative in the ordinary sense of the word. Our suburb was more Republican than Democrat; the local Republicans often were so conservative that they believed Ronald Reagan had become a liberal once he was elected president. They were always careful, however, to appear flexible and relaxed in their conservatism. True believers we didn't want in Forest Springs.

A true believer George Wholey was.

George embarrassed Forest Springs. The country club rejected him twice; they accepted him the third time because his lack of self-respect shamed the members into letting him in.

George was not so much ignorant as uneducated and unsophisticated. He also lived in a world without hues, a world of one-dimensional, one-directional good and evil.

He broke up his daughter Michele's romance with young Dan O'Rourke because Dan was a graduate student in economics at the University of Chicago and therefore a "pinko," if not a Communist. In vain did I point out that the Chicago department was conservative and that it included such well-known free market economists as Milton Friedman, George Stigler, and Gary Becker. George had never heard of them; when I said the first two had already won the Nobel Prize, George made up his mind: the Nobel Prize was a Communist front. Had it not given an award to Martin Luther King, a notorious Communist agent?

In this day of militant feminism, Michele Wholey had begun to work as a receptionist in her father's offices the day after she graduated from Mother Mary High School in nearby Yorkville Center. Women, George insisted in the vocabulary of the early 1950s, didn't need college education. George Junior, two years older than Michele, had been forced into the army when he graduated from high school. The army, his father decreed, would be good for him, though never having served himself, George Senior could know this only by hearsay.

The kid had been in and out of trouble all through high school and, despite high grades, "didn't deserve a college education, huh?"

George Junior (always "Junior" or "Sonny" around his family) found the military a happy refuge from the oppression of the big house on the hill, rose to the rank of master sergeant, chose to make the military a career, married himself a German wife, and fathered two children.

To Jill Wholey's agonized dismay she was not permitted to visit her grandchildren or to invite them to her home. At the urging of Father Louis (né Luís, I suspect), the Corpus Christi priest in charge of George's "cell," the Wholeys had disowned their son because he had married Frieda in a civil ceremony.

I believe that Father Louis's exact words, as quoted to me, were "Hand him over to Satan as a chastisement for his sins."

Saint Paul, if you hadn't noticed, was torn from context, a favorite practice of Father Louis.

The third child, Anthony (never Tony; Father Louis did not approve of nicknames—they were disruptive of family authority), was a quiet, sickly-looking eighth grader—the butt, I fear, of his classmates' jokes. His other offspring hated and feared George. Anthony, alas for his own well-being, adored him.

George was the kind of person who would announce proudly with his wife present: "We never once used birth control. We went the abstinence way with the Church. It wasn't hard on Jill—women don't need it—but it was tough on me."

For all his rigidities and ignorances, George had a certain hangdog charm about him; he'd become popular with the locker-room gin-rummy set at the club. You could like George until you discovered that, deliberately or not, he was a mean son of a bitch.

Then, maybe, if you were in a good mood, you would feel sorry for him because the meanness was a protection for his own fear.

Father New Priest would have to find that out for himself.

"In a minute, if you don't mind, sir." Jamie motioned gently to George. "I must finish this conversation before starting another one."

A point to the New Priest!

George and his entourage dutifully retreated to the sidewalk, notebooks at the ready.

The notebooks were used to record our sermons for review by Father Louis, who would determine whether one of us ought this week to be denounced to the Chancery or the Nunciature or the Vatican.

If the latter two were offended by what we said, they would relay their complaints back to the Chancery, and Joe Simon would call to complain to me.

Well, Joe doesn't call on that subject anymore—not after I demanded a session with the Cardinal in which I would give him the choice of accepting my resignation or ignoring the Corpus Christi complaints.

I believe I referred to them as "fucking freaks," for which God forgive me if S/He disagrees, which I doubt.

Impenitent, I phoned George and told him that he could take notes if he wanted, but that since there was a shortage of priests in Chicago, the Cardinal would pay no attention to him.

They continued to take notes at Father Louis's demand. The dossier with my name on it in the Corpus Christi headquarters in Rome (in a secret subterranean room probably) was doubtless telephone-book thick by now.

When I was in impish moods I would spell out words for them during my sermons: "That's E-z-e-c-h-i-e-l, folks, Ezechiel, he's a prophet, not a Communist spy."

They would dutifully spell out the word while the rest of the congregation chuckled. Many of them might have agreed with George that I was a mite too liberal. They were, however, embarrassed by his lack of style.

"All the parents," Jackie had said decisively, her tone of voice precluding any hint of disagreement, "say that Mr. Wholey is totally too gross for words. He chills them out, you know? Yucky, I mean, REALLY. Barf city."

Barf city, indeed.

"Father," George flipped back a couple of pages, "that was a cute story and the congregation did applaud it, but they cheered for Jesus on Palm Sunday, didn't they?"

I had stationed myself close to them so I could listen to the conversation. Eavesdrop, if you insist.

"I wasn't here on Palm Sunday, Mr. . . ."

"Wholey, George Wholey. My wife, Jill." He offered his massive paw, which Jamie enclosed in his own equally large, if more graceful, hand. "No, I mean the real Palm Sunday. In Jerusalem, huh?"

"This congregation wasn't in Jerusalem in A.D. 29."

"A.D. 33, Father. The Bible says so. What I mean is that those cheers for your sermon could lead to your destruction. What does it profit a man if he gains the whole world and suffers the loss of his own soul, huh?"

"An apt observation, Mr. Wholey."

"It was a cute sermon." George frowned and leafed through his notebook. Perhaps he had missed a heresy that Father Louis would catch. "The problem is not what you said, it's what you left out."

That's always the problem for the Corpus Christi heresy hunters: you must repeat the traditional doctrines every time you open your mouth, and you must parrot them in the traditional catechism language.

"What I left out?"

My New Priest was at his urbane, wealthy Irish best. Charming, patient, and indestructible. A veritable Michael Jordan of New Priests.

"You didn't say that Mary represents the contemplative life and Martha the active life and that the contemplative is better than the active. Isn't that right, Jill?"

Jill Wholey nodded her head, all that was required of her and indeed usually all that was tolerated. She was a tiny woman, wispy and weary seeming. Her youthful prettiness had faded away rather than eroded, the process accelerated by worry over her husband and children. Although a sullen Michele, deprived of her Dan, lived at home, Jill had already lost her older son forever and would probably lose Michele, too. Doggedly she tried to intervene between George and the children to prevent worse from happening, and just as dog-gedly George ran over her.

"Everyone knows that." Father Jamie smiled disarmingly.

"No, Father, they don't." George flipped more pages. "We didn't realize it till Father Louis explained this Gospel to our discussion group."

So now he was telling them what to insist on in our sermons before we gave them.

"Patti O'Hara!"

"Yes, Father Jamie!"

The worthy President of our High Club, dressed in a light gray autumn dress, was standing with her faithful Vice President, Patrick McNally, waiting for the New Priest's attention. Patti was five feet eight inches of supple, poised young woman athlete, whose brown eyes either laughed at you or read the depths of your soul. Sometimes she was just a teenager like the porter persons. Other times she seemed as old as Lady Wisdom Herself. I told her that after she was an all-American basketball player, she probably would end up as a United States senator. Patti O'Hara (the two names usually elided so they sounded like one word) wanted to be a priest.

"What do the two women in the Gospel represent?"

"The active and the contemplative lives, Father Jamie, and," she replied in catechism-class voice, "and Jesus is saying that the active, no, I mean the contemplative, is better."

"See?" my New Priest murmured mildly.

"That's what he wanted me to say, isn't it, Father Lar?" She whispered to me. "I mean what Jesus was telling us that it is better to love than to bustle, but we have to do both—and love more. Right?"

"Patti O'Hara, they'll ordain you a monsignor."

"Bishop," she sniffed.

"I'm not sure, Father." George closed his notebook. "We can't be too careful about confusing the faithful."

The laity were never the laity in the world of Corpus
Christi. They were always the faithful. Usually the simple
faithful. Sometimes the poor, simple faithful. Whom God had
designated the Corpus Christi to protect from the preachers of
heresy.

Like me.

"I agree completely, George."

"Yeah, well, gee, Father, we'd like to invite you to stop by
our house this afternoon for a drink. It's the big white one up
there on the hill. Get to know you. Welcome you. Tell you about
our group. Maybe we can ask Father Louis over, huh?"

No way that Little Louie, slimy, sallow-faced twerp, would
try to match wits with New Priest, whom he had undoubtedly
checked out.

"Wonderful! I'll try to stop by after I help the pastor to prepare the money for the bank."

None of the three earlier associate pastors had offered that
help, and I didn't want them messing with the Sunday collection.

Give Jamie Keenan two weeks and he'd be doing it by himself and I would be taking a Sunday afternoon nap, like Red
Murphy used to do.

Sure sign of aging.

The discussion split up. Jamie turned to Patti and Patrick;
the Corpus Christi gang, notebooks closed now, descended on
me.

No matter how rude I had been to them—and I can be rude
when my county Kerry genes are in charge—the Corpus Christi
people never seemed to realize that I despised the ground on
which they walked.

"I have a problem of conscience, Father McAuliffe," George
began.

"So what else is new?"

"It's serious."

"Aren't they all?"

George's perpetual frown grew deeper, as if he were trying to understand me.

"You should get rid of that hussy. She doesn't belong around the parish. It's a disgrace and a temptation the way she flaunts herself. She's a scandal to the honest women of the parish, isn't she, Jill?"

Jill nodded on schedule.

"Isn't she, folks?" He turned to his supporters who were content to let George do the talking, since they were less articulate than he.

They nodded, too.

"Father Luís suggest you say this to me?" I always used the Spanish pronunciation with George. The twerp, by the way, was transfixed when I spoke to him in Spanish after I had heard him discussing my antecedents with one of his clerical stooges in their native language.

"Well, I brought the problem to him for counseling. I mean, she's shameful. Isn't she, Jill?"

Jill nodded again.

While George may have abstained from sex with his wife during her fertile years—which ought to be just about over—rumor had it that he was less than abstinent with the women who worked for him.

One of my staff members was planting dirty thoughts in George's pin head. Who was it? Jackie? Patti, poor Linda, recovering from the Condon snit? Jeanne? Surely not poor Sister Cunnegunda!

"Which one is tempting you, George?"

"It's not me, Father. It's the young kids. Anthony's age. She's as bad as an issue of *Playboy*."

Always someone else's temptation or sin.

I must be getting old if this near-centerfold person had missed my attention.

"I can't consider firing her, George, till you tell me who she is."

George knew that as surely as the sun rose in the morning, I would not fire anyone because he complained about her. His struggle was not with me but with his own conscience. Having warned me about the serpent in the parish, he would rest more easily because he had done all he could to banish the source of his dirty thoughts.

Then, son of a bitch that he was, he'd enjoy the dirty thoughts with a clean conscience.

Too harsh? Well, maybe. I don't like George, you see.

"I mean that cook of yours, don't I, folks?"

They nodded in solemn unison again.

"Brigid O'Shea!"

"I guess that's her name."

Brigid was not, God knows, stiff in her bearing and gave no signs of being ashamed of her sexuality. A frigid Irish virgin she was not. A west-of-Ireland, Irish-speaking virgin she surely was, or I knew nothing about Irish women (a subject on which I have had extensive experience). George's mind was unspeakably dirty if he felt she was as bad as a *Playboy* centerfold.

(With her clothes off, God forbid, Brigid would be more devastating than any centerfold; that, however, was beside the point.)

"I'm astonished, George," I said, trying to control my laughter.

"She's as bad as a *Playboy* centerfold, Father."

My resident imp got the best of me, as it usually did these days with the Corpus Christi mob. Another sign of aging.

"I don't read *Playboy*, George, and you shouldn't, either. I've never seen Brigid with her clothes off, worse luck for me. I suspect she'd be a good deal better."

Disgraceful, disgusting, unconscionable, right? I should never have said it. Like I say, I'm getting old.

Jill actually smiled. A secret ally for my side? Has she finally had it with all the hypocrisy?

"I'm serious, Father."

"I understand, George."

"Promise me that you'll give my suggestion serious consideration."

"I certainly will, George. I'll take it up with Father Jamie, too. His hormones are probably more powerful than mine."

Jill smiled again. Second point for Father Old Priest.

Her husband missed my irony. "I'd appreciate that, Father."

He insisted on shaking hands with me, as did the four men in his entourage. The women, knowing their place, did not offer me their hands; rather, they departed in pious silence.

While the Corpus Christi crowd was monopolizing my time, I had noticed that the three Condons, beaming happily, stopped to chat with Jamie and his High Club elite.

He had done that quickly, hadn't he?

Coady Anne had been salvaged, redeemed from a boarding school in California—and not by me, either.

In the rectory Ed and Maria Sullivan were waiting for me, an appointment about which I had forgotten—or more likely, which I had repressed.

I was a bargain-basement therapist for them. When one was ready for family therapy, the other was not and vice versa. So it was my fate to listen to their rage at one another, secure in the knowledge that I could do absolutely nothing for them.

"Would you tell Maria that she has to do family therapy with me, Father? Tell her that it's her obligation to me and the kids?"

"I don't want to," his wife chimed in. Maria was a tall, slender Irish aristocrat from Philadelphia whose manners were far too refined for us Chicago Irish. She seemed always to be talking out of and slightly down her nose. "He'd expect the therapist to side with him all the time. When she sided with me, he'd quit."

So we played the tape over and over again.

They are an attractive couple in their early forties with five kids, two in college, three in high school: the last of the Catholic baby boom. He was a senior partner in a prestigious Loop law firm. She had wanted to be an interior decorator when she graduated from college, but married him the same summer and settled down to raise the kids while he made the money—in the last couple of years before feminism had surfaced.

Now the kids were growing up, the nest would soon be empty, and she was going through a midlife crisis. She had wasted her life, she insisted; she was worth nothing; she wanted to be her own person; it was his fault that she was no one besides his wife; she wanted out of the marriage so she could be her own person.

When a woman looks back on her life, sees no accomplishments (and five kids don't count these days), and is angry at herself, she turns that anger on the first available target—almost always her husband.

Wounded, angry, confused, Ed reacted the way men like him always do. It wasn't his fault. He had encouraged her to go back to school, offered to set her up in a "little" business of her own, as far as he was concerned she could do anything she wanted.

He did not say but implied by his manner, that her "little shop" could not possibly be as important as his work at the law. One world, his, was real. The other world, hers, was make-believe.

Maria had turned to jogging and body building ("Nothing wrong with her body, Father," he would say with a leer, a true statement and as irrelevant as it was tasteless in her presence) and fallen in with some newly independent divorced women. They persuaded her that she too wanted to be free of husband and children. ("She'd be all right, Father, if she stayed away from those bitches. Tell her she should stay away from them.")

So Maria found herself a divorce lawyer in Cotton Wood, a

nearby suburb, whom her husband promptly dismissed as a shyster—because he didn't work in the Loop.

Neither said anything about their sex life, which I was sure was not all that exciting. You can become furious at a man who is an effective lover. You don't walk out on him because you're bored. Murder, yes; divorce, no. (Ditto for a woman, by the way.) Ed was too busy with office politics to care about anything else, except in the short run—like five minutes.

It is the prerogative of the professional celibate to marvel at how insensitive married men can be to their wives, especially when a wife is so alluring the celibate thinks to himself that he would spend all day Saturday in bed with her instead of chasing a ball and clients around the golf course.

Personal taste, I suppose.

Could their marriage survive? Sure it could. There was a lot of residual love and the bond of five bright and lively kids.

Would it survive? That I doubted. The pull of the "free life," a "life of her own," was powerful. She'd find out how lonely such a life was when, after a furious divorce case with bitter quarrels over custody of the children, she was on her own. Then it would be too late.

She would not regret what she had done until after Ed had remarried and dumped five angry stepchildren on some poor woman who would probably not be older than his oldest daughter.

What could I do about any of this?

Nothing.

"Father, would you tell her—"

"Ed, how many times do I have to tell you that it is not my job to tell either of you anything—except that you should be at a therapist's office."

"I don't—"

"Damnit, Maria, I know what you don't want, you don't have to keep telling me!"

"I'm not sure whether I want to save the marriage. It's been a joke. I'm married, Ed isn't."

"That's not true! I've never been unfaithful to you!"

"Then why don't you try being unfaithful for a change!"

"That's an irrational statement if I ever heard one."

"Ed," I interjected, "would you talk to another lawyer, one with whom you're trying to work out a compromise, that way?"

"My legal colleagues are rational. Maria isn't!"

And so it went.

At the end Ed played his last and best card. And he played it well.

"I love you, Maria. I'd die without you. I haven't been as attentive as I might have been. If you want, I'll quit the firm and open an office out here so we can be together. There's enough money to see the kids through college. You could have your office right next to mine."

"It's too late for that." Her lips tightened in white anger. "You'd just slobber over me all day. I tell you, I want a life of my *own*."

Out of sync.

He threw up his hands. "What more can I do?"

"Let her have the divorce she wants." I glanced back and forth, pretty sure that Maria would reject that.

"I'm not sure whether I want a divorce."

She was at dead center, wanting out of the marriage and yet unable to make a decisive move. Eventually she would force Ed to make the choice, so she could blame him for the rest of her life.

"I don't want to lose you," Ed repeated, close to tears.

"You did that long ago, when you decided that all I was good for was being a housewife."

So they left the office, and I sat slumped in my chair. In the old days, when divorce was unthinkable for Catholics, they would have worked it out. Now they probably wouldn't. I was all for freedom, being a liberal like I was. Still . . .

"Bank deposit is ready, Father. Next week the 360/20 will fix it all for you. . . . Hey, are you sick or something?"

"No, just another woman wanting to be her own person."

"Most of Mama Maggie's cases are like that." He nodded sympathetically. "They drive her up the wall."

"Tell me about it."

"She's pretty successful at them—talks tough to the woman, I guess. Tells them that divorced freedom is no damned good. Will these people see Dr. Carlin?"

"No way. When one wants to, the other doesn't. . . . Are you on your way to visit the Wholeys?"

"Yeah, poor people. So frightened and so confused."

"And dangerous."

"Don't worry." He waved his hand. "They won't call my parents to tell them to pray for me. Not twice."

I had warned my Michael Jordan New Priest that calls to his family from the Corpus Christi gang was what finally drove poor Ron Lane around the bend.

"The Corpus Christi goons are the real enemy."

"They're entitled to their opinions, Father."

"Hoisted on my own liberal petard, huh, Jamie?"

"I wouldn't dream of that, Father." His blue eyes wavered anxiously, afraid that I was serious.

"The hell you wouldn't, Jamie." I forced a grin of my own. "That sainted mother of yours is probably an imp, too. The trouble is that we have to respect their freedom, but they don't have to respect ours."

"They won't give me a nervous breakdown." He rose from the chair across from me.

"I'd bet that you might give them one."

We both laughed, neither of us realizing how dangerous the Corpus Christi mob could be when antagonized.

"Did you set Patti O'Hara up with that answer?"

He grinned. "Not me. You'll never have to set that one up. She wants to be a priest?"

"By her own admission, a bishop!"

"Figures! Hey, what did Mr. Wholey want from you?"

"He wanted me to fire Brideheen!"

"Fire Biddy?"

I told him the story, including my line about Brigid with her clothes off, of which, God forgive me for it, I was inordinately proud.

To my surprise, the New Priest slapped his thigh in delight. "Wonderful, Father, wonderful! I hadn't considered the matter from quite that angle. You're undoubtedly right!"

"Lucky man that marries her."

"As my mother would say, apropos of her own marriage, the poor man would never have a bad meal or day's peace for the rest of his life. I bet I hear more about Brigid this afternoon. I'll have to find an equally clever answer."

My new associate pastor was not easily shocked, even by my more outrageous comments about womanly dress and undress. Not a prude, it would seem.

"Be careful."

"Now *you* sound like my mother. . . . Oh, yeah, what's the word on Pat McNally?"

"Patti O'Hara's equerry? Patrick, always Patrick, never Pat. Good kid, a bit mystical sometimes, solid. Smart, popular, generous. Why?"

"Well, Patti says he should be a priest."

"What?"

"She's a terror, isn't she? It turns out he thinks so, too. Has for years. Is afraid to talk about it. So Patti made him ask if he can see me."

Sure, see the handsome young priest.

I considered. "He has all the moves for sure."

"You don't mind?" Jamie leaned against the door frame.

" 'Course not. Be my guest. I suppose his father will oppose it."

"Why?"

"You have a doctor in your family, and so do I. So I mean no general slur when I say that Doctor Scott McNally is one of the great medical nerds of Western history."

"Cardiac surgeon?"

"Like my brother. Unlike Micky, this guy is so arrogant that he doesn't talk to other cardiac surgeons."

"Sounds like fun. Well, I'll be seeing you, and I *will* be careful."

Exit novus sacerdos, ridens.

I had not filled Jamie in on George, Junior, and Michele. Why prejudice him in advance? Besides, he could take care of himself, couldn't he? I didn't have to warn him again to be careful with that crowd of heresy hunters.

Late Sunday afternoon in a rectory is barf city, to coin a phrase. It is usually quiet—the kind of quiet you long for all week. It is a lonely sort of quiet, like a funeral parlor with the corpse present and no one else.

The priest who's on call wonders if he's the corpse.

Or short of that, whether he should have married himself a wife long ago.

Someone like Maria Sullivan. I couldn't do as badly with her as Ed had done.

Ed was a real idiot.

If I were a married lawyer in a high-powered Loop office or, for that matter, a world-famous cardiac surgeon, I might be an idiot, too.

Maybe, I reflected as I went upstairs, Father Louis will show up. I'd like to have a ringside seat when he takes on my New Priest.

9

My New Priest broke up the first staff meeting he attended and thus unleashed the whirlwind.

On himself, as it turned out. And thus revealed his tragic flaw, the full dangers of which I was too dumb to notice.

For those of you fortunate enough not to have experienced the contemporary suburban upper-middle-class Catholic parish from the inside, let me tell you about the horror of that neurotic exercise of pseudodemocracy which we call the staff meeting.

In the old days the pastor made the decisions by himself. Right or wrong, he was the pastor and that was that. When the chips are down, that's true even in my parish; I'm the one who writes the checks and worries about the bills. I do my best to see that the chips are never down.

Theoretically the staff meeting provides the other members of the staff, lay and clerical and religious and somewhere in between, a chance to "communicate" or "advise" or "participate," depending on how you want to define cautiously controlled democracy. It is usually, however, a sounding board on which everyone (except, normally, the pastor) vents his or her frustrations and dissatisfactions.

The nonclergy staff are various varieties of ex-clerics and would-be clerics. In the former group one finds sometime nuns, priests, and seminarians. In the latter group one encounters music directors, laymen who feel they should have gone to the seminary, and laywomen who are convinced that if there were

any justice in the Church, they would be sitting in my chair—
a conviction which I would not necessarily dispute.

As you can imagine, such a staff is beset by a multitude of
hidden agendas. Almost as soon as it assembles, the group becomes a substitute family in which all the unresolved sibling
and parent conflicts of childhood can be gloriously reenacted.
In the early years, staff meetings put not a few hapless elderly
pastors in Guest House for long periods of time.

Eventually we learned. First, you hire those staff types who
seem to measure in reasonably well on mental health signs (informal; you don't give them personality tests like you do college-
age seminarians).

Second, you prevent the staff meeting from becoming a
group therapy session in which the staff and its relationships become the end and the parish becomes an unimportant and often
unnoticed context.

Third, the best way of doing that is to enforce a strict time
limit. Otherwise, the staff meeting can consume the whole
working week. Easily.

So our meetings last an hour and a half to the minute. They
start promptly at four on Friday afternoon and end, equally
promptly, at five-thirty. (Drinks afterward in the pastor's parlor, if anyone wishes. Jeanne, who doesn't drink—or smoke or
eat meat—never wishes.)

The wisdom of this tactic, for which I expect appropriate admiration, is that those with substantive matters—Thanksgiving
Liturgy at this time of the year—will exercise strong social control
over those who want to devote time to "process" or "dialogue,"
both of which are euphemisms for psychotherapy.

We met in the "community room," which in the Founding
Pastor's day was his parlor. It is a two-story Gothic space across
the front of the rectory whose rafters could easily hide vampire
bats. It would have made a grand boardroom for the CEOs of

ghoul corporations. I get the creeps sitting in it for more than five minutes. So I moved out, brought in a large table of the sort used for parish dinners in the school hall and announced that it was now the community room. I hoped that the atmosphere would discourage long meetings, though I was the only one who seemed affected by it.

Jamie arrived in the community room ten minutes before anyone else, clad in a clerical collar and black suit, and looking like a bright young priest from the middle 1950s—indeed, looking like me when I ate dinner at Red Murphy's table (where Roman collars were required and cassocks preferred).

As the others came in, they greeted him, with varying degrees of friendliness, as "James" or "Jim" or, from Linda Meehan, our youth minister (glowing with the joy of an "unofficial" engagement), as "Jamie." The teens had briefed Linda about Father New Priest's proper name.

He smiled his most Redfordish smile and called them all by their proper titles—"Reverend Michaels" for the permanent deacon; "Sister Cunnegunda" for the doughty school principal; "Dr. Ronzini" for our dreamy-eyed music director; "Dr. Carlin" for our quarter-time psychological consultant; "Ms. Meehan," with a hint of a conspiratorial wink, for the youth minister, who was about his age; "Ms. Lane" for the adult education programmer; and "Sister Jeanne" for the DRE.

"I'm not a nun," she said crisply. "If you insist on professional titles, Jamie, Dr. Flavin will be fine."

Score one for Jeanne.

"Your mystical eyes must have reminded me of a picture of a discalced Carmelite," Jamie replied smoothly, utterly unperturbed by his faux pas.

"Teresa of Ávila eyes?" Jeanne blushed and smiled, two phenomena I had never seen before. "You must have kissed the Blarney stone in Ireland."

"Swallowed it, Doctor Flavin."

She laughed. No kidding.

Game point to Jamie.

"If we can have done with this west-of-Ireland happy talk," I said, not at all displeased with the events thus far, "it is time to begin the staff meeting."

A few points for the poor old pastor. Right?

Jamie: "The others aren't here?"

Cunnegunda: "What others?"

Jamie: "The porter persons."

Jeanne: *"Who?"*

Jamie: "Jackie, Lisa, Sarah, and Jennifer."

Ms. Lane: "They're children, not adults."

Jamie: "I don't believe in ageism."

Deacon Michaels (who is not all that swift): "What's ageism?"

Jamie: "Discrimination against an age group—young, old, middle-aged, whatever—by another age group. Those porter persons are an integral part of our parish ministry. One thing which has not changed in most Catholic parishes since the Vatican Council is the long wait at the rectory after you've rung the doorbell—so long that you ring it again because you figure it might be broken. Then the person who answers it makes you feel as welcome as a witch at the Inquisition. Our porter persons answer the door promptly and with a smile and a laugh and charming courtesy. They say, in effect, to the People of God in Saint Finian's parish, 'You're welcome at our house.' Besides, since they're biddies in training, I bet there's nothing that happens in the parish they don't know about. Finally, their youthful vitality might be sacramental for us."

He remembered what I'd said about the kids verbatim. A real Michael Jordan of a New Priest. Was he putting them on?

Dead silence.

Ms. (or Dr.) Flavin: "They're not professional."

"They're an underclass, I admit," Jamie ran on, half-fun

and full earnest, as my mother would have said. "It's always hardest to be fair to the underclass closest to you. We exploit them. We pay them next to nothing and use their charm and intelligence and responsibility to keep this place running smoothly in the evening. It's unjust to exclude them from our consultative process."

"We pay them fifteen dollars an hour," I noted. "That's three times what they'd get at fast-food places."

No one listened to me, not because my remark was false but because it was irrelevant.

"They don't miss much, that's for sure," Linda mused thoughtfully. "If they came, one of two things would happen. Either they'd giggle and squirm and act like it's all BORING! or they'd take over the meeting."

"The next thing," Sister Cunnegunda huffed, "Father Keenan will want to invite the cook."

Jamie: "Cook is a darn smart lady—pardon me, person. Her boyfriends are not IRA gunmen, either. They're merely illegal Irish immigrants, most of them college graduates like Brigid."

"A college graduate who is a cook?" Dr. Ronzini protested.

"Hotel and restaurant management. She likes to cook. She's saving her money to start her own Irish gourmet place."

That's more than I ever got out of Biddy.

She could invite George Wholey to lunch at her place when she opened it.

"Astonishing," murmured Jeanne.

"Yes," Jamie continued his argument, "yet isn't Marx right in the eighteenth Brumaire when he says that the underclass nearest to us is the underclass that's the hardest to recognize?"

If you've read Marx, which I did in the next couple of weeks, you'll be aware that Father New Priest had made up that quote, like all his quotes, out of whole cloth.

So it went, for the hour and a half, while I maintained a nonthreatening and clinically neutral silence (barely restraining my laughter). Jamie, God forgive him for it, had them on the run.

Jeanne was especially furious. "When you quote Marx, Jamie," she exploded at him, her face crimson, her eyes glowing with most enchanting fury, "it's like the devil quoting scripture."

"If there's an exploited underclass in our society"—Jamie was his charming, smiling, tolerantly patient Michael Jordan best—"it's teenagers. More to the point, can we not have the courage to break with our own grown-up ideology? Can't we admit that while they must learn from our wisdom and experience and patience, we must learn from their innocence and enthusiasm and boundless energy?"

Linda Meehan tried to play the "third force" role in the argument, proud of her charges, and realistic about their flaws and faults. "Teenage boys are as innocent as gang rapists."

"Is there not a saving adoration in their attitude which redeems the crudity of their imaginations as they routinely undress every woman they see, an adoration which is less likely in older men?"

"On that dubious note"—I asserted the privilege of the chair—"I must declare that our time is up."

"We didn't discuss anything important," Jeanne pleaded. "We've wasted our time."

"The rights of a permanent and unacknowledged underclass are important." My New Priest had the last word.

"Drinks as usual in the pastor's suite." I cut the rest of them off.

While it lasted, it would be interesting.

Jeanne Flavin came to the vespers libations for the first time since she had joined the staff. Game, set, and match to Father New Priest.

She accepted a Waterford goblet with a hefty shot of my precious Black Bush. From Jamie of course.

"It was shameful the way you distracted us through that whole meeting, Jamie." She had returned to her old, unsmiling self, despite the first sip of Bushmills. "An intolerable exploitation of your verbal facility."

"I'm complimented, Dr. Flavin." He bowed to her and lifted his goblet in a respectful toast. "I'll stand by my point and adhere to my favorite philosopher, William James. On sheer pragmatic grounds, apart from all questions of justice, charity, oppression, and the secondary labor market, we owe it to ourselves to see whether they have an input of which we ought not to deprive ourselves merely because of outmoded ideology and prejudice."

Half-fun and full earnest, all right, my New Priest had persuaded himself by his own rhetoric. It would not, I expected, be the last time.

"It would shake up our usual agenda." Linda held out her goblet for a refill of the rapidly diminishing bottle of Black Bush.

"It is delicious, isn't it, Linda?" Jeanne extended her miraculously empty glass. "I never drank anything like it before. So smooth. . . . All four of them, Jamie?"

"What do you think, Linda?" Jamie filled all the new goblets. "Four of them might outnumber us?"

"Let them pick two and rotate every three months." Linda sipped her Black Bush thoughtfully—a new discovery to share with "Arthur," as the teens had dubbed her beau.

(His real name was Brendan, she had whispered to me before the meeting, a better name than Arthur.)

"It'll be Lisa and Jackie, of course. Father Lar?"

"Everyone wants to try it?" I looked around the room incredulously.

They nodded solemnly.

"Jeanne?"

"Doesn't the Bible say that we should learn out of the mouths of infants?" She laughed a second time.

"Do you mean me or the kids?" Jamie enveloped her in a dazzling smile.

"Do I have to choose among infants?" She tilted her goblet in his direction, a toast that was also half-fun and full earnest.

Staff meetings would never be quite the same, I reflected as I drove Jamie over to the club for dinner—Friday being Cook's night off. My New Priest, true to his promise, had fixed something that I had long supposed to be unfixable.

We settled ourselves at my usual Friday-night table at the club, whose dining room is an unsuccessful attempt to duplicate the Polo Lounge Bar in Beverly Hills—tacky for an elegant old club into which Catholics were not admitted till 1950.

"Nice going." I raised my glass of soda water. "I hope that the kids end up on our side. They're smarter than all of us put together."

"Have you ever seen such pain in a single pair of human eyes?"

"Whose?"

My New Priest was displaying more sensitivity than I had anticipated. He was practically perfect, a Mary Poppins as well as a Michael Jordan of associate pastors. I should sit back and enjoy the show.

"Jeanne's, of course. She's a stunning older woman, isn't she? Resents and denies her sexual appeal. Yet, perversely, one flatters her when one hints at it discreetly. Wonderful, classic breasts, even without a bra. Greek-sculpture type. It's the eyes that get you. So luminous and so hurt."

"We shouldn't be mentally undressing woman staff members at our meetings." I tried to sound like a feminist and not a prig.

"Oh, we all do it, Father." He dismissed my protest with the characteristic wave of the hand that I had begun to resent. "It's the way God designed the species. I'm sure Jesus himself admired a well-shaped pair of breasts. Why not? His father in heaven devised them to be exquisite, didn't He?"

"We must treat women as persons," I sputtered, "not sex objects."

"Sexually appealing persons." He winked like a small boy with a great secret. "Don't worry, Father, I'm not going to undress her. I take my celibate commitment seriously. That doesn't mean," he said with a sigh, "that I don't imagine it as a pleasant exercise. Most pleasant." He rolled his eyes. "Moreover, and more to the point, someone ought to be doing it on a regular basis. God knows the poor woman needs all the affection and love she can get."

"Is Freud that popular in the seminary again?"

"Sexual love is no solution to any problem." Jamie dug into his spinach salad with gusto. "It may make solutions possible— motivation for therapy, courage to grow, faith to take risks. I bet our tall, shapely friend could use a lot of all three."

"Her Marxism is the result of sexual frustration?"

"Stalinism. Let's just say that if she experienced more love, she might be less angry."

"Some people are beyond help, Jamie. Whatever it is with Jeanne, she's locked herself into loneliness. Even with intense therapy, she probably won't give up the home she's built for herself. There's a lot of people in the world like that."

Mind you, only a few days before I had been praising myself for the progress Jeanne had made.

Jealous? Who, me?

"Tell me about her."

"Affluent North Shore family, debutante back in the middle sixties. Given your tastes, I suspect you would find her presentation-ball photograph quite impressive."

"They wore bras in those days, didn't they?"

"Full armor. I may have the picture around someplace. She

majored in music and drama at the Catholic women's college she attended, hung around with the nuns a lot, and entered the novitiate after graduation—there was a disappointed young man lurking in the background, unofficial engagement. A lot of kids like her were . . . well, I'll use the word, seduced into the orders by crushes on nuns. They left by the thousands after the council. Jeanne was smart and able and beautiful, so they sent her off to Wisconsin to get a Ph.D. in educational administration. They were grooming her to take over as president of the college."

"She would have been superb at that."

"You betcha. And would still be a nun, because unlike a lot of the others, she claims to have been happy, didn't mind the rules or the long hours at prayer. The sisters gave her better advanced education than her parents would have tolerated in those days if she had not entered the order."

"Alive?"

"I don't believe so. Unlike many folks from that background, they were proud of their daughter the nun and proud of her doctorate—at the head of her class."

"All perfectly reasonable," Jamie agreed. "I wonder how many of her professors considered making a pass at her and gave up because of superstitious fear."

"A lot of other women like her around the country are doing splendid jobs as college administrators"—I noted that Jamie was now systematically demolishing a steak—"talking feminism with a vengeance, running their schools with slightly frantic autocracy, and keeping alive a tradition of support for young women that it would be a shame to lose, and to which they can't give a name."

"It all turned sour when she went to the Philippines?"

I pushed aside my plate. Eating and discussing Jeanne's tragedy seemed incompatible, though such a juxtaposition hardly bothered my New Priest.

"Those were the days when the religious orders decided that they were failing in their obligations to the Third World. Overnight they dispatched tons of"—the kids are ruining my English vocabulary—"unprepared and ill-equipped young men and women to the Third World nations. The idea was that you stopped doing what you did well for people who wanted it in this country and went to the missions to do the same thing badly for people who mostly didn't want it."

"The result was culture shock, anger, and sympathy for revolution. A lot of them"—Jamie shook his head in disapproval as he polished off the last bite of his steak—"left their communities, some of them went native, and the others came back permanently angry and alienated."

"Jeanne was about to take over as dean of her college when her provincial told her, with twenty-four hours' notice, that they needed her for the same job at a school for rich young women that her community ran in the Philippines. It was in the Third World and the Third World clichés were more persuasive in those days than they are today. Although I suspect she had some secret regrets, she departed for Asia enthusiastically. Then came the culture shock. Few Americans could understand why the Church was so heavily into serving the rich in those days—they knew nothing of the history or the culture of the countries to which they were sent. The contrast between the Church's enormous efforts for the few and disregard for the impoverished multitudes seemed to them an intolerable retreat from the Gospels."

"Which of course it was." Jamie was eyeing the pastry cart; he would have to wait till the end of my story.

"Exactly. They wanted instant change. Jeanne, whose family had as much money as the parents of her students, was horrified by the suffering of the poor and guilt stricken about her own comfortable past. So, before the phrase was coined, she exercised the preferential option for the poor and demanded an assignment down island to a missionary secondary school. The order, having invested a lot of time and money in her, agreed. Not like the good old days in which you did what they told you to do and that was that. Period. Paragraph. End of revelation."

"And became involved with the revolution." Ignoring all proper clerical protocol, my New Priest signaled the waitress and took possession of two apple tarts from the pastry tray. À la mode.

"The priests there were already into it up to their necks. They were not doing the right thing for the wrong reason exactly, though there was some of that, too. They were doing the wrong thing in the wrong way. They gave her a hard time about being a rich kid in a rich order. She read some of the liberation theologians, experienced consciousness raising, as she calls it, and turned her school into a 'people's center.'"

"And then the government didn't fall over and play dead like bad guys do in the movies?"

My New Priest, addiction to apple tarts notwithstanding, had the grace of a saving cynicism.

"I'll spare you the gory details. The real revolutionaries wanted the bleeding heart Americans out of the way. I suspect that they set up Jeanne and her crowd. So the army came, burned the church and the school, shot some of the Catholic laymen, raped and molested some of the women, beat up everyone else they could."

"Not the Americans!" Jamie's massive left hand clenched into a fist which kind of reminded me of Dan Hampton of the Chicago Bears. His right hand, however, continued the pious work of demolishing the second apple tart.

"No," I sighed. "It wasn't El Salvador and these troops knew exactly what they were doing. They slapped the missionaries around a bit, threatened them, questioned them, harassed them, and then put them on the first plane back to San Francisco. The order breathed a sigh of relief. Their lovely young college administrator was home. A few sessions of therapy and then on with the work. She had become a dedicated Stalinist, convinced in theory—not in practice—that justice can be achieved through ruthless violence."

"So they eased her out of the college and sent her to parish assignments." Jamie considered the pastry tray and virtuously resisted temptation. "No, thanks, ma'am. I don't want Father to feel he has to keep up with me at the dinner table as well as at the basketball court."

"She left the order and drifted from parish to parish teaching religion and revolution, till she eventually ended up here. Kind of back where she came from. She's quite close to Blaise and Sheila Ferrigan-McKittrick, our local Catholic leftists who make sure that she isn't corrupted by our affluence."

"He's an inactive priest, isn't he?"

"A classmate of mine and a jerk. They teach at the public high school and sit in judgment on everything we do here. You won't have any trouble spotting them. They both try to look like the prophet Jeremias."

"Sad."

"That's one word for them. . . . The difference between them and Jeanne is that they talk radical and live comfortably while she talks radical and has suffered for her convictions, which they never will."

"Poor lost soul. . . . Not all pastors can absorb such staff, I suppose." Jamie beamed benignly. "There must be pressures to get rid of her."

"I suspect she'll leave next year. Expiate, expiate."

"She's too important to give up on. Don't worry, Father." He grinned impishly. "Like I say, I'm not planning to go to bed with her. Not, to repeat myself"—he winked again—"that it wouldn't be an interesting experience."

"You've proven to me, Father New Priest, that you can fix a lot of things. You can't fix Jeanne."

"Mind if I try?"

In the old days the pastor would have simply said that indeed, he did mind, and that would have been that. In the months ahead I often wished I'd tried that technique on Jamie Keenan. He was so respectful of me that he might just have obeyed me.

For reasons of principle and personality, I couldn't do it. "Suit yourself, it's your funeral."

"Lovely, lovely breasts," he murmured as we climbed into the car. "Wondrous!"

"That does not mean she does not have vocation to perpetual virginity," I insisted, turning over the ignition key.

"I have." He sighed wistfully. "I don't think she does. No happiness, Father, no happiness. God wants us to be happy."

An inarguable point.

Before I slept that night, I wondered about Jamie's fantasy of Jeanne Flavin in bed. Doubtless he was right—in the short run and the narrow context. Perhaps there were smoldering passions in that tall, graceful body. Perhaps it would be pleasurable to awaken them. So long as you could avoid her ideology the day before and the day after. Which you couldn't. Confronted by his earthy realism, my romantic attraction for Jeanne Flavin began to fade.

For the moment.

CHAPTER

10

"Lar? Packy."

"Who else?" I was never quite sure when Monsignor Keenan was joking. I had a hunch he was mocking my telephone style.

"How you doing, Lar?"

"Breathing in and out. How about yourself?"

Monsignor Patrick James Keenan and I were not exactly close friends. I admired his ebullience: he never wanted for energy and enthusiasm. He found my weary cynicism amusing. Or maybe only droll. We tended to drift together at clerical gatherings because we shared basic values although our styles were different.

I found him amusing, too.

We may have talked on the phone once every five years.

We liked one another.

"Well, Lar, I wondered whether you would mind if I applied for the job as promoter of your cause for canonization."

"Your nephew has signed on already."

Loud guffaw from the Monsignor—who would have been a bishop, should have been a bishop, if the Church were as well run as God wants it to be.

"I tell you, Lar, I never realized that you were so wise or profound or sensitive or gifted."

"He probably inherits his perceptiveness from his mother's side."

"You meet her yet?"

"I'm waiting eagerly."

"She is something else. That novel of Jerry's is an understatement."

"The kid has a lot of ability."

"He didn't get along too well with your friend Tim Aherne over at Saint Symp and the Seven Wimps."

"Gee, Pack, you know how flexible I am."

"Yeah, that's what they all say." Another loud guffaw. "Especially Joe Simon."

"Asshole."

"You can say that again. I don't know why the Boss puts up with him."

"Does the job, I imagine."

"Yeah, except the job ought not to be done. . . . The kid is doing all right?"

That question was the point of the call. The Keenans knew what the New Priest thought of me. They wanted to find out what I thought of him.

"Michael Jordan, Walter Payton, Wayne Gretzky, Sean Elliot, Mary Poppins."

"Not too pushy?"

"Pushy as all hell but irresistibly charming. Runs in the family."

"The push or the charm?"

"What do you think, Pack? Both. He's doing all right, better than all right. I think I'll retire."

"A Luke Delmege?"

"You're probably the only other one our age who's read the book. No way. Like I say, he's practically perfect. Asks my permission every time he does something important."

"What happens when you say no?"

"I'm too smart to try."

Yet another guffaw.

"Talking about Luke Delmege, listen to this: I found him looking over the clerical novels section of my library the other day. He goes—Damnit, I sound like one of the kids. He says, 'Most of these are about new curates, aren't they.' And I say, 'Associate pastors.' And he says, 'Do you mind if I read them?' And I say, 'You looking for role models?' He says, 'Only for symbols,' and wonders whether I know where he can find tapes of the Bing Crosby films. So I pull my copies of *Going My Way* and *The Bells of Saint Mary's* out of the cabinet. He carries them off and brings the whole pile back next day."

"With what comment?"

"He grins at me and says, 'Gosh, Father, I must be a terrible disappointment.'"

"Meaning?"

"I didn't ask."

"Why not?"

"I didn't want to know!"

Yet another explosion of laughter.

"Anyway, the family is very grateful to you, Lar."

"And I to the family, at least I think so."

I ambled down to the office to report to the New Priest that I had talked to his uncle. Before the day was over his family would be on the phone to him to ask whether I had told him. They would have thought it very strange if I did not.

I didn't want the Clan Keenan thinking me strange.

Not any more than they already did.

I heard laughter in the small office on the first floor, a mix of male and female laughter. The male was the New Priest.

I knocked politely.

"Come in, Father." The kid knew my knock already.

The female was Jeanne Flavin, looking happier than I had ever seen her.

"Sorry to interrupt," I said, trying to sound casual.

"You're not interrupting at all, Lar." She smiled up at me. "The New Priest thinks we ought to work up a Liturgy for Halloween."

"A blessing for trick or treaters?" I asked facetiously.

"Then you agree that it's a good idea?" Jamie leaped out of his chair enthusiastically. "See, Jeannie, I told you he's flexible."

Two conspirators planning a coup against the pastor.

"That's what I told your uncle."

"Uncle Packy?" He beamed.

"Yeah, he called to check on you."

"On you, I bet." Jeanne—or Jeannie, if you want—actually laughed at me.

"He says"—I ignored her—"that he'll tell his good friend Father Simon that I can stay on here for another year or two till you're ready to take over."

"You know how families are, Father." He shrugged disarmingly. "They want to make sure that I'm not disgracing them."

"What did you tell him?" Jeanne demanded.

"That the parish would never be the same."

"Is that good or bad?"

"Jeannie, I told you that you should never take Father seriously when you see those lights dancing in his eyes."

"I'll wear sunglasses to the trick-or-treat blessings."

I withdrew to protect what little dignity was left to my role as pastor.

Lights dancing in my eyes, indeed.

It was in Jeanne Flavin's eyes that the lights were dancing, lights of hope and love.

CHAPTER

11

"Nice, Lar." Mama Maggie tilted her pert nose and sniffed the atmosphere of the rectory conference room. "Very nice. Do you have Bela Lugosi over in that closet with the lock on?"

"You're dating yourself, Mom."

She rested a firm right hand on her towering son's arm. "Hush, dear, you'll disturb the spirits."

"Are there spirits here?" He glanced admiringly down on his mother.

"Not a one, though we mustn't say that—it will break your pastor's heart."

There was no doubt now why Jamie Keenan had such a magnetic effect on women. His physical attractions were a minor part of his charm. If a man grows up in a warm relationship with such a mother as Margaret Ward Keenan, he could not help but be sensitive, tender, sympathetic.

Dressed in autumn brown—dress, hat, gloves, shoes—Maggie was five feet three inches, perhaps 118 pounds, of slender, intense womanliness. Utterly self-confident about her power over men and amused by it, she took adoration for granted. She was almost sixty, looked ten years younger, and moved with the controlled energy of someone thirty years younger.

Maggie Ward was a handful. A handful with a Ph.D. in psychology.

"I'm sure the Founding Pastor glances over my shoulder."

Both her son and her husband—Jerry Keenan, a tall broad-shouldered man with glowing white hair and a red Irish face to match—seemed to assume that if there were spirits present, Maggie would sniff them out. Was she an exorcist and a psychologist?

It would doubtless be a useful combination.

"The Founding Pastor may well do that. If he does, he's not your standard-issue haunt. Packy says it would be beneath the dignity of the Founding Pastor to haunt a rectory. A basilica, not a rectory."

"Packy would know," I agreed. Jerry's inimitable brother had once been an associate at Saint Finian's.

"My wife is thick as thieves with my brother." Jerry Keenan grinned amiably—a man who could not quite believe in his good fortune to have such a woman love him. "If he wasn't in the seminary, she might have married him instead of me."

"Hush, dear." The firm fingers on her husband's arm patted it twice. "Packy is cute, but he doesn't have your inexhaustible patience, which"—she glanced at me as though I were someone who would understand what a difficult woman she was—"I have been trying to exhaust for forty-two years."

"I believe it," I said with a laugh. "The poor dear man looks like he's barely survived."

"I'll go make the drinks," her son walked toward the door of the parlor-turned-conference room, "so you can talk about me behind my back."

"Nothing to say," I called after him. Then as his parents and I arranged ourselves in the Founding Pastor's enormous leather chairs, I added to them: "He's an admirable young man. You both have a lot of which to be proud."

In the act of paying that compliment, I discovered that I believed it to be true.

Maggie flushed with pride. "We think so. Yet it's nice to hear it from someone else."

"We hope he will be a good priest." Her husband frowned for a moment. "It's harder these days than when my brother was ordained."

"You have to be skillful at three things to be a good priest, Jerry: preach a decent sermon, smile at people in back of church after Mass, and be friendly with the kids. Jamie does all those already better than most priests."

I did not add that he seemed remarkably skillful at rehabilitating battered directors of religious education.

The scene in the small office had repeated itself more than once. During the week after our first staff meeting my New Priest and my Old Stalinist were often together, preparing for the coming year of religious instruction and "reviewing" the present methods of "sacramental catechesis" in the parish. From the discreet and I hope not dyspeptic distance of my observation of this odd couple, Jamie seemed to be doing most of the talking and Jeanne most of the listening.

Jeanne worshiped the ground on which he walked, followed him like an obedient Irish setter. Sexual love? Well, since they were male and female, there was a sexual dimension to it. Jamie continued to praise (to me) Jeanne's womanly endowments—which somehow seemed to have improved notably since they met.

It certainly wasn't a mother/son relationship. Jamie had a mother of his own, and Jeanne was not old enough to be his mother.

What kind of love, then? The best I can do is say that it was like the love between a little sister and a big brother, except with a much stronger erotic charge to it. My two staff members found each other physically attractive.

I was tempted to jealousy, an experience not unlike rolling in cow dung. Well, I never rolled in cow dung. I imagine that jealousy is almost as vile as envy.

I guess I was more pleased with my achievement in keeping the poor woman in the parish for three years and marginally improving her life than I had realized or than I was willing to admit to myself.

The love between her and Jamie transformed her subtly. She was less assertive and yet somehow more confident, more serious, but also happier. She was now careful about her clothes and her personal appearance and looked beautiful enough when she came to work in the morning to stop traffic on Elm Street.

My erotic images about her, which had languished through the summer, now became vivid and demanding. Jamie was right: naked, our DRE would be a classic Greek sculpture. My male hormones insisted that I ponder that possibility in all its rich details.

"You look lovely this morning, Dr. Flavin."

"Cook's blarney is contagious." She flushed happily.

"I'm not sure I want a DRE that is so beautiful. She'll distract the young men from their studies."

"Like your New Priest distracts the young women?"

"Touché!"

Jamie's cure seemed to be working. I didn't resent his success, not exactly.

Would you want to have Mary Poppins working for you? Or Michael Jordan?

So I called my spiritual adviser, the one woman in my life with whom I could have been happily married. As usual when I was troubled, I poured out my fears and worries in a rushing torrent.

"Poor Lar"—she sighed in mock sympathy—"someone has stolen one of your women."

"That's not fair!"

"Sure it is. She belonged to you, and now you have equal shares at most."

"We're not feudal lords."

"No, darling, males of a hunter-gatherer species. What I'm saying is that jealousy is a perfectly normal reaction in a species which hasn't yet evolved out of the rain forests. This new priest is intruding into your turf. You like him, and he's successful in his work—too damn successful. Hunter-gatherer males are easily threatened by people they like."

"I feel like I've been rolling in cow dung."

She laughed, a cry of pure delight. "Oh, Lar, your imagery is so wonderful!"

"Yeah, but I shouldn't be envious."

"Envious and jealous both. Envious of his talents, jealous of your DRE's worship." My adviser is a pedant about words. "You figure you're an archangel?"

"No."

"If a beautiful woman came into your office now, would you find her sexually stimulating?"

"I'm too old."

"Don't give me that."

"Sure I would. You of all people must realize that."

"Would you make a pass?"

"No."

"OK. Why is one emotional reaction understandable and the other cow dung? You won't do anything to undercut this young man, will you?"

"I hope not."

"*Of course* you won't. How many times do you tell your people that normal human reactions are not sins, not necessarily even temptations. Why does that sage wisdom apply to one capital sin and not the others?"

"Envy . . . and, OK, jealousy too . . . are the worst of the capital sins. Worse than lust."

"*D'accord.*"

She likes to talk to me in French.

As always, when our conversation was over I felt better, not because of her insights—which I could have anticipated—but because of her confidence in me.

I would have been more uneasy about the budding "romance" between my associate pastor and my director of religious education if Jamie had not continued in almost single-minded pursuit of his goal of the physical and social rehabilitation of the parish—which seemed to include the improvement of the pastor's basketball game.

"Like, does he ever sleep, Father Lar?" Jackie demanded. "Yesterday he ran as much as any freshman at the teen club picnic. We're all, like, totally cashed out. Even Linda had to crash. And like he's up on the roof, fixing the leaks."

"Father Jamie is like totally larger than life, Jackie."

"Fersure."

Something, I decided the next day, ought to be done about Cook.

"Aren't you a terrible woman altogether, Brigid O'Shea?"

"Ah, sure, Your Reverence, aren't you finally seeing through my act?"

The conversation took place in my fake county Kerry brogue

and her ever thicker west-of-Ireland accent, the only rhetoric available for a serious conversation between us.

"And yourself a university graduate and you never telling me."

"I never said I was a university graduate, not at all at all."

She was sitting at a table in the kitchen, clad in jeans and sweatshirt, smoking a cigarette, drinking a cup of coffee, and reading a cookbook.

"Weren't you after telling that to the young priest?"

"I never said that at all at all. Sure, wasn't I after saying it was only the higher education institute in Limerick?"

"And isn't that as fine as a university away in Dublin? Maybe better?"

"I never said it wasn't, did I now?" She ground out her cigarette in the saucer with a grimace.

"And yourself working for practically nothing for the priests?"

"Isn't it better than not having a job at all in Ireland these days? And aren't priests nice to work for? Do they ever complain about my experiments? And don't they always say thank you when the food tastes awful? And sure, do you ever hear a word of protest from them about jeans and sweatshirts?"

"And aren't we a terrible disgrace paying you less than a university graduate ought to receive?"

"And sure, if I wasn't being paid enough, wasn't I free to complain?"

"Well, like it or not, woman, I'm giving you a forty percent raise."

"Och"—she glowed happily—"won't you be in trouble with your frigging finance committee?"

She put her fingers over her mouth, shocked at the word which came out.

"I'll worry about the finance committee. Now, are you after wanting to take some classes over at the community college?"

"Well, wasn't I thinking that a course or two in accounting and computers would help when I finally save up money to open my own gourmet Irish restaurant?"

Tears were streaming down her lovely face—the slender face of the Princess Ethain herself.

"All right, then, woman, send us the tuition bills, and I'll be hearing no more complaints from you at all at all. Is that clear?"

"Thank you, Father Lar. . . ." Tissue held to her eyes, she dashed from the kitchen. Then she peered around the door, tissue on her face, "And I'll never smoke again, either, and yourself not making that a condition!"

Cook was most appealing. Yet she didn't wrench my imagination the way Jeanne did, despite George Wholey's dirty thoughts. I guess I was getting old.

I wandered up to the New Priest's room. He was working at his computer, rearranging the style of the born-again parish newsletter—called now *The Bells of Saint Finian.*

"Well, I've finally settled with that terrible woman in the kitchen," I announced, continuing my attempt to sound like a Cacnon from the county Kerry (properly called the kingdom of Kerry by us Kerry militants).

"Have you now?" The New Priest matched my brogue perfectly. A mimic, too.

"I have indeed."

"You've fired her like Mr. Wholey wants you to?" He didn't believe that for a minute.

"I have not. I have given the poor woman a raise."

"Glory be to God! What will the finance committee say?"

"The frigging finance committee—her words, and appropriate—won't be able to say a thing when I point out that she's a college graduate. I've told her that she has to take some courses over at the community college, too. I'll not be cheating the laborer out of her wages, not at all at all."

"You never did give her a raise!"

"I did, too, and wasn't she after promising that she'd stop smoking?"

"Ah, His Reverence is too nice to say it, but he doesn't like me smoking, and isn't he right, too? Isn't it a terrible thing for your health?"

"Well, that's that." I sank into his easy chair. "Would that all parish problems could be solved so easily."

I had missed something important about Ethain or Maeve or whoever she was. It would come back later to haunt me.

The New Priest was looking thoughtful, troubled.

"What a dummy I was not to figure that out! You grow up in a place like River Forest, always having more money than you need, and you never imagine about what it's like to be poor."

"You don't have to think of everything, Jamie," I said mildly.

"That's what I have a pastor for! Speaking of which, I've scheduled you and Jackie for your first lesson in Microsoft Word tonight. Do you mind?"

"She'll learn quicker than I will and show me up again. I guess I might as well get used to it. . . . Hey, that's looking more like a corporate report every day. People will say it's too expensive."

"I'll tell them what I told you: it costs the paper it's printed on." He grinned proudly. "By the way, I suppose herself broke down."

"Wasn't there more water flowing than the River Shannon? And wouldn't your friend George be furious if he knew?"

"He'll never hear about it from me. When he told me that Brig was an occasion of sin, I told him that I hadn't noticed at all. That stopped him."

"For all their piety, they make women into things."

"Mr. Wholey quotes Father Louis as saying that members of Corpus Christi should have lots of children so there will be more priests. The marriage bed, according to Father Louis, is an altar of sacrifice."

"For the woman."

"Naturally."

"A bit late for poor George."

"He says that he and Mrs. Wholey are sorry that they couldn't do it again and have ten children."

"Ten sissies like Anthony."

"Father! He's an attractive little kid once you get to know him."

"They're miserable people, Jamie. You're right about the Wholeys, or at least about George. He's a simple soul who needs rigid answers and clear orders and a hint of being inside a secret conspiracy. The real evil is in men like Father Louis and his bosses in Rome and their friends in the Vatican Palace."

"What do they want, Father?"

"Power. That's all they care about. And they're well on their way to taking over the whole Church."

"They won't, will they?"

"Not quite, but it won't be for lack of trying."

"Do you believe I can win the poor Wholeys away from them?"

"George? Not a chance. Jill? Maybe, just maybe. How did she react to the total fertility suggestion?"

"She didn't say anything; she never does. She just drew her lips tighter. She was on Michele's side about poor Dan, too. And she wants to see her grandchildren, even if Father Louis says they are bastards."

"A real sweetheart, Father Louis. He's not as bad as the Cardinal and Joe Simon, who tolerate him and ride herd on those he criticizes—and for nothing more than continued clout in the Vatican."

"That's harsh, Father."

"What does Uncle Pack say about the Cardinal and Joe?"

"Unprintable words."

"Wait and see. The Cardinal lacks the cardinal virtues, except maybe prudence."

"Most scholars think they are different aspects of one virtue. In the Pastoral Epistles the author doesn't even mention prudence."

"Saint Paul."

"Come on, Father, you can't kid me, you know that Saint Paul didn't write the Pastorals. You're not *that* old! Anyway, they're not particularly Christian virtues. You can find them in Diogenes Laertius and Aeschylus and some of Plato's earlier works."

"What's the proper Christian virtue for a Cardinal?" interjected Mike Quinlan, who had drifted into the room to join our clerical rap session, his eyes dancing.

"You're putting me on, Father Mike. It's charity, same as for all of us."

"Except pastors," I insisted.

They laughed at me.

Although Brigid's eyes were red at supper (lamb stew, Irish fashion, she told us), she hummed Celtic melodies as she whisked the food back and forth to us. She wore a soft green dress, and her hair was done up in a vast blond roll on her head.

"What's with herself?" Mike gestured with a fork on which a potato had been impaled.

"Would I be after knowing? Sure, it couldn't be that she got a big raise, now could it?"

"Pay her what you pay a DRE," Turk said, his mouth full of lamb stew. "She's worth at least that."

Brigid ended the meal with a Bailey's Irish Cream Malted Milk, which was not a fit preparation for my first MS/Word lesson and was probably venially sinful.

I did not do all that badly at the lesson. Nonetheless, Jackie was quicker than I—I suspect because of the influence of Bailey's (Cook has a heavy hand). As I told Jackie, she was a lot younger.

Jackie: "Barf city."

Just as we were winding up and I was thinking of my last (and first) sip of Bushmills of the day, the phone rang.

"Mr. Riordan, Father Lar." Jackie was suddenly sad. "From the hospital."

"John? Lar. What's up?"

"It's the end, Father. The doctor says an hour at the most."

"Dear God!"

"She's been anointed and all, if—"

"I'll be right over."

"Mrs. Riordan?" the New Priest asked.

"Yeah. You want to come and see how a brave woman dies?"

"Certainly."

Gerry Riordan was one of the great women of the parish—wife, mother, friend, coworker. She had laughed her way through the troubles of a life that had plenty of heartache, including the death by drowning of one of her eight children (a magic young man). Nothing ever restrained her generosity or dimmed her glow or silenced her wit—not even the cancer that now had filled her body and was choking her life at the young age of sixty-two.

Through her last illness, she seemed to be taking care of her husband and children and grandchildren, protecting them from suffering and worry instead of being cheered by their visits.

"They'll do all right without me," she confided to me one day, "once I'm gone. So I want to make the good-byes as easy as possible for them."

I'm afraid the tears came to my eyes.

"And you too, Lar." She touched my arm with her scrawny fingers. "There'll always be someone else to take charge of the High Club parents' committee."

What do you do with that?

A light rain was falling as we parked the car in the lot at Forest Springs Community Hospital. A chill wind blew across the lot, stirring ripples in the tiny puddles that were forming on the asphalt surface.

"This is an all right place," I told the New Priest as we walked rapidly to the door of FSCH—a twelve-story concrete block with four wings jutting out to the points of the compass. "Yet at times like this I yearn for the old Catholic hospitals like Saint Mary's over in Yorkville, with the crucifix and the statue in the room and the elderly nun already saying the rosary when you come in."

"Like Oak Park where all of us were born. Dad and Packy, too."

In the death room, an elderly nurse was leading the rosary. Someone had brought a crucifix and a modern statue of the Madonna and child, mostly lines and curves.

Gerry winked as I walked in and tried to talk.

I bent over, my ear next to her mouth.

"You won't have to be spending any more time coming over here."

"I'll miss you, Gerry."

"See you later." She managed a tiny smile.

"You bet."

"That the New Priest?"

"Right."

"Cute," she breathed, a last soft whisper, winked again, and closed her eyes.

We began the prayers for the dying:

In the name of God the Almighty Father who created you,
In the name of Jesus Christ, Son of the Living God, who
    suffered for you,
In the name of the Holy Spirit, who was poured out upon you,

Go forth, faithful Christian.
May you live in peace this day,
May your home be with God in Zion,
With Mary the virgin Mother of God,
With Joseph, and all the angels and saints.

The dying woman opened her eyes again, looked around the room, smiled at her family, then fixed her gaze at the end of the bed where no one that we could see was standing.

The end was now very near.

Lord, Jesus Christ, Savior of the world,
We commend your servant Geraldine to you and pray for her,
In mercy you came to earth for her sake,
Accept her into the joy of your kingdom.

Just a few seconds more.

"Let's sing the 'Hail Holy Queen.' It's her favorite hymn."

" 'Hail Holy Queen enthroned above,' " we began, the New Priest's voice firm and strong, " 'O Maria!' "

Gerry Riordan opened her arms, struggled almost upright, and smiled again, this time in ecstasy.

Then her eyes closed for the last time, and she fell back on the bed, dead.

We finished the hymn. Jamie Keenan did not sing with us.

"We commend our sister Gerry," I began after a moment's silence, "to You, Lord. Now that she has passed from this life, may she live in Your presence. In Your mercy and love, grant that Your light may shine on her for ever and ever."

"Amen," they all responded.

Then the final prayer, the death knell.

"Eternal rest grant to her, O Lord," I began.

"And may perpetual light shine on her," they responded.

"May her soul and all the souls of the faithful departed rest in peace."

"Amen."

The Riordans were not the kind to let their mother down by breaking up: many tears, no hysteria, no despair.

Jamie and I lingered for a bit and then softly stole away.

"Gosh," he said as, wipers swerving furiously back and forth in a kind of dance of death, we drove through the storm and out of the parking lot.

"The name of it is faith, Jamie. At its best. I hope I have half as much when my time comes."

The New Priest said nothing at all on our ride back to Saint Finian's.

The Riordans were in full control again at the wake, grieving, yet totally Irish in their ability to turn a watch with the dead into a party where there were smiles and laughter. It was not like the legendary wakes in the old country or in the old neighborhood— no one drunk, no fighting, no loud outbursts. Both the grief and the hope were more subdued and just as intense. We who were Catholic took the gallantry of the family for granted.

"My mother would have loved this wake," said her oldest daughter. "She would have stayed all night and come back the next night."

"And made those who were suffering the most smile."

"So," the woman added, laughing through her tears, "we have to do that for her."

My New Priest watched it all, silent and stricken. I guessed what he was thinking: someday this will happen in our family.

I noticed Ed Sullivan corner him the second night of the wake. Jamie nodded impassively to some request Ed made.

You're welcome to the two of them, kid. They're nothing but trouble. Gerry Riordan never worried about being her own person.

An unfair comparison. Everyone has their own hill to climb.

I preached the homily at the Mass of the Resurrection as we now call it. My text was the "steadfast woman" passage from the book of wisdom. I'm afraid that most of what I said was about the funny things Gerry had done when she was with us. She was, I insisted, always her own person (note that, all you Maria Sullivans out there) because she had always been a person for others. I took the risk of quoting her last words to me. The congregation laughed as they often had during the homily, Jamie along with them.

The storm that had lingered for three days finally cleared away at the cemetery. We said the prayers under a freshly washed, crisp blue sky. Summer was over and autumn upon us. Winter was on its way.

Back at Saint Finian's I broke all my rules and poured a one-o'clock drink—in one of my new Waterford tumblers.

Silently Jamie joined me.

"Ed Sullivan cornered me at the wake," he said dully.

"About his marriage?"

"Yeah. He's leaving his law firm and opening an office over in the new professional building by the interchange."

"And his wife is furious."

"Right." Jamie's smile was thin. "Because he did it without consulting her."

"Typical."

"She claims that now she worries about their financial future."

"Ed has his faults, but he always brought in plenty of money."

"He says that most of his clients will come with him. He claims that he won't miss the office politics."

"That's precisely what he will miss. The law he does is dull stuff. The political battles inside the firm provide fun and excitement."

I poured him a drink.

"So they want me to see them. Do you mind?"

Automatically, as if he hardly realized what he was doing, he accepted the glass from me.

"Why should I mind? Be my guest. If you can get them both to accept family therapy, more power to you."

"I don't want"—he seemed unaware of his tumbler—"to seem like I'm taking over everything."

"Envy," I said, "is like rolling in cow dung."

"Barf city." He grinned listlessly. "I have the feeling these days that I'm a clumsy young bull in a shop with delicate china."

"Harnessed to an equally clumsy old bull."

"What's out of bounds, Boss? Where should I not butt in?"

"Nothing is out of bounds, Jamie. I mean that."

Well, I did—mostly.

"That's generous."

"The Holy Spirit blows whither She will. No point, as I see it, in trying to budget Her time or arrange Her schedule. Drink your Black Bush. It's good for you."

He glanced at the tumbler, as though seeing it for the first time.

"Don't hesitate to tell me when I'm doing something wrong."

"How would I know? I'll offer my opinion sometimes; your opinion is likely to be as insightful as mine."

"You have more experience." He drank a tiny sip of the whiskey.

"And you have more energy. It all evens out."

I was doing remarkably well at saying the right things. The words came easily because I believed them—or the man in me who wanted to be as generous as Gerry Riordan believed them.

"Is there any hope for the Sullivans?"

"Hard to say. More than for some who have the same problem. He's not the most insensitive husband his age, though he's up in the top quartile. She is not as filled with illusions as some women who want to be their own person."

"Attractive people." He sipped again, as if he was afraid there was a shortage.

"Sex hasn't been important to them for a long time, more's the problem."

"One chance in three?"

"Six."

He nodded and drank a sizable gulp. "Do you have the feeling, as I did, that it would be hard not to be empathetic to a woman like Maria?"

"Yep, but neither of us is her husband."

"What do you mean by that?" He drained his glass in a single massive swallow.

"If you're afraid of intimacy deep down in your soul, as a lot of men are, a wife like the lovely Maria would scare the hell out of you. You're not afraid of her personality or character as much as of her raw physical presence. Her sexuality—I almost said 'her genitality'—is a frightening demand, an assault on your existence."

"Gross." He glanced at his empty glass.

"You don't admit it to yourself, and surely not to her. So she thinks you're an insensitive bum and not a frightened boy-child overwhelmed by what could be an all-devouring mother. You get your kicks out of office politics."

"You're saying he feels sexually inferior to her?"

"Absolutely."

He took my tumbler and filled both of them again. "We're both going to need a nap when this is over, Father."

"Can't beat them."

"What if he admits it and tells her?"

"It's a whole new game then. I doubt that he could ever admit it to himself. It's the beginning of wisdom for men to admit women scare us and make us feel inadequate and that we're afraid of losing ourselves inside them. We are as dependent on them as we were at the breast and within the womb—helpless, satiated, powerless, content."

"Not a bad way to start a seduction, too, I imagine." He grinned briefly.

"I'm sure Mama Maggie has a couple of words for it."

He drained his second glass. "She calls men the personification of conceited vulnerability."

We both howled at that.

"Anyway," he said, changing the subject, "I've had a couple of conversations with Patrick McNally."

"And?" Bushmills Black, I decided once again, sure beat sleeping pills.

"He has 'priest,' as Uncle Pack would say, written in great big cardinal red letters across his forehead. The ineffable Patti O'Hara sees it, so do all his friends. He's afraid of his father. No, that's not quite right. He's too mature for that. He doesn't want to hurt his father and, through his father, the other members of his family."

"Did you meet his dad at the wake?"

"I guess so—medium size; kinky salt and pepper hair— looks like he's getting ready for a game of racquetball, on the winning of which his life will depend?"

"You got him. Top-quality asshole."

"What will happen?"

"Depends on how much Patrick wants to be a priest. What are his plans for next year?"

"His father's plans, which are all that count in the family, are Notre Dame, where he went. Patrick wants to go to Niles."

Niles is the seminary college, an ineptly rehabilitated Polish orphanage.

"Wants to or intends to?"

"Somewhere between."

"So you listen to him while he makes up his mind."

"I guess. . . . These last few days"—he touched his temples with long, graceful fingers—"have been overpowering."

"Tell me about it."

"My brother died in Vietnam when I was a kid. Mom lost her first daughter in a crib death back during the Second World War. Her first husband, too. I guess he was killed in action."

"I didn't know that."

He shrugged. "It was a long time ago. She has a snapshot of the little girl. Cute tyke. Sometimes I see her glance at the picture and smile with a mixture of sadness and love. After four decades . . ."

I listened.

"I've had a golden life so far, no great tragedies at all."

"As my mother used to say, 'God shapes the back to fit the burden.' "

"I heard that from Cook just the other day. The Irish never change."

"There's a woman who will scare the hell out of a husband."

Jamie rolled his eyes. "You better believe it. . . . The problem is, what do I know about life compared to the Riordans? Or compared to my parents? Or anyone who has suffered?"

How do you answer that?

"And," he continued, "we all die."

"We sure do, Jamie. We die as we live. If there's any lesson in the last couple of days, that's it."

"You're right, I suppose. . . . I'm going to leave before you fall asleep on me. Thanks for listening."

I doubt that he went to bed. I was sure that if I went down to his room, he'd be hunched over the computer, making *The Bells of Saint Finian* as perfect as possible.

I didn't sleep, either, although I certainly tried to.

I had dismissed my New Priest's fear of death briskly. Yet I was a lot closer to following Gerry Riordan higher up than he was.

Again I wondered, as I often had recently, whether it was not time for me to give up the parish and return to work in the inner city to prepare for death.

Most of what we did was so trivial, so unimportant, and so hollow.

I pondered calling my adviser again and gave the notion up for the moment. She would recognize instantly that I was tuned.

So a couple of days later, Margaret Ward Keenan tapped her trim foot on the floor of the Founding Pastor's parlor and continued to talk about her last-born child, my New Priest.

"I worry about him sometimes, Lar," she said gently, as though he were a babe in arms. "He's such an innocent."

Mike Quinlan's words.

"Now, Maggie." Her husband took her fingers gently in his. The mighty matriarch clung to him for protection.

"I mean we've raised him in an atmosphere of warmth and love, just like my books say we should have. I'm afraid that he hasn't acquired any of the nastier human traits that you need for survival in this world."

"Like?"

"Anger, hatred, ambition, envy. . . ."

"I'll take Jamie, thank you," I said firmly. "Best associate pastor I ever had, not that, as Pack might tell you, the competition has been all that great."

We all laughed.

"And don't worry about his survival," I added. "He's a shrewd one."

"Like his mother." Jerry Keenan squeezed his wife's tiny hand.

"You bet," I agreed vigorously.

"Time's up! No more talk about Father New Priest!" Jamie swept back into the room with a tray of drinks and snacks. "Cook calls this hors d'oeuvres Kilarney. Note that they consist of smoked Irish salmon and cold roast lamb on brown Irish bread."

"Cook is a piece of work." Maggie nibbled on a smoked salmon tidbit and nodded her approval. "Small drink for your father, dear, big one for me. He's driving."

"Already done." Her son bowed respectfully.

Possibly he is Billy Budd.

CHAPTER

12

Jackie and Lisa showed up for the next staff meeting in skirts, blouses, heels, and nylons. Solemn high event. Jeanne wore a black T-shirt, black jeans, and white windbreaker, all neatly molding her tall, slender, and decidedly feminine body. She had rearranged her hair, skillfully applied makeup to her Teresa of Ávila face, and made use of an appealing scent.

She was, I might remark, wearing a bra this time.

Had she dressed for Jamie? Or the kids?

"I want to begin," I said at the appointed witching hour, "by welcoming our new members to the staff meeting. I'm sure we can learn from honest dialogue with them. I wonder, Lisa, Jackie, if you would like to say something at the beginning or if—"

"WELL!" they began together, glanced at one another for reassurance, and did exactly what Linda Meehan had predicted—took the meeting away from us. Even from Jamie Keenan.

They gave us detailed and critical descriptions of everything that was wrong with the parish—our homilies were dull; the Mass schedule was inconvenient; the office hours were too rigid; the flow of traffic in the parking lot was gnarly; the daily Liturgy and the Sunday Liturgy were chill pills; the hymns we sang were for dweebs; the system for the distribution of the Eucharist at Mass was designed for losers.

There were also major problems with wedding rehearsals, funeral and wake services, the religious instruction classes, High Club, the state of the basketball courts (gross discrimination against girls and against volleyball), grammar school graduation customs, our indifference to college- and postcollege-age young people, lack of democratic procedures in decision making and the expenditure of funds—and, of course, our "total" absence of appreciation of the services of the porter persons (the last with nervous laughter).

"And Father Lar, like, is everywhere, you know? Nothing goes on in the parish that he doesn't find out about. I mean, there's no privacy for anyone. He wanders around kind of pretending that he doesn't see anything, and he's watching everything. I bet even a cop on the beat wouldn't know as much about everyone's life as he does. It's like the Gestapo, you know. Really. It makes everyone feel like losers. Can't he just stay in the rectory and not pry into everyone's life, especially their love lives. I mean, he knows about every romance in the parish! That chills us out!"

It was like a thirty-day retreat. The little witches had us cold. Like all bureaucrats, we had become sloppy; we had not been listening for feedback, not carefully; we had not been critically evaluating our efforts. We were making mistakes, partly because summer had just ended and partly because our jobs did not depend directly on the quality of our work.

The two young women had apparently collected all the complaints that were simmering just beneath the surface of the parish and repeated every one of them. Much of what they said was exaggerated—their adolescent passion for honesty not yet tempered by experience. Yet, allowing for that, they were giving us for free what would cost thousands of dollars from a management consultant firm.

Their philippics were well rehearsed; when one fury ran out of breath, the other took over. Finally, Lisa, a honey blond with slight tendencies to plumpness, sighed deeply and said, "WELL, that's almost all."

I took notes. Linda strove mightily to restrain a grin. Jamie didn't even try. Sister Cunnegunda, who had presided over these young Furies a few years ago in grammar school, huffed early in the onslaught and turned away with ill-concealed disgust—making clear to all that she was washing her hands of the project. Dr. Carlin took careful notes—for a professional article I suspect. Dr. Ronzini and Reverend Michaels looked confused and hurt (the latter seemed especially hurt when the kids told him that when he read the Gospel he made "people fall asleep or want to fall asleep. Really!").

Jeanne Flavin was furious, I suppose because our youthful assailants insisted that, "Marx is like totally irrelevant."

"When Jeanne talks about him," Jackie informed us, "she is totally BORING! When she talks about Jesus, she is cool. Totally."

I figured that it was up to me as pastor to break the frigid silence that followed Jackie's call for a cease-fire.

"Do you guys want the parish checkbooks?" I asked.

"Father Lar!" Lisa giggled.

"That can wait till next week!" Jackie giggled, too.

"Well, one thing I have to say is that you two gave us candid feedback. We would have had to pay a lot of money for a management firm to do a survey to obtain this reaction."

"Then give us a raise!" Jackie struck for the main chance.

"I can't do that till I talk to the finance committee, like you said I should."

Uneasy laughter.

"I wonder what makes you girls think you are so smart." Jeanne's lips were a thin, angry slash, made all the more vivid by the touch of lipstick that decorated them. "Do you realize how fortunate you are compared to most young women your age around the world?"

"What does that have to do with it?" The indomitable redhead was not going to roll over and play dead. "Sure we're lucky. You asked us our opinions about the problems of the parish. We told you."

"You have no experience to justify the judgments you made," Jeanne's voice was shrill, her face deadly white. "You're two spoiled brats."

"Really!" Lisa observed.

"You're just saying that"—Jackie, a pirate queen in action, was enjoying the battle—"because you don't want to hear that all the kids go that revolution is BORING! They don't go YOU'RE boring. They like you. How many times do I have to tell you that, anyway?"

"I don't care whether they like me or not. I'm here to tell you spoiled rich kids about Jesus's love for the poor. You're too self-satisfied to care about poor people."

So it went. Jeanne's clichés became more incoherent; Lisa said "Really!" periodically, and Jackie didn't give an inch.

I should have intervened and called the game because of darkness. I was fascinated.

"WELL," Jackie called on her impressive resources for hauteur and ended the discussion. "I don't care. Sure, we're dumb teenagers. Didn't Jesus say that out of the mouth of teenagers you hear truth? We have something else to say, don't we, Lisa?"

Lisa: "It's not fair that we don't tell you what people are saying about Father Jamie."

Jackie (breathlessly): "They go he's like totally running for Pope."

Lisa: "He's campaigning, you know, to make himself popular with everyone, even more popular than Father Lar."

Jackie: "Like, he has this need to make everyone like him."

The community room was as silent as a funeral home when

the undertaker closes the casket. Jamie Keenan's eyes narrowed as though he was resisting the pain of a fractured leg, his face turned chalky, his fingers compulsively opened and closed.

The princeling was under assault.

Lisa: "He cultivates and flatters everyone, you know, I mean, especially the women on the staff—Ms. Flavin, Sister, Cook, Linda, even us."

Me: "That shows excellent taste."

Jackie (stormily): "Father Lar, we're SERIOUS. People say that he has too much charm and he's too pushy for a New Priest and that he should learn to listen to people and wait till he's had more experience before he tries to take over the parish."

Lisa: "They're like it's totally gross when a priest fresh out of the seminary who knows nothing about life tries to tell everyone else what to do. Father Jamie has a lot to learn."

The silence of the graveyard after the cortege has left followed. If my New Priest, I reflected to myself, says the wrong thing now, they'll both retreat to hysterical weeping.

"I appreciate the feedback." His voice faltered. "I have a lot to learn." A wan smile. "I guess I'll have to change my style."

Lisa and Jackie (in relieved unison): "REALLY!"

By which they did *not* mean that they wanted him to change at all. They meant, rather, that they were glad he wasn't going to jump on them the way Jeanne Flavin did.

With the unerring instinct of the young, they had pried open the secret of my New Priest's weakness: in the depth of his soul he feared that others might see through his charm and energy and find nothing there. Such is the fate of the adored boy-child whose siblings did not push him around.

"Do you agree with these charges?" I asked.

Surely they did not. They were repeating what some people had said because they believed fairness required it.

The two kids were nonplussed.

"We're just telling you what some people say," Jackie couldn't make sense out of the question.

The parish would quickly settle back to normal. The New Priest would begin the slow process of learning his trade by experience and mistake. The black hurricane would blow itself out on the continental land mass of everyday life.

I sighed with relief. The crisis was over.

Graveyard silence resumed.

Me: "Is that all?"

The porter persons nodded solemnly. Linda Meehan and Jeanne Flavin both opened their mouths as if to dissent; both remained silent.

Linda understood the process: the kids, with the transient passion for justice which characterizes sixteen-year-olds (especially women sixteen-year-olds), had repeated the complaints of those parishioners who would grumble about the archangel Michael if he were a newly ordained priest.

"It's time," I continued smoothly, "to turn to the question of the Thanksgiving Liturgy."

The rest of the meeting was nervously uneventful. Jamie Keenan participated with quiet restraint. The pain in his eyes showed that the porter persons had scored direct hits on him.

Like dive bombers sinking Japanese aircraft carriers at Midway Island.

The kids were afraid to look at him.

The demoralized staff voted to end the meeting early, a quarter of an hour later. I invited the two teens to join us for drinks—"Tab or something like that?"

"No way," Lisa shook her blond curls vigorously.

"We figure"—Jackie smirked like a precinct captain who has just won the promise of your vote for a candidate you don't like—"that we ought to respect your privacy. Besides," she added with a crooked grin, "you probably want to talk about what geeks we are."

"Space cadets," Jamie corrected her.

Which is precisely what we did for the first quarter hour, Jeanne leading the attack. Then Mike Carlin gave the signal for reappraisal. "Of course, as Lar said, we learned a hell of a lot from them."

Having vented their outrage and protesting with Sister Cunnegunda that the kids were guilty of great oversimplifications, they considered the criticisms objectively and began to plan sensible responses. The music director even admitted that it had been a helpful and "healthy" experience.

After everyone else had left, my New Priest filled two Waterford tumblers with the precious Black Bush. I noted that the supply was declining rapidly.

"Well," the New Priest laughed weakly, "I guess I realize now how Doctor Frankenstein felt."

Poor Jamie Keenan, adored golden child, had at last revealed his tragic flaw: he needed love from those he loved.

Welcome into the human condition, kid.

I should have played the wise pastor role, like Canon Sheehan's Daddy Dan in *My New Curate*. I should have said something like "You have a lot to learn, Jim—we all do when we're young. You're smart and you learn quickly. The kids did you a big favor."

That's what I should have said. An answer right out of one of Canon Sheehan's books.

What I said was, "They're full of bullshit."

Jamie swallowed a large gulp of Bushmills.

"What . . . ?"

"They were right, but they were wrong. Kids are clear-sighted and rigorously logical. They don't have the experience to distinguish between bullshit and wisdom."

I was, God help me, refueling the black hurricane.

He turned his tumbler carefully, not looking at me. "Are you saying, Boss, that they were right about everyone else and not right about me?"

"What about their description of me as, like, the Gestapo?"

"Absurd," he said fervently. "It was a job description of a good pastor, a cop on the beat, like your father, who knows what's happening on his beat."

"They would be terribly disappointed if I lost interest, but they reported what they'd heard the chronic gripers say. The kids would be the first ones to complain if you reef your sails."

I was pouring gasoline on an ember. What the heck, fires keep you warm in the winter.

"Reef my sails?" The New Priest began to grin.

"A metaphor, Jamie."

"Yeah . . . another wee drop?"

"Why not?"

"Hey, the supply is running low. How did that happen? I guess we need a miracle to produce some more, huh, Lar? Single malt this time? Red and green label, you know?"

"You can't get it in America."

"My dad can."

The black hurricane was up and running again.

CHAPTER

13

Jeanne was waiting for us in the office when we returned to the rectory after dinner. She seemed still not ready to accept the new consensus about the attack of the teenage dive bombers.

"They're spoiled little brats," she protested. Her face was lined, her eyes red, her fists clenched. She was, I thought, trying to persuade herself.

"Takes one to know one," Jamie, nothing if not resilient, responded with more candor than I would have dared.

Her eyes flashed with momentary anger, and then she laughed wryly, "You didn't have to remind me. Or maybe you did." Then, in the face of my New Priest's charming smile, her resistance collapsed. "I suppose I should update myself on the parables of Jesus since that's what they think my classes want. Do you have any suggestions, Jamie?"

Only love can produce such rapid turnarounds. Jeanne loved my New Priest, no doubt about it.

"Well, definitely John Breech's *The Silence of Jesus.*" He sat on the edge of a chair. "And Bob Funk's book and of course anything that Shags has done in the last couple of years. I'll get copies to you. You, too, Father, if you want them."

"Why did you let them do it to us, Lar?" she asked, her voice cracking and her shoulders slumping. "They assaulted the dignity and integrity of all of us. A couple of hearts were almost broken in there, mine included."

"Blame the New Priest," I said shamelessly. Then thinking about envy and jealousy, I hastily added, "It hurt like truth always hurts, but it will prove to be a useful growth experience for all of us."

When necessary, I can use jargon with the best of them.

The New Priest, his own broken heart mended, was much less gentle. "Cut it out, Jeanne. You talk about revolution, you've just witnessed one, a classic contradiction that your friends Hegel and Marx would have loved. The old parish power structure— us, or we, as our grammatical-perfectionist pastor with his degree in literature would insist—were the thesis. The little monsters were the antithesis. The meeting was the revolution, and we're already working out a synthesis. Aren't you the one who says that revolutions can't be painless? As Marx says in the Eighteenth Brumaire, it is easy to support revolution until one's own social class becomes the target."

Jeanne opened her mouth to disagree, hesitated, then buried her face in her hands and wept softly.

For once my Mary Poppins associate looked as powerless as I felt. He seemed eager to embrace her so she could weep against his broad chest, and yet well aware that such an action would be a mistake.

"What a shit I am," she murmured. "Everything I would condemn in others. They are brave young women. Prophets in a way. I treated them like dirt. Poor little tykes. They've been so kind to me so many times."

"Prophets is a bit strong," I protested. "Sometimes they're real gelheads, like totally."

She snickered through her tears.

"I'd better phone them and apologize."

"That's not necessary," I argued.

She struggled to her feet. "Oh, yes, it is. I must be true to my own principles. . . . Why do you two put up with me?"

"You're good at what you do," I said, compromising with the truth.

"And we love you." No compromise for the New Priest.

She searched our faces. "Then you have bad taste."

"No way," I insisted.

"Go in hope," Jamie saluted her.

"I'll need it." She grinned weakly and looked very attractive.

"Call the kids as soon as you walk in your apartment," Jamie warned her as she left the rectory.

"Before I lose my nerve?"

"Right."

"Yes, Father."

The two of us stood in the hallway, staring at the door after she left, still hearing in our imagination the click of her heels on the terrazzo floor.

First I'd noticed she'd been wearing heels.

"Like Mama Maggie says"—the young priest turned to walk up the spiral staircase to our rooms—"God sure was ingenious when She made us male and female."

"Ingenious or troublesome."

"Is her bra a net improvement, you should excuse the expression, or not?" he asked at the top of the stairs.

"The poor woman has been weeping"—I did my best to sound like a stern moralist—"and you're asking that kind of question."

"Perfectly valid question." He waved his hand. "If admittedly not the most important. My reaction is that it rearranges the scenery and improves the fantasies. Now there is more to take off. It does not, however, fundamentally—again you should excuse the expression—alter the general situation."

"It's your fantasy life, Jamie."

"Right, boss." He chuckled. "You didn't notice anything, I'm sure."

"I didn't say that. Even at my age you notice."

We both laughed.

Then I became serious, my conscience catching up with me. "She's not an object."

"Do I treat her like an object?" He seemed surprised.

"Hardly."

"Are my remarks about her fabulous breasts sniggering?"

"No."

"Then why should either of us pretend that we're not males and do not observe, in minute detail, her attractions?"

"She would be humiliated if she heard us."

"Well, she didn't hear us. And I'm not so sure. Women enjoy physical admiration so long as we respect and love them. God knows we both respect and love her."

"Do we?"

"Sure we do. How could we not?"

"You sound like Mama Maggie again."

"Who else? . . . Anyway, to the important question." He turned grimly serious. "She might fall apart. Been heading in that direction for a long time. She feels that she has wasted her life. The kids hit that pretty hard without realizing it."

"Prognosis, doctor?"

"Guarded at best, poor woman."

"Careful, Jamie."

"We can't just stand around and let her go psychotic, can we?"

I paused at the door to my study. "Sometimes, often even, standing around and doing nothing is the best thing to do."

"She's too precious to lose."

When a man uses that word of a woman, he's already deeply in love with her.

CHAPTER

14

The porter persons, as I had predicted, forgot completely about their dive-bomber attacks on the New Priest. The next day, Saturday afternoon, while another autumn rain beat down on the various gables of Saint Finian's rectory, they gathered in the basement meeting room with a half-dozen others of their ilk to collate the first issue of Father New Priest's bulletin.

"WELL, Father Jamie, I HOPE your new collator comes before next week. We're not JUST cheap help, you know."

"The collator won't spill popcorn on the newsletters, Lisa. Or diet cherry cola."

Giggles.

"WELL, you can run off another thousand of them, just as quickly as Dr. Flavin turns the page of a book."

Dr. Flavin giggled, too, basking now in Jamie's smile and her renewed friendship with the kids.

Oh, yes, she was there, too. Recruited by the kids. She had abandoned her jeans and sweater for a beige knit dress and was wearing discreet makeup and scent. She seemed both vulnerable and happy—a prisoner who had been pardoned but was as yet uncertain about her renewed life.

Because of a couple of apologies?

And some love.

As far as the monsters were concerned, nothing had happened the night before, no confrontation, no bitter argument with Dr. Flavin, no attack on Jamie. And in their world nothing had happened. The staff meeting had been a "weird" experience that could be completely forgotten without any notable emotional effort.

Dr. Flavin's apology to them? That too had been swept away in the decision that she was "kind of cute." She was one of them.

"Doesn't she look pretty, Father Lar?" Jackie whispered to me as we stacked newsletters in a carton. "I mean, like totally cool? Really?"

"Who, Jackie?"

"You KNOW."

"Dr. Flavin?"

"Fersure."

I pretended to consider.

"Not quite awesome yet, but on the way."

"Really out there, you know what I mean?"

"I think so."

"She like totally likes us now, isn't that radical?"

"Maybe she wishes she had daughters like you."

That stopped the usually unstoppable Jacqueline.

"Who'd want a teenage kid if they didn't have to have one?"

"Maybe Dr. Flavin."

"Gee . . . is she too old to have children of her own, Father Lar?"

"No."

"Then maybe she should get married and have some, huh?"

Well, someone said it, and now it was out in the open.

"Maybe, Jackie. Up to now she has not wanted to marry. Maybe she'll change her mind."

That seemed to satisfy Jackie for the moment. "Doctor Flavin" became "Jeanne" and then "Jeannie" by the time we had finished the newsletter collating, at first tentatively, and then firmly, as though she never had another name.

"It looks great, Jamie," I told the associate pastor. "A lot of work went into it."

"Anal-retentive personality." He shrugged ruefully. "Obsessive-compulsive. . . . I've prepared a database of quotes and proverbs and other forms of spiritual wisdom. So it'll be easier from now on. The bulletin," he said, becoming serious and professional, "is a major means of communication between priests and people, and like everything else we do, we should do it well or not at all. Right?" He glanced up for my approval.

"*D'accord,*" I said, using my adviser's favorite expression—though on her lips it often meant she didn't agree at all.

A company that specialized in publishing Catholic materials had assembled the bulletin in its previous form. The company collected money for the ads from local business firms and then printed the bulletin and shipped it to us for distribution. Most of it was boilerplate, including the column called "From the Pastor's Desk." Only the announcements varied from parish to parish. It was, not to put too fine an edge on things, unattractive and sloppy.

I didn't like it. I particularly didn't like their dunning undertakers and car dealers for ads, not in Forest Springs anyway. I had not found any time to change it—not until the black hurricane arrived.

The Bells of Saint Finian had to be the most elegant parish bulletin in the archdiocese. It looked like an interim report from a medium-size corporation. Or maybe an in-house publication from an advertising firm. Moreover, the contents—quotes from scripture and other sources (like Chesterton), parish announcements, brief notes from various members of the parish staff—were lively and well written (usually rewritten by the New Priest). It was certain to be a success.

That prediction showed how isolated a pastor can be from reality.

We have four Masses on Sunday at Saint Finian's and one on Saturday at five-thirty. Each of us says one of the Sunday Masses, and in addition I say—nope, I've got it wrong—I preside over the Saturday Eucharistic Celebration.

I figure a pastor shouldn't ask someone else to do extra work when he's still capable of doing it himself. The opposite of Red Murphy's philosophy.

Thirty years later, long after his death, I'm still fighting the SOB.

Incidentally, the rectory was deluged with calls on Friday and Saturday by people wanting to know "what time the new priest is saying Mass."

I cautioned Mrs. Clarke on Friday and Brigid on Saturday not to tell anyone about the calls.

Mrs. Clarke nodded wisely, a woman who understood all that there was to understand about clerical culture because she had two sons priests.

Monica Clarke, a white-haired mother of six and grandmother of seventeen, was, I often told her, the one thoroughly sane and reliable person who worked for the parish. Including the pastor.

She would laugh her quiet little laugh and not deny the truth of my assertion.

Turk and Mike were not easily threatened. Yet such calls are a grave danger for a priest. There is nothing more likely to stir up clerical envy than a hint from the people that one priest is a better preacher than others. Some young priests are transferred out of their first assignments because there were too many calls about when they were saying Mass.

One of my classmates, who didn't used to be a fool, inveighed from the altar against calls about the Mass schedule. "You should," he insisted, "come to hear the Word of God preached and not a specific preacher."

You can imagine what his people thought of that.

I told him that the people had a right in strict justice to hear the Word of God preached well and that our generation had run up a debt comparable to the American trade deficit.

He was not happy with my remark.

The priest who was the object of the calls was transferred a few months later. Attendance at my classmate's parish (and Sunday contributions) promptly declined as his people voted with their feet.

Did the calls about Jamie's Mass time bother me?

They used to call and ask what time I was saying Mass.

Well, that was the end of my tenure as the best preacher in our part of the suburbs. Now I was second-best.

I consoled myself with the rationalization that Saint Finian's, like the Bears, was still number one and climbing.

So I told myself as I repressed the notion of another call to my adviser.

After the Saturday Mass, in back of the church, I watched people pick up *The Bells,* glance at it disdainfully, and then either put it back down on the table, or stuff it in pockets or purses.

"They don't seem to like it, Father," my New Priest was puzzled.

"Five-thirty crowd isn't much into reading matter," I said, an observation that had never occurred to me before.

Nothing to worry about yet, I told myself uneasily.

At the first Eucharist—got it right—the next morning, the complaints became explicit.

"I liked the old bulletin."

"I suppose this is a lot cheaper, but the other was worth the extra cost."

"The parish ought to do its own bulletin, instead of farming it out to professionals."

"I miss the ads, they give it a local flavor, don't they, Father?"

"This is too bland, Father. Doesn't have the vitality of the old one."

Usually such judgments were offered by people who had not bothered to read the text.

The old one, I almost said, was crap.

"We've gone slick, huh, Father?"

"Are we making more money on this thing?"

How could we be making money when there were no ads? Jamie was dumbstruck.

"They don't like it, Father."

"My fault," I said. "I should have prepared them for it. People don't like change in their Sunday routine unless they're warned beforehand."

"People are shits," Turk said audibly. "This is the best bulletin in the archdiocese."

A rare compliment from his lips.

"Thank you, Father," Jamie murmured automatically. And then to me, "The objections are all contradictory!"

"People are contradictory, Jamie. Don't worry, at the next Mass I'll make an announcement that will appeal to their parochial chauvinism."

"Would that be right?" he asked dubiously.

"You listen and judge."

The old pastor was perhaps falling behind the porter person in learning MS/Word, but he was still good for something.

What?

Bullshit. I've been number one at that for a long time. No competition.

"You'll notice," I told the congregation at the nine-o'clock Eucharist, "that we have a new parish bulletin—*The Bells of Saint Finian*. Some people have said that it looks like something that a hundred-million-dollar-a-year corporation would produce. Well, unless the finance committee hasn't been telling me the truth lately, we're not at that level yet.

"In fact it's entirely a homemade product, produced in the rectory by a bunch of fancy programs the names of which I can't remember for five minutes. Its predecessor was mass-produced for parishes all over the city with a few items changed for each parish. It was nice, though not of the professional quality of *The Bells*. It was financed by seeking ads from local businessmen who didn't prefer us to TV commercials. In their hearts they often felt they were being black-mailed, and I can't blame them. Now we don't have to do that anymore.

"*The Bells* doesn't cost us any more than the price of the paper on which it's printed—and some hard work from the New Priest. We don't ordain them anymore, you see, unless they can work these electronic gadgets. And we don't accept them in parishes unless they bring the gadgets with them.

"Actually, Father Keenan is a bit ashamed of the present product, even though it is certainly the most professional bulletin in the archdiocese. He doesn't have a four-color printer yet.

"I'm delighted with *The Bells* because he does all the work on it. The time I used to spend worrying about the bulletin I can now devote to lowering my handicap so it is only maybe eight strokes above his."

They applauded the new bulletin, sight unseen, as I knew they would.

And swarmed around the New Priest after Mass to congratulate him—the product as unread as it had been after the seven-thirty Mass.

Although Jamie seemed bemused, he accepted the compliments graciously.

"Totally radical," he murmured to me.

"Barf city," I replied.

There was no need, however, to fend off critics of *The Bells* after twelve-thirty, the New Priest's Eucharist. Alas for our side, the Bears were playing a Monday-night game that week (which they usually lose) and the twelve-thirty was crowded.

Jamie's homily was a Chippewa story of why the leaves change color in the autumn, a perfect theme for the day since Forest Springs was dappled in red and gold that Sunday.

It was a beautiful story, as I knew beforehand because the New Priest had played a videotape the night before of Ron Evans, a Chippewa/Cree storyteller, recounting the tale.

Earth Maker ("A process theology God if I ever heard of one," Mike Quinlan had chuckled) had encountered the problem of how to protect the "little people"—cricket, grasshopper, dragonfly, frog—from the cold of winter. The tree people offered to shed their clothes to provide a blanket for the little people. And Earth Maker rewarded them with wonderful colors just before they doffed their garments and turned them into blankets.

Lovely tale and one with a lot of religious truth—including regard for subhuman species.

Jamie told it with marvelous skill, recounting it as something he had heard from an Indian storyteller and then putting himself into the storyteller's role (a "Keeper of the Talking Sticks") so that he actually became a Chippewa/Cree. I didn't think that he would end the story the same way Ron Evans did, however.

"So the old man said to the little children. 'Look up at the mountaintops. They are the breasts of Earth, our Mother. She has already taken off her clothes and bared her breasts to the cold so she can wrap us up in her garments and keep us warm during the winter.'"

No applause this time, just stunned silence.

You don't talk about baring breasts in church—not even if Jesus describes himself as a nursing mother in the seventh chapter of Saint John's Gospel.

I suppose that 90 percent of the congregation liked the story and were not offended by the conclusion. On the contrary, they probably were happy to see the taboo ended, if ever so slightly surprised. And they would never forget the metaphor.

It was a new experience at Sunday Mass, just the same. Sunday Eucharist that is.

The other 10 percent, far more than George Wholey's redoubtable little band of true believers, were shocked to the depths of their pious souls. Women had breasts, indeed, but that was mostly because of an error in esthetic judgment on the part of God.

To refer to that error in church was worse than heresy, it was immoral.

There would be more calls to the rectory to find out what Mass Father Keenan was saying. Now half of the callers would want to avoid his Mass.

Well, there was no help for it.

To hell with them anyway.

The crowd that swarmed around Jamie after Mass was not quite as large as the previous Sunday, but it was every bit as enthusiastic. I wondered if he noticed those who strode sullenly by him. Or those who stormed over to me to protest.

"You gotta cut that young fella down to size, Father," an elderly businessman raged at me. "Put a lid on him. Wash out his mouth with soap."

"I beg your pardon."

"That sermon was a disgrace."

"Why?"

"You know why."

I was trying to make him say the word *breast* to a priest.

"I'm afraid I don't. It was a lovely story."

"The way it ended."

"God doesn't keep us warm during the winter?"

"The way he said. It's immoral."

"You mean suggesting that Earth Mother bares her breasts to the cold so she can wrap us in her clothes to keep us warm?"

He turned purple. "That kind of language has no place in church or on the lips of a consecrated priest."

"Jesus uses similar imagery in the seventh chapter of Saint John's Gospel."

"I never heard of such a thing!"

"I'm sorry that you didn't like the sermon."

"If you don't cut him down to size, I'll find another parish after twenty years."

"I'd be sorry if that happened."

"Are you gonna take him down a peg?"

I was keeping my temper under control, with difficulty.

"If you mean am I going to censor Father Keenan's sermons, the answer is no."

"Then I will find another parish."

"Suit yourself."

The other complaints, maybe a half dozen in all, were less emphatic. There'd be a few phone calls this afternoon and a letter or two, probably anonymous.

In Red Murphy's parish that would mean the sack for the priest responsible.

Not in my parish.

The complainers were more sophisticated now than in my youth. Three or four of them would phone the Chancery and a couple would write to the Nuncio, Cardinal Ratzinger, and the Pope.

Joe Simon would call Monday morning with his characteristic greeting designed to scare the daylights out of you: "What the hell is going on out there!"

I sighed. A part of me was already welcoming the chance to shoot Joe down again.

You must understand about me and Joe. We had been programmed by our genes to dislike one another. Contemporaries in the seminary, we were as dissimilar as any two men could be. He was as ambitious and servile to authority as I was disrespectful, as pushy with those in power as I was indifferent to them, as obsessed with the niceties of clerical protocol as I was disdainful.

He hung around with those who wanted to get ahead in the Church even when he was a seminarian, and pressured the seminary rector to recommend him for graduate work in business administration at De Paul even though his grades were not all that good.

He elbowed his way into the Chancery during the reign of the previous Cardinal and took over on his own initiative the task of organizing pilgrimages and clerical tours. He hung around with politicians, usually those who were fat and sloppy like himself. There was a scandal over money for a pilgrimage which had disappeared at a fly-by-night travel agency run by a friend of Joe's. Somehow he managed to escape unscathed. He managed always to be around when someone higher up wanted something unpleasant done and earned himself, heaven knows how, a reputation as an efficient administrator, when the truth was that his administrative abilities depended on his being stubborn and dumb.

A good second in command and occasional hit man for a Mob boss.

I may overstate the case. He was as loyal a man as anyone

who ever served a Cardinal. He worked long hours and never took a day off (like me in that respect, my adviser would probably say). He was generous with his money—though where he got it was another question.

See, I can't even pay him a compliment without being nasty. I'm on occasion ashamed at the reaction Joe produces in me. Not very Christian, I guess.

Corrupt? Well, no. Unsavory? Yeah, a little bit. Indispensable? He sure had made himself that.

So I enjoyed my fantasy about his call the next day and felt guilty about enjoying it. Not too guilty, however.

While I was fending off those who were sure that *breast* was a dirty word—and wondering what they would have said if Jamie had dared to use the even dirtier word *nipple*—I noted with some dismay that George Wholey was angrily waving a tape recorder at the New Priest. The rest of his crowd were also carrying recorders, a motley collection of tiny handheld dictators, old-fashioned Sonys, and even one huge "ghetto blaster."

"There's gonna be hell to pay, Lar," Turk muttered to me. "The kid stepped over the line."

"Fuck Joe Simon, the Cardinal, the Nuncio, and the Pope," I replied.

Turk Nelligan chuckled "Atta boy. But, say, it was one hell of a good sermon, wasn't it?"

Turk had never said anything quite like that in all his life.

"Sure was."

"Jamie's going to let me watch all those tapes. I may turn storyteller. The people eat it up."

Now I had heard just about everything.

I was also beginning to feel regrets that the elderly businessman had made me lose my temper.

I didn't believe that when he cooled off and talked to his wife and kids (who also lived in the parish with their own kids), he'd desert us.

It wouldn't be my fault if he stayed. I'd been cold and rude to the poor old guy.

Later in the rectory, the money presumably prepared for the bank, Jamie came into my parlor, the Roman collar out of his clerical shirt, an astonishing informality.

"Have a hard time with George?" I looked up from my copy of *Castle Richmond* by Anthony Trollope.

"Wow! Did you hear any complaints?"

"A few."

"What did you tell them, Father?"

My New Priest was worried.

"Told them," I dismissed the complaints, "to read the seventh chapter of Saint John."

"Seven:fourteen," he said automatically. "I figured that Mr. Wholey would object that I didn't explain the story and that I didn't insist that our God, the real God, is not as experimental as Weesak Itsak. I didn't think the allusion to baring of breasts would send him up the wall. What else does a mother do for her children?"

"It's the word, Jamie. You might have got away with *bosom*. Thank heaven you didn't use nipple."

"Saint Bernard—"

"I'm aware of the quote. Saint Bernard didn't live in Forest Springs."

"I shouldn't have done it?"

Another chance to shoot him down. Or more reasonably put, to protect him from his own innocence.

"I'm not going to tell you what metaphors are appropriate for your preaching the Word of God. Hell, it's a biblical metaphor."

"I don't want to cause trouble or offend people."

"In a neighborhood like this, you offend people if you draw in a breath of air too deeply. Fuck 'em. It was a great sermon, keep it up."

"I suppose they'll send a tape to the Chancery." He bowed his head abjectly. "I didn't intend to make trouble for you."

Another chance to trim his sails if I wanted.

"If there's any complaints, I'll take care of Joe Simon, with a great deal of pleasure, almost as much as your uncle has when he tells that fat slob off."

"Father!"

"Stick to your guns, Jamie Keenan. Most of the people loved the story. You can't please everyone."

"I suppose so." He rose.

"You're going over to the Wholeys' place again?"

"He invited me. I'd like to meet this Father Louis fellow."

"He won't show, but know thy enemies."

"Poor George and Jill have so many problems."

"Tell me about it. Father Louis is the cause of most of them."

"Maybe he only makes it worse."

"I suppose so." I picked up Trollope again. His Castle Richmond was almost certainly the same town as the one in which Thomas Flanagan located *Tenants of Time*.

"Is there much hope for them?"

"Look, there's not much hope for the Sullivans, and they're a lot brighter and more flexible than George. How is that case coming, by the way?"

"I see them later. She's still not speaking to him because he quit the law firm."

"No trip to River Forest?"

"Late supper." He smiled cheerfully. "I wouldn't dare miss it."

"You'd better believe it."

Off he went to find his lance and his Rocinante. Don Quixote, Saint Joan, and Billy Budd all rolled up into one Mary Poppins of an associate pastor.

Or Michael Jordan.

I felt old and tired and cynical.

As predicted, Joe Simon called promptly at nine-thirty the next morning.

"Lar, what the hell is going on out there?"

The first time he shouted that at you it was a little intimidating. After a while it became, as the kids would say, BOR-ING!

"Get a new opening line, Joe. That one is BORING!"

"The Cardinal is upset by the complaints he's receiving about Father Keenan's sermon yesterday."

"Homily."

"Huh?"

"Homily, not sermon."

"Yeah, well, they're inundating us with complaints."

"What's an inundation in your world, Joe?"

"Huh?"

"How many complaints does it take to create an inundation—four, five?"

"That's not the point. The people that complain have the right to their point of view."

"When their masters have more clout in Rome than the Cardinal does."

I was, as you can see, building up a head of steam.

"Well, the Cardinal is upset."

"Have either you or the Boss listened to the whole tape?"

"We have better things to do than to listen to a sermon by a kid just out of the seminary."

"You'd both learn a lot from listening to him."

"We've heard enough. What he said is inappropriate for a priest."

"Try John seven:fourteen."

"What?"

"Jesus uses a similar metaphor. Compares himself to a nursing mother."

"That was Jesus.".

"Look, Joe, this is a waste of both our time. If you and the Boss won't listen to the whole homily, I'm not going to discuss it with you."

"Will you warn Father Keenan?" He shifted his ground, an exercise at which Joe Simon was instinctively good.

"Warn him yourself."

"We might call him down here for a session with the Boss and me and the Vicar for the Clergy."

"Star chamber, huh?"

"His remarks were inappropriate."

Joe didn't understand what a star chamber was.

"The people loved the story."

"I'll see what the Boss wants to do."

"Great idea, Joe."

"I'll get you someday, Lar. You and that rich young punk, too."

"I can hardly wait."

I hung up before he did.

There wasn't much chance of their summoning Jamie to account for his metaphors. The Cardinal would listen to Joe's report of his conversation with me. He would lament how "abrasive" I was. His sense of fairness, however, would constrain him to listen to one of the tapes from beginning to end. Maybe twice.

Then he'd remark to Joe, "Actually that was a pretty good homily. If only he'd left out those last couple of lines."

That would be that.

The star chamber sessions lost their impact on people when they used them too frequently. So they would reserve them for more serious clerical problems than Jamie's image of nature taking off its garments to keep us warm in wintertime.

The purpose of Joe's call was to intimidate me into intimidating Jamie—a strategy that still worked often in many places.

Not, however, in Forest Springs.

By now both Joe and the Boss ought to have understood that I don't intimidate anymore.

I wouldn't even mention the call to my New Priest. He had too many problems as it was.

CHAPTER

15

His dignity in extreme jeopardy, the pastor still made an occasional appearance on the basketball courts.

On a late October afternoon, with gray clouds racing across the sky, and the bare trees standing in mourning for summer like relatives at a wake, I ventured forth.

I was afraid that I was losing touch with the adolescent world. I'd heard from Linda four days after the event that Patrick McNally had actually danced with Coady Anne Condon at the High Club dance, causing that young woman to glow with happiness.

The next morning Coady Anne and Patti O'Hara were seen by Cook to be shopping at the Forest Springs Mall.

I wondered if Martina Condon knew. And what she might do to reassert her control over her daughter.

On the courts the aforementioned Patti O'Hara, in a green sweat suit, was playing twenty-one with three senior boys— one of them her faithful knight, Patrick McNally—and the New Priest. Patti was on a run—ten long shots in a row.

New Priest wore a sweat suit, too, multiple shades of blue,

the sort which would do credit to *Esquire* or the "Men's Fashion" edition of the *New York Times Magazine*. When he finally shed his clericals, he dressed the way you'd expect of a kid who had grown up in River Forest.

"She's winning?" I asked the girl who was leaning against the volleyball pole, someone in a maroon sweat suit whom I didn't recognize.

"Naturally."

The voice was familiar. I looked more closely.

"Jeanne Flavin! Am I paying you a salary to watch kids play basketball? You're DRE, not athletic director."

She laughed happily. "I'm studying the cultural milieu of my charges."

"In running shoes?"

"Patti insists that I jog every day. It's foolish to argue with her."

"Tell me about it. . . . The next thing I hear my DRE will be lifting weights just like the young women basketball players."

"Oh, I do that already!" Her eyes were bright, her face shining. "Our bodies are gifts from God. We must show gratitude for the gift by taking good care of the body as well as the soul."

"Really!"

"Well," she considered thoughtfully, "I don't like that body/soul bifurcation. If you care for the body, you care for the self. Right?"

Jeanne still needed theological or ideological justification for everything she did. Now, at least, she was doing something for herself. The New Priest's magic was still working. In overdrive.

"Next thing, you'll be wanting to join the club."

"Golf does not provide much exercise."

Patti shouted gleefully and leaped several feet into the air. She'd won again.

Naturally.

Neither the senior boys nor the New Priest were humiliated. Patti was, by common consent, not only the greatest, she was also "one of the guys." To lose to her was not defined as a disgrace.

"FATHER LAR," she yelled at me. "Free throw contest?"

"NO WAY," I yelled back.

"YES, YOU WILL!"

"Lots of luck," Jeanne murmured.

"Go run another mile!"

I approached the knot of players. Suddenly several score kids of all ages seemed to appear, eager to watch this war in heaven.

"I don't like free throw contests," I protested. By which I meant that the last time I had taken on Patti O'Hara she had beaten me nine to three.

"One on one, full court?" She flipped the ball up and down.

"I won't permit it," the New Priest chimed in. "I can't do ALL the work in the rectory if he collapses and is taken off to the hospital in an ambulance. Free throws it is."

I sighed in resignation. "Only one."

"Unless I lose."

"Only ONE." I insisted. "You shoot first, Patti O'Hara, because you're younger."

"NO WAY!"

"All right, you shoot first because I own the court!"

"All right." She shook her curly head. "Authority, authority, always authority."

The preliminary rituals over, Patti took her place on the free throw line and, having bounced the ball in preparation à la Michael Jordan, began to shoot.

She made four in a row, missed the fifth, hit three more and then, horror of horrors, missed the last two.

"Beat seven!" she challenged, not altogether pleased with herself.

I made the first seven, reducing the group to silence. One more of the last three and I'd beaten her—for the first time, since the memory of humankind runneth not to the contrary.

Just one more, I told myself.

Number eight hit the rim, bounded in the air, and collapsed through the net.

There were shouts of protest, dismay, outrage.

"I'll take it," I announced and casually sunk the ninth.

No way I was going to miss number ten.

Wild cheers from the onlookers.

"Go, Father Lar!"

"The perfect score," my New Priest announced to all, "from the perfect pastor. M.A. in counseling, M.A. in literature, Doctor of Ministry, and ten free throws against Patti O'Hara!"

The loser shook hands warmly. "You'll play me again, won't you, Father Lar?"

"Yeah, but not today, Patti O'Hara!"

"Fersure. Come on, Jeannie, let's finish our running. No way he'll give me another chance today."

We were all laughing, priests and young people—and refurbished director of religious education—enjoying a wonderful day, despite the clouds, in autumn.

Then Father Mike appeared and put out the lights and laughter.

He was staggering down the middle of the street, clad only in his undershorts, a bottle of whiskey in his hand, singing "My Wild Irish Rose."

We were all silent, paralyzed. We stood frozen to the ground as a car swerved to avoid hitting him.

The New Priest came to life. He snatched up his down jacket and galloped across the courts to the street. He threw the jacket around Mike's shoulders, wrenched the bottle from his hand, scooped him up from the ground, and dashed toward the rectory, half a block away.

"Dear God!" Jeanne exclaimed.

"Poor Father Mike." Patti O'Hara was crying.

"Poor Father Jamie," murmured Patrick McNally.

"That's right, Patrick," I agreed. "Poor Father Jamie."

Poor Patrick, too, if his vocation to the priesthood dried up now.

"I'd better go and see if I can help," I said. "Patrick, you guys keep playing. Jeanne, you and the boss lady finish your jogging."

"Yes, Father Lar," they responded in dutiful chorus.

Just like they believed the pastor knew what he was doing.

CHAPTER

16

"He's sleeping it off." Jamie closed the door of Mike's room. "Already he feels guilty."

"At least he kept his shorts on this time. He lost his pastorate when he strolled naked into the back of church during the twelve-o'clock Mass."

"Dear God!"

We were walking down the dimly lighted corridor toward the New Priest's room.

Jamie had treated Mike with the skill of a professional nurse. Was there nothing he couldn't do?

"He's a man of enormous gifts, Jamie, perhaps the most gifted priest in the archdiocese—scholar, writer, speaker, he knows everything. He always tended to have a few too many drinks, but drinking never got in the way of his work. Then they assigned him a new parish, a couple of acres of land and four big housing developments. No associate pastor. The strain was too much." I extended my hands in a gesture of futility. "They carted him off to Guest House. He's been there a couple of times since then."

"On the wagon for three and a half years?"

"That earns you no points from anyone, not even yourself when you fall off. Three and a half years down the drain."

"It doesn't seem fair."

"Who ever said fair?"

"Will he have to leave the parish?" Jamie flipped on the lights in his own room. The computer screen was alive and waiting.

"Only if he wants to. The people are aware of his problem. He attends the AA meeting in the basement every week, along with some of our outstanding parishioners. They love him. It's too bad we couldn't have found one of them before the drinking began this time."

"Downtown?"

"Take him out of here? No way. Where would he go? There're not many places that would take an alcoholic resident. They're grateful I take care of him—as grateful as those people can be."

"What starts it?" Jamie sat wearily in his stiff-back chair in front of the implacable blue screen.

"Who knows? One of the self-hate demons inside poor Mike flips out."

"We should watch him more closely."

"We should, Jamie. The signs of trouble are hard to see and he's been so good for so long."

"I'll try to keep an eye on him. Kind of make sure he attends the AA meetings."

"He should do the ninety and ninety."

"Huh?"

So there was something that my Michael Jordan of a New Priest didn't know.

"Ninety meetings in ninety days . . . a solid technique."

"OK. I'll see that he does it."

"You can't do everything."

"Why not? You do." He punched a key, and the screen turned crimson.

Suitably put in my place, I returned to my room. Trollope and not Black Bush would have to put me to sleep this night.

I was wrong about downtown. Promptly at nine, the Vicar for the Clergy, the clerical babysitter, was on the phone.

"Hi, Lar," he said brightly. "How you doing?"

"Fine till I heard your voice."

"Ha, ha." He laughed weakly.

I didn't like Joe Simon, but for Wayne Rogers, the Vicar for Priests, I felt contempt. Joe didn't pretend to holiness. He might believe in God (though that was problematic), but his currency for dealing with us was power. No one ever heard him speak of religion. Wayne oozed piety.

"What do you want, Wayne?"

"It's a terrible shame about Mike Quinlan, isn't it? The poor man deserves our prayers. The Boss said he was already praying for Mike."

"If the Boss said all the prayers he claims to say, he'd never get to bed at night."

"Don't you think it would be a nice idea, for the good of Mike's soul, if he did another term up at Guest House?"

"No, I don't, not unless he wants to."

"You could double up on Sunday Mass, couldn't you?"

"We call it the Eucharist now, Wayne, and I already binate and that's not the point."

"Well, we have to worry about the simple faithful, too, don't we? Their religious needs are part of the equation."

"You mean the laity?"

"Why, yes. It must be a shock for them to realize that one of their priests is a drunk."

"Mike isn't a drunk. He's a recovering alcoholic, and I doubt after the last twenty years of clerical misconduct anything can shock the laity."

"It's not generally known in the parish that he drinks, is it?"

"Sure it is, we announce it at all the Eucharists on Sunday. Just in case people are asleep, we put it in the parish bulletin."

"Now, Lar, you're pulling my leg!"

"God forbid."

"You see, we get complaints down here. Some people are scandalized that a drunken priest would walk naked through the parish in broad daylight."

"He wasn't naked."

"How can you be so sure?"

"I was there."

"Well, the Cardinal worries about such things, you know."

"Sure, they add to the burden of his prayers. . . . Look, you receive one complaint and you call me and waste my time and yours. I'm not letting Mike go to Guest House unless he wants to."

"We worry about every complaint."

So I had guessed right.

"No, you don't. Ron Fallon drives a third of the people away from his parish and runs through half a million dollars of parish funds, and you guys ignore the complaints. All you care about are the complaints from the right-wingers, the people with clout in Rome."

"We feel it would be better if Mike took some time off. These events have been frequent, you know."

"I know no such thing. This is the first time in three and a half years."

"Really?" He seemed genuinely surprised.

"Really. Look, Wayne. You tell the Cardinal that Mike hasn't had trouble for almost four years and that I don't believe a trip to Guest House is appropriate at the present time—that's a phrase he likes, isn't it? Then if he doesn't like it, he can call me and argue."

"Well, I don't know, Lar—"

"I do, Wayne. Good-bye."

"I'll pray for you, Lar," he said just as I hung up on him.

Damn, damn, damn!

Hand on the phone, I pondered for a moment. Then I punched in a number on the house line.

"Jeannie? Lar. Was Anthony Wholey in the yard yesterday when Mike went for his walk on the wild side?"

Pause while she remembered.

"Yes, I'm sure he was. Is there trouble?"

"The Chancery wants to ship him off to the tank."

"Will you let them?"

That's what I like on a bad morning: a woman who feels you have the power to fend off all foes.

"Certainly not. I just want you to tell me the name of the one who complained."

"Don't be rash, Lar."

"Who, me?"

I meditated for another few moments, looked up Wholey Development and Construction and punched in that number.

"Michele, Father Lar. Can I talk to your father for a moment?"

"Yes, Father."

Poor kid. She surely still loved her Dan.

"Good morning, Father." George at his most respectful.

"I hear you had a nice little chat with the Chancery, George."

"They promised me confidentiality!" he exclaimed.

"They lie all the time, George."

I hung up as he sputtered. Then I turned to the house line again.

"Dr. Flavin."

"Jeanne? Lar. I wasn't being rash. He just admitted it."

"How terrible."

"And, Jeanne, this is between us. The New Priest is taking good care of Mike, as we both might expect that he would. No point in adding to their worries."

"I hear you."

"Great."

My heart was pounding fiercely and my breath coming in gasps. Damn, I'd let them make me angry again.

The Catholic Church with its centuries of rich tradition, the archdiocese of Chicago with its immense resources and horrendous problems—both were at the mercy of a small-minded, petty, ignorant suburban real-estate developer. He held his power to disturb and disrupt not because he represented anyone, not because he was important or influential, and not because the Cardinal and his stooges believed his complaints. He was a problem because he belonged to a secret society of which they were frightened. George's distant masters had behind-the-scenes clout in Rome. The Pope's press secretary was one of them, as was the press secretary of the American hierarchy and, for all I knew, so too the creepy nun who was the Cardinal's spokesman. So everything possible must be done to keep George's rigid, scrupulous conscience at ease.

How many man-hours a week downtown were devoted to George and those like him around the archdiocese?

Too damn many!

In the meantime vocations were drying up, the Hispanics were deserting the Church by the hundreds of thousands, and we were running out of money.

The Boss wasn't running for Pope, as most people said. His argument was that his influence in Rome was essential to prevent them from making worse mistakes. Perhaps a good argument.

In what kind of an organization does one of the most im-

portant leaders get held hostage—or hold himself hostage—
to the complaints of cranks?

What's the point in being Archbishop of Chicago if you have
to worry all the time about the George Wholeys of the city?

Such reflections did not calm me down. They only made me
more furious.

It was time that I followed my New Priest's example and
tried praying.

CHAPTER

17

I'm getting old.

I don't have to tell You that because You know how old I am
to the minisecond. In fact, I don't need to tell You any of the
things I'm trying to talk about tonight because You are reputed
to know everything.

We pray, I insist to the people, not because You need to hear
our prayers, but because we need to pray.

I wonder if that is completely true, however. You may not
need our prayers, although I suspect You may like to hear
them. No one ever objects to being told that they are loved.

Anyway I'm getting old. I'm burned out.

I don't like that phrase because a lot of my colleagues use it
as an excuse for laziness.

I wander. Distractions during prayer. Remember when we
used to confess them?

My work has become routine—same talk to the school kids
every September, same jokes to the women at the fall luncheon,
same remarks to the finance committee in November, same
Christmas sermon. Oh, a few things changed, so only those

with good memories notice how much is a repeat from last year.

A lot of people could probably repeat the substance of my comments without my showing up.

Too many communion calls to the sick, too many death-bed prayers, too many wakes and funerals, too many marital quarrels, too many staff meetings.

The other night I called Jackie "Millie," the name of the girl who was the first porter person six years ago.

It was like totally barf city.

She told me that, like, I was getting old.

Too many teenagers.

Too many weddings and first communions and grammar school graduations.

Too many Christmases. Dear God, why does everyone feel compelled to go crazy at Christmastime!

Too many women!

The fall luncheons didn't used to disturb me in the old days of Red Murphy. Just a bunch of middle-aged women, I used to contend, dressed up in fancy clothes, often tasteless, and more than a little tuned before the afternoon is over.

Now they drive me crazy with desire.

Forest Springs women have better taste than women did in my first parish and, because of the fitness movement, are in much better shape. They are more erotically attractive, however, because I've been around long enough to realize that there are infinite varieties and nuances to womanly appeal. A woman doesn't really begin to be interesting till she's thirty-five. At forty, if she's taken care of herself, she's ready to be devastating. Forty-year-old women have the same effect on me now as nineteen-year-olds used to.

Moreover, I'll not try to hide from You the fact that some of the matrons of the parish my own age and older are a sexual challenge, too.

I never expected I'd have to admit that a sixty-year-old woman could fill my head with dirty thoughts. However, Mrs. McElroy . . . well, we don't go into that. I'll refrain from fantasizing about taking a shower with her.

You don't have to fantasize. That is one of the advantages of being God. You can enjoy women all the time. Men, too, I guess.

I wander.

I had intended to spare the New Priest the ordeal of the fall luncheon. Then at the last minute I brought him along for insurance, just so I wouldn't have too much to drink and make a fool out of myself.

I've never fallen apart at the luncheons before. Now I no longer trust my own reactions.

When does it stop? When do women cease to affect you?

I suppose fifteen minutes after you're dead.

If then.

The New Priest was charming and won the hearts of all of them. As usual, the swarms around him were bigger than the swarms around me. As usual, I felt hurt and left out. As usual, I deliberated calling my adviser—for whom, by the way, I want to thank You again—for sympathy.

This is a long distraction, but give me a chance and I'll get to the point.

During the obligatory fashion show at the fall luncheon, all eyes turn to the pastor and the associate pastor when models appear in swimsuits or lingerie. My mind was not on the models, however, but on a dozen or so women of the parish and pictures of what they would look like in their lingerie.

What was on the kid's mind? Damned if I know, except he is probably polymorphously perverse and feels no guilt about it.

He's like I am. Mentally undressing women. And enjoying it with a clear conscience. The last unlike me.

He doesn't seemed plagued by anxiety about sex, which makes a big difference.

I realized that some of those women who had invaded my fantasy life would not be all that pleasant to come home to. At the moment it didn't seem to matter. And there were others who would be splendid mates, in and out of bed.

Do they sense their pastor's reaction to them?

Sure they do, some of them. And they like it. They're flattered by the attention my imagination pays them, and at their age they sense pretty well the details of my fantasies.

A few would be profoundly offended. Most much prefer a pastor who finds women alluring to one that doesn't.

I assume that You know what I'm talking about since in your human nature you *had* to find women disturbing and wonderful.

Now the point of all this—I understand You've been waiting patiently—is that celibacy is possible and even rewarding when you like your work and are challenged and satisfied by the demands made on you as a priest.

When you run out of gas, when your reactions become automatic, when your responses are routine, then the absence of a woman of your own in bed next to you at night becomes intolerable.

I'm not quite there yet; I have the feeling it won't be long before I am.

I'm tired. Tired of the complaints, tired of the interruptions, tired of the idiots, tired of the noise, tired of the running around in circles, tired of the failures and the frustrations.

And sick—I'm sick of the good kids who get into trouble for no reason. Sick of the marital fights which ought never to happen. Sick of young women who have abortions because to tell the truth to their parents "would break their hearts." Sick of surly teenage males and giddy teenage females. Sick of fawning ushers and quarreling staff members. Sick of phone calls from the Chancery.

Sick of being a priest?

Kind of sounds like I am, doesn't it?

Most of all, I'm angry. Oh, God, so angry. Rage seethes just beneath the surface almost all the time. Sure, I'm mad at pests like George Wholey and his crowd of simpering creeps. They're only the result of all the other and worse things I'm angry about.

I'm furious at those who destroyed the euphoria of my youth at the end of the Vatican Council. It all looked so hopeful then, and they killed it. I'm outraged at that sissy Pope and his goddamn birth control encyclical that wiped out the council and drove all kinds of good men out of the priesthood—as well as, I freely admit, some that never will be missed.

I'm equally bitter at the guys that ran out on their commitments. Some of them told the whole world that all the good priests were leaving and that only the sick and the sexually neuter were remaining. They destroyed the image of the priesthood; they destroyed vocations; and they made it much harder on those of us who kept our promises.

Since when is it fucking wrong to keep your promises?

I'm pissed off at all the false prophets who came down the pike with the new answers that were supposed to solve all our problems—salvation history, sensitivity training, kerygmatic catechesis, client-centered counseling, the Third World, fundamental option for the poor, the Rite of Christian Initiation for Adults, etc. etc.

Do You remember what all that shit was about? If You do, You're about the only one who does. Nothing but empty slogans parroted by frightened men and women looking for security blankets to which to cling in time of change. Then they clung to one another and got married and skipped out on the rest of us.

Dear God, I'm irate at all of that shit and the people who peddled it.

Most of all I'm enraged at the goddamn fools who are

supposed to be our leaders—the Pope, the bishops, the Cardinal, the morons around him.

We are ruled by juvenile delinquents!

They've sold out to institution worship and power and their own fucking careers.

Excuse my language, but You want me to tell You how I feel.

I'm *not* angry at the young priest You sent me. How can anyone be angry at Jamie? Who gets mad at Mary Poppins? Or Michael Jordan?

He's responsible for this outburst. I see in him the enthusiasm, the illusion of omnipotence, the energy, the charm, the dedication—all the stuff I had when I was his age and have lost along with my youth.

Except, God knows—You know—that James Stephen Michael Finbar Keenan damn well might be omnipotent. Or close to it.

Jamie Keenan has not made me feel hollow. Rather he's made me face the hollow feeling that's been there, deep down inside of me, for a long, long time.

Does this mean that I'm thinking of leaving the priesthood and taking a wife unto my bed so I might romp with her every night—well, a couple of nights a week?

Barf city.

Of course, I'm not going to do that! I'm a priest and I'm going to stay a priest.

That's that.

Or that I'm going to seek the one or two delectable matrons from the fall luncheon that might enjoy a relaxed and intermittent affair with their pastor? Not bad women, just bored and a little curious and ready for a fling that's interesting.

Both You and I know the likely prospects for that, don't we?

Damn it, I'm not likely to do that, either.

Unlike that bastard Red Murphy, I'm capable of imagining it.

So what does this outburst mean?

It means that I'm tired and sullen and discouraged and worn out. It means that I've got to do something about it.

What?

I don't know. If I did, I wouldn't be bellyaching at You like this.

My reaction time is terrible. Did you notice how quickly the young priest scooped up poor Mike, while I stood there as paralyzed as any fifteen-year-old?

What kind of a priest acts that way when his good friend is in trouble?

So back to the question: I need rejuvenation. How do I get it?

Maybe I should resign Saint Finian's and take another sabbatical. Slow down and think and pray for a while.

Get my golf handicap back where it ought to be.

Except that I love this place and its people, and it would break my heart to leave.

That's inconsistent with what I've said before?

You never said we had to be consistent!

Anyway You made us the way we are!

So what do I want?

I need help!

Dear God, I need help!

I love You—more than all the others!

CHAPTER

18

The next morning Mike Quinlan was a shambles, a football player who had lost a game, a defeated veteran home from the wars.

"I let you down, Lar," he said, weeping, "I let all of you down."

In pajamas and robe, he was sitting in a chair next to his bed in the tiny resident's room and poking away at the enormous breakfast Cook had prepared and New Priest had brought to his room.

"I don't feel let down, Mike."

"Three and a half years. Three and a half years and I blow it."

"Jesus fell under the cross and got up again."

"Yeah, I know the answers. I mouth them all the time at the AA meetings."

"There's no reason you can't start again."

"What happens three and a half years from now and then seven years and then ten . . . ?"

"You tell me."

"I start over?"

"I guess that's it."

"If I only hadn't felt so damn cocky, like I had it all licked."

"Is it ever licked, Mike?"

"No, I guess not. . . . Do you want me to go away?"

"Certainly not."

"Back to Guest House, maybe?"

"Only if you want to go."

"Not yet. I can beat it this time with the AA group."

"Then give that a shot first. We want you here, as I've told you many times."

"The Chancery harass you about me?" He cocked a shrewd eye, behind his thick glasses, at me.

"They know better than that."

Well, they did now anyway.

"I guess they'd have to pay for it. They lost a lot of money in the Black Monday crash."

"Did they?"

Mike didn't play the market, except in his head, where he was good at it.

"Oh, yeah, I figure their income from investment is down by half."

"So's why they want me on the finance committee downtown?"

"They want *you*?" His eyes lighted, as they did when archdiocesan gossip was the subject.

"Desperation, I guess."

"Your old friend Kenny McGuire won't like it all."

The Most Reverend Kenneth McGuire, D.D., is an auxiliary bishop on the verge of retirement. He always signs his name with the letters "D.D." at the end, claiming an honorary Doctorate in Divinity as bishops did forty years ago (even though he's been a bishop only for a few years). He's never liked me very much because I am, as he will tell you, "uncouth."

It didn't help when he sent one of his form letters, with the usual "D.D.," announcing that the finance committee would be interested in my input and I wrote "honoris causa" after his "D.D," and sent the letter back to him.

He's one of the great pompous assholes of the free world—a designation well-earned, not merely honorary.

The New Priest's Uncle Packy should have been the bishop, but Rome imposed Kenny on the Cardinal instead.

"Well, they must realize what they're getting."

"Which is?"

He dismissed the question with a short wave of his tiny hand. "A guy who has forgotten how to bullshit."

"That's what you call it?"

"Sure, what else?"

"Do you have any idea what keyed it this time, Mike?"

"The drinking? Oh, the same old thing. Regrets about the parish—*my* parish, that is. Thoughts about how it could have been different, about how I blew it. Dreams that I could start in again."

"They still love you over there, Mike."

"Sure," he snapped bitterly, "fine old man. Too bad he was a drunk."

"That's not the way I hear it. Maybe you should save it for the AA meeting."

"Tonight. I need a meeting tonight. . . . I should have called my sponsor to talk it out before I bought the bottle."

"Why didn't you?"

"Too goddamn irate at myself."

"Why?"

"Why?" He took a deep breath. "That kid's enthusiasm made me hate myself. I used to be that way, too."

I couldn't help laugh.

"What's so funny?"

"Like the kids say, tell me about it."

"He gets to you, too?" Mike didn't seem to be able to believe it.

"Hell, yes. Not only because he has so much energy, but because, unlike us, he'll never lose it."

"God, he's been good to me since night before last."

"What else? He does all things well. The Mary Poppins of associate pastors—practically perfect."

"Still a Billy Budd, though, Lar. They'll get him, mark my words, they'll get him. Just like they got me."

I didn't say that the only one that got Mike was himself. Maybe it wouldn't even have been true. Whoever was responsible for sending him to a brand-new parish knew they were doing him no favors.

"Over my dead body, Mike."

"I sure as hell hope not."

I left for sick calls at Forest Springs Community Hospital

with the warning stuck in the back of my head. Jamie could take care of himself, couldn't he?

His Uncle Packy and his mother and father and his sisters and brothers were all on his side. What could the ecclesiastical power structure do against them?

That night in the rectory office, Jackie announced, as she pondered a social studies textbook, "WELL, Father Jamie sure has shaped up Jeannie, hasn't he, Father Lar?"

"Has he?"

"Her classes are so good that some of us from Catholic high schools are attending them."

"No kidding."

"She's a sharp dresser, too. Have you seen those skirts and blouses she's been wearing?"

"Maybe we're paying her too much."

"Barf city!"

"Really!"

"And she's happy most of the time and she's working out a lot and she's getting into excellent shape and she like totally likes us kids now."

"You're just checking her out so you can attack again at the next staff meeting."

"NO WAY. She's actually kind of cool. Funny, too. And like totally cute."

"Really?"

Jackie nodded enthusiastically, causing her red hair to fall across her face like a caricature of a wimple. "Really excellent boobs, right?"

"Jackie! Is that a nice thing to say?"

"I DON'T CARE. It's true."

"Did you hear me deny it?"

"Patti O'Hara goes, like, 'We should find Jeannie a man, like someone to marry maybe, you know what I mean.' "

"Patti O'Hara said that?"

" 'Well,' she goes, 'we can certainly find her a date for the Christmas dance, you know?' "

"Like you find dates for your classmates so they can go to proms?"

"Radical!"

"Jackie, Dr. Flavin is not a teenager, and you can't intrude in her life the way you would in a classmate who wants you to intrude anyway."

"Patti O'Hara goes, 'It's only a date and she hasn't had one for a long time and she doesn't have to go anyway, you know?' "

"It's not a good idea."

No way I was going to stop them. Maybe I could talk the New Priest out of it, and he could restrain Patti O'Hara and her troops.

"She's a bitchin' woman, Father Lar. She shouldn't be so lonely."

"Some people like being lonely."

"Jeannie doesn't." Jackie's Irish jaw set stubbornly. "I KNOW she doesn't."

"It's terribly risky, Jackie."

"Like Father Jamie goes, we have to be certain that we find her the right man. Otherwise, we'd better not do it. I mean, like, we're not crazy or anything."

A pope delivering an *ex cathedra* definition could not have been more positive.

"Father Keenan," I protested, beating a hasty retreat, "is corrupting the morals of the young."

"Don't be a geek," she yelled after me. "You know it's true."

Not a word about the assault at our staff meeting a few weeks ago. Indeed, the porter person delegates came only occasionally to such meetings and said almost nothing. Some revolutions don't last long when you're a teen. The synthesis, to use Marxist terms, comes quickly.

And is abandoned for more interesting projects.
Such as finding people dates for the Christmas dance.

CHAPTER

19

I Liked Brendan Murray, and I felt sorry for him. His woman
was losing her nerve. He couldn't figure it out.

"I *do* love Brendan," Linda Meehan insisted, tissue clutched
tightly in her hand, awaiting the inevitable return of tears. "If
I'd marry anyone, I'd marry Brendan."

"But . . ."

"I don't know whether I want to marry anyone. Not now,
anyway."

"I don't know whether" in such a discussion means "I don't
want to." Or sometimes "I'm afraid to."

Linda, tearful, and Brendan, confused, had cornered me in
my first-floor office after a High Club dance. I was too tired to
catch the signs at first. I greeted Brendan warmly and told him
that I was happy to meet him after all I had heard about him.

"My name is not Arthur." He smiled wanly. "I'm not sure
tonight what it is."

First warning sign.

Brendan Murray was a solid, brown-haired young Irish
American—short hair, quick movements, tough jaw: he looked
like a middle-weight CYO boxer of yesteryear. He was a commodity trader at the CBOE and, judging by the Jaguar in front
of the rectory, a reasonably successful one.

He also adored Linda Meehan and was gentle and sympathetic toward her problem, although he could not understand it.

"We're not exactly engaged, Father," he said with a quick, winsome smile. "I'd sure like to be."

"I'm not ready for engagement, Father," Linda pleaded. "Not now."

"Not ever?" Brendan frowned.

"I don't know."

"I don't want to lose you."

"I'm not yours to lose," she snapped.

"I didn't mean it that way."

"I know you didn't. I'm sorry."

Most young women and many, many young men go through an interlude of serious doubt as they approach marriage. As a general rule of thumb, those who should hesitate don't and those who shouldn't hesitate do.

The rule of thumb, alas, doesn't always work.

I remember from my time at Red Murphy's parish one couple who did hesitate. Well, the young woman did and not without some reason. Her man was secretive or maybe only shy. He fled from intimacy into job, working many more hours at his law office than he needed to. He swore that he would change after they were married.

"I'll have someone to come home to then, Father."

"Do you believe him, Terri?"

"I think so."

"I promise."

"What will you do if he doesn't keep his promise?"

"I'll walk out on him."

"You won't have to do that."

"If she does?"

He grinned at me. "Then I'll beg her to come back, make my promise again, and keep it."

Fair enough?

They were married. He didn't keep his promise. She came to see me. I reminded her of her threat. She didn't walk out on him and thus broke her own promise. Both accused me to their friends of trying to break up their marriage.

It has not been a happy marriage.

I learned my lesson, though I'm not sure what it was. Maybe only to listen more carefully and say less in such situations.

"You see, Father," Linda began. ". . . You're sure this isn't unprofessional? I mean you're my boss."

"If you want to talk to me, Linda, it's not unprofessional."

"I have to talk to someone."

"I'm not opposed to her working for the Church, Father," Brendan cut in. "I think it's great. My family was active in our parish when I was growing up. I love parish life. Linda is great with the kids. She'll be a great mother."

"I quite agree. Linda?"

"I don't know whether I want kids."

Linda adored kids. What the hell was wrong?

"I can't figure it out," Brendan said with a sigh. "I'm trying, but I still don't get it."

"A wife has to earn money for the family if she is to be a full partner in the family, doesn't she, Father Lar?"

A dangerous question.

"Not necessarily, Linda. My mother was as full a partner as you could imagine, and she didn't earn a cent."

"I mean *now*. If you're economically dependent on your husband, you're not a full equal."

"I don't mind you working, Linda."

"I *intend* to work, except perhaps when the children are little." She dabbed at her nostrils with the tissue. "If I ever have children."

"I see."

I didn't see.

"The problem is with the work she does, Father."

"I see."

I still didn't see.

"A woman can't be a full partner on a parish salary, Father," Linda argued. "I mean, you pay me more than any of my friends earn in business. But most pastors aren't like you."

"Wages will go up in the Church, Linda. They'll have to."

Over a lot of my colleagues' dead bodies.

"You see, Father, Brendan is a very successful trader. We'll never need the little bit I earn from a parish. So I won't be essential to the family's economic welfare." She dabbed at her eyes. "Not ever."

Well, I'll be damned. And I thought I had heard them all.

"If I should die young—" Brendan tried manfully to say the right thing.

"I don't even want to think about that." She burst into tears. "I'm so confused."

So was I.

"I bet, Linda, that you can find a parish worker somewhere in the city who is married to one of these freebooters from the commodity exchanges and that they work out their financial problems just fine. Well, as fine as anyone else."

"I know THAT." She laughed through her tears.

"Try to explain it to me, Linda."

"Well, I had a long, long talk with Jeanne Flavin—I admire her so much—and she convinced me that women have to be independent and that it was hard to be independent on parish salaries, and so I started to worry and . . ." More tears.

So that was it. Jeanne was messing in someone else's romantic life. Damn the woman. She'd fed Linda's free-floating anxieties and gave them something to fixate on.

"I think, Linda, that your real problem isn't money so much as it is cold feet."

We pursued that subject for another half hour, making little progress but not confusing things even more.

"Well, I didn't say I wouldn't marry you." She dried her eyes at the end.

"You didn't say you'd accept my ring."

"You didn't try to give it to me yet." She sniggered. "If you could be patient a little longer . . ."

He rested his strong hands on her shoulders. "As long as you want, Lin. Understand me: I don't intend to lose you without a fight."

She leaned her head against his chest, hopelessly in love with him. "I know that."

"A good investment, Brendan?"

"I'm a bull, Father. I'm going long on Linda."

So our conversation had provided some temporary relief.

Prognosis for the future: pretty good if I could shut up Jeanne Flavin.

I stormed up to the New Priest's room. He was bent over his computer.

"I'm on the verge of a major breakthrough in the human condition, Father." He did not look up.

"Oh?"

"Right. I'm on the verge of designing a program which will distribute altar boy, uh, Mass server, uh, Eucharistic minister appointments with total fairness."

"We can all retire on the income from that. . . . Will it eliminate all complaints?"

"It will minimally give the illusion of fairness."

"Can't beat that."

"I admit"—he glanced up at me—"that I've met my match."

"Impossible."

"Truly. Eighth-grade altar persons. You can't train the boys and girls together. The former fight and show off. The latter giggle. Chaos."

He turned back to his keyboard, then glanced up at me again.

"So what do you do?"

"I've decreed that they will be trained separately. It doesn't

take any more time because we save all the time expended on a
hopeless fight for order. God may have created sexual differen-
tiation, but She made a mistake with eighth graders."

"Or we do when we put them together at that age."

"Maybe. . . . I confess that I like the boys better. They're
more predictable and less snooty. . . . Something wrong, boss?
You look perturbed."

"Linda's romance is in trouble. Probably not fatal, but your
friend Jeanne is responsible!"

His friend Jeanne. Get it?

"No!"

I told him the story.

He carefully saved his program and turned off his 386/20.

"I'm sure she didn't mean any harm. Jeanne's not vicious.
There's not an ill-intentioned cell in her body."

"Intentional or not, she's created problems for Linda and
Brendan."

"Would they have had a problem anyway?"

Good question.

"Probably. People are scared by marriage. My point is that
dumb Jeanne with her one-dimensional ideology has made it
worse for them."

Jamie nodded solemnly. "One damn thing after another.
Let me talk to her about it. She's so dependent on your approval that it will shake her up badly if you reprimand her."

"I wasn't going to reprimand her."

"Just raise bloody hell?"

"Something like that."

"I'll do it, if you don't mind. She'll feel awful."

"She ought to feel awful. It's damnably insensitive behavior."

"Absolutely. She's badly confused these days. Maybe"—he
smiled, too gently, I thought—"we can turn this into a maturation experience for her."

"I'd probably lose my temper. It's in your court."

"I don't think you would, Father. You only lose your temper with the Chancery. Not with people."

"I like the distinction."

"I'll take care of it, then?"

"Naturally."

If I decided to resign as pastor—maybe when I decided to resign—I wouldn't be leaving Forest Springs in the lurch.

The New Priest would take care of everything.

CHAPTER

20

Just before Halloween another Irish female tried to thrust her long nose into our parish staff. She was a real bitch.

On Friday morning I was at the breakfast table, poring over the sportswriters' analyses of the chances of the Chicago Bears against the hated 'Niners. I heard heavy breathing and looked up to see the intruding bitch staring at me with large gray eyes. I suppose you could call the expression on her face an ingratiating smile. She wagged her tail suggestively.

"Cook," I bellowed, "get this shanty Irish bitch out of my rectory this moment."

Normally I say "our rectory."

Cook had been waiting behind the kitchen door anticipating my reaction.

"Her name is Norah, with an haich. And isn't she the darling thing?"

"In English-speaking countries, young woman, we pronounce it 'aich.' I don't want her in the rectory for more than five minutes."

Norah with an aich rose from the floor, put her front paws on Cook's shoulders, and tried to lick her face.

"Sure you're just a friendly puppy, now aren't you, you darling thing!"

"Puppy? She's a small horse!"

Norah forsook Cook and returned to me. She rested her enormous muzzle on my thigh and looked pleadingly at my English muffin, drenched in Cook's raspberry jam. She pawed at my arm insistently.

"You can't have any," I informed her sternly and broke off a piece of the muffin. Her vast mouth was a bottomless pit.

"She's an illegal alien," Cook insisted, "well, in a manner of speaking. Immigration deported her owners because someone snitched—they usually leave the Irish illegals alone till someone snitches. Father Jamie said that she could stay here till I found a home for her. Otherwise, the poor little thing will have to go to the dog pound. Get off the table, Norah, don't make His Reverence any more grouchy than he is."

Looking guilty, Norah withdrew her massive paws from the table and slunk away into a corner, knocking over one of the dining room chairs in the process.

"Clumsy bitch," I murmured.

"She's got papers and she's house-trained and she's got a license—see it on her collar?—and she's got all the right shots and can I keep her till Monday? In the garage? The young priest said I could."

"Irish wolfhounds are too valuable to have to go to the pound," I said, "and too dumb to comprehend when they're in the doghouse."

I added the latter because Norah had quickly left her corner and returned to me, her mouth hanging open, her tail wagging furiously.

"Just till Monday morning," Brigid begged, dangerously close to tears. "The young priest said . . ."

Norah sat obediently at my feet and raised a paw in a gesture of friendship.

"Who's the pastor of the parish, young woman?"

I shook hands with Norah, a gesture that caused her to grin happily.

Dogs don't grin? Wolfhounds do.

"You are, of course, Your Reverence. The young priest says you have a collegial relationship—"

"Woof!" Norah barked, demanding a pat on her head. I obliged, and she snuggled up to me, an immense and friendly puppy.

"Till Monday morning, not an hour later."

"Thank you, Your Reverence," Cook enthused. "She won't be any trouble at all at all. Come now, Norah, me fine lady, and leave the parish priest to his breakfast."

Norah didn't budge. She constrained me to present her with half an English muffin before she agreed to be more or less dragged out of the dining room.

I have nothing against dogs. In fact, I'm a pushover for them when I meet them on the streets of the parish. Dogs, nonetheless, don't belong in the rectory. For generations pastors' dogs have oppressed curates, as we used to be called. Red Murphy bred Chihuahuas. One of my responsibilities on his staff was to go forth into the parish late at night when his Chihuahua bitch—Queenie—was at large. This became a serious charge when Queenie was in heat and hence in danger of violation by one of the local mutts.

Her confinements were a grave crisis in the rectory: all parish activities were more or less suspended when Queenie went into labor. Red would awaken me at five o'clock in the morning with instructions to call Mount Carmel to seek a "monk" (as the pastor called them; actually the Carmelites are friars) to take his Mass so he could be obstetrician for Queenie.

"Why the late call?" one of the Carmelites asked me on a subzero morning.

"The boss's bitch is in labor," I explained.

Once a whole litter died. I wondered whether Red was going to order black crepe to hang in front of the church as we did whenever a bishop or a pope went home to whatever reward the Almighty might have prepared for him.

I discovered the tragedy late the night it happened. I had decided to raid the freezer for the remnants of the chocolate ice cream that I was pretty certain was there.

Someone had pasted a sheet of paper to the ice cream carton. On it the same someone had scrawled in large block letters the word "Puppies." I told myself that it was one of my colleagues' idea of a joke, till I opened the top of the carton and plunged my spoon into five dead puppies.

I vomited in the sink.

The next morning, I confess it, I called a dozen of my classmates to tell them the story of the emergency morgue in our rectory.

I swore that day that if I were a pastor, I would not impose a canine pet on my staff.

I planned to keep my oath.

Before I had time that morning to worry about the new bitch in the house, the Catholic Left, slower than the Catholic Right, expressed its displeasure with the New Priest.

I received a letter of complaint from Blaise and Sheila Ferrigan, or as they styled themselves, Blaise and Sheila Ferrigan-McKittrick.

He was an "inactive priest," as he described himself, she a sometime nun. They both taught at Forest Springs Township High School, as they had before they "withdrew from the ministry." Neither of them, however, would give up involvement in clerical activities. They laid claim to the title of "theologian" on the basis of their master's degrees from Marquette. (That program in the late 1960s had been the most efficient marriage market in the country for priests and nuns planning to decamp.)

Blaise was a classmate of mine, our class intellectual. If the archdiocese had sent him away for a full-fledged doctorate in theology, he would never have left the priesthood. Today he would be a competent but undistinguished professor of theology at a small Catholic college. Probably he would be working on a book which he would never quite finish.

Although they were "inactive" in the "exercise of the ministry," Sheila and Blaise could not, as many former priests and religious have, relinquish their fixation on the ecclesiastical institution. Although Father and Sister were playing house together, the parish was still their obsession. They felt quite confident that they would have done a much better job "evangelizing" (one of the currently fashionable buzzwords) Forest Springs than I was doing.

They were sad, lonely people. I felt sorry for them and appointed Sheila a minister of the Eucharist and, despite the Polish Pope's ban, I deputed Blaise a lector so he could read the scripture at the beginning of the Mass—oops, Eucharist.

Neither of them were good at their "ministries." The people avoided Sheila's line at Communion time because she was so slow, and Blaise mumbled so softly at the scripture readings that no one could hear him.

"You'd fire him if he wasn't a priest," Turk insisted. "You're discriminating."

"I feel sorry for them."

"Rotten excuse. Blaise Ferrigan always was a jerk."

In person the two of them are shy, diffident, gray-tinged people—an underplayed Jessica Tandy and Hume Cronyn. They would scurry away from the sacristy with hardly a word after the Mass was over. The most I ever heard from either was a faint mumble.

They took out their anger in the printed word—letters to the *National Catholic Observer* (the *NCO* in clerical jargon) and to me.

I would reply politely, usually denying their charges.

I knew they'd eventually go after Jamie. He was a perfect target for their small, envious souls.

Dear Larry [sic],

If Father James Keenan is typical of the young men ordained to the ministry of Eucharistic President at the present time, the condition of the Church is even worse than we had thought.

He is the spoiled son of celebrity parents. He has no concern for the poor or the oppressed of the world, no sensitivity to the suffering of women, blacks, browns, Palestinians, Salvadorans, Angolans, and gays. He never preaches on the fundamental option for the poor, to whom all Christians are bound. He does not use gender inclusive language. His homilies are devoid of theological importance. He is apparently unaware of his obligation to denounce with prophetic vigor the American consumerist system of waste and war. He tries to compensate for his intellectual and spiritual deficiencies with an artificial charm more suitable for the country club than for the altar of the Eucharist.

We wish to impress on you your solemn responsibility to demand of this young man authentic ministry. If he does not respond to your demand, then you should replace him.

Cordially in the poverty of Jesus,
Sheila Ferrigan-McKittrick
Blaise Ferrigan-McKittrick

The Poles had not made the honor role of the oppressed. Too bad for you, Lech Walesa.

I crumpled the letter to throw it away and then decided that I should warn the New Priest about them.

I ambled down to his room and gave him the letter. "You've got the Catholic Left down on you now, Jamie. Indeed, the whole Catholic Left of the parish."

He read the letter and frowned, taking it more seriously than he should have.

"Like the kids and Jeanne combined."

"You don't use sexist language."

"I've preached about poverty and suffering—my homily last week about Conor and Seamus Sean the Leprechaun."

"It won't do, Jamie, not for this twosome. They're just like George Wholey and his bunch: you have to preach it in language of which they approve. Sound like an *NCO* editorial or you're just a spoiled rich kid. I'm only warning you about them. No point in taking them seriously."

"They have the right to their opinion." He puzzled over the paper.

"Sure they do, but their reality is in their heads, not in the world outside."

He pondered and then grinned happily.

"I've been thinking of a 'Voice from the Pews' column in *The Bells*. How about beginning with this one?"

I gulped. "Give them a pulpit and you'll never get rid of them."

How innocent could this young innocent be?

"Well, it might not hurt them if they had to listen to replies."

"Most of the parishioners wouldn't take this bullshit seriously. They won't bother to reply."

"Not unless we ask them to." He laughed merrily. "Nothing like dialogue in a parish, is there, Father?"

Not innocent at all.

I had said nothing to him about Norah with an aich. Let him bring up the subject.

"Norah," he gazed out the window, "must feel she's died and gone to heaven."

"Umm."

"Wolfhounds dote on kids. She's got a whole school yard filled with them. Take a look."

Reluctantly I glanced at the school yard. Norah was truly having the time of her life. Her only problem seemed to be that she couldn't play with all eight hundred kids—and twenty staff members.

"Even Sister Cunnegunda is petting her," the New Priest observed.

"Overgrown bitch."

"Handsome though."

"Let that outsize nose in the door and she'll take over."

I was about to tell him about Red Murphy's Chihuahua. He prevented me from repeating a story told him four times already.

"It's not like Monsignor Murphy's Queenie, Father. Norah isn't the pastor's dog, she's the parish's dog. Saint Finian's needs a parish dog."

"I don't see why. My decision is final. Handsome or not, the bitch leaves on Monday morning."

It was, naturally, already too late.

Back in my study, I called the Ferrigan-McKittricks and they granted enthusiastic permission for their letter to appear in *The Bells*. At three in the afternoon, I was in the office with a committee of the Woman's Society. Cook buzzed me from the kitchen.

"The fifth-grade girls are at the back door, Your Reverence. They're after wanting to have a wee word with you."

An innocent to the slaughter, I went to the back door. Eyes dancing with glee, a gaggle of young women awaited me.

"Father Lar . . ." one of them began breathlessly.

"Can . . ." a second one added.

"Norah come out and play with us?" a third burst out. "PLEASE!"

Before I could reply, like a herd of antelope escaping from a leopard, their playmate bounded up the steps from the garage and out the door.

"We'll take her over to Myrtle Park," the kids yelled, as they dashed after the manic wolfhound.

None of them seemed to care that in her rush for the outdoors, the shanty Irish bitch had knocked the parish priest off his feet.

Well, almost.

"She's just a wee clumsy puppy," Cook said cautiously.

"Monday morning!" I gathered the shreds of my pastoral dignity and went back to the office. My committee was watching Norah's progress down the street toward Myrtle Park.

"Is *that* Norah, Father Lar?"

"Isn't she cute!"

"The kids just love her."

"It's wonderful that you have a dog."

"When you breed her, can we have one of the puppies?"

"If they're not in the chocolate ice cream carton."

"She's not a Chihuahua," one of the women laughed, with no respect at all for an aging pastor's propensity to repeat his stories.

"That she's not. And she's not the rectory pooch. On Monday morning she goes!"

"Oh, Father," they chorused, "she's so cute!"

The chief of police arrived at four-thirty. I knew what he wanted as soon as I saw his fat face.

"I've come to make inquiries, Reverend, about your dog."

"I don't have a dog, Captain."

He sighed heavily. "I have been given reason to believe that the subject is a resident of this house."

"She's no perpetrator, Captain. She has all the proper licenses and immunizations."

"I realize that, Reverend." He shifted his heavy weight on the hard chair to which I had shown him. "We checked the subject's tags."

"Fine."

"We received a call from a citizen who said there was a dangerous dog in Myrtle Park."

Forest Springs has liberal ordinances about mutts. So long as they are properly immunized and don't bite anyone they are not subject to either leashes or muzzles.

"Norah is not a dangerous dog, Captain, She's nothing more than a puppy."

"The subject"—he rested his hand on his gun—"is a very large animal."

"And as gentle as a newborn kitten, officer. Irish wolfhounds were bred long ago to be gentle, especially with children. They are, according to experts, the most intelligent and most friendly of all canine creatures."

I was quoting the New Priest, who had also informed me at lunch that the wolfhound would only harm someone in defense of its owner: "She wouldn't do anything more than knock an assailant down unless ordered to do more. The Irish had too many drunken fights with their best friends to risk a killer dog. Norah looks like a fierce watchdog and growls like one, but she's a pushover."

"The subject is a very large animal, Reverend," the cop repeated. "People might be frightened."

"Did the subject resist apprehension when you inspected her tags?"

He blushed. "She tried to lick my face."

"Promiscuous bitch," I murmured. "Wolfhounds are like that, Captain. They have no taste in their choice of friends."

He didn't get the joke.

"Well, Reverend." He rose ponderously. "I sincerely hope it will not be necessary for us to take action against the subject."

"If you do anything to that harmless pooch, Captain, the village will have a major lawsuit on its hands."

You'll notice that I said nothing about her leaving on Monday morning. Nonetheless, I was still firm in my intentions: the bitch would not stay in Saint Finian's rectory for more than an hour after breakfast on Monday morning.

I introduced her to the staff at their meeting. I didn't have much choice: she sauntered in like she was on the payroll. She promptly made friends with Jeanne and curled up at her feet. They all insisted that she was a wonderful dog.

"Like radical, you know, Father Lar," Lisa enthused. "I mean, like totally out there!"

"That's where she's going to be Monday morning: out *there!*"

Jeanne and Linda had come into the meeting together, whispering happily to one another. The engagement was back on.

"Thanks for listening the other night, Father," she murmured to me in the libation period after the meeting. "I feel kind of foolish because I was such a little twit. Everything is fine now. Jeanne has been a big help to me. I can't believe how patient Brendan was. I think I would try the patience of a saint."

"I like him a lot, Linda."

"So do I, Father. So do I."

Well, that was that. The New Priest scores again.

Now, if the marriage doesn't work out, both of us are to blame for helping it along.

At supper that night Norah charmed both Mike and Turk. The latter was so busy sneaking her snacks when he imagined that I wasn't looking that he ate something less than his usual massive meal.

Father Keenan's eyes twinkled with delight.

Norah with an aich, indeed!

After Mass on Saturday morning a professor of veterinary medicine who lives in the parish arrived at the front door to visit Norah. She promptly jumped all over him like he was an old friend.

"Fine dog, Father. Fine, fine dog. Almost a show dog. Quite valuable, I should say. Picture of health. Very intelligent. When she's ready to be bred, I'd be happy to find the right mate for her."

"He'd better be Catholic."

He glanced at me uncertainly before he laughed.

Norah saw some kids outside and began to scratch insistently at the front door. I let her out. She took the front steps in a single vast bound, fell clumsily on her face. Then she jumped quickly to her feet and, with an embarrassed glance back over her shoulder at me, raced off after the kids.

The professor asked for her papers.

I didn't know there were any such. Cook told me that the "young priest" had them.

I buzzed Jamie, who appeared with the papers in his hand.

The veterinarian glanced at them. "Impressive, Father. She's a wonderful addition to the parish. If I can be any help with her, please call me."

Even now I'm not altogether sure that Cook and the New Priest were telling the full truth. I'm sure that someone had to return to Ireland lest they be deported (and probably fly back on the next plane on another tourist visa). I'm not so certain that Papa Jerry and Mama Maggie weren't involved.

The veterinarian's visit was likely part of a carefully staged scenario. Someone decided that since the pastor couldn't have a wife, he needed an Irish wolfhound.

Saturday night was, in retrospect, my last chance to get rid of the bitch. The whole parish was agog about her. As she greeted people coming out of the five-o'clock Mass, they all seemed to know her name—even the toddlers she nuzzled.

That's right: after the Saturday Mass there were four priests and one Irish wolfhound puppy waiting for the congregation. She received more attention than any of us.

She accepted it as a matter of right.

She went too far on Sunday morning when she strolled into the sanctuary during my homily.

"Norah," I yelled in my most pastoral voice. *"Out!"*

With a reproachful wag of her rear end, she departed.

The congregation applauded.

I was not yet ready to admit that I was finished.

Almost no one seemed to notice the Ferrigan letter. A few men asked whether the authors lived in the parish.

"Sure. They teach at Forest Springs Township."

"I've never met them. Never heard of them."

"They don't belong to the club."

"I would hope not."

So on social-class grounds, the Ferrigan-McKittricks were dismissed.

On Sunday evening, the Bears triumphant, the Sunday crises all successfully averted, I settled down in my study with Mozart on the CD player and Trollope in my hands. Norah, whom I had sternly banned from the second floor, peeked around the corner.

"Out!"

She withdrew.

A minute or so later, I looked up and saw her sniffing at the speakers out of which the Posthorn Serenade was coming. Without exactly looking at me, she meandered over in my direction, turned around a couple of times—to make sure her tail was still there I suppose—and sank contentedly to her stomach.

Before I could order her out, she fell asleep.

"All you need is a pipe and a peat fire," my New Priest said when he put his head in an hour later.

"And a blackthorn stick to chase all responsible for this bitch."

He just laughed.

Norah opened one eye, saw him leave, rose to her massive four paws, stretched, and walked out of the room after him.

"Unfaithful, like all Irish women." I went back to *Castle Richmond*.

In a minute or two, having put the New Priest to bed, I figured, she returned and made herself comfortable again.

She was most indignant when I banished her to the garage before I went to bed.

She was waiting for me when I went over to say the first Mass the next morning, participated in the Liturgy from the sacristy, and accompanied me back for breakfast.

"Me friend Timmy will come before noon to take herself away," Cook informed me uneasily in the dining room, as Norah stationed herself by my chair and watched the English muffins.

"Woman, would you be after wanting another parish priest?"

"Glory be to God! Why would I ever want that!"

"That big Irish bitch owns the parish now. If they have to choose between me and her, she'll win. When the New Priest comes in from his hospital calls, tell him your conspiracy has been a success."

There were three brief signed responses to the Ferrigan-McKittricks the following week. (I had banned anonymous letters as a matter of principle: "Young man, someone has the right to express their opinion only when they put their name to it.") One asked what two teachers from Forest Springs Township High without children knew of poverty since their joint salary was well over a hundred thousand dollars. A second, from a woman M.D., refuted the accusation of sexist language. A third, signed by the ineffable Patti O'Hara ("Ms. Patricia Anne O'Hara"), insisted that "all of Father Jamie's homilies have social implications. And anyway, what kind of Catholic liberal is it that wants to use authoritarian tactics to silence a young priest?"

"I didn't have to plant any of them, Father," he said, beaming at me as I read the letters.

"Not even Patti's?"

"No way. Maybe Patrick McNally helped her to write it."

"Bet on it."

That was the last we were to see from the Ferrigan-McKittricks for a while. Neither of them appeared the following weekend for their "ministerial" work.

"Did we offend them?" Jamie was anxious.

"We permitted others to disagree with them. By definition that is offensive. Don't worry. We're well rid of them."

Such sentiments did not please my New Priest.

"Poor people."

We were not, however, rid of them at all. Our exercise in parish dialogue would later come back to haunt us.

Their letter was the beginning of the Christmas craziness. I don't mean the extra work and the extra ceremonies. I mean the lunacy that seems to affect so many people during the holidays, as they yearn for their own particular version of *A Child's Christmas in Wales,* for the reincarnation not of the Christmases of their childhood, but for their nostalgic recollections of impossibly wonderful Christmases past.

Mike was shaky for a week and then seemed to settle down to his old cheerful self again. The New Priest and Mike had become inseparable friends. Jamie would drift into Mike's room at the end of almost every evening's work and listen admiringly to Mike's stories.

Mike had gained a better keeper—or maybe "minder," as the Brits say—than I could ever be.

Jamie announced triumphantly one Sunday afternoon after his routine visit to the Wholey residence that George Junior with his German wife, Frieda, and their two children were visiting the Wholeys at Thanksgiving. They would be on their way to their new assignment at Fort Ord. George Senior had finally accepted the wishes of his wife and Michele that he be reconciled with his son. Jill and Michele could hardly wait to embrace their grandchildren and nephew and niece, respectively.

"Do they have Father Louis's permission?" I asked somewhat cynically. "Without that it could turn into a nightmare."

"Maybe we've outflanked Father Louis."

"Maybe."

"Anyway, they have invited you and me to their house for brunch the Saturday after Thanksgiving to meet George Junior's family."

"Do I have to go?"

Jamie was getting to know too much about me. "Come on, Boss, you're dying to get a look at Frieda."

"And the kids."

Later in the week, Jackie buzzed my room late in the afternoon after I had returned from a session with Dr. Flavin's confirmation class—the only one of the religious education groups that was to be trusted to the pastor this year.

"Mrs. Sullivan to see you, Father Lar."

"Which Mrs. Sullivan, Jacqueline? There are nine in the parish."

"Mrs. Sullivan," she whispered, "who has that real cute son, Neil, that goes to Notre Dame."

"Oh, THAT Mrs. Sullivan. Tell her I'll be right down."

I put on my Roman collar and black jacket. My New Priest's clericalism was contagious. Moreover a little authority might be useful in dealing with the stubborn Maria.

At the confirmation class, I had crossed everyone up by telling them stories I had listened to on Jamie's inexhaustible supply of cassette tapes.

Jeanne, pretty as a picture in a light gray suit, white blouse, and more makeup than I'd ever seen on her before, shook her head in mock dismay.

"You're nothing if not flexible, Father Pastor."

"You've heard some of those stories before?"

"All but one of them. They're good stories, however."

"I only steal the best ones off his tapes."

"It's nice to see how well you two relate to one another."

"It's easy. I just do as I'm told."

"Isn't it wonderful how nice he is to poor Father Quinlan?"

"He's begun a reconciliation in the Wholey clan."

"Will that work?" She was walking me to the door of the school.

"No. We might smoke out Father Louis Whatever-his-name-is."

"Jill Wholey will put her foot down someday, and that will be the end of Father Louis."

"You think or you hope?"

We paused at the door of the school.

"I *know*."

A woman's insight into another woman or just a fervent wish?

"Incidentally, that suit looks sharp. Or should I say, like totally radical."

She blushed with pleasure and turned away from me. "I used to be quite the fashion plate when I was young. In a parish like this I suppose I ought to look like a professional instead of a bomb-throwing radical."

She peeked up shyly at me to see if I would rise to that bait.

"All power to the people!" I said as I went out into the cold November wind and hunched my shoulders under the scant protection of my Chicago Bears windbreaker.

She still needed a rationalization to explain her behavior.

Now it was rationalization in defense of the self.

And a quick jab at the poor pastor too.

Jamie's magic was working all too well.

He could deal with Maria Sullivan too as far as I was concerned.

She had asked for me, had she not?

No, more likely she'd asked for the young priest. Since he was at a grammar school basketball game, she settled for the pastor.

I glanced into Jackie's cubbyhole. She was entering some mysterious stuff into the associate pastor's computer which, she had informed me, was transportable but not portable.

She nodded at the mink coat on the coatrack and rolled her green eyes.

I made a face and walked across the hall to the other office, where Maria Sullivan was waiting.

CHAPTER

21

"Father McAuliffe." She rose like the convent schoolgirl she had been, and extended her gloved hand respectfully.

"Nice to see you, Maria." I shook hands with her. "Please sit down."

Maria was not the kind to throw a down jacket over jeans and a flannel shirt to visit the rectory and see a priest—even if any priest would do. She felt obliged to dress as if she were paying a visit to a doctor or a lawyer, a divorce lawyer perhaps. She was wearing a blue checked suit, a black blouse, with large white buttons and a full array of jewelry.

I was glad that I had the foresight to put on my Roman collar.

She gestured nervously with her right hand. "I'm not altogether sure why I'm here, Father."

I waited. Maria had seemed to me to be aloof, reserved, distant—light brown hair in place, makeup perfect, Middle Atlantic diction a little affected in my flat prairie ears. Frigid, I would have insisted once. Perhaps terribly shy, I would have said later. Maybe both, I would guess now. And scared.

"I want to talk to you."

"I'll try to help, Maria."

"Yes, Father," she choked. "The problem is I'm not sure about what it is I want to talk. . . . Do I sound a little strange?"

"Just honest, Maria."

"I'll try to be honest."

"And a little frightened."

She considered that. "Perhaps. Surely baffled."

I waited again.

Maria was not one of those attractive matrons who, in my argument with God a few days before, I would have pictured as open to the chance of dalliance with her pastor. Nor was she engaged in seduction now. She was rather working up the nerve to be vulnerable.

That made her more attractive than she had ever seemed before.

"As you know," she began carefully, "Ed and I have been seeing Father Keenan periodically. Ed goes all the time. I go some of the time."

I nodded my head.

"As you may also know Ed has resigned from his law firm and is seeing a therapist, about neither of which actions did he consult with me." She frowned, upset by the irresponsibility inherent in such behavior.

"I didn't know that, Maria. We priests do not violate the confidences of the rectory office, not even with one another."

"Sometimes it might help." She smiled briefly. "It would make it easier for people like me."

"Only when we have explicit permission—under ordinary circumstances."

"I see." She tapped her finger lightly on her knee. "Then perhaps I should tell you that Ed has moved out of the house into an apartment in one of the town houses over near the station."

"I see."

"He did so at my request."

"I see."

"My children are furious at me."

"Children are usually sullen when their parents seem to be separating."

"I don't want to hurt them." She sighed. "I have my own life to lead."

"I understand."

"Do you?"

"I didn't say I approve. I merely said I understand."

"You think, I would imagine, that they are wonderful children. . . . Your young aide across the way was most interested in the health of my son, Neil."

"She is part of the admiring consensus for your children."

"I daresay." She lifted her shoulders slightly, a deftly controlled shrug. "Does anyone," she burst out, "understand how much of a mother's life goes into raising such young people? How much her own life she must bury in theirs?"

I chose my words carefully. "If I may dare to interpret the consensus about Maria Sullivan and her children, the admiration extends to both."

"You're clever, Father McAuliffe. I suppose you imagine that I'm just another silly premenopausal woman in a midlife crisis."

"I would never dare put you in a category, Maria."

She colored slightly. "Indeed? In any event what I want to ask you is whether it would be possible for me, perhaps on only one or two occasions, to seek counsel from you, apart from my husband. There may be, once in a great while, some matters about which I would wish to consult if I go ahead with plans for a divorce."

"Certainly."

I suspected that she would never file the divorce suit, about which she would talk for a long time. As I had told Jamie, Ed might sue eventually to escape the intolerable—and thus be guilty.

"I'm grateful, Father."

She rose to leave.

"Maria!"

"Yes, Father?"

"Sit down."

Her eyes widened in surprise and she sat down.

"You did not get dressed up like a proper product of the Religious of the Sacred Heart and come over to see the parish priest merely to assure yourself that on a possible future occasion you would have a counseling resource available."

She bowed her head and bit her lip.

"No, Father . . . and when the pastor tells me to sit down, like the docile Sacred Heart girl I am, I sit down."

"So tell him why you're here."

Did she already have a lover?

Maria?

No, that would be utterly without class.

"Yes, Father. . . . I am frightened and I don't even know why, isn't that strange?"

All my life in the priesthood, women have astonished me by their willingness to trust themselves and their most intimate problems and fears to a priest confidant. Some of them were targets for seduction by priests during the terrible years of the late sixties and early seventies; but that did not seem to have shattered their confidence in us, although now they are perhaps a little more careful in choosing whom to give their trust.

"You can't beat it," Mike Quinlan says, "if you're a woman. The local priest is a man to whom you can give a lot of yourself and still feel reasonably secure that he's not about to take that which he shouldn't take. It's a good argument for women priests. Men should have a similar supply of confidantes available."

"I wonder they still trust any of us after all that has happened."

"They'll always trust you, Lar." The Turk jumps into the conversation, looking up from his potatoes. "You're handsome and sympathetic, and they understand that if they ever put a move on you, you'd run at a speed only slightly less rapid than light. So a crush on you is fun and safe."

"God knows," Mike concludes, "they may even get a little help in the process."

The New Priest merely laughs.

Thus for Laurence McAuliffe, the last playboy of the Western world.

"Not strange at all, Maria."

"Father . . . are most men afraid of women?"

Had Jamie planted that idea in her head? If he had, it sure had hit home.

"As a general rule they are."

She shook her head in disbelief. "I have the impression that Ed is trying to tell me something like that, either because of his conversations with the young priest or the therapist or, arguably, both."

"You don't want to hear it."

"Of course not." She clutched her gloved hands together, fingers working back and forth against one another. "I will not permit him to continue such a line of conversation."

"Why not?"

"I do *not* want to hear such matters."

"Why not?"

She paused, searched my face carefully, and then said, "They are profoundly disturbing . . . arousing even."

"I see."

Which I didn't.

"There is an implication of power that I do not want and won't have."

"What kind of power, Maria?"

She shut her eyes. "When Neil was a tiny baby and I held him naked at my breasts, I experienced a feeling of enormous power over this tiny male and"—eyes still closed—"considerable arousal, too."

"I see."

She opened her eyes. "Does that shock you, Father Mc-Auliffe?"

"No, Maria, it doesn't. I would have been more shocked if you had denied ever having such emotions."

"They are not uncommon, then?"

"No more uncommon than women bringing men into the world."

"I see." She sighed with relief. "I had wondered. Logically it seemed to be as you say. I never had the courage to ask any-one."

I was silent again.

"Is my husband afraid of me, Father?" She closed her eyes again, dreading the answer.

"I assume so, Maria. He has no sisters, as I remember. You're a—how shall I say it?—a strong womanly reality. It would be most improbable that he would not be afraid of you."

"I don't see myself that way." She opened her eyes. "I'm a little . . . a little nothing. Why would anyone be afraid of me?"

"If you are a threat to men, it would mean you aren't a little nothing, and that would, right now, be profoundly disturbing, wouldn't it?"

"Of course it would. . . . Are you afraid of me, Father McAuliffe?"

"That's direct, Maria."

"I'm sorry if I shouldn't have asked it."

I took a deep breath.

"It's a legitimate question in the circumstances, Maria. I am not involved in anything remotely resembling a relationship as intimate as your relationship with Ed. If I were, I assume that I would be frightened of you. As it is"—I hesitated, searching for exactly right words and phrases—"what else can I say except that you are certainly a disconcerting presence?"

"I can't believe it!" She threw up hands in dismay. "I don't want to be that at all!"

"Or you don't want to consider the implications of that?"

"Is it because I am physically attractive—though in truth I can't quite believe that, either?"

She was sitting on the edge of her chair, stiff and erect, her hands clutched together as if in desperation.

I continued to tred on eggshells: "I don't like to separate body and character, Maria."

She grimaced. "I want to become someone, my real self. Now you and my husband are telling me that I am someone, someone who I don't want to be—a . . . a biological symbol, or something of the sort."

"You're much more than that, Maria, but you're that, too. Why don't you want to be a person who is a symbol?"

"Because that would change everything, don't you see?" her hands unclutched and reached out to me in entreaty. "It would close off my last escape hatch."

"I don't quite understand."

"The image of little Neil haunts me. I don't want that kind of power over another man. Ever."

"It's not quite the same."

"I know that! It's even worse when the defenseless little man-child is an adult like you, capable of a response besides passive acceptance of mother love! I tell you," she shouted, "I don't want that!"

"That image disturbs you?"

"Tremendously . . . and since I'm being more candid than I have ever been with anyone in my life, it arouses me terribly, too. It makes me want to find a man and quickly!"

"You're afraid you might close the escape hatch yourself?"

She nodded and bit her lip to hold back the tears. "I do not want my own earth-mother inclinations to trap me."

Maria's problem was that she was sufficiently intelligent to recognize her own emotions—I would not have imagined that before this session—and not yet so brave to trust them. It was likely that she would never be that brave.

On the other hand, recognizing the existence of an emotion and giving it a name does let it half out of the box.

"Why should men be afraid of me?" she murmured, almost in a whisper.

"We men are afraid of you women, Maria, because you have so much of what we need and can't possibly obtain by ourselves."

"Men take what they want!"

"No, Maria, they take what they can, which is infinitely less than what they want."

"We have to give it to them," she snarled.

"Only if you want. That's why you're so powerful against us."

She nodded. "I guess I understand. Maybe I'd figured it out myself, more or less. I needed to have someone tell me what I figured out is right. It's not fair, Father, it's not fair. It puts all the responsibility on us."

"How so?"

"Not only must we be both wife and mistress to them, we have to be mother, too."

"It's not possible to separate the roles that sharply. If you want, yes, women play a mother role to their men. How could it be otherwise? Men play a father role to their women, too, but it's not nearly so important."

"That's why it is so unfair."

"If there's one thing I've learned in almost thirty years in the priesthood, Maria, it is that we can never judge the relationship between the sexes appropriately by the norms of fairness."

"You have had all the legal power over us down through the centuries."

"We sure have. And that is changing and has to change even more. You have all the other kind of power over us and that will never change—not as long as women carry men in their bodies and nurse them and then eventually permit them back into their bodies."

A bit of the conversation with Jamie had come back and was proving useful. He had probably planted the idea in Ed's head. Ed, thinking it was his own, talked it over with his psychiatrist and then had tried in his inarticulate and clumsy way to share it with his wife. The implications terrified her.

"Dear God in heaven!" she shouted, "how terrible!"

"And how beautiful."

"I suppose so. . . . Yes, of course it is. 'A terrible beauty,' to quote Yeats out of context. I'm sorry for shouting, Father."

"That's perfectly all right."

"If you men can persuade us that all of this fear is true, then we will be pushovers for you, just like we are for little boys like Neil."

"That would be so terrible?"

"You'd fuck us to death!" she snarled again. "Oh, Father,

I'm so sorry, I didn't mean that. I've never said anything like that before, and certainly not to a priest. I'm so ashamed."

She buried her face in her hands.

I grinned. "To tell you the truth, Maria, I am kind of proud of you for saying that. Realistically, it wouldn't be quite to death. Live women are much more fun than dead women. And in all honesty, you might not find the experience completely unsatisfactory."

She removed her hands from her red face. "That's the problem. I might not want my escape hatch."

We were silent again, Maria struggling to assemble her thoughts and I trying to recoup my energy. These kind of confidant talks were emotionally draining—not unpleasant, God knows, but exhausting.

"He's trying to seduce me again by this power and fear theme."

"You're right but there's more to it. He also has learned more about himself and about his relationships with women than I would have expected Ed ever to learn."

"A complex, intricate, and clever come-on." She reached for her purse and took out her car keys.

"Yes indeed—and you're not sure you can resist it. Sometimes you're not even sure you want to resist it."

She sighed, deeply this time, and her shoulders lost some of their convent-school stiffness.

"You know me better than I know myself, Father McAuliffe."

She rose to leave, sensing that we had said all that we could.

"One more thing, Maria." I rose with her.

"Yes, Father." She actually smiled. "I wouldn't dream of leaving without giving you the last word."

"You better not, or I'll report you to Reverend Mother. Freud was wrong, biology isn't destiny. It is, however, an important part of destiny. Right now you mostly don't want your new power, or your old power newly discovered. It's not an option. You can stop your exercise and abandon your diets. You can stop reading and let your mind rot. You can break away from your commitments and responsibilities in the name of being your own person. You can't change who and what you are."

"A woman?"

"No. The woman that you are."

She stared at me uneasily.

"I'm not sure I believe you, Father. . . . I understand you."

We walked out into the corridor.

"I'll get your coat," I said.

I did not want little miss busybody with the green eyes trying to check out Neil's cute mother to see why she had shouted.

"Thank you, Father," Maria said as I helped her on with the mink.

"You're welcome."

"Nice doggy." She patted the now ever-present Norah. "Remember: I get one of your first puppies."

Norah arched her back in clear agreement.

I had given up trying to banish her from the front office in the evening. The one night I had locked her in the garage, every single caller asked where the big bitch was. Well, they didn't call her that. I did.

At the door we shook hands. "You've been a wonderful priest to me, Father McAuliffe. Whatever happens, I'll always be grateful."

"I'm here to help, Maria. Anytime you want."

Outside, as the fog and the mists swirled around, she turned toward me.

"I frighten my husband?"

"Woman, you scare the hell out of him!"

"You, too?" she said softly.

"After this conversation, a lot more than before."

She turned and ran down the steps.

I glanced at my watch after I had closed the door. No time for a drink before dinner. God knows I had earned it.

I poked my head into the throne room of the Empress Jackie and pointed my finger at her.

"Don't ask."

I was not hopeful about Maria Sullivan. Other women in the same situation had arrived at the same place to which she had come and then turned and run away. She was more intelligent than the others and hence more articulate about it, not necessarily braver.

There was a net around her, a benign spider's net whose silken cords bound her throughout this crisis in her life, a net spun by her husband and his therapist, by her priests and her children. She would have to decide for herself whether freedom was inside the net or outside.

In most such dilemmas these days, the woman chose to break out of the cords and find freedom somewhere else.

CHAPTER

22

"There's a geeky boy here, Father Lar."

"Ah?"

"He wants to see you."

My night was crowded already—two wakes, a wedding rehearsal, a finance committee meeting, and if there were time, a hospital call. My end-of-the-day tranquillity—Black Bush, Trollope, and Mozart—was in jeopardy.

"Should I see this boy?"

It was a rhetorical question. Jackie had already made up her mind that I'd better see him. He was doubtless grinning across the desk at her.

"I wouldn't if I were you, Father. Except that he like kind of works for Patti O'Hara, you know, and she goes, 'Father Lar better see him.'"

"Patrick?"

"Yeah, what can I tell you."

"He's come to help you with your homework?"

"Father LAR!"

I hung up as she sputtered.

Patrick McNally was sitting across the desk from the redhead, slouched in a chair, hands jammed in the pockets of his blue and silver Saint Edward's jacket, grinning at Jackie. He wore an earring in his left ear, an affectation which did not bother Norah in the least. She had snuggled her massive skull into Patrick's lap.

If Patrick McNally wore an earring, then it had to be all right.

"How do you stand her, Father? She's SO bossy!"

Jackie's freckled face was redder than ever, and not from anger, either. Patrick had been charming her. The unflappable Jackie was flustered.

"He's the worst geek in the whole parish, Father Lar. He chills me out. Why does Patti O'Hara put up with him? He is so excessive."

Patrick's hair was black and curly, his chin dimpled, and his smile quick and lively. On other occasions I had been told, "He's a geek, but he is like totally cute."

"Like me," I suggested, "Patti O'Hara is a total saint."

"Father LAR!"

"Come on, Patrick, we must let the porter person finish her homework. Maybe she'll even find time to do some work for us—on Father Keenan's computer."

Patrick patted her on the head as we left the room. "Back to the books, small one." And to the rectory wolfhound: "You stay here, Norah, like a good girl. Make sure Jackie finishes her homework."

"Space cadet!"

"She's a neat girl," he confided to me when we had reached the safety of the other office. "Lots of fun."

"I've never seen her quite so flustered."

"I told her that her hair looked pretty with the green ribbon in it. You pay Jackie a compliment, and poor kid goes all soft and mushy. Then she's not bossy for about two minutes."

"You kind of like her, Patrick?"

"Sure, Father. I like them all, some more than others. I like her a lot. She'll grow up to be a fine woman."

"Your judgment from the wisdom of your advanced age?" We both sat down in chairs by the coffee table. No desk needed for a protective barrier as when Maria Sullivan was present.

"Right!" he grinned. "But won't she?"

"No way I'm gonna deny that. . . . You can't object all that much to bossy women. Your friend Patti O'Hara is even more bossy than poor Jackie."

"Patti?" he shrugged. "She's a cupcake, Father. The woman senator is an act. A good act, an effective act, God knows, but Patti is as fragile as they come—even if she is all-conference power forward."

"You seem to figure out women pretty well, Patrick."

"Too well maybe, Father. For me it might be either celibacy or polygamy."

I almost laughed. Then I realized that Patrick McNally was mostly serious. He'd come to talk about his vocation to the priesthood. Another reference from my tireless new priest.

"They're not incompatible, Patrick."

"So I've noticed!"

We both chuckled.

"I want to talk about being a priest," he said easily. "I have some questions—well, one question—that Father Jamie said you could answer better than he could, you being an older priest."

"Totally old."

"Not quite totally."

"Ask away," I continued after a pause in which Patrick searched for opening words.

"How do you avoid discouragement in the priesthood as the years go on?"

"Pardon?"

"I mean, I look around the neighborhood and see all the men my father's age. They're mostly worn-out and discouraged and maybe even sorry that they chose the careers they did, and I wonder how you avoid that if you're a priest. A disillusioned priest must be an unhappy man."

"You underestimate the morale of most men of the parish, Patrick. A few of them are burned out completely. Most of them have bad moments. I'm not sure all of them are that unhappy."

Dear God, this is going to be one serious conversation.

"Maybe I see them at bad times. Take my father." He grinned ruefully. "I mean, I like him. He's a good guy, when he gets around to spending time with us. He's living on a knife all the time, Father, or maybe I should say a scalpel. He's the best cardiac surgeon in the Midwest, at least. He'll tell you that, too, maybe once too often. Then you realize he's unsure of himself and afraid of the younger men who are coming after him. He's not all that old and already he's certain he's over the hill. He's a great surgeon, he makes a lot of money, and he talks about the thousands of men and women who are alive today because of him. Yet he doesn't like what he does."

It was an extraordinary speech, far more perceptive and nuanced than one would expect from a seventeen-year-old boy. He'd figured his father perfectly—and yet did not dislike him.

"He's not happy?"

"Not happy and he doesn't quite realize that something is wrong with his life. So he blames other doctors and the hospital staff and his patients and once in a while his family. He doesn't give himself time to think, so he'll probably never realize he's unhappy until it's too late to do anything about it."

A faraway look crept into Patrick McNally's eyes, the look of a man somehow on the fringes of the Ultimate.

"Poor man."

"Yeah. The only time he seems content is when he's working in the garden, which you can't do too much this time of the year."

"Garden?" It was a picture of Dr. McNally that I couldn't quite imagine.

"Out of sight, huh?" Patrick shifted in his chair. "He'd probably would have made a hell of a florist. His father was a surgeon, too, and he didn't have much choice. Not that there's anything wrong with being a doctor, so long as you don't expect it to deliver happiness that no job can deliver."

"You want to give one of the sermons next Sunday, Patrick?"

"I'm already sounding like a totally old priest, huh, Father? I guess I was born old."

"More likely born thoughtful."

"Priests get that way, too, don't they? I mean Father Nelligan and Father Quinlan don't seem all that happy."

I rubbed my tongue over my lips. The answer would have to be both delicate and true.

"They're both good priests in their own way, Patrick. No one is better than Father Nelligan at his work in Catholic Charities. Father Quinlan has had a rough life, but he hangs in there."

"I wouldn't want to be like either of them." His blue eyes, almost silver in color, bore straight into me.

"There's not much chance of that, Patrick. You could end up more unhappy than they are, in your way not theirs. We all have the seeds of unhappiness inside ourselves."

"There must be some way to beat it." He leaned toward me, his elbows on the coffee table. "How can you stay happy as a priest?"

"Lots of us don't, Patrick. That's why there are so many resignations. Men didn't use to leave the priesthood, say, twenty years ago. A lot were unhappy."

"Yes," he said solemnly.

People fool you. Until this conversation Patrick had been the occasionally dreamy-eyed, mostly happy-go-lucky squire of Patti O'Hara. Now, having precisely located that young superstar as a cupcake, he was wrestling the problems of the ages—and with more insight and concern than I would have expected of someone twice his age.

"Most of the time they wouldn't have been happy anywhere else. . . . No, that's not what I mean. Some of us were never meant for the priesthood. What I mean is that the problem of unhappiness is not just a problem for priests. With us it's just more obvious because we don't have the distractions of family life to blur the question for us."

"Why are YOU never discouraged, Father Lar?"

That question stopped me dead in my tracks.

"I'm discouraged every day, Patrick. Several times a day."

He laughed easily and leaned back in his chair. "I don't mean that kind of discouragement."

"What do you mean?" I didn't like this development in the conversation at all. Patrick McNally should not, I repeat, *not* identify with me.

"You never run out of gas, Father. You're bubble with energy and enthusiasm, no matter how tired you are. You seem to love every day of your life as priest. Nothing ever gets to you."

"Um . . . I don't quite see myself in that mirror, to tell you the truth."

"I was in sixth grade when you came, your first altar boy—Mass server we have to call them now." He grinned and nodded his head in the general direction of Jackie. "Every morning you came into the sacristy with a smile. That's when I made up my mind that I wanted to be a priest."

Oh.

Oh, my God!

"I see."

"Your example means so much to me that I could hardly talk to you about my vocation. I wonder if I can be as enthusiastic as you are when"—he smiled sadly—"even when I'm my father's age. What's your secret, Father?"

All right, Laurence McAuliffe, what do you say now?

"I'm not sure I have a secret."

"I asked Father Jamie, and he said I'd better ask you."

I swallowed.

"That you're able to ask the question, Patrick"—this was even more difficult than coping with Maria Sullivan—"is a money-back guarantee that you'll find the answer as your life goes on, whether you become a priest or not."

"Oh." He dismissed that issue with a flick of his fingers. "I'm going to be a priest, fersure."

"Discouragement," I tried desperately, "weariness, wanting to quit—they're part of the human condition. The secret is not finding a way to avoid them. You can't avoid them. The secret is bouncing back, usually one day at a time. Each of us has to find our own tricks for doing that. Love of people helps, I guess. You'll never have any trouble with that."

"Woman people especially," he chuckled.

We waited again while Patrick digested what I had said.

"Yeah," he began softly, "YEAH, that makes a lot of sense. Gee, thanks, Father Lar, I knew you'd have the answers."

What the hell answers did I give the kid?

"It's never easy, Patrick," I warned him. "So far, never dull, either."

"You think I can do it?" He cocked his head to one side.

"Fersure!"

"Great!" He bounded up, the enthusiastic senior boy again. "Thanks a lot, Father Lar."

We paused to pay our respects to Jacqueline on the way out.

"Stay out of trouble, small one"—he patted her cheek— "and have a nice Thanksgiving."

"Geek!" she screamed and blushed furiously.

"You ought to get a new record for your answering machine, Father Lar." He nudged the sleeping Norah with his toe. She opened an eye and then bounded to her feet to escort him to the rectory door.

The rest of the evening was even more chaotic than I had expected—made worse by the snow flurries that imperiously reminded me that winter was breathing down our necks.

The baby I baptized at the community hospital didn't have a chance. I stayed with the mother and father a long time. It was their first child. They would have others that would be healthy. They knew that, but it still hurt.

Still their world had come to a temporary end, an end that they could not quite believe would be temporary.

The finance committee haggling didn't seem so important.

The New Priest was waiting in my study.

"A pastor should not be up this late," he said piously.

"Bad night."

"The baby?"

"Not a chance."

"Poor people. My good news doesn't seem important."

"Young man, we take our good news where we can find it. . . . Someone offer to donate a color printer?"

"How did you know?" he exclaimed.

"I'm on a roll, I guess. Or maybe turning psychic like your mother."

"That'd be the day. . . . Anyway, Pete Maher, the ad man, called. They're upgrading their system, and he's willing to donate their Hewlett-Packard color printer to the parish. It's not a bad deal for him, actually, because as a contribution it's probably worth more than as a resale."

"What'll it do?"

"A hundred and sixty-four colors!" My New Priest beamed happily.

"Not quite state-of-the-art, though, is it?"

"It was a year ago," he sounded defensive.

"Saint Finian's only uses state-of-the-art, Jamie."

"Even its pastor?"

"Especially!"

"We can take it, then?"

"Sure, why ask me? Did you say yes on the spot, before Pete could change his mind?"

"I never make major decisions without my pastor's approval."

He laughed.

Just the same he meant it.

Time, long past time, for Mozart, Trollope, and Bushmills Black Label.

And Norah stretched out in front of the speakers like they were a fireplace.

CHAPTER

23

I understand I am late for prayers tonight. Moreover, they won't be long because I'm too tired.

I could have omitted those last fifteen pages of *Castle Richmond*. They'll be there tomorrow, too.

I had to finish my drink, didn't I? You can't pray and drink at the same time, can you?

Incidentally, since I am in a grateful mood tonight, I want to thank You for Bushmills Black Label. Just to show that I am not a puritan or a prohibitionist, in case You had any doubt.

I'm also grateful for my adviser. She was marvelously gentle and loving on the phone tonight. She always fools me. When I expect she'll be reassuring, she's sarcastic. When I think I deserve to be told off, she's so tender and good that it takes my breath away.

When I was listening to Maria Sullivan tonight, I remembered about Mike Quinlan's comment that women should be ordained so men can have confidantes like women do with male priests.

It's a good idea, as I'm sure You agree, despite Church leaders—who figure they know more than You do. The women priests would have to be celibate, or much of the magic which exists in the priest-confidant relationship today would go away.

Maria would not have given so much of herself to me and in such trust if I were married to another woman. Poor thing, she's not likely to make it. She's dug herself into a hole out of which she doesn't want to climb. You will have to help her pull herself out, because I'm not going to be able to do it.

I'm not in love with her, by the way. I do care about what happens to her.

I'm one of the lucky ones. I have a womanly confidante who has other commitments that are inviolable. I have been able to give her more of myself than most men give to any woman. Still, it's a good thing our conversations are always on the phone. I love her too much to be alone with her in a room.

Maybe Turk is right, maybe if a woman ever did hit on me seriously, I'd run in terror.

This has been a crazy night, but, hell—You should excuse the expression—what night hasn't been since I came here?

I don't pretend to understand why You reclaimed that poor young couple's first baby, not that the kid would have much of a life if she had survived. You'll have to heal their wounds and give them a couple of healthy kids with whom they'll be happy.

The real subject tonight, however, is, as I'm sure You've guessed, Patrick McNally.

The priesthood is such a mess these days, I don't understand why any kid in his right mind would want to be a priest. Yet we ordain people like Jamie and attract young men like Patrick.

They're rare. A lot of the newly ordained are assholes—not that we were all that much better in our day. The assholes don't surprise me. It's the good ones that surprise me and give me hope. As long as we ordain a few of them—it won't even require all that many—we'll survive through these horrible times.

What do they see in the priesthood? Jamie saw his uncle Packy, who is a pretty good, if somewhat ebullient—You like that word?—example. Patrick sees me, of all people.

He doesn't see the last three curates—a loafer, a womanizer, and a creep—he doesn't see them at all. Rather, he sees me and worries that maybe he won't be as good a priest as I am when he's my age.

Which we both understand, You and I, is a farce.

Dear God—that's You—I hope he's not as pissed off as I

am when he's my age. By which time I'll be in whatever You have in mind for me in the World to Come.

He doesn't see my rage.

What the hell does he see?

I'll be damned if I know!

Mind You, I'm flattered. I love it. I just don't understand it. And I worry about him.

What will happen to his enthusiasm and his idealism when he finds out that our leaders are slobs like Joe Simon and attractive and well-meaning cowards like the Cardinal?

Every human must experience disillusion. What was it Your friend T. S. Eliot said? "Disillusion, if persisted in, is the ultimate illusion?"

I can't protect him from it, any more than the clergy of my own youth could protect me. I just want him to escape it unscathed, if that be possible.

That's Your job, isn't it?

Funny, twenty-five years ago, I wouldn't have had a second thought about encouraging a kid like Patrick.

I still believe in the future of the priesthood, more or less. Most of the guys who don't believe that the priesthood has a future would discourage someone like Patrick. Tell You the truth, I don't think anyone could talk him out of it.

You have Your hooks into him pretty well. The assholes will worry him even less than they worry Jamie—who is a lot less concerned about them than I am.

Still, parentlike, I worry about Patrick.

I worry about his father, too, who sounds like the kind who will soon need a cardiac surgeon himself.

He could scream bloody murder about Patrick going to Niles for college, and the Boss and Joe Simon wouldn't pay any attention. The Romans believe in vocations, even if they don't believe in anything else.

Geeks!

I'm not going to lose my temper at them tonight. They're not worth it.

Dr. McNally might want to put up a fight. Well, that would be interesting.

Anyway, take care of them all, Patrick especially.

Also Patti O'Hara, who may, after all, be a cupcake, though I never noticed.

Help me to be patient. It becomes more difficult every day. I had no trouble with Patrick, some trouble with Maria, though not much because she was so trusting. And a lot with those idiots on the finance committee who figure my appointment on the archdiocesan board is as a delegate for them. I'm supposed to tell the Cardinal, they insist, not what I think but what they think.

As You've doubtless noticed, even in this prayer I have damn little patience for other priests and particularly for the poor Cardinal and poor Joe Simon. I would not trade jobs with either of them for anything.

Note that I did *not* say "poor dumb Joe Simon"; much less, "that dumb slob Joe Simon."

I am probably going to have erotic dreams—confusing Maria Sullivan with my adviser. I am assuming no responsibility for them. They're Your fault for providing me with hormones and then sending attractive women into my life.

Mind You, I'm not complaining.

Lest I forget, thanks too for the color printer, which has made my New Priest so happy.

And for that stupid, clumsy wolfhound bitch, who, I suppose, is a metaphor for the hound of heaven.

Dear God, take care of us priests and the priesthood, which is in such an awful mess.

24

The night before Thanksgiving, with the rain pounding mercilessly against our windows, Jamie appeared at the door of my room.

Norah opened one eye, noted that it was him, and went back to sleep.

"Boss," the closest he'd come to "Lar" or "Father Lar," "I need advice."

"I will call Lincoln Park to check on the spots on the other leopards."

"Funny." He smiled wanly.

"So what's it about?" I asked, as if I didn't already know.

"It's about Jeanne. I was right about her problem. She finally admitted it to me."

"And the problem is?"

"Incest."

Brigid, Patrick, and Columcille, as Cook would say.

"It's an epidemic," he continued, "they're crawling out of the woodwork these days, now that it's kind of all right to talk about it. I had three cases in the parish where I was a deacon. How much of it there must have been down through the ages."

"Some men think they own their women." I had never encountered a single case. "They believe the stronger have, by right, power over the weak."

"Her father"—Jamie was not disposed to discuss the general causes of daughter abuse—"he didn't rape her exactly. He felt her up for years. She blames herself: only daughter manipulating father's affection, which is an idea he planted in her head. Then she blames her mother. Slapped her when she tried to talk to her. The old man finally left her alone when she went to college. She never spoke to anyone about it. Never confessed it until her senior-year retreat."

"In high school?"

"In college. The damn-fool retreat master stirred up a storm of guilt about the seductiveness of women. She went to see him, told him everything. He hit the ceiling—all those sacrilegious confessions and Communions—you know the whole line. In the late nineteen sixties, too! Unfit to marry a fine, decent man. Only hope was a life of expiation—his very word, would you believe? She was worried about married sex anyway, felt filthy and used. So off to a life of perfect and perpetual virginity, as we used to call it. Her father felt her up for the last time the day she left for the convent."

"Ought you to be telling me all of this, Jamie? Isn't it confidential?"

He waved his hand as he rose from the couch, and began to stride back and forth by the window looking out on the courts.

"She wants you to know. She says you were the first man who ever treated her with affection and respect. If it had not been for you, she would not be able to talk to anyone about it. You, and I quote, made her begin to believe once more in the goodness of her womanhood."

"What?"

"Come on, Boss"—he would not be distracted from his principal concern by my stupidity—"that's the way you treat all women, even those little airheads down in the office. You don't realize you're doing it. Must have had a good relationship with your mother or something. Anyway, Jeanne adores you and wants you to know and at the same time is drowned in her own shame."

"She sees the molestation as the cause of her Marxism?"

"She's too confused to explain anything just now. It was the kids. Jackie and Lisa. And that super gelhead, Patti O'Hara."

"Huh?"

"She loves them like everyone does. Realizes that if she'd not listened to that asshole she might have teenagers of her own. Doesn't understand that to have little dolls like that around the house on a twenty-four-hour basis, more or less, is a recipe for insanity. I ask her what it must be like at the O'Hara house with a United States senator cum Cardinal Archbishop for a seventeen-year-old daughter. She giggles and says it would be kind of fun."

"Peg O'Hara might agree."

"Sure she would." Jamie continued to stalk back and forth. "She's an airhead, too."

"Maternal instinct? Is that why she teaches high school kids?"

"She's brokenhearted that she has no kids of her own and probably won't ever have any."

"She needs therapy," I began. ". . . Jamie, the odds against it working are enormous."

"She understands that. In some ways she's quite sensible. Other ways off the wall. She needs to be loved, too, and she knows that and there's the problem and the possibility."

"Who might love her?" I asked uneasily.

"The kids want to find her a date for the Christmas dance. At first I thought it was a gnarly idea. Now I'm not so sure. The ice floes are breaking up inside her; she's hungry for love, a man's love, a man's physical love at that."

"It would never work, Jamie. She couldn't let a man touch her without remembering everything. Life is not a woman's-magazine romance."

"I wouldn't know, Boss." He managed a faint grin. "I don't read those journals. Much too sexy for me. I suppose it wouldn't work, but what if it would? What if this is God's grace for her? A chance for a resurrection? How can we say that it isn't?"

"It's not our right or duty to suggest that to her."

"What are priests for except to suggest that we should run risks?"

"What if it's a mistaken risk?"

"What if it's the right risk? Boss, she's ready to fall for the right man if he comes along; unless I'm completely off base, she wonders whether she could seduce him."

"JAMIE!"

"Easy, Boss, I don't mean drag him off to bed, though there's no telling what she might do now that the glaciers are melting. I merely mean that she might lure him into marriage— after explaining what went wrong the first time."

"You've discussed this with her?"

Why was I so peevish? Hadn't he done a splendid job in helping the poor woman to talk about her wretched life?

"Not in so many words. She's willing to take a chance. Eager to take a chance before it's too late. Hell, Boss, it only took a tiny nudge. She *wants* to do it. You and the kids turned a blowtorch on all that ice, and it's melting like an April thaw."

"It's a long shot, Jamie, a wild long shot."

"Tell me about it." He sagged back into the couch. "At this stage in her life only long shots have a chance. You'd do it, too, if you came along not at the beginning of the thaw like you did but at the end like I did."

25

I spent Thanksgiving night reading about incest.

When I came home from Thanksgiving dinner at my sister's, I put on six Mozart compact discs, poured myself a large jolt of Black Bush, and settled in. The books and articles on child molestation and incest Jamie had given me were not light holiday reading.

Thanksgiving is the official beginning of the Holidays—a season extending from the latter weeks of November to New Year's Day and peaking (in lunacy, as I argue—not altogether facetiously) at Christmas.

As Patti O'Hara says, it's a shame that Christmas has to come during the Holidays when we have so many other things to do.

The Church's Liturgy manages to be out of sync with this rhythm. Thanksgiving does not formally exist (though the American bishops did manage, with difficulty, to arrange for a Mass text to be inserted in our missals). December is a time of mildly penitential preparation. Christmas is celebrated until the Feast of the Epiphany (better known as Twelfth Night or Little Christmas). Epiphany used to be on January 6 (and had been for seventeen hundred years or so) but now is a wild card and not necessarily Twelfth Night any more.

Talk about airheads!

So we are praying penitentially to prepare for a festival that the secular world is already celebrating. And we are celebrating the festival when the secular world sighs with relief that the festival is over.

I have argued with Jeanne for the three years she has been here about the "Holidays." Until now she has opted for the liturgists and against reality. This year, however, when I asked her and Jamie to plan a Liturgy for the Thanksgiving Friday Mass for the college kids, she agreed that the Holidays have already begun by then, haven't they? Not a hint that she'd changed her mind.

Poor battered, wounded woman.

The return of the collegians on the weekend before Thanksgiving is the beginning of the Holidays. I could never figure out why the educational administrators drag them back to campus for a week or two afterward.

The freshmen are close to despair. College life is a terrible trauma for young people who've had their own room, their own bath, and their own mother to care for them for all their lives. They discover that they are nothing more than student numbers in large classrooms. The college is a total institution that does not love them the way their mothers love them. It does not, in fact, give a damn about them. Moreover, dorm living is marginally better than prison living and those confined to them are likely to be terrorized by young people of different cultural backgrounds just as are convicts.

They are homesick, lonely, and frightened. The occasional campus rape (like once a week) makes the terror even worse for the seventeen-year-old girl who has never been away from home in her life.

So they're mighty happy to come home, to family, community, and old friends.

The older kids are more sophisticated and better able to protect themselves but are not loath to return to comfortable beds and home-cooked meals.

None of them wants to contemplate the endless purgatory (the real Lent of the modern world) that stretches out like a vast Sahara from the first week in January to spring break (without which the natives would destroy the institution).

During those months, I pile a Mass kit into my Taurus and visit the schools where we have large groups of parishioners—Northern, Southern, Loyola, Marquette, Notre Dame, Loras, Saint Ambrose, U of I. I say Mass for them and take them out to eat and remind them that there still is a Forest Springs and that we still care about them.

At a couple of the schools, the local clergy are not happy to see me. They have charge, they tell me, of the souls of the young people on campus. I should leave the responsibility to them.

My reaction to that depends on my mood. When I'm in a good mood, I just laugh at them.

This year I'll ask the New Priest if he wants to visit a few of the schools. I'll give him the ones where the clergy don't want to see the parish car appear.

I'll warn him beforehand. Naturally.

Anyway, the collegians are so happy to come home for Thanksgiving week—a down payment on Christmas—that their exuberance sweeps the town. We do our best to harness that exuberance by having a party for them one night and a Mass and brunch for them and their parents the day after Thanksgiving. The latter is an occasion to remark, *sotto voce,* that the returning collegians are adults now and not the children who went off to school a few months before. Parents nod their heads in agreement, and then they continue to treat their sons and daughters like they were freshmen and sophomores in high school. Hence tension and conflict often ruin the long-awaited (on both sides) Holidays. Time for special ministry if there ever was one.

The people who do the Liturgy books are quite unaware of this phenomenon.

Naturally. They're more concerned about the "Third World," where they have no influence, than they are about the problems of a parish where maybe they can have some impact.

So we try to make Thanksgiving week, the first week of the Holidays, a festive interlude.

The church is jammed for the two Thanksgiving Masses, almost as crowded as Sunday. We deliberately omit a collection. The idea is to show the people that we are not money grubbers like Red Murphy and his ilk were in days of yore.

I usually launch myself on an emotional high during Thanksgiving week, one that lasts until about the Feast of Saint Nicholas on December 6—when the Christmas lunacy does me in. The next four weeks are a fight for survival before the winter vacation about which I annually fantasize and never take.

The fantasy, however, is by itself salvific.

The Masses on Thanksgiving were as crowded as ever. I smiled cheerfully at everyone and told them not to eat too much turkey.

Martina Condon may have actually moved her lips in a hint of a smile when she passed by me on the way out.

"Happy Thanksgiving, Father Lar," burbled little Coady Anne. "Wasn't Father Jamie's story really excellent?"

"Out there, Coady Anne, out there."

Linda and Brendan swept by me beaming happily.

"Thanks for the help, Father Lar," he said. "We're back on track again."

"Brendan, you don't have a chance of escaping now."

"Father!" Linda protested. "That's not a nice thing to say, even if it is true."

"Never can tell with these youth ministers, can you, Father? See you around."

"If I don't see you, Brendan, I'll be disappointed. And astonished."

Linda blushed furiously but not unhappily.

No ring yet, probably one by Christmas. A slight sign of rationality in the midst of the Holiday lunacy. One disaster had been averted.

I was faking the good spirits. My annual early Holiday euphoria had ended with Jamie's revelations about Jeanne's victimization.

So I should not have read the incest material after a pleasant day with throngs of nieces and nephews. I figured—wrongly as it turned out—that I could not become more depressed.

My first reaction to the articles was anger at the Church. Our ecclesiastical leaders rant about respect for life, yet this particular disrespect for life doesn't seem to attract their attention, not even when the victims are almost always potential bearers of life. Our leaders are normally unconcerned about women victims. No one ever phones from Rome on their behalf.

The incest victim's situation is worse than that of other child molestation victims because she is usually confused and uncertain about what is being done to her. She is betrayed both by a father whom she loves and by a mother who sacrifices the little girl for the sake of family peace. Often the mother refuses even to listen to the girl's questions or complaints.

Had that happened in Jeanne's family? Probably. Her father had corrupted that which was most beautiful and most womanly in her with the connivance of her mother and the willing aid of that retreat master and perhaps many other priests and nuns, too.

I felt my hand gripping the pages of the book, like I was going to tear it apart.

She had been a defenseless victim at a turning point in her life—without hope or help.

Such events mark the victims for life, "as would any catastrophic childhood experience," one author remarked. "Prognosis for recovery must be guarded."

Another, more hopeful author said that there was often substantial recovery and that in many cases there was a chance for a happy and fulfilling life "in which the horror of the incest experience is integrated into the personality and becomes possibly even a source of maturity and sensitivity to other victims."

Still other young women recovered simply because of raw personality strength.

To whom would this felicitous outcome be likely to happen?

"Young women with strong egos—though the experience itself often precludes the maturation of a strong ego."

"Luck," according to another expert, "genetic or psychological."

"A sympathetic and understanding husband, successful motherhood, a productive career, early and skillful therapy," said a third.

Jeanne didn't seem to measure in on any of these. Perhaps a strong ego, though that might be a protective coating.

My eyes closed as Mozart's piano trilled a melody that was both sad and joyous. I sipped a tiny draft of Black Bush.

We understood little about the incest phenomenon. The victims were horribly brutalized. The victimizers were either monsters or unimaginably sick. The women in *The Color Purple* weren't the only victims of incest. Father incest was more likely among the affluent than among the poor. Jeanne was North Shore aristocrat. One of the articles mentioned a wealthy surgeon who raped all five of his daughters when they were teenagers.

Lovely man.

Another article said 16 percent of the girls in the country had been the targets of "attempted incest," 5 percent by their fathers.

That was one out of twenty kids in the teen club—at least.

What was the Church doing about the problem?

Nothing. Too busy with nuclear weapons and the Third World—and covering up for the priests who played with little boys. And keeping the patrons of the Corpus Christi thugs in Rome happy.

I'd do something.

What?

It shows how dependent on my new priest I had become that I thought I'd have to ask Jamie what he would recommend.

As for Jeanne—a long, long shot. Impossibly long.

Suppose that Jamie, with the help of the bossy, busybody young people, who thought they were doing no more than finding a prom date for someone, actually found her a man who would be interested, then what?

A forty-year-old virgin with a history of molestation by her father? Who would want that?

An attractive forty-year-old virgin who had recaptured some of her youthful fashion flair and had been running and working out?

In preparation for a search for a man?

Jamie thought so. I wasn't so sure. Jeanne had ideological answers that would justify in her own mind the effort and the agony of getting back in shape.

On the other hand, it did not follow that beneath the veneer of ideology there was not also a lonely woman's hunger for a man.

If Jamie were right, she was growing through a crisis of change.

Such transformations don't happen.

No, that was not true. They were psychologically improbable. Yet they happened. Some people, as a psychoanalyst remarked to me, mature despite our efforts or without our efforts.

Jeanne must have a strong will; I could not question that. Otherwise, she would not have survived at all.

A forty-year-old virgin with spectacular breasts, a flat belly, and by now, solid muscles? And a first-class, if somewhat rigid, mind? Well, if a man were free and lonely, she might be appealing.

The first time he touched her, even in the most modest way, she would freeze up, turn him off, and send him on his way. He would not try again, not with that cold shoulder.

I pondered the scenario carefully.

One date, engineered by the busybodies, and that would be that. No harm done, except perhaps to Jeanne's self-esteem.

What if, with her sturdy willpower, she mandated herself not to act that way. Suppose that she gritted her teeth mentally and tolerated affection from a man, even led him to believe that she enjoyed it.

I couldn't rule out the possibility of such a scenario. It might happen.

Suppose they eventually went to bed together.

That was hard to imagine—Jeanne naked in bed with a man. It was even more difficult to imagine her as anything but cold and rigid if she did go to bed with a man.

If she had the willpower to force herself that far, with the help of ideological rationalizations, she might be able to grow through the motions of passion.

She would have read all the books and would know all the expected reactions. Doubtless she could reproduce them if she made up her mind to do so.

Would that be any worse than not a few marriages in the parish?

It would not last, it could not last. She could by sheer will perhaps endure it in the short run. Not in the long run. She'd drive the poor man crazy, punishing him for what her father and her Church had done to her.

I sighed. That was the best-case scenario, and it was none too promising.

Would she tell this highly hypothetical man about her experiences?

Almost certainly. Her ideology would require her to be honest about them. Up front at the beginning.

Let's process that possibility through the scenario.

A wise man would decamp posthaste. A wise man would not want to become involved with such a flawed woman, no matter how attractive she was.

What about a wise man who was also kind?

Her wounds might make her more attractive.

Then what?

The picture didn't change much. Maybe he'd suffer more as he tried to break through the hatred that she had built up around herself as a defense. He'd understand much, if not everything, and would be able to do nothing.

Poor man.

I reviewed the bidding. Perhaps I had missed something.

If she became involved in a love affair that was passionate for the other person and terrifying and disgusting for herself, what ideologies would she activate?

First, she would conjure up all the feminist rhetoric about being objectified and dehumanized—becoming a plaything for a crude, lustful man. Ugh.

But then she would also fall back on the alternate version, which said women were as much entitled to sexual pleasure as men. If she bought into this possibility, she would dedicate herself to a resolute and frantic quest for as many orgasms as possible.

The net result in the marriage relationship would not be much of an improvement. Serious sex, terribly serious. But no fun.

Jeanne was quite incapable of having fun.

Was that true?

She had laughed a lot lately with her teenage patrons. Giggled even. Second adolescence.

Prognosis poor, very poor indeed.

I wasn't leaving much room for grace. We humans rarely permit the Spirit much freedom.

Nor it did matter much about my prognosis. Less experienced and less wise heads than mine had decided what was to be done. My convictions forbade me to interfere.

Maybe, despite all odds, the Spirit would sign on with them. Maybe She'd make their zany plans successful.

That possibility made me feel happy. I told myself that I was not afraid of losing Jeanne to a husband who would bring her happiness. On the contrary, I wanted it with all my heart. There was no doubt in my mind anymore: I did love her, not the way a future husband might, not even the way Jamie did. Yet I loved her.

A long and useless reverie, designed to screw my head on straight more than anything else. Not one erotic feeling about her during my reflection, not even at the thought of her naked in bed.

"They're bastards, Norah," I informed the ever-present hound of heaven. "Like total bastards!"

Norah rose from her peaceful sleep and began to prowl the room. She didn't like it when I lost my temper.

"Go back to sleep, you overgrown bitch," I instructed her. "I don't want you tired tomorrow when the other kids come to play with you."

Obligingly she settled in for the night.

Goddamnit, I prayed, Jeanne's an innocent victim. You put her, without protection and without hope, in a family which destroyed her.

Now, with my tenderness for her, there do come erotic feelings. That's better: I shouldn't try to evaluate her clinically. That's no way to treat someone you love.

Dear God, You owe her a second chance.

Please.

I beg You.

26

Father Louis was in attendance at the Saturday brunch *chez* Wholey.

I had the impression that he had invited himself.

It felt like Jamie and I were walking into a wake.

Since I had suspected that Father Louis was trying to take over my parish, I had done some checking on him. He was in his early forties, had studied at the Corpus Christi seminary in Rome, was one of the local superiors, and was destined for great things in the Society and in the Church—hence his assignment to be superior of their Chicago house for "seasoning." It was said that when the secular institutes had taken complete control of the Congregation of Bishops, he would be the first member of Corpus Christi to be named head of a prominent American archdiocese, even if he was born in Spain. He was just the opposite of Joe Simon, smooth, elegant, aristocratic, charming—a somewhat sawed-off Mediterranean-lover type.

The Cardinal was reported to dislike him intensely and to resent his conspiratorial activities in the archdiocese, especially since in the present regime the local bishop, even if he were a Cardinal, had little authority over the Corpus Christi and similar societies and institutes.

To paraphrase Jean Sulivan, the French novelist, such groups wanted to save the Church. The means were simple—piety, virtue, money, power, and military force. The time for nuances was over. Now was the time to influence public opinion, organize, get hold of the levers of power, convert if possible, and reduce whatever can't be absorbed. "There could be no coexistence between good and evil: it was the language of the apostles before the crucifixion."

And, I would add, the language of the Spanish Inquisition. Why would they bother with George Wholey?

Mike Quinlan had an answer: "They want to get *you*, Lar. Those guys enjoy doing other people in. It makes them feel powerful and important and virtuous. You know, the Inquisition type."

"I'm not the type for an auto-da-fé."

"Just don't turn your back on that smooth little operator. He'll stick a shiv into you."

"He won't try a second time."

Anyway, when we arrived at the Wholey house, George was glowering in one corner of the vast and tasteless recreation room of the family home—confused, hurt, irate.

Jill was bustling with the last preparations for a brunch that would feed three times as many people as the eight adults who were there.

Michele was holding the little girl, maybe a year old, as though she were the most precious girl-child in the world. Frieda, the child's mother, a tall, pleasant-looking, blond woman, was trying to keep her three-year-old son out of trouble.

George Junior—"Sonny" in the bosom of his family—in full uniform, was looking very, very military.

Father Louis was smoking cigarettes, a habit I despise and about which I am rarely silent. I was especially likely to despise it today because the New Priest had reported on the way over that Father Louis had an interesting theory about how to deal with women.

"They appreciate being chastised by their husbands because it reminds them of their proper place."

"You'll not try it twice in my part of Ireland," I commented through clenched teeth.

"Or in my part of River Forest," the New Priest laughed.

Until I heard about Father Louis's advice, I was in a reasonably good mood, considering the circumstances. The college Mass and brunch had been a huge success. The Jamie/Jeanne Liturgy was both fun and brief. The crowds around the New Priest were no more than twice as large as the size around me.

Jeanne herself, in a smart maroon dress trimmed in white and surrounded by the porter persons and Patti O'Hara, seemed happy.

"They really are wonderful people, aren't they, Lar?"

"For capitalist parasites."

She wrinkled her nose at me. "I haven't said that in a month. You may actually have to keep me another year."

Was she worried about her future?

"You have a job here, woman, as long as I have."

"Thank you, Lar." She turned away hastily, as if to hide tears.

The glaciers were indeed breaking up. And spewing icebergs into the bay. Icebergs are dangerous.

Nonetheless, I felt a touch of envy for the man who won the raffle for her.

The three weddings on Saturday afternoon promised to be joyous events—no one was contracting an outlandish match to punish parents.

I figured that brunch at the Wholey house was tolerable.

Until I heard about Father Louis on women.

And saw him in the recreation room, smoking.

"Ah"—he flashed his neat, even teeth—"the distinguished pastor and new member of the archdiocesan financial committee!"

Louis—né Luís—was not, as I have said, without considerable Mediterranean grace. Although he might have been a good foot shorter than me, he had smooth, dark skin, bedroom brown eyes, wavy brown hair and an accent that hinted at a bit of

Castilian lisp. He was a polished, urbane, sophisticated cleric of the world.

As Mike said, the kind who would slip the shiv into your back.

"*Buenos días, Padre Luís*," I reminded him of my Spanish fluency, Mexican accent and all, and introduced him, in Spanish to "*Don Jamie, mi vicario asociado.*"

Don Jamie spoke to Father Louis in polished Castilian. Where the hell had he learned that?

Why hadn't they sent him to a Hispanic parish where they needed someone who could speak the lingo that well?

Father Louis complimented Jamie on his fluency and accent—and did it in English: he was uneasy about the Spanish, not to say Falangist, influence in his order. Or society. Or whatever the hell it was.

"I'm surprised, Father"—I lifted my eyebrows in what I hoped was an expression of astonishment—"that you are smoking with children present in the room. The data on the horrific effect of nicotine smoke on their lungs is quite persuasive."

I knew of no such study, but I was sure there had to be one.

The associate pastor rolled his eyes, a phenomenon that had come to mean "there he goes again."

It did not hint at disapproval.

"How right you are." He turned crimson and quickly snuffed out the cigarette. "So sorry."

That'll show the bastard.

Young George treated me like I was at least a full colonel. He shook hands formally. "Nice to see you again, sir. I hope you've been well, sir."

"Sir, Georgie?"

He grinned broadly. "Sorry, sir, er, I mean, Father Lar."

"I am not a full colonel, Sergeant."

"I'm aware of that, sir. At least a three-star general."

"At least."

Even when he was in the depths of teenage trouble, even when he was thrown out of Saint Ed's High School for smoking pot on campus, he was good for a laugh.

"What happened to your hair, George?"

"Military cut, sir, uh, Father. Don't you like it?"

"Makes me feel a lot more confident that the Russians will not march on the Wabash River anytime this week."

George Senior continued to glower in the corner; Jill continued to fuss with the food; Jamie engaged Frieda in conversation in German. Michele played with both of the kids. Anthony was in another room watching a football game on television. Father Louis entertained me with rumors about episcopal appointments in the United States and changes in Curial leadership in Rome, as if I cared about such matters.

"The new man in sacraments is quite sound," he babbled, "East German, you know. Very close to us. Understands from his own experience how critical it is to maintain uniformity of practice in this time of trial."

There was something wrong in the Wholey home, something in addition to what was ordinarily wrong. I tried to sniff it out. The big reunion celebration was not working out.

"Probably would not approve of our celebrations of Thanksgiving, huh?"

"He insists quite seriously in the importance of Advent."

"What about the polygamous bishops in Africa? Is he going to put a stop to that?"

I didn't much care. No one could put a stop to it, any more than they had in Ireland for a thousand years. I was merely making trouble.

"I am reliably informed that the Congregation for the Defense of the Faith, the Holy Office, you know—"

"Yeah, I know. The Inquisition."

"—will have a statement on that subject. It will be quite stern, in fact. Such abuses simply cannot be tolerated."

Well, at least he wasn't denying them.

"Too much like the Irish?"

"Like the Irish?"

"There was an item on the agenda of the Synod of Maynooth in 1560 to ban concubinage among the lords, the ancient Brehon right to have four wives. The proposal wasn't voted on because all the lords, temporal and spiritual, were practicing concubinage."

"Really?" He looked around nervously as though he were afraid the image of white bishops with several wives might shock the poor simple faithful present.

"Yeah. I could never understand it myself. I figure one Irish woman on your hands would be plenty. Four would drive you up the wall. I sure wouldn't want to bed four of them every night, even if you gagged them so they couldn't talk."

Frieda, who clearly was no fool, turned away to suppress a smile.

New Priest rolled his eyes again.

Father Louis reached for a cigarette and thought better of it.

George Senior continued to sulk.

"These are difficult times for the Church, Father McAuliffe," the Corpus Christi priest continued, "we are under assault on all sides—materialism, consumerism, Communism, paganism. . . ."

"So I've heard the Pope say."

"In another era we could afford to be more relaxed about traditional doctrines and practices. Now, however, the worst enemies of the Church are inside it. We cannot be too careful of their pernicious influence. The Holy See is our only protection."

Undoubtedly Padre Luís believed his rationalization—just like Joe Simon did. Sincere they both were, and both equally devoid of self-critical instincts. Neither realized that the means of power to be exercised in defense of the Church had become an end in itself; the "good of the Church" had been converted from an end to a rationalization.

Not that I was innocent of rationalizations myself.

"Well, I gotta say that I've always admired curialists who would never lie and cheat and steal except for the good of the Church. Like the guys that diverted all that Banco Abrosiano money for the Solidarity in Poland."

"That is not exactly what happened," he murmured, missing my heavy-handed irony.

It probably suffered in translation.

When we had collected our food for brunch, the trouble came into the open.

I had heaped my plate with four cinnamon rolls, not as good as Cook's and certainly not as good as Jamie's. But you take your cinnamon rolls wherever you can find them. Also a half-dozen slices of bacon, so they wouldn't go to waste. I had just seated myself next to Frieda and placed my food on the coffee table in front of us when Father Louis cleared his throat for attention.

Is this sumbitch going to try to give a sermon?

I cut him off at the pass. "Maybe the young priest can ask a blessing for us."

He did, in German—and probably a Lutheran formula because Frieda seemed quite pleased with it.

George Senior, a cup of coffee in his hand, was not amused.

And Father Louis was not to be denied.

"Perhaps, Father Pastor, you can lend your official and canonical support to a work of the Church I have begun here this morning."

"Possibly and then again possibly not."

"I have been taking the opportunity provided by this reconciliation of the generations which you have so wondrously organized—"

"My *vicario* deserves the credit, Father."

Jamie was silently laughing. At me? With me? Both?

"I'm sure, like the good young priest he is, he worked under your direction and control."

Barf city.

"In any event," he tried again, "I have been urging our two young friends here to regularize their marriage in relationship to the Church so that their children may be recognized as legitimate by the Church, such an important gift to the children. And, naturally, their parents would no longer be living in sin, and hence could be a channel of grace for them."

The girl-child, one Hilda, was creeping toward me, her blue eyes wide open in awe of the silver-thatched giant. I made a face at her. She returned it in kind, as women will do.

"Sonny wasn't married in church, Father," George finally spoke. "It's high time he get himself squared away with God."

Hilda rose to her feet and tottered in my direction. I held out my hands to her.

What the hell was Louis doing? Maybe he actually believed the crap he was dishing out. Maybe, in addition to their power hunger, they were actually sincere in some warped, conservative way. Nonetheless, he was a sumbitch.

"I do not understand any of this," Frieda spoke with heat. "I do not consider my marriage to be displeasing to God. I do not believe my children are illegitimate."

Hilda collapsed into my arms and gurgled happily as I lifted her into my lap. I was, to judge by her smile, a very funny man.

Most babies, regardless of sex, seem to think so. Her brother Stefan wandered over to me, too.

Jamie was grinning like a Cheshire cat. He probably had guessed what was coming.

"My dear, I understand that completely." Father Louis tried to pour soothing oil on the troubled waters. "However, you see, from the point of view of the Church, regrettably they are not legitimate."

"I said I was not a Catholic," George Junior insisted.

"And I said"—his father clenched his fists—"that you are a Catholic and that it's about time you got yourself squared away."

I lifted Hilda high in the air, she chortled like one who had found ultimate beatitude.

"This is the most lovely blond girl-child I have seen all day. We will be lifelong friends, won't we, Hilly kid?"

She cheered the suggestion and grabbed for my silver hair, doubtless to discover whether the metal was authentic.

"You do go to Church every week." Jill tried to find common ground, as she had through her whole marriage to George. "And receive Communion."

"As I do," Frieda said stubbornly. "The chaplain is a good man."

"Colonel Grace." I pushed Hilly up and down, to her enormous joy. "Good man."

"You know him, Pastor? Is he not wonderful?"

"You agree, Hilly, you like old Jim Grace, do you?"

Stefan was now at my side laughing at his little sister.

"Those are all sacrilegious Communions!" Father Louis insisted. "In the eyes of God they are heinous sins!"

Jamie swung Stefan into the air. My friend considered her brother's sudden rise to prominence and decided to ignore it.

"I'm not a Catholic, so they're not sins," George Junior argued doggedly. "I believe in God and I like the chaplain, so why can't I go to Communion?"

George Senior stood up, fists still clenched, now menacingly. "I *said* you gotta get yourself squared away."

"For the good of your children," Father Louis agreed.

"I do not understand this at all." Frieda had started to cry. "I came here to meet my husband's parents and be reconciled, and I and my children are insulted. . . . Hilda, do not dribble on the nice priest."

"My silver hair gets them every time."

George Senior was only a few feet away from his son, his face twisted with rage. The young man was as skillful as ever at the art of infuriating his father—an automatic action that required no conscious effort.

"Sonny, you goddamn well better get yourself squared away now so your mother won't worry about you anymore."

"In God's time, George. And no one else's." I stood up and sort of drifted between father and son. "We don't pressure people anymore in the Church. And especially not in this parish."

I continued to cuddle Hilly in my arms. She seemed prepared to call it a day and settle in for a nice nap.

Jamie was at my side, not that I needed his help to flatten George Senior if needs be.

"Why not now, today, during this glorious time of reconciliation and Thanksgiving?"

"Father Louis"—the damned New Priest stole my thunder—"why don't we postpone this conversation until another time. It is embarrassing to Frieda, who is a guest in our parish."

Louis flushed angrily and shrugged his shoulders. "Of course, if you wish."

"We wish," I put in my two cents.

George Senior, looking confused and uncertain, settled down. I returned the sleeping Hilda to her mother, who smiled gratefully at me. Jamie took Stefan to the TV room to watch football with Anthony. Father Louis departed, pleading that he must attend a wedding. I finished the last cinnamon bun and made the same excuse for my associate pastor and myself—in our case, I told myself, with more honesty.

"You haven't changed a bit." The soldier shook hands vigorously at the door.

"Carry on, Sergeant."

"Didn't I tell you, Frieda? Didn't I tell you that there are lots of priests like Colonel Grace?"

His wife's eyes were filled with tears—of gratitude, I think. "Yes, you did." She smiled at me again. "You didn't say that there would be two of them."

"Oh boy," George Junior enthused, "there sure are."

"Just think of how much trouble we can cause together," my New Priest said.

We didn't know the half of it yet.

CHAPTER

27

They gathered in my office on the first floor, Norah naturally in attendance, the night they were raffling off Jeanne Flavin.

At least I told them it was like a raffle.

"You're wrapping her up in tissue paper and raffling her off as a Christmas surprise."

"Gross." Patti O'Hara turned up her nose.

"Barf city." Jackie frowned dangerously.

"Transparent tissue paper," Patrick laughed.

"PATRICK!" both young women protested loudly.

"She is not a pig in the poke," my New Priest insisted. "The man who wins the raffle will see what he's getting."

"One totally GORGEOUS mature woman." Patrick shook his head in approval of the woman, as though it was not fair that he should not be given a chance to win her. "Tissue paper or not."

"PATRICK!!"

They had piled the desk around which they were sitting with phone books and lists.

"I'm surprised that Father Jamie hasn't started a database on his computer."

"I've thought about it."

"I don't want to know what your strategy is," I insisted. "What are you up to?"

"WELL," Patti O'Hara, alias Cupcake, took a deep breath. "We figure that if she can meet someone this weekend and they hit it off and then if she invites him to the Chicago Symphony concert next week with Father Jamie's tickets and if he has a good time and if he invites her to the Christmas dance at the club, THEN, we'll have made a really excellent beginning."

"A lot of 'if's."

"We can't waste time."

"Why not? What's the rush?"

"WELL"—Jackie joined the argument—"she isn't getting any younger."

"Biological clock," murmured Patrick.

"PATRICK!"

"They're talking a best-case scenario, Father," the New Priest said soothingly. "I've told them that we must be prepared for miscues and failures and must be ready to assume fall-back positions."

"Of course," I agreed.

"You don't like our plan, Father?" Patrick studied me closely.

"No, Patrick, to tell the truth, I don't. I want no part of it."

"Why not?"

"I'm reluctant to mess around so directly in anyone's future."

"It's no different than finding a prom date for somebody." Jackie set her jaw stubbornly.

"Yes, it is, Jackie, much different. Younger people are resilient. Older people have a lot more trouble rebounding from heartbreak."

"We don't want to break her heart, Father." Jackie seemed ready to cry. "We love her. Really."

"Her heart seems to be broken already." Patrick considered the issue carefully. "Maybe we'll make the break worse, but maybe we'll make it a lot better."

"Do you agree, Father Keenan?" I nodded at my New Priest.

"As you keep saying, it's a long shot." He licked his lip with his tongue. "I kind of agree with Patrick: nothing much can go wrong and maybe we'll be a big help."

"She doesn't have to fall in love with him." Jackie had recovered her élan. "And if she doesn't, so what's wrong?"

"What if she does lose her heart to him, Jacqueline, and then it doesn't work out?"

"That would be SO gross. That CAN'T happen!"

"It might."

"My mother," Patti O'Hara chimed in brightly, "introduced eighteen couples who got married, not counting herself."

"How many worked out, Patti O'Hara?"

"Thirteen, counting herself, are still together anyway."

"That's a pretty good average these days, and your mother's friends were all much younger when she introduced them."

Grim silence.

"You think we should forget it?" Patrick asked.

No, I didn't want them to forget it. I wanted them to do it because the Spirit might through them be able to bring a tiny bit of happiness to Jeanne. I wanted the risk taken; I didn't want to be responsible for taking the risk.

"The Holy Spirit, being an Irish womanly type, blows whither She wills. I'm not sure that you're wrong. So I won't tell you not to try."

"You'll pray for us?" the New Priest asked.

"You'd better believe it."

"Radical!" the ineffable Jackie announced. "We'll do it, I just KNOW we will!"

Ah, to be young and credulous again.

"I don't suppose you want to know," Patti O'Hara cocked a teasing eyebrow, "who our number one prospect is?"

Cupcake, huh?

"Certainly not. . . . Who is he?"

"Mr. Lyons! From Park Hill." She waved a paper at me. "Isn't that really out there!"

"Don Lyons?"

"Ria and Helen and Ken's father," Jackie enthused. "He's awesomely nice and awesomely CUTE!"

"Do you know him, Father?" Jamie asked cautiously.

"Oh, yes, I know him. Play golf with him a couple of times a summer."

"Like his wife died in an accident two years ago," Jackie noted, ticking off the details, "and he's really awful lonely and all his kids want him to marry again and Ken and Helen are already in college, you know?"

"And Ria has been coming over to our CCD class all year and likes Jeannie a lot," Patti O'Hara continued.

"You'll make them part of the plot?" I asked dubiously.

"Patti O'Hara's idea," Jamie said, "is that if we decided on Mr. Lyons, we'll ask Helen to come to the CCD class next week, and if she likes Jeannie a lot, then she and Ria will invite her to a party at their house next week."

"Without telling their father?"

"Of course they will tell him they're inviting their teacher," Patrick interjected, "these plotters are not total geeks. They'll just put the two of them together for an hour or two next Friday evening and see what will happen. Nothing much risked, is there?"

"Not if there's no chemistry between them."

"And if there is?" Patrick was still watching me very closely, studying my reactions.

"Then they're both on their own, aren't they?"

Silence around the raffle booth.

"You didn't express an opinion on Don Lyons?" Jamie noted.

"It's not all that bad a choice."

It was in fact a brilliant choice. He was a handsome, compassionate, admirable man. Maybe he deserved someone less troubled than Jeanne.

Maybe, just maybe, the tragedies that had hurt them both could be the basis for something wonderful.

I sure as hell wasn't going to tell the conspirators that.

"Will there be, ah, chemistry between them, Father?" Patrick asked.

"Maybe."

Jamie and I shared a drink later in my room.

"How's Mike Quinlan doing?" I asked him.

"It's not easy, Father. He's so hard on himself. Christmas will be tough. He'll see all the excitement here and dream of the Christmases in Saint Esther's. Not ready to forgive himself."

"You're not sure what might happen?"

"Not at all."

"Christmas is a bad time for lots of people, not excluding priests."

"Strange, isn't it. . . . I couldn't read your reaction downstairs about the conspiracy."

"It really isn't yours, is it? It's the brats'."

"I certainly didn't suggest it." He put down his Waterford glass. "I'd thought about it, as you know, but I'm not as reckless as they are, not quite. I didn't stop them, though."

"Who would have imagined a couple of months ago that Jeanne Flavin would be a folk heroine to the teen establishment?"

"It started the night she apologized to them. She was changing anyway—mostly, like I say, because of your support. By the way, she went home and cried after the brunch when you guaranteed her job."

"Dear God, that's not worth crying about."

"She thinks it is."

"Poor woman."

"Boss, you still haven't said what you think about the plot?"

"What can I tell you, Jamie? I hope it works. I think they will like one another. They probably have more in common than the kids realize. What happens if intimacy blossoms? I'm not worried about Don exploiting her. He doesn't have it in him. How will she react to a man who wants to be close to her, really close? That's when it will turn sticky. Maybe it will work. I don't know."

"Still a long shot, huh?"

Absently he patted Norah's massive skull, which was jammed against his hand—a plea for attention whenever the subject of the conversation seemed to have wandered from her.

"Real long, Jamie, real long!"

I did not add my usual "impossibly long."

I prayed for her later that night.

"If Your friend the Holy Spirit planted the name of Don Lyons in the little brats' heads, She's got good taste. You can't let Jeanne down. Or Don, either.

"They both need help, even without one another.

"So, goddamnit, You'd better help them!"

CHAPTER

28

"Can you cope with a secret marriage, Boss?"

"A secret marriage?"

"Yes, dispense from the banns. Pastors can do that these days."

"I seem to remember," I said with a touch of sarcasm. "They need a good reason."

"What's a good reason?"

"Anything the pastor says is a good reason. . . . Who are the lucky couple?"

"Michele and Dan."

"Aha! Father Louis loses another."

"They love each other very much."

"So it seemed last spring until George broke it up."

"She's afraid of her father."

"Reasonable reaction."

"She made up her mind after we left on Thanksgiving Saturday. Mr. Wholey went after his son, tried to beat him up."

"In the name of the Church. Get Sonny squared away with the Church."

"I suppose it's an old scene, poor Mr. Wholey attacking his son?"

"Weekly occurrence when the kid was in high school. So what happened this time?"

"Frieda and the kids became hysterical. She swore she'd never set foot in the house again. They left right away."

"And the fight?"

"Nothing much to it. George simply pushed his father off.

He's a combat infantryman now, not a teenager. The incident was the last straw for Michele. She wants out."

"He's dominated her all her life."

"She's afraid she'll cave in again if he forbids the marriage."

"Does he push her around?"

"Beat her? Or chastise her, as Father Louis says? Sometimes, I guess, though she won't quite admit it. The threat of violence is usually sufficient to intimidate George's womenfolk."

Had he beaten Jill? Probably.

And enjoyed it, too, the son of a bitch.

"That's more than adequate reason to dispense from the banns. We'll wait till a week before to make it official, so we can use the argument that there was no time to apply for Chancery office approval."

"There'll be trouble there?"

"Sure there will. Father Louis will probably stir up friends of his in the Congregation of the Sacraments."

"Do we worry about them?"

"Not in the least. I merely want to be able to say the right things when idiot Joe Simon calls and asks what the hell are we doing now!"

Jamie laughed uneasily. He still was not accustomed to my contempt for ecclesiastical authority—though heaven knows he'd heard enough of the same, I was sure, from his outspoken uncle.

"Dan has a tenure-track job at Washington State beginning the next semester."

"Pullman, Washington."

"Right. They want to be married at the seven-thirty Mass the Saturday after Christmas, drive to the airport, and fly to Seattle."

"Practically elope."

"Escape from George. By the time he finds out, they'll be safely in Pullman, and George is afraid of flying."

"OK." I ticked off the facts of the situation on my fingers. "They both were raised in the parish, even baptized here, so we have all their records in hand. We are morally certain that neither of them have ever been married before. The marriage has to take place because the groom is leaving that weekend for a new job and has to be in Pullman by January first to prepare for the coming semester. There is reason to believe that they have grounds for grave fear of her father. . . . Open-and-shut case, Jamie. Even the Pope would have no reason to object."

"It's between you and me and them. They'll tell the two witnesses the night before."

"Not Jill?"

"Better that she be able to say that she didn't know when George erupts."

"What a jerk!"

"Poor confused, frightened man. I still hope we can help him. The young people are what counts now. They want you to officiate at the marriage."

"You've been their coconspirator."

"They worship you, Boss. They're grateful because of the support from you the last time. Michele feels guilty for letting you down as well as Dan."

Better that I could tell Joe Simon that I had presided over the "secret marriage."

Joe would raise hell, though he would know that *(a)* he didn't have a leg to stand on and *(b)* it would have no impact at all on me.

He and the Cardinal could, however, report to Rome that they had made a thorough investigation and had given an appropriate reprimand to the pastor involved. They would add that, unfortunately, the marriage had already been consummated, so there were no grounds for an annulment.

"Perhaps you could quietly suggest to them that they might

stop at a hotel in Seattle—the Four Seasons there is nice—and consummate the marriage as soon as they can."

"Really? Who would try to annul it?"

"George, who else."

"He'd have no grounds!"

"They'd find grounds for him."

"That would be wrong!"

"Jamie, how many times must I insist that his friends are corrupt, power-hungry bastards and that our beloved Cardinal and his Vicar General are scared shitless of them. Father Louis is under no illusions, I'm sure, about George. He is well aware that he has a stupid dolt working for him. However, he's a useful dolt. Besides, they'll leap at every opportunity they can find to cut down the legitimate leadership of the American Church."

"Wow!" he breathed softly. "Maybe you shouldn't get involved."

"Come on, Jamie. You've been around me long enough now to know me better than that."

"You'll love every minute of it!"

"Who me?"

"Just like Mile Hi!"

"That name rings no bells at all. . . . Does Michele love her father?"

"She hates him, Boss, with quiet fury. And she fears him. Whatever love there might have been once was wiped out when he stopped the marriage the last time. It was only a month before the wedding when he made her break it off."

"She's a good kid, Jamie. So's Dan. They have half a chance of making a go of it as long as they never are closer to her father than Pullman, Washington."

"One more Christmas crisis, huh, Father?"

"And the great day itself is still a long way off."

"We'll survive."

"One way or another, Jamie. One way or another."

"You simply must take a vacation after Christmas, Father. Get rid of that cold."

"It stays all winter, Jamie. Part of the environment."

"You still should get away. We all need change."

"You're skiing at Steamboat Springs?"

"With the family."

"Associate pastors take winter vacations these days, not pastors."

He laughed at me, like I'd said something very funny. I had not taken a winter vacation since I came to the parish.

That night as I was falling asleep, I resolved that someday, someday, I'd get rid of Father Louis.

CHAPTER

29

One evening in the third week of December, I wandered into the office to find Jackie bent over the word processor, banging away on one of her term papers.

Cook had just "confessed" to me that she had smoked three cigarettes since her vow to abandon them.

"All of them three weeks ago. I've been clean ever since."

She was sitting at the kitchen table, still in the beige sweater and skirt that was her school uniform, a stack of accounting books in front of her, Norah at parade rest next to her.

"Well, for your penance, you'll have to climb Crogh Patrick on your knees three times when you go back to Ireland."

"Ah, aren't you the terrible priest, now?"

"Worse than any of the canons in the West of Ireland. I'll have no cigarette smoking in my rectory, woman, haven't I been telling you that?"

"Seriously, haven't I been thinking I should give you back some of my wage increase?"

" 'Tis not the money I want. 'Tis Crogh Patrick for the likes of you, Brigid O'Shea. And this terrible canine bitch with you."

"Arf!" commented Norah, as she usually did these days when I spoke about her to others—confident that I was paying her an extravagant compliment.

"Sure, am I not a terrible lost soul?"

"You are indeed. And I suppose you've been lollygagging your time away in school, flirting with the boys and not paying attention to teacher."

Cook in a beige sweater and skirt would lead most boys to flirt.

"I never flirt with boys. I don't even talk to them. No good ever comes of talking to boys. And I don't drink, either."

"Is that so? Sure, aren't you a paragon of virtue?"

"Well, I lie a little."

"And you're not getting A marks in your class?"

"I never said I wasn't! And the teacher saying I should try for an M.B.A."

"As if a cook needs an M.B.A."

"That's what I told him."

"Register for it, Biddy Mike."

"Yes, Father. And myself always doing what the priest is telling me to do."

"When it suits your purposes. . . . Now, do you want to go home for Christmas?"

"To Ireland?"

"Where else?"

She shook her head firmly, all trace of the bantering woman leprechaun gone.

"Saint Finian's is my home, Father. I have no other."

It had been a long way around to her question about the

M.B.A. That's how you deal with the Irish—if you deal with them at all.

If I had listened to the full implications of her remark at the end about home, I might have avoided a lot of trouble later on for all of us.

I went out to check the front office, Norah dutifully in train behind me.

"What's going on, Jackie?" I asked, the usual prelude to her filling me in on all the gossip in the parish.

"WELL, you know that gross Christmas display in front of the Maloney house?"

"The one with the life-size crib and the floodlights that make their front yard look like Soldier Field at a night game?"

"It really chills me out. ANYWAY, you remember last year when the geeky sophomore boys drew funny faces on the wise men? And a beard on the baby?"

"Space cadets."

"Really! Anyway, this year all the crib statues are electrified, so if anyone touches them, they get a shock! Is that the most gross thing you ever heard!"

Noel, noel!

"Do they have a warning sign?"

"Like they didn't at first, but then Mr. Geary, you know the lawyer who lives next to them, he's like, 'If you don't put up a warning and somebody gets hurt, you're liable because it's a detractive nuisance.'"

"Attractive nuisance."

"So Mr. Maloney is like, 'I can do anything I want on my property.' But Mrs. Maloney, she goes, 'You better talk to our insurance broker,' and Mr. Hickey—you know, Jennifer's father—he's like, 'Our policy doesn't cover that.' So they put up a sign. Now the geeky sophomores—this year's sophomores—are trying to figure out how to short-circuit the wires. Isn't that really gross?"

"Right in the Christmas spirit—down, Norah, can't you see that Jackie and I are having a serious conversation."

"Really!" She patted the pooch's snoot and returned to her keyboard.

"And Ms. Flavin?"

As usual, Jackie, perhaps occasionally in error, was never in doubt.

"WELL, Ms. Flavin is in love."

"Really?"

"Uh-huh." She didn't look up from the screen. "She looks totally cute and acts really icky."

"Ah? You won't be happy till you tell me all the details."

"The Thanksgiving party was neat and she asked Mr. Lyons to the concert and he asked her to the Christmas dance and he can't take his eyes off her and I still think it's kind of schmarmy. Right?"

"You're disgusted?"

"Don't be a nerd, Father Lar. You're not as out of it as you pretend. Teenagers are not the only ones who fall in love. You know that. Doesn't he, Norah, dear?"

Jackie was right, as always. Except that I was really as out of it as I pretended. I had not noticed that Jeanne was "schmarmy" until Jackie called my attention to it. Our stern-visaged Stalinist seemed complacent, happy, ready to burst into song. Score another match—no, score five or six—for the New Priest and his merry band of conspirators. Not that I could close the Jeanne Flavin file yet.

I figured that if I was so out of it not to notice the change in Jeanne from dour to schmarmy, I really did need a vacation. So I checked with Jamie about his Steamboat Springs weeks and muttered that I had often thought of going to Barbados for a few days.

"Crane Beach Club! It'll be perfect for you. I'll arrange the reservations."

CHAPTER

30

The fight between the New Priest and the director of religious education caught at the low point of my pre-Christmas gloom.

It was some fight. I didn't think that Jeanne Flavin knew all the words she used. She probably didn't think she knew them, either.

My bad mood was not helped by the book I had been reading—one of those "cute" Catholic nostalgia books by someone who hadn't been inside of church for twenty years and was on her third "relationship" but fondly remembered the dear, lost days with the Religious of the Sacred Heart.

I figure that anyone who has copped out on the Church of today has no right to be nostalgic about the Church of thirty years ago, which was a lot worse than the newer model for all the faults the latter has.

"McAuliffe," I snarled into the phone.

"Boss?" The New Priest sounded surprised.

"Who else?"

It was almost eleven o'clock, long after the ministry center activities for the night should be over.

"Would you come over to Dr. Flavin's office in the ministry center? Right away?"

"Why?"

"We're having a fight."

"One on one."

"Yes, so I'm outnumbered."

He sounded more rueful than comic.

"OK. I'll be right over. Tell her she's excommunicated if she slugs a priest."

"I don't think she cares."

That bad?

Well, it was bound to happen.

Yeah, but you're not ready for it, idiot.

I whistled.

The hound of heaven came hurtling down the corridor like a space shuttle striving for orbital speed.

"Come on, bitch, we have to settle a war in heaven."

"Woof!" exclaimed my companion.

It was cold in the yard between the rectory and the ministry center. Big-deal pastor doesn't have to put on a jacket because he's immune to the cold, right?

Norah wanted to chase sticks. I ignored her. I was working out a sneaky, corrupt, dishonest strategy for mediating the fight.

"Fucking asshole," Jeanne snarled as I walked into her office.

"Me or the New Priest?" I asked innocently.

Jeanne was wearing a white blouse and gray slacks—business-like, yet still feminine. Her face was pinched, her eyes were red, and she looked terribly unhappy.

"Both of you." She bit her lip holding back more tears. "Nice Norah." She patted the hound of heaven, who had snuggled up to her. "You weren't part of the conspiracy."

"Neither was I." I sat on the edge of her desk, my usual place. "It was all his idea." I pointed at the New Priest. "And your teenage friends."

Jamie cocked an eyebrow, trying to tune in on my strategy. He seemed casual and relaxed for someone supposedly under assault. Mama Maggie's "client-centered" manner, no doubt.

I noticed that two red and white tickets lay on the floor between the New Priest and the DRE. Chicago Symphony Orchestra, no doubt.

"They had no right." Jeanne burst into tears. "You didn't stop them. You knew about it, didn't you? And you let them . . ."

"Raffle you off?"

"Fuckheads!"

"You've picked up Cook's bad habits. Like I said, they wrapped you up in tissue paper and raffled you off. In transparent tissue paper, as Patrick McNally said."

"Bastards!"

Jamie frowned—not, God forbid, displeased with me, but not yet digging my strategy.

"The young women persons promptly reprimanded Patrick for his chauvinism."

"You didn't say anything?" She stopped crying and stared at me, preparing for another outburst.

"Not at the time. I confess that I still have enough male hormones in my bloodstream to have reflected that you would be most attractive wrapped in tissue paper."

"Father!" Jamie protested.

"Woof!" Norah erupted in confusion.

"Fucking male chauvinist shithead!"

"Since we're being open and honest and candid, transparent tissue paper or not," I concluded.

"You make me a sex object!"

"Sexed person," Jamie interjected.

Norah, true to her own gender, decided that she was on Jeanne's side, parked her large self next to the DRE, and glared at us.

"They intruded themselves into your personal life and engaged in behavior that might well be called manipulative," I continued serenely, "I was aware of it. However, it seemed improper and authoritarian for me to intervene to prevent them. You have confronted me many times, Jeanne, on abuse of authority. You can hardly blame me for not abusing it now."

A faint smile appeared on the New Priest's face. He thought he saw where my sneaky strategy was headed. He was wrong. Even when he was as old as I am, he would not be nearly so sneaky.

"We did it out of love," Jamie interjected, trying to defend himself and his coconspirators. "It was kind of like a prom date."

"I am no fucking prom queen. And I can find my own dates if I want to become a sex object again."

"Right," I said firmly.

She wiped away her tears and glared at me. "You opposed them because they were violating my freedom and privacy?"

Cross your fingers, guys.

"Well, more because I didn't think it would work. I felt that at the present time in your life, you were not ready for heterosexual intimacy."

Jamie rolled his eyes. Norah pawed at the hardwood floor.

"I'll make the determination about that," she snapped. "It's no one else's fucking business. I reserve the right to my own freedom."

"Absolutely. That's why I don't believe they really manipulated you. Intruded in your life, yes. Unconscionably, perhaps. But they didn't take away your freedom. I was sure they couldn't do that."

"Oh?" She narrowed her eyes suspiciously. "What kind of pissant dishonesty are you up to now?"

"You can pick up your phone"—I shoved it across the desk toward her—"and call Don Lyons right now. Cancel your, ah, date for the Christmas dance. No one can prevent you from doing that. Your freedom is preserved completely. You have the right to be offended. Exercise that right by terminating the whole sorry raffle affair."

"No pun intended," the New Priest snickered.

"JAMIE!"

Hand on the phone, she glanced suspiciously back and forth at each of us.

"If I want an affair, I can arrange one for myself."

"Precisely."

Jamie picked up the tickets from the floor and placed them on her desk. "And you can also assert your freedom by tearing up these tickets."

"You'll paste them together again."

"Flush them down the toilet."

"You're absolutely free," I continued. "Go on, phone Don Lyons. I'm sure the conspirators will back off after such an exercise in freedom."

I wasn't sure of that at all.

Her anger faded. Now she was anxious, vulnerable, and utterly delightful.

"That might not be fair to him," she pondered. "Poor man has suffered a lot during the past two years."

"There are costs to every exercise in freedom."

Norah sensed that the fighting was over; she settled down on the floor for a snooze.

"You're manipulating me, Lar," she protested sadly. "By telling me to cancel, you're putting me in a position where I can't cancel."

"And tear up the tickets," the New Priest added.

"That would be destructive," she murmured.

"Suit yourself, Jeanne." I stood up. "If you want to be free to cancel, think of me as telling you not to cancel. . . . Come on, Jamie, let's leave Dr. Flavin to her decision making. There's nothing more for us to do here."

"Yes, Father." He was smiling broadly, admiring, no doubt, my sneaky strategy.

Tell Mama Maggie about that one, kid.

"I'm sorry about my language," Jeanne said contritely.

"It's not skillful enough yet to merit promotion to pastoral associate."

She smiled and rose to bid us good-bye. "I'll work at it."

Norah stirred from her sleep, stood up, stretched, and yawned.

I cupped Jeanne's chin firmly in my hand. "Listen to me, Jeanne Flavin, and listen carefully. This is a turning-point decision in your life. It would have come anyhow. All your friends did was to make it more dramatic. Make your own decision, no one else's. Understand?"

"Yes, Father." Her sadness broke my heart.

"God bless," said the New Priest.

Back in the yard, Norah began bounding about, eager for sticks to chase.

"That was marvelous, Father." Jamie said, "You set the question in just the right context. I couldn't figure out how you were going to arrive there. You sure did, however, right on target."

"Take herself for a long run down to Myrtle Park and back. Puppies should be able to run."

"Yes, Father."

He didn't ask what decision Jeanne Flavin would make. With his youthful enthusiasm, he assumed that when given a clear choice, people normally opt for life.

As I settled back to my nostalgia book, I told myself that the normal choice is against resurrection instead of for it.

CHAPTER

31

"The New Priest," I informed herself, "is getting on my nerves."

"Woof," Norah rumbled, a mild protest that I was disturbing her rest.

She had parked herself in front of one of my stereo speakers—in lieu of a fireplace I presumed—and was currently absorbing Joemy Wilson playing Christmas carols on a hammered dulcimer. The tapes of Ms. Wilson's delicious music were, need I say, gifts of the aforementioned New Priest.

"I can't figure him out," I continued. "Is he innocent or shrewd? Is he radical or a reactionary? The ordinary labels don't fit."

Norah shifted her large haunches and rested her head on an ottoman in front of the speaker. She was uninterested in my reflections.

I was not about to tell her or anyone else that I was upset with the New Priest because of Jeanne Flavin. I was now almost as responsible as he was for her plight—and I with less reason and against my better judgment. He was to blame for involving me in a wild-eyed scheme that would never work.

If I had kept my mouth shut that night in her office, the whole escapade would have been history. Now it was still alive, though not exactly well. There was about as much chance of Jeanne actually going to the Christmas dance as there was of the renegade Phoenix Cardinals (whom my father had adored in their Chicago days) capturing a wild-card berth in the NFL playoffs.

Oh, yeah, I had been brilliant that night in her office—Old Priest as folk hero. Why didn't I keep my big mouth shut?

I knew the answer to that. I had been trying to prove that I was more skilled at coping with a frightened and vulnerable woman than the New Priest was.

Big frigging deal.

Now Jeanne drifted around the parish like a zombie fresh out of the tomb, pale, preoccupied, scared. That made me love her all the more and yearn to take her in my arms and exorcise her pain.

Not that there was even a remote chance of my doing that. If I tried, I would make her problem worse instead of better.

So I blamed Jamie for causing all the trouble—and had a fight with him about the Christmas reconciliation service.

It was not exactly a fight. You don't fight with someone like Jamie. He's too elusive to pin down.

My feelings about the reconciliation service had not been helped by a call from the ever-slimy Vicar for Liturgy, Dolph Santini, on the subject.

"The Cardinal wanted me to check with you about Christmas confessions," he began suavely.

"I'll mail you a copy of the bulletin."

"The Cardinal takes very seriously the prohibition of general absolution at Christmas, Lar."

"Does he really?" I replied in a tone of voice appropriate for being told that Mike Ditka wanted to win football games.

Many Catholic parishes in this *fin de siècle* era have "reconciliation services" before Christmas as a substitute for the old custom of last-minute Christmas confessions that used to extend up to just before the beginning of Midnight Mass. Properly done, such services can be deeply moving and very effective. They also make Christmas Eve in the parish a little less irrational. The major issue is whether at the end of the readings and the prayers and the hymns and the examination of conscience, you give general absolution to everyone or demand that they traipse off to the waiting confessionals. The Vatican takes a very dim view of the former alternative.

"He wants me to remind pastors that the Holy See explicitly forbids general absolution as a substitute for auricular confession except in dire emergency."

"That sounds dirty, Dolph."

"What?"

Dolph was not behind the door when wit was distributed; he was ten miles away walking in the opposite direction.

"That adjective you put before 'confession.'"

"Auricular confession means that the penitent confesses his sins in both species and number."

"Grave sins."

"That is correct." He was flustered that I had caught him in an inaccuracy.

"You're calling all the pastors with this reminder of the wishes of the Vatican?"

"No . . . only certain ones."

"Those whom the Cardinal suspects of breaking the rules?"

"Well . . ."

"Has someone denounced us?"

"Not exactly. . . . Some of the guys think you do grant general absolution. . . ."

"Guys?"

"You know . . . some other priests."

"Who?"

"I can't tell you that, Lar."

"Look, moron, when you tell me who my anonymous accusers are, I'll respond to your question."

"Now, Lar—"

"I must cut this conversation short, Dolph. I'm taking an engaged couple out to supper. We do that here with all our engaged couples. Talk to them about how they came to know and love one another. Do you do that, Dolph?"

"Ah, well, no."

"Tell the Cardinal why I didn't have time to answer your question."

I hung up, fuming. I then stormed down to the New Priest's room and—gesticulating wildly, I fear—told him the whole story of the conversation.

"Very nice." He smiled appreciatively.

"Huh?"

"You distracted him from his question most skillfully." His deep blue eyes danced.

I flopped into a chair. "No complaints from people this time. Even George Wholey likes the reconciliation service. Incidentally, they've heard my homily for six years. Would you mind having a try at it? We do it on a morning and an evening and a Sunday afternoon."

He leaned over to the big calendar on his desk and made notations in precise handwriting. "I'll be glad to. I'll have to find a story by then."

"Naturally."

"How would you have answered his question if you weren't able to distract him?" His eyes were still dancing.

"I would have said that we make no mention of general absolution."

"I see."

"We don't," I insisted piously. "We simply impart it. Some people still want private confession. Others come up to the altar, kneel down, and say they're sorry for their sins. Then we repeat the absolution. Others ask if they still have to go to confession, and I tell them no. See? Not a word about general absolution!"

He frowned. "So you do violate the law?"

"No way. General absolution is permitted for the good of

the people when there isn't time for private confession. As pastor, I judge there isn't time."

"Doesn't the Vatican say that the only justification is a very large crowd or a dire emergency."

"They can have their interpretation of the law, I can have mine."

"Indeed." His frown deepened. "Do the people know that we're breaking the law?"

"Some do, and they couldn't care less. Look, Jamie, it's all a power game to those guys. Forcing the laity into a confessional is one of the few controls they have left. If they give up their domination of the sacraments, how can they compel people to do what they want them to do?"

"You disapprove of private confession, Father?" he asked mildly.

"Not at all, as an option, not something into which we terrify people. Hell, Jamie. I don't want to force you into something that's against your conscience."

"I don't have one, Father." He waved his hand. "Not about sacraments. They're for people, not the other way around. I don't see any difference between absolution in the confessional and at the beginning of Mass. God has forgiven all their sins anyway, hasn't he?"

That's the sort of response which was getting on my nerves. He had begun the conversation sounding like a conservative who was very dubious about my bootleg Christmas general absolution. Now he was admitting, quite cheerfully, that he dispensed general absolution at the beginning of every Mass.

"Sacramental absolution at the beginning of every Mass?"

"I don't think God bothers sorting out the different kinds of forgiveness priests give in His name, do you, Father?"

"Probably She doesn't." I struggled to my feet. "So you won't mind preaching at the service?"

"And I won't tell anyone that we're dispensing sacramental

absolution free of charge." He grinned. "Jeanne will organize the Liturgy for the service?"

"Who else? How's she doing by the way?"

"Struggling. I think she'll be all right."

"I sure hope so."

"Don't worry, Boss. God will take care of her."

"She'd better. We're not doing very well."

The New Priest laughed cheerfully. "By the way, have you made a decision about the Christmas carol event?"

"The Christmas carol event?" I searched in my aging memory for a recollection of what that was supposed to be.

Jamie smiled tolerantly, "You remember, Father. I spoke to you about the hayrack and the horse and buggies we are renting to carol through the community on the night before Christmas Eve?"

"I don't remember it," I temporized. "I surely don't object to it—so long as we don't violate any of the local noise ordinances."

"We have a permit from the village council." He waved his hand. "The question that the Christian Family Movement group had me raise with you two weeks ago was whether you would ride on the hayrack and lead the carols."

"Me?"

"You!"

"I'm sure I don't remember."

"Mama Maggie would say you're repressing."

"I'm not the carol-singing type."

"They say you are."

"I'll think about it."

"You said that before." He was grinning at me, as if he had dispatched a boxcar load of canaries. "I'll tell them that if your voice survives the pre-Christmas strain, you'll be happy to join us."

"Maybe."

If God gave me life till the day before Christmas Eve, there was not a chance in the world I would escape the hayrack and the belting out of carols. Why couldn't the New Priest be the liturgical type that worried about the arranging of flowers in the sanctuary on Christmas Eve?

Hell, he'd probably do that, too!

Uneasy about Jeanne and dissatisfied with my failing memory, I walked down the corridor to my own room and turned on the stereo. Norah bounded up the stairs.

Was the kid a naive innocent or, like Mark Twain, had he really killed his conscience?

Norah dashed down the corridor to pay tribute to the New Priest before settling down in front of the stereo.

"There are two possibilities," I said to her when she finally got around to me as I was putting on my coat for supper with the engaged couple. "Either I know something that kid doesn't know, or he knows something I don't know. About everything."

Naturally his story of love and forgiveness (based on a medieval legend of which I had never heard and which he later admitted he had made up) delighted everyone at the reconciliation services. Even George Wholey admitted to me that it was "kinda moving, you know?"

I took it for granted that half the congregation would tell me how wonderful the young priest had preached as they walked out of church.

To which I would routinely reply, with my best county Kerry smile, "We sure are lucky to have him, aren't we?"

Or sometimes, "Give us a few more priests like the New Priest and we'll change the Church."

To which exercise in blarney they would assent enthusiastically.

After the Sunday afternoon service an older woman stopped at the rectory to "register in the parish," a custom to which some Catholics are still seriously committed.

Mrs. Fred Grant. Anne. She was in her middle sixties, pleasant, handsome, and respectful. Her clothes and jewelry hinted at tasteful affluence.

"You and your husband live at the corner of Linden and Elm?" I began to write down the data on a card, which one of the porter persons would later transfer to the parish computer, using one of the New Priest's programs.

"Does every town in America have an Elm Street?" she asked with a light laugh.

"Also an Oak, Pine, and Maple. . . . Just you and your husband?"

"Our two sons and our daughter are married, Father. They live in the city. Yuppies, I'm afraid."

"I see." I really didn't. Folks in their middle sixties don't as a rule buy a home in the suburbs, especially with their children living in town. "And you're new in Forest Springs?"

"Oh, no, Father. We've lived here for twenty-six years."

I looked up from the card. "Twenty-six years?"

"Well"—she laughed again—"I've been meaning to come over and register. It's a long story, Father."

"I'd like to hear it."

"My neighbor brought me to the reconciliation service today. It was so lovely," she said wistfully. "I felt like I was a Catholic again. The only other times I've been in Church since 1948 were for our children's weddings. They all married Catholics."

"Nineteen forty-eight?"

"I want to be Catholic again, Father. I really do. Does the service tonight make me a Catholic again?"

"It sure does."

"Good." She rearranged her purse on her lap. "I'll bring my husband tomorrow night. He wants to be Catholic again, too. He told me to see what it was like."

"Nineteen forty-eight?"

"We're not validly married, Father, not in the Church's eyes.

We felt that we could not be hypocrites and attend Mass after we'd been excommunicated. We've always missed it."

"Were you married in a Protestant church?"

"Of course not, Father. We're Catholic. Our kids were baptized and made their First Communion. We were afraid to send them to Catholic schools because we were excommunicated."

"I'm sure you weren't excommunicated," I said.

"Father Scott said we were excommunicated. Father Michael Scott at Saint Agnes."

One of the all-time great clerical assholes of the Western world. This gentle woman and her presumably gentle husband had been messed up by dippy Micky Scott.

"Why did he say that?" I asked patiently as I clenched my fist to contain my anger at Micky Scott.

"My husband had been married before, Father, to another Catholic. He was an army flyer during the war. They were both nineteen. She divorced him while he was in a prison camp in Germany. I met him after the war was over."

"They were both Catholic? I presume they were married in church?"

"Oh, no, Father. It was a hurry-up marriage. She said she was pregnant. They found a justice of the peace somewhere up in Wisconsin. Father Scott said it didn't make any difference: a marriage between two Catholics was always a sacrament."

Dippy Micky Scott had made up his canon law as he went along—and always to make life as tough as possible for those unfortunate enough to walk into his rectory. Hence these two good people had been excluded for forty years.

"I'm sure there would be no problem in blessing your marriage, Mrs. Grant." I thought about it and added, "God approved it long ago."

"My husband and I have always thought so." She sighed.

"At first we were very angry at Father Scott and the Church. Fred and I have never been very good at staying angry. We hoped that someday we'd be able to come back."

They could have been married in church forty years ago. Like so many others who had been hurt by dumb and vicious priests, they took his word as gospel. It would never have occurred to them to ask for a second opinion.

"You're most welcome, Anne," I said. "We're glad to have you back. In truth," my voice choked, "I don't think you've ever been away."

Her eyes began to tear. "I didn't believe it was possible. Joy Allen, my neighbor, insisted that I come. The young priest's story was so lovely." She reached into her purse for a tissue.

"We are certainly lucky to have him," I said automatically.

"Everything was so wonderful," she murmured through her tears. "So different and yet so Catholic."

"We try, Anne. By the way, we'll get you a set of collection envelopes in a couple of days."

She laughed through her tears. "You can't fool me, Father McAuliffe. Joy says you don't have envelopes at Saint Finian's."

"I wanted to make you feel at home. . . . Look, Anne, you and Fred were treated shamefully forty years ago. I'm sorry. In the name of the Church I apologize. We'll try to make it up to you."

"I'm happy to be home, Father, so happy." She struggled to control her tears. "Please tell the young priest how much his sermon meant to me."

"I sure will."

"You've been so kind." She shook hands with me. "I'm looking forward to being part of Saint Finian's."

I told Jamie the story the next morning at breakfast.

"It's hard to believe that Father Scott was so uninformed."

"He was, God be good to him, one of the all-time great

assholes of our galaxy. And not the only one, Jamie. There were and still are a lot of idiots messing up people's lives. Anyway, you brought them back in."

"I think the parish did, Father. Wasn't Jeanne's Liturgy wonderful. Maybe it will help her to forgive herself."

Don't bet on it.

"If I had listened to the Vatican and Dolph Santini"—I gave Norah a bite of an English muffin—"Mrs. Grant would never have worked up enough nerve to find out if we wanted her back."

"She would have found a way, Father." He wolfed down a couple slices of bacon. "Still, it's good that the parish was able to help."

"Why the hell," I demanded of God that night, "do we have to spend so much time undoing the hurt that the assholes have caused?"

Naturally there was no answer.

She could have noted that I had enjoyed welcoming Anne Grant back in.

I would have insisted in reply that I wanted substantial points for feeling only modest tinges of envy about the New Priest's homily that had occasioned Mrs. Grant's return.

I was, however, still angry at him because of the Jeanne Flavin problem.

Hence my outburst to an indifferent Norah the night I insisted the New Priest was getting on my nerves.

The phone rang. Norah's ears perked up as they always did when the phone rang: maybe there would be action that would require her attention.

"Saint Finian's, Father McAuliffe."

"Lar? Jeanne. . . . Hmm, nice music."

"Hammered dulcimer."

"Little three-string instrument."

"That's the plucked dulcimer. The hammered dulcimer is so

called because it has at least ten strings, which are pounded by little hammers. Came from Syria to medieval Europe. Ancestor to the piano."

"The New Priest gives good lectures, huh?"

"Not much choice about listening, either."

Norah sensed the tension in my body. She rose from her place of rest, ambled over to my chair, and nudged me with her vast snoot.

"I'm sorry for calling so late. Again."

"No problem."

"I have a question which I wouldn't dare ask you face-to-face."

"Ask away." I pushed the hound of heaven away. She backed off a couple of inches.

"You know about my past, don't you? I mean—"

"I know."

"Do you think"—she drew a deep breath—"do you think that I am a good prospect at my age in life for an intimate relationship?"

The final words tumbled out in a rush.

The most honest answer was no. A gentle answer would have pointed out the problems, run through a sanitized version of my Thanksgiving reverie.

"Quiet, Norah," I shushed the eager pooch, who was whimpering—loudly—for my attention. Then I answered Jeanne Flavin's question, on which her whole life might well depend.

"Sure you are, Jeanne. You're intelligent, determined, sensitive. You've deepened your life in the last year or two. Moreover"— why couldn't I stop this outpouring of nonsense—"you've always been a passionate person. I can't imagine any reason why, with the proper help, you couldn't channel those passions in positive and constructive directions."

"Thanks, Lar," she sobbed into the phone. "That's what I was hoping you would say."

"Oh, damn!" I exploded after I put the phone back on its cradle. "Why did I speak such damn foolishness?"

Norah pranced excitedly around the room, looking for a fight.

"Come on, bitch." I forced myself out of the comforts of my easy chair. "Both of us need a long run in the dark."

CHAPTER

32

"You totally won't believe it," Jackie exploded on the phone. "You gotta come down and see it."

"I gotta come down and see what?"

"Jeannie in her dress for the Christmas dance. She's like totally out there. Really bitchin'!"

"You sure I gotta come down? I'm writing my Christmas message for Father Jamie's bulletin."

I was also trying to recover from my first session with the Cardinal's financial planning committee, a session devoted to attacking my success at raising funds in Saint Finian's. It was an example of clerical envy in its most convoluted nastiness. Nothing you could put your finger on, just mean little jabs.

My success was, it seemed, not only a threat to the rest of them. It was an attack on them and their work.

I should have expected it. That's the way a lot of priests are. I hadn't anticipated it would happen at such a high level as a committee on whose work the future of the archdiocese might depend.

The Cardinal tried to fend it off, in his gentle, nondirective way.

"We are not here to pass judgment on, ah, Larry's plan. We asked him to join us so we can benefit from his input."

"I don't see," said a priest from a working-class suburb, "what we can learn from a fabulously wealthy parish."

They didn't want me on the committee. My appointment, halfway through deliberations, was an affront to them all.

"We can learn from him, if not from the parish."

Another priest, a classmate of mine who had never liked me, opened his mouth to reply and then decided that it was best not to take on the Boss, not directly.

I was unprepared and inarticulate at first. Then I recovered my composure and, naturally, became furious.

"You can learn one thing, Your Eminence: unless we act like every other religious body in America and invite our lay people to participate in decisions about how we spend their money, the contributions will continue to decline."

Joe Simon, who lurked protectively near the Boss at these meetings, sometimes with his hands on the Boss's shoulders, even if he wasn't sitting at the table or even on the committee, signaled me with a hasty negative shake of his head.

Everyone else ignored my comment.

I almost walked out on them. One more time I told myself, then I quit. If this is the Boss's idea of teamwork, I want no part of it.

So I was ready to inspect a beautiful woman emerging from her cocoon.

She took my breath away.

Her dress was ankle length and dark blue, edged in white, with a broad white belt that emphasized her tiny waist. It just barely clung to the edges of her shoulders and thus revealed a lot of pale, smooth white chest. It was a deeper décolletage than I thought Jeanne would ever risk—though by most standards she could be said to be quite modest.

Norah was pacing up and down, aware of the excitement in

the room and proud of it because, she assumed, she was the reason for anything that happened in her rectory.

I whistled.

"Lar!" she protested weakly and quite insincerely.

Jackie was ecstatic. "Like, Father Lar, I'm like, 'Wow, no way you bought that at our mall. You had to go over to Oak Brook or downtown to Water Tower' and she's like, 'I made it myself,' and I'm like, 'No way you made it yourself,' and she's like, 'I did, too,' and I'm like, 'Wow!' "

"That's an understatement."

"You're both embarrassing me."

"Are we, Jackie?"

"Don't geek out on us, Jeannie. You know you're totally out there."

"Did you face the RCIA class in that?"

"I'm terribly sorry," she replied nervously. "There wasn't time to go back to my apartment and change. Don—Don Lyons, my date—he insists you play golf with him, beat him usually—said he'd pick me up here. I hope you don't mind?"

"How did the Catholics-to-be react?"

"They cheered."

"Good for them. We'll have to make it part of the program. They can see for themselves what we mean by the Catholic imagination."

"LAR! You're really embarrassing me."

"I bet. Come over to my office for a moment. Jackie, you keep an eye open for Dr. Flavin's date."

"Fersure."

"Calm down," I said when I had her ensconced in one of the easy chairs by the coffee table. "You look wonderful and you'll have a wonderful time unless you panic."

She took a deep breath. "I won't do that, Lar. Absolutely not. Do you really think my gown is all right? It isn't too . . . too extreme?"

"It's perfect, Jeanne. All the men will ogle you. Some of the women will admire you and some will envy you. Thus the fate of a beautiful woman at a formal dance."

"I don't know."

"And the décolletage is sensational."

"LAR!" Her hand flew to her chest.

"That's what you wanted to know, isn't it? Don't pretend it's accidental and that men aren't supposed to notice."

She blushed to the roots of her careful coiffure, black hair tinged with silver.

"You're sure it's all right?" She closed her eyes. "I can't believe I made the dress this way myself." She gestured in front of her breasts. "Something reckless inside of me took over."

"You're a beautiful woman, Jeanne. It's time you come to terms with that."

She opened her eyes and leaned forward. "I'm scared, Lar." She held out her hand, seeking not me but some magic help that would exorcise her fear. "Terrified. I'm like an adolescent girl on her first date. Only it's much worse because . . . because of all that has happened."

"Not only beautiful, but brave."

Pile up the reassurance, that's the name of the game.

"Or foolish or reckless or crazy."

"I insist that you have a good time tonight. That's an order from Superpastor."

Jamie's latest title for me.

"Yes, Father." She bowed her head demurely. "Oh, Lar"—she looked up, her eyes filled with terror—"I'm afraid I'm falling in love. I've been there before—when I was in college—and I know the feeling, but now it's crazy."

"It's not crazy at all."

She lowered her head shyly. "I really made an ass out of myself the other night, didn't I?"

"I never said that."

"You thought it."

"I didn't. You had every reason to think you were being set up, because you were being set up. You had a right to find out whether they were trying to take away your freedom. Even love doesn't justify that."

"They weren't, not really. It kind of looked that way."

"Not even manipulating you a little?"

"They were." She turned back to face me and stopped my heart with her smile. "They were creating a situation in which I could exercise a free choice about a notable and maturing change in my life."

"The New Priest speaks!"

"Naturally..." Her nerve faltered. "...I still think it's crazy."

"Who says?"

"It's too risky. I shouldn't let it happen. I don't care, Lar, I won't stop now. Crazy or not, I'm not going to fight it."

A strong-willed declaration if I ever heard it.

"Mr. LYONS's car has just pulled up," Jackie yelled, "like his Jaguar, you know!"

"Jacqueline, I'll answer the door."

"Gross," a disappointed voice echoed from the other office.

I opened the door as soon as Don had pushed the bell.

"Yes?"

"Lar." He grinned. He looked quite suave in his evening dress and did not seem a bit embarrassed.

The sad lines at the corners of his eyes were still there, perhaps not so deep.

"Do you want something"—I shook his hand firmly—"or someone?"

"I've never come to a rectory for a date," he said as he entered. "It's an interesting experience."

"Well, we have a supply of grand duchesses on hand," I swept a bow toward his date. "Will this one do?"

He gasped, just enough so you could tell. "Quite nicely."

Jeanne was both miserable and delighted. Two men whom she liked were sweeping her with their eyes, devouring her from head to foot. She stood still and permitted us our admiration, shy, confused, and regal.

"Acceptable, Don?"

"Breathtaking, Lar. I may join this parish."

Don walked up to her, touched her chin lightly, and brushed his lips against hers. "You look lovely, Jeanne. Glorious."

"Thank you," she stammered.

Jackie's red head had peeked around the door, just in time for the kiss. She grinned wildly.

Don did not move for a moment, but continued to hold her chin and gaze into her eyes.

Oh, the chemistry was there all right. So thick you could cut it with a knife.

Norah emitted a low growl that sounded like a sign of mild displeasure and fooled no one. She snuggled up to Jeanne's thigh, wanting some of the emotion for herself.

Jeanne's right hand touched the hound of heaven's head, and her left hand slipped gently to Don's and held it against her chin. Her smile enveloped him and all the world—he was all her world for that moment. And she his.

"Be sure you get her home early," I adjured Don as I handed him her white cloth coat and broke the magic.

"Anything you say, Father." He slipped the coat on her, touching her bare shoulders lightly. "I understand that this is a busy time of the year in a parish."

Jeanne had shivered with pleasure at the touch of his hands. The past had been repressed if not exorcised.

We shook hands again. Jeanne pecked at my cheek.

"Thanks, Lar."

She was wearing a decidedly inviting scent. Our plain-Jane Stalinist had become a siren.

"Have a good time, both of you," I shouted after them as I closed the door.

Norah echoed my sentiments with a happy bark, a sound that would have scared off half the coyotes in the United States.

They turned and waved, a strikingly handsome couple.

Jeanne was not the only one who was falling in love.

"Out of sight," Jackie exulted.

"Schmarmy."

"Totally cute."

"Soap opera stuff."

"You're IMPOSSIBLE, Father Lar."

"Yes, Jackie, now finish your homework."

"Before I do, Father"—she didn't move from her post at the doorway of her office—"Patti Anne says I should tell you that Coady Anne Condon is really bummed out."

"Oh?"

"Her mother like goes, 'You're too young to go to the Saint Ed's Christmas dance, and I don't care whether everyone else in your class will be there.' She goes 'that's up to their mothers, and I'm your mother.'"

Sounded exactly like something Martina would say.

"Coady Anne is upset about it?"

"Like she's really flipped over this dreamy boy from River Prairie that goes to Saint Ed's. He's supernice, too. But Mrs. Condon doesn't like him, you know."

"I know." I sighed wearily. "Keep me informed."

One damn thing after another.

Jeanne had so invaded my imagination that I forgot that night to pray for Coady Anne—my list of people for whom to pray was not as long as the Cardinal's alleged list, but it was growing rapidly.

My dreams were filled with Jeanne and other women in

my life, all confused and combined—and all breathtaking as she was.

That night, at any rate, Jeanne didn't need my prayers.

Poor Coady Anne did.

CHAPTER

33

The Christmas madness finally began.

With a vengeance.

Sister Cunnegunda expelled fourteen eighth-grade boys, almost half the class, because someone had scribbled obscene words on the walls of the boys' washroom. The obscenity of the words would have seemed highly advanced to anyone who did not remember the verbal environment of his own eighth grade.

The parish school board overruled her and reinstated the kids. The boys' language was not acceptable, the board ruled, and they should be "appropriately punished"; they did not, however, merit expulsion.

I ordered the kids to clean the washroom walls. Naturally they did what the pastor told them.

She refused to let them in the classroom.

Two parents appealed over our heads to the Catholic school board downtown. They were a good deal more courteous in their phone call than Joe Simon and backed off quickly when I said, "We'll take care of it."

"She won't budge, Boss," said the New Priest. "I can't change her mind. She doesn't even offer to resign."

"For once a woman resists your charm, young man."

"She won't let them in the school. And she's so fierce that the kids are afraid to try to walk by her. The eighth-grade teacher is afraid to let them in the room."

"So?"

"So it's a case for Superpastor, even if he has a terrible cold."

Before Superpastor could resolve the Cunnegunda conundrum, Mrs. Clarke summoned him to the office to visit with the Forest Springs chief of police.

My father, as I think I said, was a cop. I like cops. But I don't like the Forest Springs cops who talk like characters on "CHiPs" and have no common sense.

"Merry Christmas, Chief."

"And to you, too, Reverend." He seemed doubtful that a college-trained criminal justice officer should be exchanging season's greetings with a priest.

His khaki uniform could have been bought from the leftovers after "CHiPs" folded.

"I'm sure this isn't a holiday courtesy call, Chief."

He was not an Irish cop, which is, I suppose, what I had against him. Or a black cop: they're indistinguishable from Irish cops save in skin color, which doesn't matter much.

"*Your* kids broke a hundred and twenty-seven windows in the Millicent Adams Middle School last night."

That was more than last year.

"I don't have any kids, Chief."

"You know what I mean, Reverend. Kids from *your* school."

"Ah, what age group, Chief?"

"Sophomores."

"Nope, sorry. We don't have a high school. They're either from Saint Ed's or Forest Springs Central."

"They went to your school once, Reverend."

"Statute of limitations, Chief."

"Well, you have to assume responsibility for them."

"Why?"

"They're Catholics, aren't they?"

"If you say they are."

"Well?"

"Would you complain to Pastor Martin if you apprehended some Lutheran perpetrators?"

"I don't suppose so. Catholics are different. They do what their priests tell them to do."

"Would that you were right. . . . I am correct, am I not, in presuming that you have apprehended the alleged perpetrators?"

I knew he hadn't.

"The subjects are not in custody yet."

"Then how do you know they're Catholics?"

"The engineer at the school said they were Catholics."

"How did he know?"

"He said he could tell. Besides, Catholic kids break the windows every year."

That was true enough. Despite the ecumenical age, the "publics" were often the enemy. When the perpetrators were taken into custody and dragged over to the rectory, shamefaced (more at being caught than at being guilty), I would routinely lecture them in my most stern and icy fashion. The effects of my anathemas, I would assume, would be long-term on teen males—perhaps twenty-four hours.

Lecturing alleged perpetrators was one thing, collecting them and turning them over to the cops was something else.

"You'll have to produce better proof than that, Chief."

"I expect your cooperation, Reverend."

"In what way, Chief?"

"I expect you to hand the perpetrators over to us."

I paused for dramatic effect.

"We are not part of the criminal justice system, Chief. I deplore the destruction of property, no matter who was responsible. Apprehending the alleged perpetrators, however, and taking them into custody is your job, not mine."

"I'm sorry to hear you say that, Reverend. Your kids are your responsibility."

"I have no kids, Chief, to repeat myself."

"The Catholic Church is responsible for what its people do. If you don't cooperate this time, we'll have to keep that fact in mind during further criminal justice efforts in this town."

"As you may have heard me say in the past, Chief, my father was a cop. He would have resigned before he made a threat like that to any church." I rose and walked to the door of the office. "Happy New Year, Chief."

I met Jamie on the stairs, in cassock, going to the church for a funeral Mass.

"I'll be over later, Jamie. The sophomore boys have given their annual holiday present to the township. Chief Dawkins wants us to give him the names of the alleged perpetrators so he could take them into custody."

"And you didn't?"

"Naturally not. I don't know who they are."

"You could easily guess." He grinned like a sophomore boy himself.

"That's different. You find out who they are and ban them from the High Club for a month. Tell them if they do it again, Chief Dawkins will roll up to their homes in his death wagon."

The death wagon was what the kids called the cops' van which looked like an armored personnel carrier.

You could never tell when the natives might turn very restless.

"Can do. Headed for the lion's den?"

"Lioness—and like I say, no problem!"

"Take care of that cold."

What cold? It was part of me and I had forgotten about it.

The sun was shining brightly as I crossed the yard toward the school. It was already bitter cold, only ten above.

Ned Reagan, our engineer, stopped me in midpassage.

"We had a hard time getting rid of last night's snow," he began.

Ned started complaining the day I arrived and has never stopped complaining. He thought the world came to an end when the Founding Pastor retired and the parish was turned over to me. He did not reverse his opinion when I discovered how little he was being paid and almost doubled his salary.

"You did a good job." I surveyed the yard, which doubled in brass as a parking lot. "Real good."

Ned was immune to compliments.

"The snowplow isn't what it used to be. You know that, Father."

"The finance committee says that it would be cheaper to contract for snow removal than to buy a new plow. It would be easier on you, too. You wouldn't have to get up in the middle of the night."

He loved rising in the middle of the night to plow snow: something more about which to complain.

"Father Delaney would have bought me a new plow, one of those big ones."

Father Delaney was dead now, God be good to him. "It's up to the finance committee, Ned, but I don't think they'll like it."

I shook him off before he had a chance to say that when Father Delaney was alive, the pastor didn't have to check with any finance committee.

Or anyone else, not even the Lord God Herself.

"Sister Cunnegunda," I strode into her office like I was General George Smith Patton, Junior—or maybe George C. Scott playing the general.

"Yes, Father." She stood up, as close to attention as her old bones would permit.

"I've come to talk about the eighth-grade boys. I admit they have filth-filled minds. They should be punished. They will spend the Christmas vacation scrubbing all the washrooms in the school and repainting those which require it. They will, however, be readmitted into school on January second."

"Yes, Father."

"Keep up the good work, Sister. This is the best school in the archdiocese, far and away."

"I know that, Father. It's nice to hear it from you. Thank you very much."

"You're welcome, Sister."

"Merry Christmas, Father."

"Merry Christmas, Sister."

"Do something about that cold, Father."

I was an eighth-grade boy myself.

"Yes, Sister."

The way I felt just then, rushing across the yard to the church, was, I reflected, the way Fred Delaney felt all the time.

And Red Murphy.

The funeral was for a great uncle of a woman in the parish. He died in a nursing home, the last of his immediate family. Our parishioners were his only relatives. Other parishes turn down such funerals routinely these days, but I figured that such poor old souls were still men and women of the Church and deserved the best we could give them.

That included the appearance of the pastor at the Mass, even if there were only eight people, including the pallbearers in church.

"Piece of cake," I said to Jamie as he removed the white vestments of the Mass of the Resurrection.

"You played Father Delaney?"

"General George Smith Patton, Junior."

"*Who?*"

"Never mind."

"Well, maybe you can play the same role with Dr. Ronzini. He simply doesn't listen to the liturgical committee about Christmas Midnight Mass."

"Doesn't listen?"

"The committee has given the choir half the carols before the Mass and the 'Lord Have Mercy.' He wants three-quarters of the carols and the 'Glory to God' and the 'Lamb of God.' And a long Communion motet. We simply can't do that. The people have the right to sing on Christmas. It's the only day in the year some of them want to sing."

"And that, badly."

"I'm my usual charming self, as you would put it. Jeanne is incredibly sweet. Linda Meehan is cool and rational. He won't argue, he doesn't hear us. We have two separate Christmas preparations in process."

"General Patton will not work with him."

"What will?"

"I'm not sure. I'll give Renaissance corruption a try."

"While I'm at the cemetery. We're running out of time."

So now associate pastors give orders to the pastor.

So what else is new?

Crossing back to the rectory, I passed Jeanne, hatless, coatless, and radiant.

"Good opera last night, Dr. Flavin?"

"What?" She looked up, surprised that someone else inhabited her world. "Oh, good morning, Lar. What did you say?"

"I said you should be wearing a coat or you'll catch a cold like mine."

"Yes, Father." Her smile was like totally schmarmy.

"You enjoyed the opera."

"*Falstaff*? It was wonderful. So funny."

All right.

My confidential intelligence reports from the country club Christmas dance were that Jeanne had been a sensation: witty, smiling, self-confident—and charming to the parents of her pupils. Don had beamed proudly all night.

"The men"—Jackie was breathless—"like couldn't take their

eyes off her. My mom goes, 'Jackie, your Dr. Flavin stole the show.' And I go, 'Do you think Mr. Lyons is in love with her?' and Mom goes, 'If he's not, Jackie, he's a damn fool. Someone better marry her soon before all the men in the community lose their heads over her.' And I go, 'Mom, isn't she nice?' and Mom smiles, like Mom does, and says, 'She thinks you're pretty sweet, too.' Isn't that radical, Father Lar?"

"Schmarmy."

Did women like Kate Walsh (Jackie does have a last name, and it is Walsh) wonder where Jeanne Flavin had come from? Or did they take it for granted that forty-year-old virgin directors of religious education would burst out of their cocoons and blossom?

I'd never know, and it didn't matter. Since she praised their kids, they were all on her side. The tender trap was closing in on Don Lyons, not that he seemed to mind.

Despite the stern orders of my associate pastor, I did not have time to speak with the director of music. Mrs. Clarke stopped me as I entered the rectory.

"There's an emergency call from Forest Springs, Father. The little Condon girl attempted suicide."

"Oh, my God!"

Ned, for all his complaints, had cleaned the snow from our parking lot, but the streets of Forest Springs were still icy, and the lot at the hospital was a mess. I had to park on a side street two blocks away and hike—no, run—through the snow to the emergency room entrance.

"Condon?" I asked the attendant at the desk next to the door. "Coady Anne?"

"Down the corridor to the right, Father. I think she's all right."

I pushed aside the curtains of the alcove. Coady Anne was on the table, ashen faced and looking like a tiny child. Two women hovered over her—one, older and white; the other, younger and black. The stomach pump was next to the table.

I figured that the black woman was the resident. Even to Forest Springs integration had come.

"How is she, Doctor?"

The black woman enveloped me in a smile. Points to you priest for knowing. The white woman, patently Irish, smiled briefly.

"She's all right, Father." Pure Mississippi. "Her mother's phenobarbital. Took a few too many. Didn't mean to kill herself. Just wanted some attention and help. Cut it too close."

"There's reason to believe she tried it before, Father," the nurse added. "Her mother is good at denial."

"Tell me about it."

Coady Anne opened her eyes and saw the silver-haired giant lurking at the emergency room table and towering over her.

"Father Lar." She clutched at my hand. "I'm so sorry, I didn't mean it."

"I know, Coady Anne, I know." I took her tiny hand into both of mine. "It's all right, it's all right."

"Am I going to die?"

"Not for a long, long time." I put my arms around her thin shoulders and held her against my chest. "Like maybe sixty or seventy years."

"Would I have gone to hell if I had died?"

"No way, Coady Anne. No way. But don't do it again."

"God isn't angry at me?"

"Maybe a little upset, but not like totally angry."

I eased her back onto the table.

"Really?"

"Really, Coady Anne. God never stops loving us, no matter how much we geek out."

"Radical." She closed her eyes peacefully.

"Nice going, Father!" The resident grinned at me. "The kid needed to hear that. Her mother is a real bitch."

"You better keep an eye on her, Father," the nurse said.

"Look, Doctor"—I had an inspiration—"hold her in here as long as you can and turn her over to your child psychiatrist who is best at dealing with overpowering mothers. Dig?"

"I dig."

In the relatives' lounge, Joe was pacing back and forth, Martina sitting placidly on a chair, serene in her own wisdom.

"Did you see her, Father?" Joe bounded over. "Is she all right?"

"Out of danger, Joe. However, she's going to need help."

"The child was upset because we thought she was too young for a date at the Saint Edward's Christmas dance," Martina said calmly. "She's punishing us because we wouldn't let her go. It would be a serious mistake to give her too much attention."

"She almost died, Martina."

"I really don't believe that."

"If she doesn't receive long-term psychiatric treatment, she may die the next time or the time after."

Martina dismissed me with a brief hand gesture. "Don't be ridiculous, Father. She's seeking attention. That's why young people attempt suicide."

She'd read that in an article somewhere.

"Attention and help, Martina. Help is the relevant word."

"No child of mine requires psychiatric help, Father. That matter is settled."

"Maybe we should listen to what Father says." Her husband rubbed his jaw anxiously. "The doctor said the same thing."

"What does she know about our family life?"

The "she" was a genteel racist sneer.

I paused to find a strategy. There was just one available, and it wasn't very good.

"Joe, I warn you solemnly, if you want that poor child to

live to graduate from college, you'd damn well better find her the best child psychiatrist that's available. She's hurting and hurting badly."

"Nonsense." Martina hardly raised her voice. "She's merely seeking attention."

"You heard me, Joe?"

He nodded miserably, caught between the real world and the world Martina had created for both of them.

Jamie and I had better keep our eyes on Coady Anne.

Back at the rectory there were two parents and a college-aged daughter ready and waiting to fight about a marriage—which the girl had designed to hurt her parents, even if it ruined her life.

The parents couldn't figure out what went wrong. My guess was that their mistake was to have second and third children. This kid had never forgiven them for sharing their love with her siblings and was now eager to deliver her ultimate punishment, a disastrous marriage to a man ten years older, twice divorced, and currently unemployed.

You listen patiently and wonder who's going to pick up the pieces.

My cold was worse.

Finally the music director strolled in, a long-haired young man who seemed most of the time to be part of perhaps the sixteenth century. You felt that he'd just returned from a meeting with Giovanni Pierluigi da Palestrina, possibly in some Cardinal's palace up in the Alban Hills with fountains bubbling in the background.

He made the proper obeisance to the Grand Duchess Norah.

"How's the Midnight Mass program coming?" I asked, hoping that the Holy Spirit would provide the words I needed.

Sometimes She does—like with Coady Anne—and sometimes She doesn't—like with her parents.

"Oh"—he gestured elaborately—"they are all wonderful. The choir will sing three carols before Mass, the Kyrie— excuse, I still call it that—at Mass and the 'Cantique de Noel' at Communion, with a soprano solo. All wonderful."

It was Jamie's program with the Communion carol—a short one—added and one pre-Mass carol removed from the list.

"Sounds marvelous."

"There were some disagreements." He flipped his fingers. "They were of no consequence. Dr. Flavin and I worked them out this afternoon."

"I'm glad to hear that."

"She is a remarkable woman, Father. Very remarkable. Quite intelligent and attractive, very attractive."

"Nice tits," I said maliciously.

He blushed at my shanty-Irish indelicacy but rolled his eyes in agreement. "She is quite overwhelming."

If she stays in love, I thought, I'll have to give her a big raise.

"You're doing well on that assignment," I prayed that night. "Keep up the good work.

"And get cutting on Coady Anne. That kid is in deep trouble."

CHAPTER

34

We had sown the wind in our response to the Ferrigan-McKittricks. With seven shopping days left till Christmas, we reaped the whirlwind.

They had disappeared from sight after the issue of *The Bells* responding to their attack on the New Priest. I sighed with

relief: good riddance. I underestimated their capacity for re-
venge.

I was eating a quiet and late breakfast after Communion
calls at Forest Springs Community Hospital. While I read the
Sun-Times analysis of the Bears-Vikings game, I broke Norah's
English muffin ration into small pieces. Jamie burst into the dining room and waved the *National Catholic Observer* (the *NCO* in
clerical culture) in my face.

"They've attacked us!"

I hate interruptions at breakfast. That hatred is not a sign of
aging. I've hated them all my life.

"By the *NCO*?" I sighed and spread a second helping of
Cook's raspberry jam à la Conor Pass on an English muffin.
"That's an honor!"

"Do you know a guy named Ted McPhaul?"

The New Priest paced back and forth, like a quarterback
waiting for the defensive team to get him the ball.

Norah paced behind him, like the high-speed wideout who
was as essential to the team as the signal caller.

I sighed again. "A classmate. Never did like me, particularly
after he'd left . . . what's the word? . . . the active ministry."

"Bastards!" Jeanne charged in, waving her own copy of the
NCO.

"Unconscionable thing to say about fellow members of the
Catholic Left." I began to work carefully and slowly on the English muffin. "I note that Cook's negative impact on your vocabulary increases."

"I don't care! The only people he quotes by name are the
Ferrigan-McKittricks."

"And some anonymous parishioners who sound just like
them." Jamie continued to pace. "He never talked to anyone
else."

"Or even visited the parish!" Jeanne shook her fist.

I sighed once more and took another bite of my English

muffin. It was likely to be the last pleasure of the day and I proposed to enjoy it.

Norah managed to interrupt her pacing behind Jamie to demand her last bit of muffin.

"First, will you two reactionary servants of the right-wing military-industrial complex sit down and let me finish my breakfast? Second, what more would you expect of Ted McPhaul? He needs to pick up a few extra dollars. He decides he'll play the game of being the Chicago stringer of the *NCO*. He wonders what sort of raw meat they would like to feed their readers during the joyous seasons. He thinks that maybe it's time to attack the suburban Church again. Then he thinks of me. He remembers our good friends the Ferrigan-McKittricks and gives them a ring. He takes a few notes as they babble. He remembers what he can about my past, and presto! he earns a couple of hundred bucks to buy Christmas presents for his kids. Do you two radicals of the right begrudge him that?"

I sound tolerant and patient, don't I?

I was faking—trying to protect the troops from the hurt which the Ferrigan-McKittricks and Teddy McPhaul had inflicted on them.

In the seminary I had despised Teddy and Blaise—two weak and inadequate men who posed as intellectuals because they were not really good at anything. I disliked them after I discovered that they resented my success at basketball—a skill which I believed earned you no grounds for admiration and thus no grounds for envy.

Without even reading their article, I wanted to strangle them for trying to settle an old score that ought not to have been a score at all.

"Look at the headline!" My New Priest waved the paper at me one more time.

I finished my raspberry-drenched English muffin and did as he requested.

EX RADICAL RELAXES IN PLUSH PARISH

I lifted my tea cup cautiously so my two colleagues would not see fingers trembling with eagerness to choke two pricks.

"Read it!" Jeanne demanded. "Bastards!"

"Now, now, Dr. Flavin"—I began to read—"that's not a nice way to talk about fellow Leftists."

"Bullshit!" she exploded. "If ever there was a real revolution in this country, they'd be put up against a wall and shot as parasites."

"So might we all."

"Not *you.*"

I finished the article. "Pretty much what you'd expect from them."

"It's filled with inaccuracies." Jamie pulled out a notebook. "Your father was a captain, not a sergeant. You did finish your degree work in both fields. You weren't injured in the explosion at Mile Hi—"

"I wasn't even there."

"You haven't had a vacation since you came here, and they talk about several vacations every year. You're lucky if you get in one golf game every week, and they say you play every day."

"They say the parish staff lacks competence." Jeanne took up the litany of rage. "Neither of the Ferrigan-McKittricks has a doctorate, and Sister, you, Dr. Carlin, Dr. Ronzini, and I have doctorates, Linda has an M.A. in pastoral theology—"

Norah growled fiercely, sensing that there were enemies about.

"Cook has a degree from the Limerick Higher Educational Institute in hotel management," I offered blandly.

"We gave a quarter-million dollars last year to the poor." Jamie continued to check off items in his notebook. "Our young people do volunteer work in the inner city. We emphasize social justice themes in our teaching. There are more women on the staff than men. . . . They're lying about us, Father!"

"Pissant blatherskites." Cook, who also read the *NCO,* appeared with another English muffin and a large smear of raspberry jam. "Frigging shitehawks."

Norah's growl rose higher. If Cook were upset, then so must be the hound of heaven.

"Brideheen," I said mildly as she stormed out of the room. "They don't accuse us"—I buttered both the muffins—"of having the best Cook east of the Mississippi!"

"Will you be serious!" Jeanne jabbed an elegant finger at me. "They've libeled us. They didn't bother to check the facts. That's reckless disregard for the truth."

"I'm sure Don would not advise suit," I murmured.

"I'm not suggesting we sue," she said, blushing. "We should at least reply and go after them for their reckless disregard for the truth."

"It is a plush parish."

"It's the most vital parish in the whole frigging archdiocese."

"Cook's really corrupting you, Jeanne." I layered the jam onto my muffin.

"Father"—Jamie's blue eyes sparked fire—"this *is* a serious matter. It's an insult to the whole parish."

"Besides the rectory, maybe two homes in the parish receive the *NCO.* The parish won't know it's been insulted."

"They didn't check their facts." Jeanne was now on the edge of tears. "They didn't check their frigging facts."

"They never do." I sighed.

"You don't feel we should reply." Jamie looked like he was convinced I was losing my mind.

"Sure." I bit into the muffin. "By all means reply. Detail the factual errors—there's at least a score of them. They won't print the letter."

"What?" Jeanne's eyes widened in disbelief. "They'll have to print it and apologize!"

"Elementary honesty will force them to print it," Jamie insisted.

"Nope." Cook's jam was pure miracle. "Tell me the last time you read an apology in that paper. Or even a letter that nailed them for inaccuracy. Believe me, as one who has been in situations they have described, this piece is right at their usual level of journalistic responsibility. They never admit they're wrong."

My two younger colleagues looked at me in disbelief.

"You don't mind if we try?"

"When have I said that you couldn't try anything? Even prom date arranging for directors of religious education."

"I always assumed these were good people." Jeanne was disconsolate, though not so disconsolate that she didn't smile—in self-satisfaction, as I thought.

"So do they, that's the problem."

"How can they get away with it?" Jamie asked, still the quarterback wanting to dash back on the field.

"They can get away with it"—I turned to the final English muffin—"because those of us who live in the clerical world love to see the mighty pulled down."

"You're not mighty," Jeanne protested.

"To Teddy McPhaul and Blaise Ferrigan I am."

They wrote their letter that day and showed it to me. I shrugged and nodded. It was a restrained and devastating response.

"Nice work," I said.

"They'll have to use it," the New Priest insisted.

"Nope."

The letter never appeared. Five weeks later they received a form response that said that because of the volume of mail the *NCO* received, it would be unable to print their letter.

We heard not a word from the Chancery. A similar spread

in *The Drover* would have produced a full-fledged investigation. The complaints of the Left, however, along with a dollar bill would entitle you to a ride on the Chicago subway.

Nonetheless, the charges of the *NCO*—that I was a lazy, do-nothing priest living high off the hog in a rich parish—were more serious than any of the Corpus Christi accusations that so upset Joe Simon.

In the Catholic Church today a priest never finds himself in trouble for being lazy or doing nothing.

I expected that the exposé would end the Left whirlwind in Saint Finian's. Sheila and Blaise, however, would strike again in the New Year—and do us all much more serious harm.

CHAPTER

35

The congregation was fretful and anxious on the Sunday before Christmas.

Fourth Sunday in Advent and the hate meter was turning as purple as the Advent vestments.

The sophomores had, by the way, figured out how to short-circuit the electricity on the Maloney's crib. They then kidnapped the Baby Jesus and were holding him for ransom.

The New Priest made them return the Kid.

You could tell from the altar how fitful the congregants were.

There were more latecomers than usual, twenty or thirty filtering in defiantly during the Gospel and homily, conveying the impression that I had better not say anything: they were at the breaking point because of the Christmas rush.

They listened to my homily attentively but shifted restlessly

in their pews halfway through the ten minutes—saying in effect, "This is Christmas and we're all in a hurry. Can't you cut
it in half today so we can all escape from church and finish our
Christmas preparations?"

The fact that I was preaching about taking time off during
the coming week for prayer had no impact.

I interrupted my planned comments to say, "Hey, I'm not
sure that I'm about to practice what I preach. The New Priest
is running me ragged. I'll make a deal, you call me to remind
me and I'll call you back."

They laughed, not as much as they should have. Laughing
wastes valuable time during the Christmas rush. Like I say,
quoting the ineffable Patti Cupcake, we shouldn't have Christmas during the Holidays.

That had been my text last year, so I couldn't use it this
year, however certain I was that no one remembered the homily of the previous Sunday before Christmas.

Our attitude toward the Mass—or Eucharist, as the purists
keep reminding me—has changed completely since I was ordained more years ago than I care to remember. We say it (preside over it) in English and face toward the people, a one-shot
reversal of a millennium and a half's practice. Those are, however, only superficial hints of the deeper change. A quarter century ago the Mass was *my* Mass, a private devotion of the priest
at which we permitted the people to be present.

They listened as we muttered this private worship of ours in
sotto voce Latin. In a rare progressive parish we permitted them
to respond occasionally, in Latin of course.

Now the Eucharist belongs to everyone. The priest presides,
but he interacts constantly with his people. Some of my generation of priests and many of those a bit older still resent that
our Mass was taken away from us and given to them.

I like it much better this way. When the Mass was a private
devotion, I did it badly, distracted usually as I went through

motions that long ago had lost all meaning. Now it means much more to me. When I'm in a bad mood, even when I have my winter cold, the Mass cheers me up—which is what good ritual is supposed to do.

For the laity, the quality of the performance of the Eucharist is almost as crucial as the quality of the homily—and as much a subject of bitter complaint.

For the pastor, among other things, this new worship of ours (or old, old worship brought back) provides a way of judging the temporary mood of his people.

On that grim, gray, cold Sunday before Christmas, with a Bears game only an hour away and six inches of snow promised that night, my people were peevish at the whole world.

God rest ye, merry gentlepersons!

Among those I noted at Communion who seemed particularly glum were Dr. McNally, Maria Sullivan, and the Condons. Coady Anne was wan and haggard, with huge black circles around her eyes.

Her parents had obviously yanked her out of the psych unit at Forest Springs Community. Damn them.

The Ferrigan-McKittricks were in the front row, returned in triumph to the parish they had punished. They looked like church mice who had swallowed a whole gaggle of canaries, to mix my metaphors outrageously.

I didn't want to stand in back of church after the Eucharist was over.

Sure enough, most people were glum and surly; only a few grudgingly admitted that it was a good homily. A wonderful old woman, well over eighty, promised to call me to check up on my pre-Christmas prayers.

"I'll keep after you, Father, you just wait and see."

"I'll be waiting, Agnes, I'll be waiting."

I stopped Patti O'Hara in midflight. "Can you spare a poor old priest a few seconds, Patti O'Hara?"

She glanced impishly at her watch. "Just a few. I gotta run home and get all my work done so I can find time to pray—except maybe I'll fall asleep."

"A serious project, Patti."

She sobered up instantly. "OK, Father."

"Keep an eye on Coady Anne for me, will you? She's having a hard time with her parents."

"So the Juniors tell me," she nodded.

"Even worse than they know."

"Oh?" Her brown eyes widened. "Real serious?"

Should I tell her? I hesitated, fatefully, and decided not to. "Kind of serious."

"I'll take care of it, Father."

Then, because Patrick McNally had said she was a cupcake, I added a warning: "Patti, you are not responsible for her, understand?"

She frowned. "Not quite, Father Lar."

"You do what you can and you can't do anything more?"

She brightened. "Like we can't make Mr. Lyons and Jeannie stay in love, huh?"

"Something like that."

"Got it, Father."

I wondered if she had.

"And leave Ms. Flavin alone. She's capable of working out her own destiny now."

"Right, Father Lar."

Sure.

At the rectory office two people were waiting, Maria Sullivan and P. Scott McNally, M.D.

Both of them were pointedly ignoring the hound of heaven, who, tail and tongue wagging, stood at the foot of the spiral staircase, waiting for attention.

"Who's first?" I tried to sound genial.

"I believe I was," Maria said.

"Madam"—Doctor bounded out of his chair—"I am a doctor. I have patients whose lives may depend on my being with them. I must ask you to defer to me."

"Maria?"

She smiled faintly. "I'm not that important."

P. Scott did not even pick up the sarcasm.

I directed him to the hard-back chair across the desk, not the easy chairs by the coffee table. He refused to sit down.

I remained standing, too.

"I absolutely forbid you to meddle in my family life." He jabbed his finger at me. "I will not tolerate it."

I remained silent, trying to hold down my temper.

"I require"—he continued pacing back and forth like a caged animal—"that you warn your young resident that should he continue to meet secretly with my son, I will bring legal charges against him for corrupting a minor."

I said nothing.

"I am prepared to take all appropriate action to bring an end to this ridiculous affair." He jabbed his finger at me again. "Patrick will be a surgeon, as I am. That matter was settled long ago."

I smiled pleasantly.

He continued to pace. "I am an important and powerful man. I can bring all necessary pressures to bear. And I will not hesitate to do so, do I make myself clear?"

"Is that all, Doctor?"

Out in the corridor, Norah growled. No one dared raise his voice with her parish priest.

"It is quite enough, I think."

"Good, then perhaps you would be so good as to leave the rectory, as there is someone else waiting to see me."

"Do you not intend to reply to me?"

"No."

"I insist that you reply."

"All right, Doctor, if you insist. First, I don't take orders from you. Second, Father Keenan is not meeting secretly with your son. Third, your hints of homosexual involvement are slanderous and could merit legal response. Fourth, if Patrick wants to be a priest, it's between him and God. You may delay that vocation for a time, but you won't be able to stop it. Fifth, you're an asshole and get out of my rectory before I throw you out."

He sputtered and fumed, then left quickly and quietly, followed by a low rumble from Norah—which, to tell the truth, speeded up his departure.

All right, I lost my temper at the end. I wasn't much better than Red Murphy—though he would never have thrown an M.D. out.

In excuse for my behavior, I plead that my cold had deteriorated. I belonged in bed, I told myself piously, as I bowed Maria into my office.

She didn't sit down, either.

"I've come to tell you, Father, that I'm filing for divorce tomorrow morning."

"At Christmas time, Maria?" I asked mildly.

"What does superstition have to do with my personal freedom?"

If it were superstition, why had she come to Mass?

"It's your decision, Maria. I hope everything works out."

"I'm demanding money for a comfortable life," she continued, her lips a thin line. "I'm entitled to that, after all the work I have done for him and his children."

"I see."

They were her children, too; she knew that as well as I did.

"He can have custody if he wants. I'm tired of them anyway. I'll keep the house. It's mine by rights after all I've done to keep it presentable for him."

Her divorced friends had won. She had made their arguments her own. They hadn't told her about the loneliness.

"What will you do, Maria?"

"Do? I'll be a free woman for the first time in my life. I'll be my own person. Perhaps later I may have a relationship. I want no part of marriage. It makes the woman a slave to her husband and children."

"I see."

"Aren't you going to endeavor to dissuade me?"

"Dissuade" was almost certainly her word, not those of her friends. So probably was "endeavor."

"I'm sure it wouldn't do any good."

The scenario called for me to argue. I was not, however, about to play her game any more than the game of P. Scott McNally.

"As a Catholic priest, aren't you bound in conscience to defend the sanctity of marriage?"

"Not to force an argument when someone has made up her mind."

"The Church is part of the conspiracy." She spit the words out in clipped segments. "You celibate males want to keep women in subjection for your own needs and those of other men. Ever since I was a child, the Church has taught me to be submissive and obedient. That is over, Father. Do you understand, *over!*"

A woman as intelligent as Maria should be able to rise above clichés. Perhaps she was too frightened to realize how trite she sounded.

"I'm sorry, Maria. I hope you don't suffer too much loneliness."

"Loneliness?" She snapped. "That's a joke, Father. I won't be lonely, I'll be *free!*"

"If you say so." I showed her to the door. Despite the thin coating of new-fallen snow, she tried to stride briskly down the stairs—a woman of the eighties, at last in full charge of her life.

High heels, however, do not facilitate such manifestations of independence. She tripped and fell. As she tumbled down the steps, she tried to regain her balance and failed. She plunged into a snow pile at the edge of the sidewalk.

Norah reached her first and began to lick her face—the wolfhound version, I suppose, of first aid.

Maria pushed her away impatiently. Norah jumped back, feelings hurt, and looked up at me for moral support.

I helped Maria out of the snow. For a moment she leaned against my arm, fragile and shaken. Her mink was covered with snow; her hose were torn; her knee was bleeding; her face was red, and a glob of snow clung to her cheek; tears were forming in eyes already haunted by fear.

She hesitated and then twisted away from me.

"You should sweep your steps."

"Yes, ma'am."

Poor doomed woman.

I went searching for the New Priest to warn him about "Doctor."

He was in the church, practicing for the Christmas Liturgy with the eighth-grade altar boys. He was persisting in his policy of sexually segregated practices. The young men were docile and attentive.

Pure adoration.

So I returned to the rectory and swept the front steps. I finished and put the broom back in Cook's kitchen closet just in time for another call, this time a married couple. Their oldest son, home from first year at an Ivy League law school, had brought his "friend" home without warning. The woman was five years older than their son, did not wash or use deodorant, was foulmouthed, insulted the other children, and openly smoked marijuana. The two of them were sleeping in the same bedroom and openly engaging in marital affection. What should they do?

The best strategy would be to throw them both out of the house. The young man, perhaps still smarting from losing his status as an only child when his younger siblings were brought home from the hospital, had found a wonderful technique for punishing his parents.

At Christmas, naturally.

"You should not put up with that behavior," I told them carefully. "In your own house you have every right to assert your own values."

"She doesn't even make the bed in the morning," the mother wailed.

"Johnny is testing your reactions. If he sees that he can annoy you, he will continue to act this way. If you draw the line now, he will probably stop eventually."

"He's offered to leave," the father said dubiously. "And take the woman with him."

"He doesn't expect you to accept his offer. Surprise him."

"He's our son!"

"It's Christmas!"

"Don't you think you have the right and the obligation to protect the rest of the family from his aggression?"

"We love him!"

I tried to explain about "tough love," about drawing lines, about asserting reality. They listened, maybe even understood. They would, however, continue to cave in.

It was Christmas and he was their son and they loved him.

And he would continue to assault and punish them as long as they lived.

God rest ye, merry gentlepersons.

I thought about warning Jamie as I climbed the spiral staircase, huffing and puffing because of my congested chest. It had been many years since I had worked with a priest I liked and respected. Maria Sullivan was confidential, I supposed. P. Scott McNally, M.D., was not. I hadn't told him yet about Coady

Anne's attempted suicide because there hadn't been time. Was that confidential?

Probably not. I'd better tell him.

"You look terrible, Boss." He was working on the final draft of the Christmas *Bells*, the first one to appear in color. It looked like a stained-glass window. "Sit down. I'll get you a drink."

"Don't bother." I sighed as I collapsed into a chair. "I'm going to bed in a few minutes, and I'll take a hot toddy with me."

"That will cure your cold?" he smiled.

"No, but it will make me feel better."

I told him about Doctor.

He laughed and clapped his hands at the end. "Wonderful, Boss, wonderful!"

"You baffle me, young man. You protest when I do or say something that is not particularly outrageous and applaud when I really am outrageous."

"You're never outrageous, Boss. Besides, he was asking for it, demanding it. You're not an orderly in the operating room."

"In Doctor's world everyone is an orderly in the operating room. I hope this doesn't make life any more difficult for Patrick."

He spun his chair away from the mesmerizing blue screen and leaned back in it. "Patrick is not deceived about his father. He expects opposition, and he knows he can surmount it."

"With difficulty."

"And pain. But Doctor won't stop him."

"My reading, too."

Then I told him about the Condons.

"She won't permit therapy for the girl?" Son of a therapist, Jamie found such a notion incomprehensible. "That's inviting another attempted suicide!"

"I've asked Patti O'Hara to keep an eye on her. Might be a good idea if you did, too."

"I surely will. What's happened to Mrs. Condon?"

"It's probably our fault in a way. We asked the kids to be nice to Coady. They decided they liked her, and she became part of the crowd. That set up a family conflict. Martina demands control of all her children, complete control. That way she persuades herself that their need for her is absolute. Coady is challenging the myth and that's intolerable."

"And Joe sits and watches?"

"That's all he's ever done."

"Asshole!"

"You're getting as bad as I am."

"You're corrupting me, like Cook and Jeanne. . . . Now take your nap before you fall asleep in that chair."

I did as my associate pastor told me.

The nap didn't help any.

Nor did I sleep much that night.

I was now into that phase of the winter months when I refought all the daytime battles at night.

I was afraid to call my adviser to tell her.

She would not approve.

CHAPTER

36

Christmas day itself was not as bad as it might have been.

The young marrieds were still pleased as Christmas punch with the success of their carol serenade of Forest Springs—an event to which our Separated Brothers and Sisters (formerly known as "Protestants" and occasionally as "Dirty APAs") reacted with fine ecumenical tolerance.

As I had feared, I was constrained to join the carolers.

In part, our Separated Brothers and Sisters accepted our noise with patient amusement because they were no more immune than the people of Saint Finian's to the charms of the hound of heaven, especially when she rolled over and played dead in the snow.

"See, Father," Jamie chortled as she frolicked with the children of the Lutheran pastor, "she's an ecumenical asset."

"Shanty-Irish bitch doesn't know a heretic when she sees one."

The five-o'clock Vigil Mass for the children went smoothly enough. A red-haired three-year-old girl-child burst into tears during the New Priest's Christmas story—with most of the kids in the parish crowded around him in the sanctuary. She wanted her mommy.

How's he going to handle this? I wondered.

He picked up the kid and cuddled her in his left arm as he finished his story.

The little brat forgot about Mommy.

The bulletin of many colors was a huge success.

The New Priest seemed modestly pleased with that development. He had another success on his mind.

"Jeanne is looking particularly schmarmy these days," I observed.

"Keep your fingers crossed." He crossed his. "A lot could go wrong."

"Are they sleeping together?" The idea hit me like a flying saucer.

"Is that"—the New Priest winked—"a legitimate question for us to ask?"

Oh, my God!

Surely they were. That kind of radiant complacency in a woman could mean nothing else.

They hadn't wasted much time, had they? Nor did fake orgasms produce such a self-satisfied glow. Jeanne had made the transition from frigidity to passion at record speed and with only one explosion and aborted regression. Shows what willpower will do.

Willpower and sexual hunger.

Had they made love in her tiny apartment before they came over to church for her to make the final preparations for the Christmas Liturgy?

I watched her movements and her gestures, her facial expressions and her sparkling eyes.

She didn't care who knew it.

Their illicit love didn't prevent them from receiving Communion, side by side, at Midnight Mass, next to Linda and Brendan (né "Arthur"), the former sporting a strikingly large diamond.

Don's three children were at Mass, too, Ria, Helen, and Ken, behind their father and Jeanne in Communion line, quite content with the presence of their father's lover.

I cornered her in back of church after Midnight Mass was over as the bells played and shouts of "Merry Christmas" cut the crisp winter air. "I hope I'm not charged with chauvinism, Jeanne, but you look gorgeous tonight. Totally."

Norah, who had been greeting people as they left Mass and barking her Christmas cheer, trotted over to nuzzle Jeanne—who was number four in the hound of heaven's pecking order, after the pastor, the New Priest, and Cook.

Except at food time when Cook became number one.

Jeanne did not show the slightest sign of embarrassment at what we would have called in ages past her fall from grace.

"Keep your fingers crossed, Larry." She squeezed my arm as she whispered into my ear. "A lot could still go wrong. I have a great record for blowing opportunities."

She looked like she wanted to kiss me, but didn't.

Don's children shook my hand with special fervor and big grins and hearty wishes for "Merry Christmas, Father Lar."

I delighted them by remembering their names.

"Our pastor doesn't know we exist."

"My father was a cop who walked a beat," I explained.

They didn't seem to mind Jeanne at all. Indeed, Ken, the oldest, helped her across the parking lot, slippery from a light snow, toward the family car.

If—no, when—the word of their "affair" spread around the parish, there would be phone calls of protest and maybe yet another anguished yelp from downtown.

Fuck 'em all. Merry Christmas, everyone, too.

"Did Don's kids seem to approve?" Jamie asked me eagerly after the ten-o'clock Mass the next morning—the first time in the Christmas maelstrom that we had a chance to talk.

"Are they aware she's already his mistress?"

"Boss, what a hopelessly outmoded way of putting it. You're trying to play Scrooge this morning. They don't care what happens so long as their father is happy. What do you think now?"

"I think they're screwing!"

"*Boss!*"

"And she's loving it!"

"You're awful!"

"It's nice to see one genuine smile at this dreadful time of the year."

"God bless us, every one." He jabbed my arm. "You're as happy for her as I am."

"I never, never expected I'd live to see the day."

"We've made a beginning, admit it, so far so good."

"Only a beginning."

"Well begun is half done."

"I hope so."

We all left the rectory after the last Mass for our various places of Christmas celebration. Cook, I gathered, had been invited to the Lyons along with Jeanne. I put the call-forwarding on to my sister's house. Christmas Day was a time when people might do odd things which would require their parish priest.

Christmas is a much better day for priests now than it was in the old days despite the dementia that goes with the season.

At Red Murphy's parish, Christmas was a plebiscite. The people, by the size of their contribution to the Christmas collection, either ratified or rejected Red's stewardship over the parish. Weeks before Christmas he would begin to analyze the reasons why there might be a decline in the contributions this year—all of them related to something his assistants (as we were in those days) had done or, more likely, were alleged to have done. The last several days before Christmas he worked himself into a state of absolute panic. Christmas itself was a day of somber gloom as we worked desperately to keep up with the collections as the nervous ushers brought them over from the church to the rectory.

Red did not dirty his hands with counting money. He contented himself with urging us on by barking imperious orders to work more quickly. Then he would fume when the ushers took too long to fetch the money that they had just collected.

He kept a running count after each Mass, muttering anxiously, "It looks bad, real bad."

He wouldn't let us see the running counts from last year; however, one of the older curates had kept his own record from the previous year and gave it to us on Christmas Eve.

It never looked bad. Although the people hated Red almost as much as we did and saw him for the phony he was, they were still generous to the parish. Since the parish was still growing, the collection always increased, and hence Red won the plebiscite—to his enormous relief at the end of Christmas afternoon when the bags of money were tied up, the bank deposit slips prepared, and one of us (you'd never know which one till the last minute) was designated to take the money to the bank, and the rest released to spend the tag end of Christmas

Day with our families. For one of us that meant about two hours, because someone had to come back and guard the rectory on Christmas evening.

Our Christmas collection at Saint Finian's is for the poor, like all our Sunday collections. It's larger than the usual collection because more people are in church that day. But it still goes in the safe, and we all leave promptly after the last Mass.

As I say, despite the cowards downtown, some things have improved.

"Merry Christmas, Boss." My New Priest waved cheerfully at me as he jumped into his car. "Have a good time."

"My best to all in River Forest," I said. "Tell them to pray for me."

"What?"

"I said tell them to pray for me."

I had no idea why I said that.

Perhaps, I told myself as I piled the last of the Christmas presents into my own car, I was anticipating the Wholey wedding on Saturday.

CHAPTER

37

Michele and Dan were married early on Saturday morning. The thermometer outside my bedroom window said that it was ten below zero. The church was warm because Jamie had remembered to turn up the heat the preceding night. (Ned turned it down before he went home every afternoon, regardless of what events the rest of us might plan for the evening or the next morning and regardless of what we told him. He had turned the furnace down every evening when Father Delaney was pastor, and so he would until Judgment Day.) No artificial warmth was needed to supplement the warmth between the bride and the groom.

She wore a white knit dress, suitable for traveling on a cold day during the Christmas season, he a business suit. They had informed their two witnesses late the previous night. Neither the bride nor the groom was nervous, though she was almost certainly a virgin and he perhaps one. They spoke their promises in loud, clear, confident voices and never looked at anything besides each other's eyes.

Two ordinary young people, it had seemed to me beforehand, forced into a small and hasty marriage because the woman's father was a stupid brute. Yet their love that morning was extraordinary. Mature emotions of power and depth and intensity that normally exist only among the most mature and experienced married lovers leaped back and forth between them, sparks closing a circuit.

Something marvelous had happened to them because of their adversity. Dan was as self-confident and gentle a bridegroom as I had ever seen in church. Michele was no longer a frightened girl, but a proud, exuberant woman. One might feel sorry for their families (though his, sitting in the first row of pews, hardly seemed despondent), but there was no reason to feel sorry for them.

The heavy hand of the past would rest lightly on their marriage.

Their union in a hotel in Seattle later in the day would not be a furtive love stolen on the run from crazy George Wholey; rather, it would be a celebration of the passion that binds the universe together.

Lucky Dan and Michele.

There was no wedding breakfast.

"George Wholey is a mean, ignorant bastard," Tom O'Rourke

said to me, as his younger son drove the newly married off to O'Hare Airport. "But nothing will ever stop that twosome."

"Are you as astonished as I am?" We both were shivering in the cold as the bridal car turned out of sight.

"Dan has been a good kid, a kind of quiet intellectual type. I hardly know the man that just carried off that splendid woman."

"George may come after you before the day is over."

"We can take care of him."

"He thinks he's pretty tough."

"He's overweight and out of condition. . . . You'll be the target before I am."

"I'm looking forward to it."

He chuckled. "Send him a mile high!"

Everyone knew. They all thought I was a bomb-throwing radical.

Except poor George.

He showed up at two in the afternoon, face red from the cold, shoulders bursting out of his big down coat, fists clenched, scowl deep and fierce.

Brigid, who was in charge of the door on this supposedly quiet day, buzzed.

"There's a frigging idjit down here, Father Lar. You want me to throw him out?"

"Biddy, such language."

"I can use a lot worse—what about a pissant shitehawk?"

"Mind your tongue, woman." I did not manage to suppress my laugh. "I'll be right down."

George had offended Cook, a bad beginning for anyone entering Saint Finian's rectory. I stopped at Jamie's door. "Condition red."

"You push the button and I'll come running."

"Remember the drill. We merely want to restrain him and eject him from the rectory because he is vile, abusive, and threatening. Brigid will listen in across the hall—with the tape recorder on—so we have a witness."

"Got it."

So I went down the spiral staircase feeling proud of our plans.

"Good afternoon, George."

"What have you done to my little Michele?" he demanded through clenched teeth.

I haven't said much about staying in condition because it's not part of the story. I weigh what I did at ordination and can take care of myself if I have to, even if I don't exercise nearly as much as my adviser, a fitness freak, insists that I should. So I wasn't afraid of him.

Besides, I was certain that Cook had Norah with her in the opposite office.

"Michele? We haven't done anything to her."

"She's gone."

"Really?"

"She's run off with that pinko punk. People are saying you married them."

"He's not a pinko and he's not a punk and they are validly married before God and Church and state."

"I'll get an annulment."

"It'll be pretty hard."

"I've got influential friends, more than you have. Tell me where they are. I'll beat the shit out of him and drag her back by the hair of her head."

"Maybe beat the shit out of her, too?"

"That's none of your goddamn business."

He was on the edge of violence now. I didn't want a fight. I pushed the button on the house phone which would summon the New Priest.

"I'll find them and cut off his balls. My friends will annul the marriage for me."

His fists tightened and he advanced toward me menacingly.

"Consummated marriages are difficult to annul, George, especially when neither party will sue."

I glanced at my watch. Perhaps not quite consummated, but sufficiently close so that it did not matter anymore.

"Consummated!" he shouted. "You mean you let that faggot fuck my little girl!"

"He's her husband, George. Keep saying that over and over. He's her husband."

"I'll be goddamned if he is! I'll stop them! Where are they shacked up!"

"I haven't the slightest idea, George."

"You won't get away with this." He slammed his fist against the wall. "I'll get you and that goddamn faggot curate of yours. I'll destroy you both."

Jamie a faggot? Pretty funny, even if the eighth-grade boys adored him.

"You're welcome to try."

Why did Louis, a man of some sophistication within his own rigid context, put up with this loose cannon? He must know that as long as George was his creature, the more intelligent and important people in the parish would avoid Corpus Christi like it was infectious. George was an interim tool that Louis would discard when he no longer served any useful purpose.

George slumped back into a chair, tugged open his coat, and sighed noisily.

"It don't make sense, Padre. The only thing that matters in life is your kids. The company, the money—all that's a pile of shit. I work for my kids and my wife." He pounded his fist into his other hand. "I bust my butt for them every day of the year, and they don't seem to care."

I felt sorry for the poor man.

"It's hard to raise kids these days, George."

"They don't give a shit. I try to tell them things for their own good and they don't listen. I'm just trying to keep them out of trouble."

"Kids insist on making their own mistakes, George." I relaxed into the chair behind my desk.

"Yeah, they sure do. It's like their parents don't know nothing. You do everything you can for them, and they screw you."

"It takes time."

"And the one I feel most sorry for is poor Jill. The kids never consider what they're doing to her. She didn't even get a chance to see her only daughter's wedding."

"I feel sorry for her, too, George. It's a shame. But maybe it will all work out after things calm down a bit."

George was an obtuse pawn for much more sinister forces, a simpleminded brute they were exploiting. I now felt truly sorry for him, as my New Priest did. I could even understand Jamie's quixotic attempts to save him.

"Geez, Padre," he said as he scratched his head. "I hope you're right. Jill has been crying all day. She says she'll never see her daughter again."

"I doubt that."

"If only they'd call so we'd know they were all right. The punk's family won't talk to us."

"I'm sure they're both fine and happy."

"Someday they'll have kids of their own and know what a hell it is to be a parent—particularly of a daughter."

I said nothing: let him talk, work it out for himself. He shook his head sadly and scratched his jaw, trying to think and finding it hard work.

"Often there's reconciliation," I said finally.

"Yeah"—tears formed in his big dumb eyes—"like with Sonny. I thought it was all gonna work out fine back at Thanksgiving. I did everything I could. He didn't want to bend."

That was not quite the way it happened; with George's

limited perceptions and Father Louis's whispering in his ears, it surely seemed by now that it had happened that way.

"I guess you'll have to try again."

"Yeah, well, all we have left is Anthony, cute little guy, ain't he, Padre? He'll screw us, too, if we give him a chance."

Now the tears were falling down his cheeks.

"Padre, I love her so damn much. Why did she do this to me?"

"She has a right to her own life, George. Everyone does. We have kids for a little while. We care for them and then give them back to God with their freedom intact."

"I guess you're right, Padre. Maybe we ought to give her a ring and congratulate her. Maybe it will all work out. What did you say their number was?"

I almost told him to call the Department of Economics at Washington State. George, you see, was almost sincere. Only at the last fraction of a second did a sly look creep into his tear-filled eyes as he realized that he could use his sadness to trick me.

"I don't know, George."

Without warning he hurtled out of the chair, hands extended toward my throat. "I'll kill you, you fucking prick!"

He managed to dig his fingers into my neck. I responded with a knee in his stomach that sent him flying.

"You sold him my little girl!" He was still sobbing.

"Stop it, George," I commanded, like I was Red Murphy.

He hurled himself at me again.

This time I ducked.

He sailed by me and into the wall. Furious, he slammed his big fist into and through the plasterboard, opening a gaping hole. He pulled his fist out and smashed it against the office window, shattering the pane.

Then he turned toward me again, a frenzied ape with a bleeding hand closing in for the kill.

I could have handled him easily; I want to make that point clear.

The New Priest, however, dashed through the door, grabbed George from behind, and pinned his arms to his side.

Behind him Norah cried like a banshee wailing at the moon.

"Now, Mr. Wholey, calm down, please, this won't help anything."

Brigid appeared behind him, one hand on Norah's collar and the other wielding a broom like it was a pike. Granne O'Malley and her hound to the rescue.

Norah snarled fiercely, as if to say, "This time I really mean it."

"Sweet, holy Mother of God, I'll make mincemeat out of you if you touch Father Lar again, you pissant fuckhead!"

"A little unimaginative, Brigid, and not up to your usual standards. Nonetheless, thank you for the support." I found that I was breathing heavily. "Mr. Wholey, however, was just about to leave, weren't you, George?"

"I won't leave until you tell me where he's fucking her." He twisted and kicked but Jamie did not permit him to move.

The kid was strong.

Norah's wail changed into a furious rumble, now really angry and threatening.

"You stay out of this rectory"—Brigid jabbed in his general direction—"or I'll feed your balls to me wolfhound for dessert."

"Queen Maeve, thank you. I'd say that I'm in good hands now."

She grinned wickedly. "Ah, no, Your Reverence, 'tis himself there that's in the good hands."

Brigid beat a strategic retreat and dragged a reluctant Norah along with her, muttering imprecations as she went, her broom still at the ready.

Thank God she had not grabbed for a carving knife instead.

"I think, Father Keenan, Mr. Wholey wants to leave now."

"I think so, too."

He literally picked George up off the floor and carried him to the front door. I opened it.

"This isn't helping, Mr. Wholey," Jamie said mildly. "You ought to go home and quiet down."

"I'll drive you out of the priesthood, you fucking faggot. I'll get you for this."

Jamie deposited George Wholey outside in the cold.

"Poor man" was all that Jamie had to say.

"We'll have to find Ned, if that be possible, and ask him to repair the damage."

We were already shivering as the minus-thirty windchill factor rushed through the shattered window.

"No problem." Jamie waved his hand. "I'll hunt up a hunk of plasterboard and a windowpane and fix it." He studied the wall. "I'll have to match the paint carefully. Hmm . . . maybe repaint the whole wall. Shouldn't take long."

"You didn't have much trouble with him, did you?"

"George? Poor man. It's lucky I got to him before Cook and Norah! Incidentally, Boss, you're still pretty fast on your feet."

"For an old man."

"Your words, not mine. Come on upstairs, let's have a drink and cool off. Then I'll fix things here."

"Cool off, man, we're both shivering."

"I mean figuratively. I suppose we'll hear from your good friend Father Simon about this."

"First thing Monday morning—no, Tuesday. Monday's New Year's Day. Happy New Year from the courageous Church of the Lord Jesus: why did you let a woman of twenty-two marry the man she loves!"

"Father!" he protested, "the Chancery is not the Church."

"They think they are," I said stubbornly. Then realizing

that I was still breathing rapidly, I yielded to his suggestion that I needed a drink.

The Chancery did not wait till Tuesday morning.

"Father Simon called while you were at Church, Father Lar," Lisa said anxiously when I came back from the ten-o'clock Liturgy on Sunday, New Year's Eve. "He said it was serious and you should call him back."

"I'll call him after the last Mass, Lisa."

"Yes, Father."

She disapproved of my procrastination; unlike her colleague Jacqueline she didn't have the nerve to tell me so.

"No big deal, Lisa."

"Yes, Father."

New Year's Eve call? Joe Simon must think it a very big deal indeed. Well, let him wait.

I took my sweet time getting back to the rectory after the last Mass.

"Father Simon again," Lisa looked worried. "He sounds awful angry, Father Lar."

"No problem, Lisa. No problem at all. If he becomes gross, I'll turn him over to you and Jackie."

I picked up the phone in the other office.

"Joe? Lar, Happy New Year."

"Don't you believe in returning Chancery office phone calls?"

"After I've finished my Sunday morning ministry to my people," I replied serenely.

"We had a call from Rome this morning, the Sunday after Christmas, do you realize how rare that is?"

"Tell me how rare it is."

"What the hell is going on out there?"

"I was afraid that you'd forgot your opening lines, Joe."

"Rape and abduction! The Sacred Congregation is mighty upset about it, let me tell you!"

"Rape and abduction!" I chortled. "Come on, Joe! Tell the Sacred Congregation that this is Forest Springs in the twentieth century and not Florence in the sixteenth."

"A forced and secret marriage? That's no laughing matter, Lar."

I was trying, oh, dear God, I was trying.

"There was no force to it, Joe. The woman freely gave her consent. We have all the documents here if you want to look at them."

"To an unemployed graduate student? Practically a vagrant, canonically speaking. And with dubious political background. Don't you ever show any discretion? Do you have any idea who this kid is or where he's from? Do you have all his records?"

"I have some idea, Joe. He was born at FSCH—that's Forest Springs Community Hospital. He was baptized, confirmed, and made his First Communion here. He attended Saint Finian's Grammar School, Saint Edward's High School, and Marquette University. I agree with the part about the dubious political background. He's a product of the University of Chicago economics department, so he's probably a Republican. He has a tenure-track appointment at . . . at a major Pac Ten university. His parents are both loyal, practicing members of the parish. What more background do you want?"

"Is the girl pregnant?"

"I didn't ask, Joe, to tell you the truth. I kind of doubt it. Do you want us to question every bride-to-be on that subject? If you do, you'd better send out a written directive."

"It's still no good, Lar, and you know it. Canonically this marriage is a case of abduction."

"Abduction?"

"An underage bride without her parents' consent—that's damn near abduction."

"How old did your Roman buddy say she was?"

"A sixteen-year-old virgin!"

"Yeah, well, that's interesting. I'll send the papers down and you can see all the facts. Then call me and we'll talk about it rationally."

"How old is she?" he shouted.

I knew he'd bite.

"As to her virginity, Joe, I have no certain knowledge. It's highly likely she was a virgin on her wedding night—that still does happen occasionally despite the way you and your friends have messed up the Church's credibility on sex. As to her age, she is twenty-two years and eight months."

"You sure?"

"No, Joe, I'm just guessing. Like I say, I'll send down the papers and you can see—"

"It was still a secret," he broke in.

"The bride asked that there be a dispensation from the banns. Using pastoral discretion according to the New Code of Canon Law—the newest one, that is—I dispensed from the banns."

"Why?"

"I did not know that my pastoral discretion was subject to review by the Vicar General."

I was getting touchy, as you can tell from the unnecessary crack about sexual credibility.

"Why?"

"If you and the Boss don't trust my discretion, you can send another pastor you do trust."

"We trust you," he said, changing his voice from a screech to a whine. "I just need facts for Rome."

"You can get them from our records. I'll put copies in the mail today, you should have them by Wednesday if the postal service recovers from its New Year's hangovers."

"They want a reply today."

"We should never have invented the transatlantic phone."

"I won't argue with that. Now, Lar, would you please give me the reason for your dispensation?"

"Well, since you said please . . . The bride was afraid of violence. Her father has routinely beaten her and her mother. He did so the last time she was preparing to marry this vagrant of yours. Apparently your good friend Father Louis whatever-his-name-is—"

"No friend of mine," Joe said fervently.

". . . advises periodic chastisement of women on the grounds that they enjoy it. That would make interesting reading in the *Sun-Times,* wouldn't it? Anyway, Ms. Wholey was fearful that her father would do it again. As a point of fact, he put his fist through the wall of our rectory office yesterday. Broke a window, too. My Associate Pastor had to scurry around to patch them both so we wouldn't freeze to death."

"Anger of an outraged father," he mumbled.

"Listen to me, Joe Simon"—I put on my no-more-Father-Nice-Guy voice—"and listen closely. That young woman had the right to the Sacrament of Matrimony and she had the right to receive it free from the threat of violence. If you try to deprive her of that right because of those Corpus Christi bastards, I'll turn the whole story over to the papers."

"Don't do that!" he begged. "We have enough trouble as it is."

"Then leave us alone."

"I don't want a fight with you, Lar. I have to make a report on this to Rome. They call us like we call you."

"They don't trust you any more than you trust us?"

"A lot less."

"Then why don't you quit?"

"You could have some real son of a bitch calling you instead of me."

How much of his time every day did he devote to phone calls like this one? We were all at the mercy of the nuts. I almost felt sorry for him.

"I'll send you our records by messenger on Tuesday morning."

"That won't be necessary. All we need—"

I hung up.

I climbed upstairs and told Jamie about the call.

"A lot of time wasted, isn't there?" He shook his head. "What a shame no one trusts anyone else."

"And everyone is at the mercy of the George Wholeys of the world."

"Poor man, he must be really hurting this morning. By the way, Dan and Michele called while you were talking to Father Simon. They're quite happy. They wanted me to thank you for being so gentle with them."

"*Me?* Gentle?"

"What else?" He waved his hand. "They said that you saved their love after the last breakup."

"You were at the wedding, Jamie. Love like that doesn't need saving."

"I'm just quoting them, Boss."

"Well, the old year ends nicely for someone anyway. . . . You're going back to River Forest tonight?"

"Naturally, the family demands one's presence on New Year's Eve."

"You mean the Mother does."

"Who else? You're going to the party at Don Lyons's house?"

"I don't like New Year's Eve parties. I'll try to sleep off this cold."

I couldn't quite stomach the adolescent happiness that radiated from Jeanne's eyes. Not now anyway. Nor the secret glances of love between the two of them.

"I'll drop by on my way home. They seem happy, don't they?"

"Don will insist on marriage pretty soon, if he hasn't already. That's when the troubles will begin."

"I'm betting on them."

"I hope you're right."

That night after he left, I played string quartets and finished *Castle Richmond* and poured myself a drink.

Then I poured the whiskey back into the bottle and, moving softly so as not to disturb the hound of heaven, turned down Wolfgang Amadeus. I rested my hand on the phone, thought about it for a maybe a half minute, and dialed my adviser's number. She was gentle this time. "You must take that vacation, Laurence. You've been working too hard."

There was music and laughter in the background.

"Yes, ma'am."

"And you must do something about that cold."

"Yes, ma'am."

"And you must permit yourself to understand that the young couple is right about you."

"That'll be harder—"

"No argument, please."

"Yes, ma'am."

"Finally, you must believe that I love you very much."

"That's a great way to end the year."

"Good-bye Laurence. God bless you and protect you. I repeat, I love you very much."

She hung up before anything I might say could spoil the magic in those words.

There are so many different kinds of love in the world.

I went right to sleep and slept through all the noise of the coming of the new year, foolishly confident that it would be better. It was my last good night's sleep for a long time.

CHAPTER

38

I was at the Cardinal's house when they took Brigid away.

It was my fate in the new year to be somewhere else when tragedy hit Saint Finian's rectory. I would tell myself that I should never leave.

The meeting with the Cardinal had not gone well, to put it mildly.

The Cardinal invited me for lunch before the meeting. "A small festive celebration of the new year," he said formally, "and a token of my appreciation of your work."

The Boss was one of the more progressive or "moderate" churchmen who had risen to power during the last papacy, infinitely better, to give him full credit, than the semiliterate fools that they have promoted in the last ten years.

My cold had not improved. I was not sleeping. I was in a blackass mood.

"Maybe we can consider this a reconciliation," he said to me over coffee and dessert, "for the misunderstanding about that secret marriage at your parish, Lar."

Well, he finally had the name right.

"I've noticed, Your Eminence, that when bishops use the word 'reconciliation,' they give it a special meaning: the other person does what the bishop wants or agrees that the bishop is right."

He winced, as he often does when someone speaks the truth.

"My name is Steve," he said mildly.

"I use first names with friends, Your Eminence. With bishops I use the proper ecclesiastical title."

"I would hope we could be friends, Lar."

"No one can be friends with his own bishop."

He winced again.

"You are really upset about that secret marriage matter, aren't you?"

"And the harassment about Father Quinlan and about my associate pastor's sermon."

"Those who complain have a right to be heard, Lar."

"Only, it turns out, if they're right-wing cranks."

I rose from the table and walked away to the meeting room.

If he'd had the guts to say that they were wrong on all three matters, I would perhaps have considered the possibility that we could be friends.

Bishops can't admit they're wrong.

I'll confess: I came looking for a fight with the committee. Like I said, I was weary and sick and in a bad mood. I was not about to endure any more harassment from other priests about our financial program at Saint Finian's.

When I came back from my sabbatical degree work in Dublin and the personnel board asked me to take Saint Finian's, I discovered the place was a financial mess. In his dotage the Founding Pastor had pretended to himself and everyone else that the parish was not running deeply in the red every year. The usual procedure under such circumstances is for the new pastor to solemnly inform the parish of the situation. Thus he attacks his predecessor who, whatever his idiocies, was dearly loved by at least a third of the parishioners. Then new pastor harasses them for the next year about the need to increase their contributions, which they do eventually, though grudgingly and resentfully.

Instead, I asked them on the first Sunday for recommendations for a parish finance committee. Two weeks later I convened the committee, turned the parish books over to them, proposed the hiring that would be required to bring the parish into the late twentieth century in its services, and outlined my ideas on parish finance.

They listened in fascination.

Each year, I suggested, we would construct a budget (the word was unknown to the Founding Pastor) and mail it to the people of the parish. We would observe what the result would be if you divided the budget by the number of families in the parish. Obviously, we would say, everyone must judge for themselves what they can pledge. We would ask that those who could be more generous than the average would try to do so.

Enclosed would be pledge cards. We would remind them each month. They could pay by using Visa or MasterCard numbers. Or if they didn't want to be bothered with notices, they could simply initial the enclosed card authorizing their bank to transfer on the fifteenth of each month one-twelfth of their pledge to our account.

There would be no money talks in church. The Sunday collection would be for the poor in the parish and the city and the world. The parish council (not the finance committee) would determine where that money should be sent.

No fuss, no muss, no bother.

My classmates told me I was crazy. I had my first call of protest from Joe Simon, who asserted that "we're getting a lot of complaints about this crazy new idea of yours."

No one apologized when the contributions doubled in the first year. We exceeded budget by 20 percent and voted (at my suggestion, I confess) to put the surplus in a fund for high school tuitions, half in our parish, and half in an inner city parish.

The reason for the surplus? Most of our people were convinced that they were earning "better than average" incomes.

Our contributions have gone up by 15 percent every year since then.

No other parish has tried to imitate us.

No priest has even asked about the plan.

After lunch at the Cardinal's house, the committee described for my benefit how wonderfully well they were doing in their parishes at fund-raising.

Ken McGuire, looking like an aging Anglo-Irish lord, with his carefully trimmed white hair and his London tailor-made suit and shirt with gold cufflinks, was at his pompous asshole best.

"As part of our ministry of sacrificial giving, Lar," he said patiently on a sigh, "and our exercise of Christian stewardship, we tithe."

The Cardinal, like most American bishops, wears a simple gold band on his right-hand ring finger and an equally simple pectoral cross—when he bothers to wear it at all. Kenny, on the other hand, wears a ruby ring and a huge cross packed with diamonds.

I happened to know that although his parish, Queen of Apostles—known popularly as Queen of All Cadillacs—was the same size as Saint Finian's and had roughly the same kind of people, his Sunday collection was 20 percent lower than ours, in part because Kenny's arrogance had driven a good number of his people to other parishes.

"You give ten percent of your salary to the Sunday collection, Ken?" I asked innocently.

His red face turned crimson. "The people tithe, following the biblical injunction," he said piously, patting his stomach as though to make sure it was still there.

"Are you going to be consistent with your restoration of the Mosaic law," I demanded, loving every second of the developing fight, "and require kosher food, circumcision, and the ritual purification of women?"

"Lar, please!" The Cardinal moved his hands as if to sooth a rumpled blanket.

"I note, Cardinal"—I turned to him—"that when many of

my colleagues talk about stewardship, they mean that they are the stewards and the people are the ship."

"At least we're not reported to Rome every week," Kenny mumbled.

I forgot to mention that when Ken retires in a couple of months (at the age of seventy), he will continue to live in the palatial pastoral suite in his rectory. He's building an addition for the new pastor (a parish improvement about which the people had not been consulted) and has announced that as a bishop, he is of course not bound by the rule that retired pastors must leave the rectory for at least six months.

"And they expect the laity to sacrifice," I continued, "but they don't offer the personal sacrifice of preaching better homilies. I wonder if Dr. McGuire has ever considered offering to his people the sacrifice of setting up a committee of laity to evaluate the quality of preaching in his parish. Maybe he'd win back some of the people that have drifted away to other parishes."

"Lar!" the Cardinal begged me.

"Just asking," I said innocently.

Clearly I was enjoying my role as the bull in the Waterford crystal shop too much. On the other hand, everything I had said was true, if impolitic—and useless.

The committee then rehearsed the old criticisms of our fund-raising at Saint Finian's. I let them continue for a while.

"Your Eminence, I was not aware that I was to be put on trial for the achievements of Saint Finian's in meeting its annual budget."

"No one is trying to put you on trial, Lar," he said soothingly.

"Don't be paranoid, Lar," Joe Simon pleaded.

"The hell they're not putting us on trial. I assure you that the subject of Saint Finian's will not disrupt future meetings, because I won't be at them."

"You shouldn't say that," one of the other priests at the table said. "You shouldn't be so defensive, Lar."

I ignored him.

"There are two observations that I do propose to make, Your Eminence, about the subject of money and the Church. They are as unprofound as they are unwelcome to this committee. First, the laity are furious at the mess we've made out of our finances and at the insensitivity of the Vatican and the hierarchy to their religious needs. Second, they will not notably increase their generosity until that day we are willing, like every other church in this land of the free, to grant them participation in decisions about how the money they give is spent."

Ken McGuire, D.D., looked like he was about to collapse in apoplexy.

Joe Simon shook his head furiously, just as he did the last time I had raised that subject.

"That's not really on our agenda, Lar," the Cardinal said apologetically.

Joe put his hands protectively on the Cardinal's shoulders and shook his head at me again.

"Don't send me head signals, Joe. Tell me why we can't talk about the subject."

"At the present time," he snapped at me, "it does not seem an appropriate subject."

"Why not?"

"Because it is not appropriate."

That was that.

I didn't walk out because I didn't want them to say around the archdiocese that night that I had stormed out of the meeting. So I daydreamed through the rest of the session and tried to figure out why lay participation in parish financial decisions was inappropriate.

As my fellow priests babbled incoherently about motives for "stewardship"—that is, guilt trips to put on their people—I pondered the problem. There was no ecclesiastical illegality to what we were doing. Maybe such experiments made someone in Rome uneasy.

Maybe the Boss was afraid that if we even talked about it at our meeting, he'd receive a phone call from someone in the Vatican.

How cowardly can you be? Or maybe he was afraid that if you permitted the laity into the action on the parish level, they would want into the archdiocesan action, too. Perhaps his financial administrators had warned him that in the perilous state of the archdiocese "at the present time," that chance could not be taken.

Or maybe Joe had told him that the pastors would not stand for lay participation.

It really didn't matter, I concluded, what the explanation was. Cowardice was at the root of it.

When the meeting finally drifted to a halt, dead in the water like the rest of the Church, I rose to leave. The Cardinal intercepted me.

"I wish you'd come back, Lar. You're abrasive at times, but at least you keep us honest."

My head was throbbing and my stomach restless. I offer those facts as an explanation, not as an excuse.

"What does a bishop know about honesty, Your Eminence," I said softly, almost gently.

He winced for a third time. "What do you mean, Lar?"

"There are two ways a man in your position can react to the present situation in the Church, both are dishonest. One is to pretend that everything is fine just the way the Vatican wants it to be and persuade yourself that this pretense is true. That's the way the dumb bishops do it. The other is to maintain the pretense even though you know it is false, because you figure you have no choice. That's the way the smart bishops do it."

"And what am I?"

"No one ever said you were dumb."

"That's harsh, Lar."

"Untrue?"

He hesitated. "Not entirely."

Which is about as straight an answer as anyone ever gets from him.

I stole out of the house alone and walked from North Avenue and State Parkway to the train station. I wasn't angry at anyone anymore. Just sad for the Church and the priesthood.

On the train ride back to Forest Springs I began to meditate once again about resigning my pastorate and returning to work in a black parish in the inner city.

I'd thought of it often before, never seriously. It was an escape from complexity to simplicity, maybe a coward's way out.

On that cold gray January day, with more snow clouds building up in the west like the national debt, I told myself that there comes a time in life when a man needs simplicity.

Snow was already tumbling down, a couple of hours early, when I left the train at the Forest Springs Station and began the hike in the bitter cold back to the rectory.

Two drinks before supper tonight. Tomorrow I'd board the wagon.

As I struggled through the blizzard, a big Cadillac pulled up next to me.

"Give you a ride, Father?" Joe Condon asked.

I would have rather walked; however, the ride would provide an opportunity to offer another warning about Coady Anne.

"Have a good Christmas, Father?"

"Not too bad, Joe. How's your family?"

"Fine, Father, just fine. Everyone's great."

"Coady Anne?"

"Couldn't be better. She's completely recovered from that silly little incident that got you called to the hospital."

"Is she receiving any help?"

"All the family can give her."

"I mean from a therapist, Joe."

He paused as he cautiously squeezed the brakes for a stop sign.

"Tina doesn't think there's any need for that, Father."

"Joe, she's wrong. Coady Anne needs a therapist and badly. With help she'll be all right. Without it, she will plead for help again with another suicide attempt. The next time she might cut it too close."

"Tina feels pretty strongly about it, Father."

"You're the girl's father, Joe. I'm warning you that Coady Anne is a badly disturbed little girl. If anything happens to her, the responsibility is yours."

"Nothing will happen, Father." He stopped in front of the rectory to let me off. "Tina is sure of it. She thinks Coady Anne is just acting up a little."

"Acting out. . . . Joe, I'm warning you for the last time."

"Thanks, Father. I appreciate your concern."

I didn't bother to thank him for the ride.

Jackie, sobbing hysterically, met me at the door. "I tried to stop them, Father Lar! They pushed me down and took her away anyhow!"

"Calm down, Jackie, calm down!" I took her strong shoulders in my hands, just as Joe Simon had gripped the Cardinal's frail shoulders. "Who took who away?"

"Brigid!" she wailed. "The Gestapo took her away!"

"The *Gestapo*!"

Mike Quinlan appeared at the foot of the spiral staircase, his handsome face even more haggard than it usually was.

"Thank God you're back, Lar." He seemed harried and battered. "I tried to stop them, too, but they pushed me aside."

"Will someone *please* explain what has happened?"

"The Immigration Service took Brigid away today. They said

she was an illegal alien. Jamie's meeting with his father now. They're trying to obtain a court order before she's deported."

"They had a warrant?"

"Said they didn't need one. They had probable cause to assume that she was an illegal."

"And they knocked Jackie down and pushed you around?"

My blood was tundra cold, much colder than the weather outside the rectory.

"Norah?"

"Thank God she was playing with the kids at the skating rink over at Myrtle. Otherwise, we might have had a couple of dead feds on the rectory floor."

"I'll get the bastards. Is she really an illegal?"

"As best as I could figure from their shouting, she was here on a tourist visa that she'd renewed twice. Now it's expired. According to Jamie's father she could have applied either for a student visa, because she's in school or a work permit, because she has a job. I guess she was afraid to try for fear they'd do exactly what they did today."

"If Jamie comes back, tell him to see me." I bounded up the stairs, three at a time, and called a certain political person.

"Yeah, Lar," he said, "I've heard about it. Immigration is no worse than any other law enforcement agency. They've got some real hard-nosed bastards in it. Hey, turn on your TV. Your parish is on channel two."

Who had tipped off TV?

Still holding the phone, I pushed the button just in time to see two goons wrestle Brigid, handcuffed and with tears pouring down her face, into the Federal Detention Center on South Clark Street. The building is brand-new proof of the decadence of Chicago architecture; with its concrete slab walls and slit windows, it is one of the most forbidding buildings in all the world. It makes Victorian prisons in England look like luxury hotels.

"Hellhole," my friend said.

"Chicago school of architecture," I muttered. "Form follows function."

Then a cut to our rectory and a red-eyed and outraged Jackie, speaking not teen English but perfect standard English.

"I said that they had no right to come into our rectory and take someone away. I told them they would have to wait till our pastor, Father McAuliffe, returned from the Cardinal's house, where he was at a meeting. They pushed me and knocked me down and dragged poor Brigid out of the rectory. They hit Father Quinlan, too, when he asked them what right they had to break in."

"What do you think about this, Ms. Walsh?" a black reporter asked her.

"I didn't know we lived in Russia!"

"Hey," my friend said on the phone, "sign that kid up! How old is she?"

"Sixteen."

"You guys grow them fierce out there. This is a big black eye for Immigration, forcing an entry into the rectory, assaulting rectory employees, beating up on a pretty redhead kid. You can really stick it to them. . . . Who's your lawyer? You have one, don't you?"

"My associate pastor's father, Judge Keenan."

"Heavy, very heavy. If there's anyone that can block them, he can. Is the kid really illegal?"

"I gathered her tourist visa expired. She could have applied for either a work permit or a student visa—she's studying for an M.B.A.—but was afraid to take the risk."

"Good cook?"

"The best."

"Bastards. That's pushing the law to an absurd limit. Look, Jerry will tell this to you, too, though in more ornate prose as befits a published novelist: if you can keep them from putting her on a plane tonight, he can obtain a habeas corpus in federal court tomorrow morning. You can stretch out the hearings for years. By then she can fit into a quota or maybe find a nice American boy, Irish-American, of course." He chuckled. "She shouldn't have a hard time doing that."

"Thanks. I guess the case is in good hands."

They didn't need the pastor at all.

Except if I had been there, both the goons would now be in FSCH.

"The best hands. Stay in touch."

"I sure will."

I hung up, thought about a drink, and decided that I wasn't thirsty.

I hurried down to the garage. Someone had provided Norah with her supper, despite Cook's absence. The hound of heaven had not touched a bite of it. She was pacing back and forth, like a wolf in a zoo, and emitting a low snarl.

"Don't worry, girl." I patted the immense head. "We'll bring her back."

She turned away from me, still rumbling.

Back in my study Jamie appeared, his blue eyes tungsten hard. He mixed two drinks without saying a word.

"I have to watch myself, Boss, or I'll use some of your language."

"Did you see Jackie on TV?"

"I just had a blow-by-blow description. It calmed her down. How about that for a punch line: 'I didn't know we lived in Russia!' "

The phone rang. I picked it up. "Is Father Jamie there, Father Lar? His dad wants to talk to him."

"I'll put him on, Jackie. You were brilliant."

"That's what Mr. Keenan said. He's cute."

I handed the phone to the New Priest.

"Yeah, hi, Dad. No, I didn't see it; herself gave me a full report. The Boss saw it. He's as proud as if she were his real daughter instead of surrogate. Right, here he is."

"Jerry? Lar."

"We're in luck. First, I think your New Priest may have exceeded his authority in hiring me as attorney for the parish in this matter."

"To paraphrase the late mayor, what kind of a son would it be that wouldn't hire his father, especially when he's a retired federal judge."

"Fine." He laughed. "If I may say so, I want to get those two brutes, too."

"Right. What's our luck?"

"The big luck is that Northwest flight forty leaves for Shannon at four—so it's already left. They couldn't ship her out there tonight. We'll apply for a habeas corpus tomorrow morning on the grounds that they did not follow the proper procedures. Aliens don't have the rights of Americans, but they have some rights. No judge is going to be happy with those clips on all the channels tonight of Immigration invading a Catholic rectory—they'll make the ten-o'clock news, too. Unless the turn of the wheel gives us one of the Republicans who sit on the federal bench, we'll probably obtain the injunction."

"That will mean?"

"They'll have to turn her over to us. Then we can stall and win on appeal or make some kind of other arrangements. We'll also enter suit in the name of the parish and of Mr. and Mrs. Dermot Walsh, acting for their daughter Jacqueline, and of Father Quinlan. That will scare the hell out of the government."

"You've talked to Kate and Dermot already?"

"Yes. And I'd say that the young woman comes by it naturally."

"Such things happen."

"You've noticed. . . . I don't want to make any promises.
You're never sure in a courtroom. Immigration can be tricky
and stubborn. I think we've got them."

"Thanks, Judge," I said, deciding that it would not be wise
to ask who sent the TV cameras racing out to Forest Springs.

"I've asked a bailiff I happen to know to keep an eye on
them down there tonight, just in case they try to sneak her out.
I've lined up two federal marshals for tomorrow in case we have
to make a few threats."

"They won't let you see her."

"Not yet."

"She was in handcuffs."

"They say she resisted arrest."

"Bastards!"

"We'll get them, never fear."

"What if the Judge doesn't give us a habeas corpus tomorrow?"

"Then we'll figure a way to get her back in. Won't take any
more than a few months."

"If she wants to come back after this."

"Lar, everyone wants to live in America."

Which was true enough.

"Do you want me in court tomorrow?"

"As her employer? Maybe, but I think it would be better if
Father Quinlan were there. He is technically an associate pastor, is he not?"

"Right."

"He can act for you in assuring the court that the young
woman attends school and has a valid job at the rectory."

"Sure can."

"Maybe it would be better for you to lurk near the phone
out there tomorrow, in case we need a wild card."

"Fine with me."

"Boss," said the New Priest grimly when I had hung up, "with

your permission I'm going to organize a demonstration for tomorrow."

"A *demonstration!*"

"Perfectly peaceful and law-abiding exercise of First Amendment rights. At the airport, if we lose in court or the INS tries
something kinky."

"Why not?"

Jamie Keenan was not only the absolute Mary Poppins of
associate pastors, he was also, when angered, a very dangerous
young man.

As is Michael Jordan of the Chicago Bulls when he's pissed
off.

I tried to pray later, after I had disposed of the evening's office calls. The emotions churning around in my head drove off
all devotion. I was annoyed at just about everyone, myself included.

So I spent the night in fitful tossing and turning.

And eager anticipation of the battle on the morrow.

CHAPTER

39

A battle it was.

Dear God, what a battle.

More fun than blowing up a real estate company.

I fretted and stewed and answered irate phone calls all
morning. Heaven knows the parish was on our side.

I wondered if they would be so militant if Biddy were a
Mexican illegal.

The blizzard had stopped. Or rather it had paused. Another
front would sweep in late in the afternoon.

At two-thirty Mrs. Clarke rang me.

"Judge Keenan, Father."

"Jerry? Lar. What's up?"

"We finally got the writ, but the bastards pulled a fast one. They've already shipped her out to O'Hare. They're going to try to put her on the flight before we can get out there with the writ."

"Why?"

"Some idiot in the middle level of the bureaucracy wants to make a fight of it, despite the bad publicity last night, maybe because of it. I'm bringing the writ and the two marshals. I've already talked to Jamie and he's assembling his troops. I want you there as the pastor and a woman from your staff who can take care of Ms. Brigid O'Shea. She's spent the night in the bullpen with drug addicts and dealers and is probably an emotional wreck by now. We're off. If the rush hour isn't too bad, we'll make it in time."

I didn't ask if the TV would be there. The Judge—or perhaps more likely Mama Maggie—would have already taken care of that.

I thought for a moment. What woman? Linda? No, it was her day off. Mrs. Clarke? No nerves for a confrontation. Sister Cunnegunda? I hesitated. No, too fierce. Cook? No, it was Cook we were trying to save. Jeanne? There wasn't anyone else. She was my first choice anyway.

"Jeanne? Lar. We're on our way to O'Hare to salvage Cook. Judge Keenan wants a woman to reassure her when she's released. You free to come?"

"You bet."

"I'll be right over."

Beneath her white cloth coat, she was wearing a brown suit, beige blouse, and a broad plaid tie.

"Professional enough?" she asked as she climbed into my car.

"Perfect. . . . More snow on the way."

"We live in Chicago and it's winter."

"You're right."

"Lar, you look terrible." She was examining my face closely. "Do you have a fever?"

"I don't think so. Cold and no sleep."

I drove carefully down the street toward the expressway interchange three blocks from the rectory.

"It's been a hard year for you. Are you really taking a winter vacation?"

"The New Priest has decided that I am."

"Good for him." She laughed.

"I'm sorry you think I look so rotten. I was about to observe that you look sensational."

"Thank you," she said cheerfully. "I feel sensational too."

"Love does that, I'm told."

I eased into the steady flow of expressway traffic, already hinting at the coming rush hour.

Rush hour and snow. Would Judge Keenan make it in time?

"There was no reason to assume we could keep it a secret."

I had meant emotional love. Had she thought I meant physical love? Did she want me to have meant that? I must navigate carefully now, and not just the expressway.

"The signs are evident, Dr. Flavin."

"Do you mind if we talk about it now?" She spoke hesitantly, almost shyly. "I know it's not exactly the right time. . . ."

"Anytime you want to talk about something to a priest, Jeanne, is the right time."

Her story was disconnected. Words, half sentences, leaps back and forth. I was astonished once more at how much women trust priests.

"I never thought I would experience physical pleasure . . . or make love to a man. . . . I was sure I wouldn't enjoy . . . I'd be cold and stale . . . frigid. . . . If someone told me that I'd . . .

well, love it enormously, even the first time ... I propositioned him you know ... the night we saw *Falstaff.* ... I felt
certain from the way he kissed me and touched me after the
Christmas dance that he wanted me. ... I'm bothered by some
guilts ... old-fashioned Catholic ... thou shalt not fornicate ...
feminism ... thou shalt not be a sex object ... not bothered
too much. I want him as often as I can have him. I'm out of
my mind with desire. ... Can you imagine that, Lar? Me of all
people become a nymph. ... It was deliberate. I said to him at
dinner that I knew he wanted to make love with me. I told him
I was a virgin, hymen long since ruptured but never a man inside me. I didn't think I'd be any good in bed; I wanted to find
out for sure. If he wished to run the risk of a dull night, he was
welcome to me. ... Long wait through the opera, heightened
expectation. ... I told him that I trusted him and he could do
whatever he wanted with me. ... I used to think I was bad because I was sexually attractive; then I thought that I wasn't attractive anymore. Now sometimes I think that if a man enjoys
me that much I might even be good. ... Are you disgusted
with me?"

"Not at all."

"Surprised?"

"Impressed at your courage."

"I had everything ready ... candles, his favorite brandy,
lacy lingerie. ... He is really a wonderful lover, patient, kind. I
mean, I can make no comparisons, but he's so good to me. ...
I thought I'd feel nothing at all. ... Men are really quite vehement when they are aroused, aren't they? ... Delightfully so."

She paused, not embarrassed but searching for words.

"I just trusted myself to him. Completely. After that it was all
golden and sweet and then like a thunderstorm of pleasure. ...
I couldn't believe it. ... I'm still young enough to have
children ... teenagers like those darlings that wrapped me up
in tissue paper and raffled me off. ... Don would like more

children, too. . . . His kids are wonderful . . . they're on my side. . . . He wants to marry me. He's the marrying kind. . . . I don't know. I'm afraid. It's been easier than I expected so far, but marriage. . . . Sometimes it all seems so ugly . . . everything that happened with my father. . . . How can I ever be happy with a man? . . . Then I'm alone with him and I can't keep my hands off him. . . . I melt when he comes into a room. . . . I see that he wants me as much as I want him, I catch fire. . . . We're never too old to love, are we, Lar? I mean to fall in love like a pair of geeky teens?"

"We lose that ability, Jeanne, if we lose it at all, fifteen minutes after we're dead."

"I've been ice and he's set me on fire and melted me and turned me into boiling water. I tell myself that's sufficient, and then I say sex can't hold a man and a woman together by itself. Then I say that it's a big help and I should find a good woman therapist and talk out this incest thing. Then I say it's a quick love affair and it can't last. . . . He'll grow tired of me, and that will be that."

The snow clouds above O'Hare, off to the west of us, were giant gray towers in the sky. Maybe they would delay Northwest flight 40 and give us more time.

"I'm sure there are lots of signs of him growing tired of you."

"None at all," she said hotly. "He seems to enjoy me more each time."

"Understandable."

"You're so sweet, Lar." Hand briefly on my arm. "If it hadn't been for you and Jamie, I'd never have dared. . . . Sister used to say during my formation year that I was a sensualist. . . . She meant that I liked to sleep late and take long showers. I guess that wasn't the half of it. . . . I revel in being desired. . . . I like undressing for him. . . . Does that make me a sex object?"

"I doubt it."

We were slowing down for the O'Hare traffic crunch. In the distance the Kennedy Expressway looked jammed. Dear God, please let the Judge make it.

"I don't think so, either. . . . Women tell such crazy things to one another . . . the first-night stuff . . . and at my age. . . . Well, I found the answer to my question. . . . If heaven isn't like that I might want to reconsider."

"All reports say it's better."

"I told him about Dad . . . the retreat master . . . the whole story. . . . He wept with me, can you imagine that? Said he loved me all the more for my courage and resiliency. . . . Am I resilient, Lar?"

"Is the Pope Catholic?"

"Silly." Hand on my arm again. Longer this time. Then a silence after she slowly removed it.

"I'm a shit, am I not? Talking about my silly self while that poor young woman is being terrorized by beasts."

"Self-hatred is banned in this battered Ford Taurus."

"You ought to buy a new car, too."

"Yes, ma'am."

"I suppose all this passion will go away. . . . I should enjoy it while I can. Fond memories of when I was a sex object, a mistress, a thing used and exploited."

"You don't mean that."

"No . . . I don't mean it. . . . I'd marry him tomorrow if . . ."

Silence.

"If what?"

I was now in a long line inching its way to the ticket gates at O'Hare's multilevel parking lot.

"If"—she choked—"I wasn't afraid that I'm such an emotional wreck I'd ruin his life."

"You'd still be fun in bed, Jeanne."

"*Lar!* What an awful thing to say!"

We were climbing up the crowded ramp, bumper to bumper with the car ahead and behind. We are destined for the roof. No protection up there from the snow.

"Aren't you?"

"Of *course* I am!" Then she added apologetically, "I can't believe it really, but he says so, and I guess he's right. I do *have* fun in bed."

"Well, that's better for a man than a cold and empty bed on a cold winter night. Most men are willing to put up with a lot from a woman who, besides keeping the bed warm, is a good lay."

"That's chauvinism."

"No, it's not. It's just the bottom line, you should excuse the expression."

"I am blushing terribly."

The clock on my dashboard said 3:25, thirty-five minutes to flight time, maybe ten to boarding time. We were cutting it close. Biddy didn't need us. She needed Judge Keenan and his writ and his two federal marshals.

"I can't see your face because I'm searching for a parking place. You understand me, don't you?"

"Yes, Lar. You're saying something truly scary. You're saying I'm worth the risk a man—any man, even Don—might take if he should marry me."

"Body *and* soul."

"You're also saying, by implication, that I should find myself a shrink—maybe Jamie's mother if she'll take me—and trust everyone. God, Don, you, the shrink."

"And yourself, especially yourself."

"I'm so frightened, Lar." She huddled briefly against me as I set the gear in park. "So happy and so afraid."

"You'll make it, Jeanne, never fear."

Very gingerly I put my arm around her.

By which I meant that the long shot was not quite so long as it used to be.

"Thank you for listening, Lar." She slipped away from me and out the door. "Now let's go liberate Cook!"

CHAPTER

40

We made a horrendous mistake.

Jeanne blamed it on her "silly babble." It had been so long since I'd flown out of O'Hare . . . it was my mistake.

I remembered that the old international terminal had been torn down to make room for the new United Helmut Jahn affair. I had heard that like any other Third World city, Chicago now bused its international passengers out to planes waiting on the runway. I assumed that we should dash to the international terminal, which was in fact part of the multilevel parking garage with walls attached.

We ran madly up and down the length of the terminal searching for Northwest flight 40. All we could find on the monitors was NW 41 which seemed to have already left.

Were we too late?

I finally asked a cop about NW 40.

" 'Tis a departing plane you're looking for, is it, Father?"

Still some micks on the force.

"I am."

"This terminal is for incoming flights. See up there on the monitor: flight forty-one is already in. You'll be wanting to walk over to the Northwest domestic terminal, the outbound foreign flights leave from there. I hear there's a bit of a dust-up over there. INS trying to smuggle out a rectory housekeeper or something. The regular customs' folks hate those so-and-so's."

"Thank you, officer."

The clock said 3:45. Jeanne and I began to run.

It said 3:55 when, weaving our way through the crowded Northwest terminal like Thomas Sanders and Neil Anderson of the Chicago Bears, we reached the departure gate for NW 40.

Dust-up was an understatement.

Father New Priest had arranged a spectacular exercise in the constitutional right of peaceful assembly.

A horde of teens and their parents, waving banners and placards, were chanting, "Give us Brigid! Give us Brigid! Give us Brigid!"

TV cameras from all four channels were grinding away. Not live yet.

Patti O'Hara, who would not have been caught dead as a pom-pom girl, was nonetheless leading the chant. A dozen of Chicago's finest were standing around, grinning at the show. My New Priest was talking to a lieutenant.

Behind Patti stood the entire defensive line of the Saint Edward Lions, all in their blue and silver letter jackets.

In the waiting lounge, Brigid, chained to two hulking characters, was cowering in a chair. A third man, a young Mexican kid, was watching nervously.

The departure time on the board was 4:30. The snows had delayed the takeoff.

"You go talk to her," I said to Jeanne. "Let's make sure the police know that I'm Captain Tom McAuliffe's son."

"Jamie wouldn't leave that to chance."

Naturally not.

The lieutenant had worked with my father a long time ago. "Most honest captain on the force," he said admiringly. "You look just like him. Your kids are wonderful. It's not them we're worried about; it's those jerks from INS. The young guy is supposed to be in charge, but the agents don't pay any attention to him."

"Give us Brigid! Give us Brigid! Give us Brigid!"

"Where's Dad?" Jamie asked, his brow furrowed for the first time since I'd known him.

"The Kennedy Expressway is a mess. How long till boarding?"

"Fifteen minutes. They won't listen to me when I tell them there's a court order on the way. Nor call their office. This could turn messy, Boss. Half those kids never saw Brigid before. They're all fired up, though, and they don't like the way she's being pushed around."

As I watched, I saw Jeanne lean over the pathetic little figure. Then the larger agent shoved her rudely away.

"They won't let us talk to her," Jamie explained. "I wanted to avoid an incident."

"There won't be an incident."

"I hope not."

In the background I heard a menacing yelp.

"Norah?"

"Not my idea." The New Priest shrugged. "I have three sophomore boys holding her."

I strode over to the boarding lounge; Jeanne dropped in behind me.

"No talking to the alien," the big guard announced.

Big he was, a caricature of the white sheriff in a dozen movies about the South; not as big, however, as your silver-haired suburban pastor.

He might push around teenagers and women and recovering alcoholic clerics. Not said suburban clerical hero.

Macho? Hell, yes.

The scene would wipe out sleep for another month. It was like Mile Hi all over. This time with the cops on my side.

"Look, buster, I just saw you assault a member of my staff. That's number three. Dr. Flavin and I are staying here until Ms. O'Shea's attorney arrives. You keep your hands off Dr. Flavin and me, or you won't have a job tomorrow morning and you'll probably end up in jail—when you finally get out of the hospital."

He backed off. Jeanne knelt next to Biddy and folded her arms around her. "It's all right, Brigie dear, it's all right. We won't let them hurt you anymore."

"Give us Brigid! Give us Brigid! GIVE US BRIGID!"

The natives were having the time of their lives and becoming even more restless.

The scared young Mexican-American kid in charge of the INS team scurried up to me.

"All three of us are Catholics, Father. We have a job to do."

"A job of which you and your families ought to be ashamed."

"Someone has to do it, Father."

"There's a court order coming for Ms. O'Shea's release. Your office knows about it. Call them for instructions."

"I can't call them, Father. We have orders."

"Then God have mercy on you!"

He scurried away again, doubtless wondering what would happen next.

He'd deported his own fellow ethnics until today, frightened, powerless victims. Now he was up against a different breed of victims—the kind that fight back. He had the Irish on his hands and he couldn't figure them out.

A TV mike was jabbed in front of me.

"Is your group planning direct action, Father McAuliffe?"

"Direct action?" I tried to look innocent.

"Those young people over there?"

"GIVE US BRIGID! GIVE US BRIGID! GIVE US BRIGID!"

"Young people? Oh, you mean the ones who are chanting?"

"Yes, Father."

"I do recognize some of them. They're from Saint Edward's, aren't they? I assume that they're merely exercising in an orderly fashion their constitutional rights of freedom of speech and freedom of assembly. I'm here as her employer."

"What will happen if the government agents attempt to deport Ms. O'Shea?"

"I assume they won't do that. Her attorney is on his way from the federal courthouse with a writ of habeas corpus. The INS is aware of that. I'm sure they won't act in contempt of court."

"If they do?"

"Then they'll have to answer to the federal judge who issued the writ, won't they?"

Cool? Your totally-in-control cleric—just before he pushes the plunger that sends Mile Hi a mile high.

What, I wondered, would we do if Judge Keenan didn't make it in time? Would we be violating the law if we physically restrained the INS people?

Twenty-five years ago, I wouldn't have worried for a moment.

Now I was concerned. Priests probably ought not to engage in riots, even in a good cause. Particularly on prime time.

The best bet would be to invoke Chicago's finest. I glanced over at Jamie and the lieutenant. The latter tipped his hat to me.

I could not possibly have predicted what actually happened.

"She's almost catatonic, Lar," Jeanne whispered to me. "They've brutalized her."

"We'll take care of them later."

Poor Cook. Sure, she had a degree from a community college in Limerick and, sure, she was bright and quick. She was also an Irish-speaking peasant kid who had grown up in a thatched cottage way out on the end of Dingle. She must feel like she was part of a Hieronymus Bosch painting.

I placed my hand gently on her shoulder. She looked up, startled, recognized me, and with great effort, winked.

"We want Brigid! Give us Brigid! WE WANT BRIGID!"

The rhythm had changed. The kids were mad now.

The hand on the clock of the boarding lounge inched, ever so slowly, toward 4:15. I saw the passenger agent at the counter, a man who looked like he was caught in cross fire during the Fourth Battle of the Somme, timidly lift his microphone.

Think quickly, McAuliffe, this is it.

"Northwest Airlines announces the delayed departure of its flight forty to Boston's Logan Airport and Shannon, Ireland. All passengers who have not received seat assignments at this time should do so. We will be boarding by rows."

As the agents pulled Brigid to her feet, a great roar rose from our peaceful exercise of constitutional rights. Judge Jeremias Keenan, former Commander USN, Navy Cross (with Oak Leaf Cluster), descended upon us—two stalwart federal marshals and one even more stalwart priestly son in tow.

He waved the writ like it was a battle flag.

"I have an order from the federal court that Ms. O'Shea be released to my custody. Who is in charge here?"

Deafening cheers from Patti O'Hara and friends.

"I am," the kid said. "I am an attorney for Immigration and Naturalization, sir. I have orders to place this young woman on Northwest flight forty. I propose to do so, unless ordered not to by my office."

"Call your office," the judge ordered imperiously.

"Sir, I have orders not to call my office."

"I must tell you, sir, that I have two federal marshals with me to enforce the writ. Please call your office so that there will be no unnecessary confrontation."

"I cannot, sir."

"Why not?"

"Standard procedure, sir. I must tell you that we fully intend to put this young woman on the airplane."

"And I must tell you that I have two federal marshals here to enforce this order." He brandished the legal document like it was a passport to heaven.

"Sir, they cannot apprehend us until we are found by the courts to be in contempt."

"Mr. Lawson?" He turned to the burlier of his two marshals.

"Yes, Judge. Sir, I am John Boniface Lawson, a United States marshal for the northern district of Illinois. I hereby serve this writ of habeas corpus, issued this day, by Judge Wilfred McCarthy."

"Sir, I decline to accept that order."

"What?" The marshal seemed astonished.

"That order ought properly to be served on our office and not here at the airport. I decline to accept it."

The TV cameras were all around us now.

"Your office has no right to limit where a federal writ might be served, young man," Judge Keenan took over. "You accept this order, or you will be in contempt of court."

"Sir, I respectfully decline."

"Mr. Lawson, serve the writ!"

The marshal jabbed the document at the INS official. He pulled back his hands and let it fall to the floor.

Impasse. What do we do now?

The kids closed in.

"Young man," Judge Keenan was terrifyingly stern. "I think you'd better call your office. Now."

The official looked around nervously and reached for a public phone on the wall. He searched his pockets for a quarter. Judge Keenan gave him a quarter.

Then, just as it looked like calm was about to tentatively rear its head, the situation suddenly turned ugly.

Or maybe comic—take your pick.

"This is the final boarding call for Northwest flight forty for Boston's Logan Airport and Shannon, Ireland. All aboard please."

The two agents, contemptuous of their boss's hesitation, jerked Brigid to her feet. So sudden was their movement that she fell forward and landed, facedown, on the boarding lounge floor, right in front of me.

Automatically, I reached down to help her up.

The burly agent swatted me. On what was now live TV.

I tumbled back over the row of seats, banged my head against a pillar, and slumped to the floor. Dazed and bewildered for a couple of seconds, I looked up into the grinning red light of a TV camera.

Later the agent would claim, after the police had arrested him on charges of assault and battery, that he had prevented me from interfering, pushed me perhaps because I was in the way.

As the videotape replays showed, however, he slugged me. Penalty stands. Fifteen yards for unnecessary roughness.

"That's the geek who hit me," I heard Jackie shriek. "And Father Mike!"

The Saint Ed's line blitzed.

"He's history!"

"Archive him!"

Dear God, now we have the riot. Make them cool it!

Then out of the dim mists and the steaming peat bogs of antiquity, there came a bone-chilling wail. Finn McCool's wolfhound Bran bounding to the attack—trailing the leash that she had yanked from the hands of the three sophomore apes who were restraining her.

Dear God, I thought again, as a vast canine shape swept by me, make them cool it.

Norah was new at the battle-charge swoop. Her leap was

effective enough but clumsy. She knocked the agent down, pinned him with her forepaws, opened her jaws so her teeth were a fraction of an inch from his throat, and draped her hind legs over my stomach.

Make them cool it, please!

"Cool it, everyone!" an imperious voice commanded.

Everyone cooled it.

"Norah, *no*!"

Norah removed her teeth from proximity of the agent's throat, looked at me stupidly, and wagged her tail.

God answered my prayers, you say?

Maybe, but through the voice of my New Priest.

The INS lawyer dropped the phone and stopped dialing.

"Release her!"

A loud cheer from our now peaceful demonstration.

I pulled Norah off the agent. She was still rumbling, ready to rip out his throat at a single word. She was also wagging her tail, ready to play if this were a big game.

Jamie helped me up off the floor. "You all right, Boss?"

"Only my dignity is offended." I found Norah's leash.

My head was whirling and I was unsteady on my feet.

"I *said* release her."

"Why?" The agent had stumbled away from us, a wary eye on the monster who had knocked him down, and dragged Brigid with him.

Norah roared, this time in dead earnest. I hung on to her leash.

"Down, Norah!"

She howled again.

"I'm giving the orders. Release her. I'll take the responsibility."

The New Priest guided me to a seat at the end of the row. The three sophs recaptured Norah who was still growling ominously.

"If the world would stop spinning, I'd go back and flatten that bastard."

"Shush, Father, there's TV all around. The police are about to arrest him anyway."

Brigid was unchained. She collapsed into Jeanne's arms. Peg O'Hara, chief of nursing at Saint Mary's in Yorkville, rushed to her side.

"Brigid! Brigid! Brigid!" cried our happy First Amendment crowd.

Still confused, her face smudged, her eyes red, her Limerick sweatshirt dingy, Brigid raised her hand in a victory sign and waved to the crowd.

They screamed in appreciation.

Norah, dragging her three retainers, stationed herself next to Cook and barked appreciatively, sure that the cheers were for her.

"Is she a rock star or something?" a woman who had just come upon the scene asked.

"A famous Irish cook," Jamie Keenan replied. "With her wolfhound."

"Do you have any final comment, Father McAuliffe?" A TV mike appeared in front of me.

Father Lar of the glass jaw, live at five.

"I'm happy that the INS has obeyed the court order. Ms. O'Shea is free because she had a fine attorney and the support of the parish at which she works and because she is white and Irish. I wonder how many other young women who are not so fortunate are brutalized every day in this land of the free and this nation of immigrants."

Not bad for someone who still saw at least three cameras for each one that was actually pointed at him.

"Jeanne and Brigid are driving back to the parish with Peg O'Hara." Jamie helped me out of the chair. "I'll drive you home in your car."

"I can drive myself," I protested.

"*Father*, I said I'll drive."

"Yes, Father," I said meekly.

It took us awhile to find my car because I had forgotten where I had parked it.

Snow was falling still, thick and heavy. My New Priest drove with confident assurance. The world inside my head began to clear.

"I suppose we'll hear complaints from the Chancery tomorrow, won't we, Father?"

"I doubt it. The Corpus Christi mob is on the side of immigrants because the Pope is. Joe Simon will take a pass on this one."

We left the airport area and were back on the expressways. Snowplows were lumbering through the gloom, spewing salt on the snow.

"Maybe," Jamie said, "school was the problem—although it will help us get her another visa."

"Huh?"

"Someone at school must have reported her. Certainly no one in the rectory or the parish could have done it."

"George."

"Mr. Wholey?"

"Sure. I assume that Padre Luís planted the idea in his head. This has George all over it."

"That's hard to believe, Father. He's been quiet lately. He's quite happy that I'm giving Anthony Mass server instructions. He's an appealing little kid."

"He won't let him be a server as long as there are girl servers on the altar with him."

"We can finesse that."

"You can depend on it. He denounced Brigid just like he denounced poor Mike Quinlan."

"Mike? Are you sure?"

I told him how I had tricked George into admitting his call to the Chancery about Mike Quinlan.

"They're dangerous people, Father. I can't dispute that any longer."

"George and his buddies?"

"No. The Corpus Christi priests. Father Louis and his colleagues."

"I can't figure out why Louis uses George Wholey. He's a shaky reed. I'm sure that Louis will drop him when he stops being useful, but I don't understand the risk."

"Oh, I think that's pretty clear now."

"What's the game?"

"Father Louis wants to get rid of you."

CHAPTER

41

I'm not in such good shape for praying, but I figured I ought to check with You.

My cold is worse, I have a fever, my head aches, and the environment still spins.

I can, however, think as clearly as ever.

Which might not be very clearly.

I've really had it out here. After I manage to organize myself, maybe after that vacation I had better take—I'm sure Jamie has made reservations for me in Barbados, so I can't plead that there are no vacancies down there—I'll write up a letter of resignation.

Maybe I've done a good job at Saint Finian's; six years is enough. My term is up this summer. I'll tell the personnel board that I am not applying for a renewal.

When professional athletes begin to go downhill, their re-flexes deteriorate. I have no reflexes.

Look at this afternoon. Jeanne finally worked up enough courage to talk about her love affair. I can't remember what I said. My reflexes are all wrong. I can't get my head straightened out about her, maybe because I'm emotionally involved. I'm sure there will be big trouble for her in the weeks ahead, as her past catches up and snuffs out the flames of the present. I'll be no damn good at helping her. I'll probably mess up, just like I've done so far.

That loony scene at O'Hare. How the hell did I permit that to happen?

All right, we saved one West-of-Ireland peasant from being shipped back, probably only for a few months. Still, we acted like she was being sent to Dachau. If my New Priest hadn't been cooler than I was and if that poor kid from the INS hadn't finally understood that we were all live at five, we could have had ourselves a nice riot.

Old priest in hospital after riot!

Wouldn't that look nice in tomorrow's *Sun-Times*?

I can't sleep, my appetite is gone, I'm no good to myself or the people here. It's time I get out.

Please help me!

CHAPTER

42

I was wrong about the Chancery.

A few days later, while the New Priest was preparing to leave for Steamboat Springs and his family's January ski bac-chanalia, John Price, the Cardinal's young secretary, called me.

"The Cardinal would like to see you tomorrow afternoon, Father. Would two-thirty at the Chancery be convenient?"

In the old days such a summons from a Cardinal would strike terror in the heart of the most innocent of priests.

The first and shattering question you would have asked yourself would have been, "What have I done wrong?"

These weren't the old days, and I knew what I'd done wrong.

"What does he want to see me about, Father?" I asked, keeping my voice cool and neutral.

"Just a little dialogue, Father. Nothing serious."

"Dialogue with a bishop means that you listen while he talks."

Even in these new days, John was not ready for such a reaction.

"I'm sure that it will be nothing like that, Father." He laughed nervously. "The Cardinal always listens."

I hesitated, tempted to say that if the Cardinal wanted to speak with me, he knew where I lived.

Not this time.

"Very well, John. I'll be there. Tell the Cardinal, if you would, that I am profoundly suspicious."

That would keep the Boss awake all night. Served him right for that sort of summons.

Jesus washed the feet of his followers, and the Cardinal sits down there like a Renaissance lord summoning his vassals to pay homage to him.

Although I had made up my mind that I was quitting when my term was up, I was not about to be forced out by their harassment.

I told the other priests at supper that night.

"Sounds like the star chamber," I concluded.

"Will they try to take the parish away from you?" the New Priest asked uncertainly. "They can't do that, can they?"

"Not without a lot more cause than they have. Don't worry, Jamie. That's not on the agenda. There's a shortage of pastors. They would have a hard time finding anyone sane who would risk coming out here after me if they sacked me. Besides, it would look bad in the papers."

"They'll try to slow you down." Mike Quinlan removed his thick glasses and began to polish them—a sure sign of anxiety.

Turk looked up from his soup. "Standard drill. The Boss, Joe Simon, Wayne Rogers, some auxiliary bishop, and John Price to jot down notes. The Boss needs that kind of crowd around him to build up his confidence when he wants to reprimand someone. I wish I could be there to listen."

"I'll make a tape. If John Price can make notes, I can record the conversation."

"If they don't let you?" Mike cocked an eye.

I spread my hands. "Then no conversation."

Brigid sortied in with the roast pork and a bright smile. She was still pale, but as cheerful as ever. Your Gaeltach peasant women are nothing if not resilient.

"Roast Pork County Kerry, Your Reverences," she announced.

"Doesn't it look like Roast Pork Dingle Bay to me?"

"Ah, sure, isn't Your Reverence still suffering from that knock on the head?"

Out she went, with a slight extra twist of her more than presentable rear end.

Mike shook his head in disbelief. "Indestructible."

" 'Tis how the race survived."

"The idea," Turk continued his analysis, "is to awe the victim. Years ago a Cardinal could do that by himself. Even a VG like George Casey or Clete O'Donnell. Now people treat Joey Simon like the shit he is, and they talk back to the Cardinal. So they assemble a solemn high team. The outnumbered defendant presumably succumbs."

"Father Lar won't," Jamie declared.

"What do they want?" Mike Quinlan was not eating his Roast Pork County Kerry.

Who would keep an eye on him while the New Priest was skiing in the Rockies?

"I'm sure it's connected with our happening up at O'Hare. I'm not sure about the angle. The Boss isn't like his predecessor—threatened every time some other priest besides himself pushed his face in front of a camera."

"Prudence." Turk attacked the roast pork. "They'll urge you to more prudence. All nice as pie, clip your wings a tad."

"Reef his sails." Jamie Keenan was not smiling.

"They may be talking to the wrong sailor," I said lightly.

I had made up my mind how I would react. I would make the meeting as difficult for them as I could. I would fight them every inch of the way. If one man gives in to such violations of human rights, it's easier for them to break the next man.

"I'm not leaving for Denver till tomorrow night," Jamie announced. "I'll change my reservations."

"Jamie, don't be ridiculous. This is nothing more than a minor episode in the ecclesiastical power game. No problem."

"I want to hear the tape."

"It'll probably be pretty tame stuff."

"Like you say, Boss, it's a long way from Jerusalem."

CHAPTER

43

I was ready for them.

I had been distracted in the morning by a drug bust at Forest Springs High School. FSHS was a superb school, one of the best in the country according to some of our parents who sent their kids to it instead of Saint Ed's or Mother Mary. "Look at all the National Merit Scholars they have."

To which I would invariably reply that Mother Mary and Saint Ed's together had more per capita. It was a useless argument against those affluent Catholics who thought their kids deserved something better than what they themselves had received from the Sisters or the Jesuits or the Christian Brothers.

It was no secret to anyone who interacted with teens that for all its academic excellence (and computer facilities, which were often cited by parishioners as reasons for choosing the public school), FSHS was a hotbed of drugs and kinky sexual experimentation.

You could maybe find pot to buy at Saint Ed's or Mother Mary if you were really interested. At FSHS cocaine and crack were so readily available that you had to fight off the pushers. School board, parents, and police looked the other way because the results of a drug bust were too appalling for the community to contemplate.

The week after Christmas four kids were banged up in an auto accident on the expressway ramp. An honest young cop found "traces" of crack in the car. The local police force covered it up. However, a resident who worked for the United States Attorney's Office heard about the case and, in what the community thought was an excess of zeal, sent in the feds for a sweep of the school the day before my appointment with the Cardinal.

Twenty kids were arrested on possession charges. Some of them sang about their sources—kids a year or two out of high school who owned formula boats and three or four foreign cars each—and these dealers were picked up.

Their parents were astonished. It never occurred to them that if their nineteen-year-old son owned a Mercedes, a Ferrari, and a Porsche, he might have an illegal income.

Those who had been dragged in for possession would get
off with probation or supervision. Five of the kids were ours.
Two of the families were not registered parishioners, so we
knew nothing about them. We knew the other three, but only
one family dragged their fourteen-year-old son over to the rectory the morning of my star chamber hearing.

Marty Regan was a little guy, still at the physical and emotional maturation level of a seventh grader. Like the other kids
who were swept up by the feds, he was an outsider and a loner,
barely known to the teenage establishment that hung out
around the rectory and the yard.

"Lynn Regan's little brother?" Lisa asked uncertainly when I
queried her about Marty.

"No, he's the oldest in the family."

"Never heard of him."

His parents were young, especially his mother, who, it soon
turned out, was in fact his stepmother. Both father and stepmother worked for a major Loop ad agency. His "real" mother
had walked out on his father for reasons that were not too clear.
That the father had custody of the son was possibly a signal of
something badly wrong with the mother.

John Regan took the offensive as soon as I walked into the
office: "Why aren't you doing more to protect the young people
of the parish from this sort of thing?"

He was an intense man with thick glasses, a high forehead,
and a squeaky voice. I felt that he was the kind of advertising
executive who drove himself to run at top speed every day
because he was afraid that such frantic activity was necessary
not to fall behind the other racers. He ran fast to stay in
place.

I listed our parish activities for teens, our drug education
program in the grammar school, Dr. Carlin's availability for
counseling one day a week.

"I think we're doing more than any other church in Forest Springs, John."

"My son isn't involved in any of those things."

"That's not our fault."

"Can't you force him to join?"

"We don't believe in force around here."

"Martin is so withdrawn," Jan, the sexy, pouting stepmother complained. "We can't interest him in anything except model airplanes."

"It is a phase some kids go through," I said.

Marty was sitting on the chair next to her, across the coffee table from me, physically present but a thousand miles away.

"You should do something special for the kids who go to public high schools," John insisted. "They're entitled to help from the Church, too."

"We have a full-time religious educator from the University of Wisconsin, Dr. Flavin, who offers classes and programs for them."

"Do you go to those classes, Martin?" Jan asked.

"Martin, answer your mother."

Martin glanced at his father, a look of intense loathing.

"Nah."

"Why not?" John demanded.

The answer was inaudible mumbles.

"What?"

"BORING."

His father turned to me. "Can't you do something to force this Dr. Flavin to make his courses more interesting?"

"Her courses. They're very popular with most of the kids. The evaluations are quite positive."

I was beginning to steam. This superannuated yuppie and his young wife had ignored Marty for years. Now they were trying to blame me for their own failures. Sure they felt guilty.

Sure they were looking for a scapegoat. Only the scapegoat wasn't going to be Saint Finian's.

"We can't hope to accomplish anything with our teen program unless parents are involved in some way."

John brushed off my suggestion. "We don't have time, we're both deeply involved in our professional careers."

"I see."

"Maybe we should send him to Campion."

Campion was a Jesuit high school in Wisconsin, famed for its successes with "hard case" kids in days of yore. Most of its success was the result of the fact that the kids got away from their families, which were the cause of their troubles.

"Campion closed years ago, John."

"Well, what does the Church do for kids who are screwed up like Martin?"

"It does what it can, especially when there is little parent interest or cooperation. It offers Catholic schools and parish activities."

"Saint Ed's is out of the question." He brushed that school off, too. "I want only the best for my son. Saint Ed's is strictly second-rate."

"Its test scores are higher than FSHS," I murmured.

"It doesn't have the facilities. I want my son to learn computers early in life. You can't succeed today without computer literacy."

"I think advanced courses in English may be more important. . . . Did you want to go to Saint Ed's, Marty?"

He shrugged indifferently. "Dunno."

I was part of the adult world that Marty spurned. He would no more talk to me than to his father, not at this age. In a couple of years, maybe.

"That's not open for discussion," John insisted. "I will *not* have my son studying under the brothers as I did. I'm still recovering from the bad effects they had on me." ,

"Look, John, the school and the parish are not in the babysitting business." I leaned forward to deliver my punch line. "We do our best for kids. We are not substitute parents. If you and Jan are too busy to have time for your son, don't try to shift responsibility to us. It may salve your conscience. It won't help him."

John began to sputter.

I held up my hand like a traffic cop.

"Wait till I'm finished. This may be an incident that will never be repeated, in which case Marty will be lucky and so will you. It may be the result of somewhat later maturation. A year from now you may have no problems at all. Or Marty may be in worse trouble. I have the following recommendations. One, computers or not, take him out of FSHS. Two, arrange for a good therapist. Three, find more time for him in your life. Four, treat him like a human being, not excess baggage. We'll try to help, particularly if you and Jan become more involved in the community and we can cooperate with you. If you don't want to do these things, then put him in a boarding school where there's lots of individual attention and he doesn't have to endure your indifference day in and day out. In any event, don't blame us for your failings."

Blunt talk. Tough love, if you wish.

And wasted energy. John Regan was so busy with his running in place that he did not have the time to think about what I had said.

He bounded to his feet. "If that's the way you feel, there's no point in wasting our time talking to you."

I shrugged. "If that's the way you feel, there's nothing we can do to help."

"I consider the conversation over," he sputtered and grabbed for his coat.

"Maybe Father is right, John. . . ." Jan held back, more clear-eyed than her husband. "Maybe we ought—"

"I *said* the conversation is over."

Jan tagged dubiously after him. Marty, hands jammed in his FSHS jacket, trudged along behind.

"Marty," I said softly.

He hesitated and turned half toward me.

"If you ever want to talk, come on over."

He grunted and turned away.

Maybe someday he would show up and maybe someday Jan would find—just as had Marty's mother—that she had married an impossible fool.

Compared with the tragedies in those four lives, the nonsense at the Chancery was insignificant. I sat in the office for a minute, half praying for the Regans. They were in God's hands now.

Well, now I was ready for the Cardinal and Joe Simon and their gang.

"Loaded for bear" might be an appropriate description of how I felt when John Price said, in the soft murmur that is required of the personal staff of a bishop, "The Cardinal will see you now, Father."

"The appointment was at two-thirty, was it not?" I glanced at my watch: 2:45.

The fifteen-minute wait was mandatory. It made the defendant squirm longer. Hence he was more ready for a "compromise" settlement—one in which the Cardinal gave the 5 percent he had been ready to give all along and the victim gave the other 95 percent.

What did they want? More "prudence"? That surely, probably something concrete. Even if it were easy to give them, I wouldn't yield. In spring they could have my resignation on my own terms and at my own time and not because they thought they could overawe me.

"The Cardinal has had a busy schedule today. He's running a little late."

"I suppose his time is more valuable than my time. He administers, I deal with the faithful."

John Price glanced at me quickly, almost as if he was looking forward to the battle he now saw looming. He opened the door and ushered me into the inner sanctum. The door did not creak as it did in the old radio horror show.

There were spooks inside, however, as Turk had predicted: the Cardinal seated at the middle of his broad oak desk (ten thousand dollars in the previous administration), Joe Simon on one side, the young Hispanic auxiliary on the other. Wayne Rogers sat at one end, and John Price at the other end. Everyone was relaxing in red leather chairs. Behind the Cardinal, windows revealed a less than spectacular landscape of Ontario Street on a late January afternoon.

"There's coffee and tea on the table, Lar." The Cardinal smiled, diffidently and appealingly as he always did. "Help yourself."

I ignored the offer.

"I had assumed this was to be a personal conversation, Your Eminence."

"I felt it proper to have a few of my staff present," his voice cracked, as it did when he was uneasy.

"I'm not sure I'm going to stay."

I fully intended to stay; we were playing a game and I was snatching the advantage away from them.

"This need not be adversarial, Lar." The Cardinal brushed back his long salt-and-pepper hair. "All I want is a friendly chat about matters of mutual interest."

"A friendly chat with the judges of the star chamber."

"Not at all, not at all," he said, chuckling uneasily. "Look around, Lar, there are no stars."

I glanced around. "Neither decorative nor human."

"Do please sit down. There's one or two matters. I'm sure we can work things out quite easily."

"This is the prisoner's dock?" I gestured at a single chair, leather like the others, black not red, across from the Cardinal's station behind his desk.

The young auxiliary, who had looked embarrassed, grinned at me. He hated himself for being here. No one ever told him that being a bishop's auxiliary demanded such dirty work.

"Please sit down, Lar"—the Cardinal was almost begging—"as a personal favor to me."

"I reserve the right to leave this trial"—I seated myself comfortably in the chair—"at any time that I deem appropriate."

"It's not a trial," Joe Simon snarled.

"The hell it's not."

The Cardinal had risen and was pouring me a cup of coffee. "Sugar or cream, Lar?"

I drink either coffee or tea.

"Tea, please, Your Eminence, black."

He replaced the coffee pot and poured a cup of tea—in china with his coat of arms on it.

"Now then"—he returned to his desk, carefully placed his own cup of coffee on a coaster (a steelworker's son from Pittsburgh would not want to ruin a ten-thousand-dollar desk) and leaned across the desk toward me—"we can begin."

I glanced at my watch. "By all means. . . . Incidentally, since Father Price is making notes, I propose to record this conversation."

I walked to the Cardinal's desk and placed my small Sony on it.

John Price lifted his notebook, waiting for a signal to close it.

"This is confidential, Lar." Wayne Rogers spoke for the first time. "Can't we be a group of brother priests who trust one another?"

"No," I said, "we can't."

"It's all right." The Cardinal raised his hands soothingly. "If Lar wants to record the conversation, that's all right with me."

I had forced them all off base. Good on me, as the Aussies would say. What a disgraceful waste of time and energy for men who were supposed to be preaching God's love.

"Well," the Boss began again, "that was quite a show you had out at O'Hare the other day."

"I'm glad you liked it."

"We've had complaints." Joe Simon spat out the words. "Lots of complaints."

"How many?"

"Plenty."

"Your Eminence, I've had quite enough of Father Simon on the subject of complaints. Either you tell me exactly how many calls you received because of the incident at the airport or I'm leaving."

There was deathly silence in the room. Someone had dared to call the bluff.

"John?"

Price looked up from his notebook, expression impassive, eyes twinkling. "Five, Cardinal."

"How many anonymous?" I demanded.

"Three of them."

I could not believe it. Five calls were "plenty"?

"With respect, Your Eminence, are you telling me that we are consuming the time of these busy and important men and my less important time because of five calls of complaint? Again with respect, Your Eminence, if this fact were known, the archdiocese would be a laughingstock."

"Those people have a right to be heard," he said mildly, "don't they?"

"How many calls does it take to convene a meeting like this? Two? Three?"

"We believe every Catholic is entitled to have his complaints taken seriously," Joe Simon shouted at me.

Joe was defending his boss, just like Jamie Keenan would defend me.

"No, you don't believe that, Joe. Only the right-wing cranks have the right to be heard in the Church today. You don't pay any attention to the liberal protesters."

"Quite apart from the issue of calls"—the Cardinal rubbed the desk with the palm of his hands as if to soothe the conversation—"there is also the fact that the Holy See is easily upset these days by involvement of priests in civil disobedience."

Aha, that was it! This meeting was to anticipate a complaint from Rome. So!

"The civil disobedience at O'Hare, Your Eminence, was by the agents of the INS. I was there as Ms. O'Shea's employer."

"All those kids . . ." Wayne Rogers never liked anyone under thirty, not even when he was under thirty himself.

"I assume they were exercising their constitutionally guaranteed rights to peaceful assembly."

"They were *your* kids."

"I don't have any kids, Wayne . . . none that I know about anyway."

The Cardinal blushed at that indelicacy.

Joe Simon took over. "Those bruisers were from your parish?"

"You mean the young men with the silver and blue jackets, Joe? The ones with the *E* on the jacket? They're from Saint Ed's high school. Maybe you should talk to Brother Mark about them."

"Pretty big kids."

"Not fat anyway, Joe."

I was having the time of my life—probably too much fun.

"There was an altercation, was there not?" The Cardinal's patience, unlike mine and unlike Joe's, was inexhaustible.

"I have a hard time remembering, Your Eminence. I was knocked down by an INS agent and hit my head against a post. The police later arrested him."

"That monster dog . . ." Joe grimaced as though Norah's teeth were next to his throat—not a bad idea, come to think of it. "Attacking a government agent."

"Norah?" I feigned astonishment. "She's a cupcake. She was defending her parish priest. When we breed her, I'd be willing to sell her puppies to other pastors. You won't have any of them killed by muggers stealing the Sunday—"

"It looks bad, Lar," Wayne interrupted me, "for a priest to be knocked down on TV, not a good example to the poor simple faithful."

"It didn't feel all that good, Wayne. I was humiliated. If he hadn't caught me off guard, I would have knocked him down. That would have pleased the faithful—a priest defending a young woman from violence."

"You don't seem to understand, Lar." There was the faintest trace of exasperation in the Boss's gentle voice.

"I admit that, Your Eminence. I was vindicating the rights of the Church, action for which I ought to be praised. I can't see why that doesn't delight you."

"The rights of the Church!" Joe Simon sputtered. "What the hell are you talking about?"

"The government invades a rectory, abducts an employee of the Church, assaults a priest and another employee, incarcerates the abductee with hardened criminals, and then tries to deport her illegally. Do you want that sort of thing to happen in every parish of the archdiocese? We nipped such violations of the rights of the Church in the bud. I am entitled to gratitude, not reprimand."

No one had thought of that aspect of the case.

Fools.

The auxiliary had closed his eyes and drawn his lips in a

tight line—to control laughter. John Price, who either had no ambitions or was secure in his role, was openly grinning.

"The young woman's lawyer is the father of your assistant"—Joe Simon shifted his notes—"isn't he?"

"We call them associate pastors nowadays, Joe. To your question, yes, Judge Keenan is Father Keenan's father. And Monsignor Keenan's brother. I'm surprised you didn't drag Monsignor down for this hearing."

"Don't you think that a little odd?"

"What is a little odd?"

"That the associate pastor's father would act as the young woman's lawyer."

"Father Keenan returned to the rectory shortly after the invasion. To paraphrase the late, great mayor, what kind of a son would it be who wouldn't call his father when he needed legal advice."

"Who's paying him?"

"The issue has not arisen. The Keenans are not poor, Joe."

"The woman *was* an illegal, wasn't she?" Joe was now so red in the face as to seem on the verge of apoplexy.

"What can I tell you? She's a hell of good cook, Joe. The court seemed to think that there were no grounds for summary deportation. How many other parish workers around the city might be in trouble with the INS if your friends in Corpus Christi start to denounce them? I'm sure you're aware that the man who reported Brigid O'Shea is the same person who has denounced my associate pastor's brilliant homilies and my resident's single fall off the wagon and persuaded Rome that the marriage of his twenty-two-year-old daughter was the rape and abduction of a sixteen-year-old virgin."

"We're aware of his involvement in this incident," Joe snarled. "He's no friend of ours."

Aha, Jamie, there's your proof!

"He's also the man who leads a group of people into our

Sunday Liturgies and points tape recorders at us. Frankly, Your Eminence, I am astonished that you'd take such people seriously. There must not be any serious problems in the archdiocese—finances, Hispanics, vocations."

"Please, Lar." The Cardinal sighed. "Can we stay on the track?"

"I am staying on the track. This fretfulness over crank complaints would be merely comic if the Church were not dead in the water and drifting. Surely you have better things to do with your time."

It was now to be a dialogue between the two of us. Good, that's what it should have been all along—two priests, one of whom happened to be president of the presbyterate.

"What would you do if you were in my position, Lar?" He raised his voice. "What would you do?"

"I'd spend all my time working on the problem of the morale of priests. The priesthood is a shambles. Morale is in the lower depths. You should be encouraging and reassuring your priests. Instead, you hassle them because of right-wing nuts."

"Lar, Lar, Lar." He shook his head sadly. "Be nice to me. When I die, they'll send a son of a bitch and you'll have to work with him."

"The hell I will. . . . And if I were you and I thought that, I'd quit!"

John Price was no longer grinning. We were playing hardball now.

"Sometimes," the Cardinal said with a sigh, "I think you're right. If you were sitting in my chair—"

I was wound up now, far more than I ought to have been. I was becoming indiscreet, and I didn't care.

"If I were Cardinal Archbishop of Chicago, I'd throw the Corpus Christi goons out of town and tell the Romans who harass me on the phone to fuck off."

More dead silence.

The Cardinal bowed his head.

"Don't think I wouldn't like to do that. However, there are other goods at stake. . . . In any event, let's try to stay on the subject at hand. That young woman is quite attractive, is she not?"

"Ms. O'Shea? Even more attractive when she hasn't spent a night in a bullpen with drug addicts and prostitutes. . . . I didn't think Cardinals noticed such things."

"We notice." He smiled briefly.

"We hired her to cook, Your Eminence."

"Some people think she's too attractive to work in a rectory."

"They're prudes and hypocrites."

"It was noticed," he continued, his eyes lowered, "that you were, ah, affectionate with her and that you reacted quickly when she fell to the floor."

"I tried to help her up when she was knocked down. That's what a gentleman does."

"Do you think that's appropriate for a priest?" Wayne Rogers rejoined the discussion.

"To help a woman up when she's been knocked down—or rather, in this case, to attempt to do so? Yes, Wayne, I think it's appropriate."

"Are you sleeping with her?" Joe Simon erupted. "People say you are."

"Dear God in heaven, Joe. You may well be the greatest asshole in the history of the priesthood."

"Gentlemen, gentlemen!" the Boss pleaded. "Please, please, let us not be abrasive." Then to me: "There is that problem, Lar."

"There are many, many women, Your Eminence, with whom I might like to make love. Not a twenty-three-year-old Irish-speaking peasant girl from Slea Head, however lovely she may be. Give me credit for good taste if not virtue."

They had not noticed Jeanne Flavin in the TV shots. Dummies. Or maybe only crude imaginations. Jeanne's appeal would elude them.

"I'm prepared to take your word for it." The Cardinal sighed heavily. "More than that, I would not credit such a rumor to begin with."

"Nonetheless, you'd call me down here to ask me? All right, Your Eminence, we've played our little game. Now what is it you want me to do?"

He shuffled his feet beneath the desk.

"Surely you do not plan to continue action against the government agents."

"I can't speak for parents of the young woman he knocked to the floor of the rectory. I presume the actions in which the parish is directly involved will remain pending until the question of Ms. O'Shea's status is favorably resolved."

"Don't you think it would be better, Lar, if she were permitted to return home to Ireland?"

So that was it. They wanted to deport Cook.

"Your parents were immigrants from Galicia, Cardinal. How can you say something like that?"

My head was throbbing again, my sinuses were blocked up, and I was feeling dizzy.

"We're worried about public controversy, Lar." Joe Simon's color had reverted to crimson from purple. "Can't you see that? And the scandal that would result. Even if what people think is not true, the problem is that they think it."

"It really would be much better," the Cardinal continued, "to drop this whole matter quietly."

"I see."

All right, we were almost at the bottom line.

"Or if you're not ready to let the government send her home, then at least you might discharge her, perhaps recommend her to another rectory."

"I understand."

"I'm glad you do." He sighed with relief.

"The answer is no."

"I beg your pardon?"

"I said no. I won't do it. You're wasting your time. You must have known that you would be wasting your time."

"You will not compromise with us?"

"I will not drop my support for Ms. O'Shea, and I will not fire her. If you don't like that, you can replace me with a pastor who will."

The Boss waved his hand. "There is absolutely no question of that, Lar. You're too valuable to the parish and to the Church to even consider that. Our hope was that you would see your way clear to reach some sort of accommodation with us."

"Is it because she's Irish, Cardinal? You and the other bishops have told the world that you're on the side of the poor, though that apparently doesn't include your own school teachers. God knows Brigid O'Shea is poor. You have personally embraced that nasty little Leninist Daniel Ortega when you visited him in Managua and broken bread with him when he came to Chicago. Is it only the Irish whose oppression you are willing to tolerate?"

That was gratuitous and totally unnecessary. It was, however, clever.

"You know that's not true," he fired back hotly.

So I had found the end of his patience after all.

"I don't know anything about you anymore, Your Eminence. Let me make another suggestion: why don't you appoint Father Louis what's-his-name. . . ."

"Almaviva," the auxiliary bishop spoke for the first time.

"No kidding!" I threw back my head and laughed. I was so manic by then I almost broke into an aria from the fourth act of *La Nozze*. "Anyway, send the count to Saint Finian's as pastor. He wants to get rid of me and control the parish himself.

So give him the place. You won't hear any more complaints from the right-wing nuts or from Rome. You might hear a lot from other people, but they don't count, do they?"

"Be serious, Lar," Wayne Rogers pleaded. "This is not a farce."

"No, Wayne," I rose and recaptured my Sony, "it's not a farce. It turns out that it's a comic opera. By Mozart. In any event, gentlemen, Your Eminence, Your Excellency," I bowed to each of them, "Reverend Fathers, read my lips: FUCK OFF!!"

At the door I turned. They were staring at me in consternation.

"One more thing." I jabbed my finger at the Cardinal. "You betrayed me today. You brought me here under false pretenses. I won't come the next time, no matter who phones me. If you want to see me ever again, you know where I live. You come to my turf"—I waved a finger deleting the rest of the court— "ALONE!"

I felt fine till I walked out onto Ontario Street. The sun had finally reappeared, after a couple of weeks' absence. The sky was crystal blue, the snow and ice were melting; Ma Nature, deceitful bitch that she is in middle western America, was making one of her periodic deceptive promises of spring.

Then I felt sick. All right, I had routed a group of fools. Ducks in a shooting gallery. Nowadays you told off Cardinals. Big fucking deal. You even beat them at their own stupid game. So what difference did it make?

It was not a game that grown men should be playing, particularly not priests. The Church was falling apart. This was the decline and fall. We had fiddled inside while Rome burned.

I was the worst asshole of all for being proud that I could play my fiddle louder than anyone else.

Big fucking deal.

I walked slowly down to Michigan Avenue: the Magnificent Mile was glistening in the newly rediscovered sunlight.

Telling off superiors is a kick the first time you do it. After that, it's BORING!

Stupid, stupid, stupid game.

Slowly and wearily, oblivious to the sunlight and the vitality of the Magnificent Mile, I walked back to the station. My head ached, my fever had somehow returned, I felt rotten.

Worst of all, my heart was sad.

For a wasted life.

CHAPTER

44

The other priests loved the tape.

Mike and Turk applauded. Jamie laughed. I felt like an even worse asshole than when the actual scene had occurred. Silver-haired comic from the suburbs, putting down all the ducks in the gallery.

Jamie did exclaim, *"Father!"* when I told the assembled crowd to fuck off.

The other two applauded.

"They'll leave you alone." Turk nodded approvingly. "They found out for sure what they must have expected before: you can't be bluffed."

"The Boss won't sleep for a week," Mike agreed.

"Poor man, I've been there."

"I'll admit that I'm shocked." Jamie refilled my drink and Turk's and put another can of Diet Pepsi next to Mike. "Faith doesn't depend on the virtue and intelligence of leaders, but they're really as pathetic, Father, as you've told me. One doesn't despise them so much as feel sorry for them."

"You noted that my surmise about the source of Biddy's troubles was correct."

"Your surmises"—he grinned happily—"are always correct. By the way, Anthony Wholey is almost finished with his Mass server training. I've been giving him special instructions. Would you run him through his final exam while I'm away? The poor kid doesn't have much going for him. Maybe we can do something to help him."

"Sure."

In our tradition the sins of the fathers are not held against the sons.

Jamie sure was correct about one thing: Anthony didn't have much of a chance.

"So," Mike said, grinning genially, "it's safe to leave Chicago for a few days. The old pastor can take care of himself?"

"In spades. And, Father, if you get in more trouble, don't call me. I'll be out on the slopes."

When I did get in more trouble two weeks later, I didn't call him. He found out anyway.

Later in the evening, when Jamie had left for O'Hare, Mike ducked into my room, polishing his glasses.

"The kid is a wonder, Lar. Absolute wonder. The parish, the priesthood, the Church are all lucky to have him."

"So, to tell the truth, is the pastor."

"I'm worried just the same."

"Worried? About Jamie?"

"As I said the night he showed up, he's an innocent."

"His mother said the same thing."

"Those guys found out today that they can't get you. They'll figure out that you like Jamie. Mark my words, they'll go after him."

"Go after Jamie? They should know by now that the Keenans

are tough and powerful people. They won't pick a fight with Packy. By their standards he's a worse sumbitch than I am."

"Joe Simon's a sociopath. Don't argue with me that he's just trying to do his job. The man has no conscience. He never has had one. For someone like him, the Keenans don't mean shit."

"Why should he bother?"

"Because Joe's insecure in his job. He'd be insecure regardless; they've made a lot of mistakes down there lately. The Cardinal likes you. That's obvious. He knows that there's no bullshit in you. He tells people how honest you are, abrasively honest are his exact words. Simon hears that and worries that you might be his successor."

"Joe doesn't think in those terms."

"He may not admit to himself that he's worried about his job. But it's in Joe's nature to be threatened by anyone who might be a rival."

"That's crazy. I'd never accept the job even if the Cardinal offered it to me, and the Cardinal damn well understands that."

"Absolutely. Yet if you see the world through Joe Simon's eyes, it might seem that Laurence McAuliffe is a serious threat. He didn't want you on the finance committee, and the Cardinal put you on anyway. So Joe tricked you into quitting."

"I didn't belong on that committee. They had made up their minds not to hear what I said."

"Regardless. Your presence there scared Joe—it's all true, Lar. As ever my sources are good."

"I don't doubt that, but I still can't believe it."

"Mark my words, Lar: before the winter is over, they will go after the kid. And it will be a bloody mess."

45

The next disaster also occurred when I was away from the rectory: Coady Anne Condon overdosed herself again.

It was a Saturday, one of the endless string of grimy Saturdays that are part of a Chicago winter. The New Priest had been away a week. After the first forty-eight hours I stopped telling myself that I didn't need him. He had made himself indispensable.

Nonetheless, I felt better despite the need to run at breakneck speed to keep up with all of Jamie's projects. My fever vanished and my cold diminished to a sniffle. I was sleeping at night.

There were no major crises the first week. Cook was singing happily in the kitchen and dating a different black-bearded Irish warrior every Saturday night (the young men didn't carry clubs and didn't come accompanied by their own wolfhounds, but you found yourself looking for both). Jeanne still glowed. ("Totally awesome," according to her patrons.) Anthony Wholey passed his Mass server test easily—he was a shy, vulnerable, but very appealing kid: perfect candidate for neurosis. His father's crowd now covered all the five Liturgies with tape recorders. I practiced on the word processor to prepare by myself the Sunday issue of *The Bells*—with substantial help from the porter persons and other authoritarian personalities. I saw nothing of the Sullivans or Patrick McNally, save in company with Patti O'Hara.

A lawyer, claiming to represent Dr. P. Scott McNally, had written a bland letter expressing his client's concern about attempts to "lure" his son into the Catholic priesthood. It ended with a warning that legal actions might be taken at some subsequent date to seek relief from such attempts.

It looked weak; a lawyer with whom I checked said that I should forget about it. Clearly the McNally lawyer had written to calm down an irate but erratic client.

"Doc McNally is so light," my lawyer said, "that you need three paperweights to hold him down when he's not in the operating room."

So I kept busy all week. By Saturday morning, however, I hadn't made a single hospital call. In a week at the end of January, the cards from the various hospitals pile up on your desk. It wasn't like the old days when all your people were in one or two hospitals. Now they were scattered around the whole metropolitan area, some in FSCH or Saint Mary's of Yorkville, but a lot way over on the other side of Chicago at the various university medical centers—Illinois, Northwestern, Chicago.

I gathered the stack of postcards, jammed them in my coat pocket, and walked down to Mike Quinlan's room.

"I'm off to visit hospitals, maybe four or five hours. No young priest to do the work this week. Would you mind?"

Mike looked up from the French theology book he was reading. "Be my guest. Delighted to help."

Maybe he didn't need Jamie's constant attention to survive. He seemed to be doing quite well on his own.

It was a long five hours. The hospital patients ran the full range of the human condition from mothers with their firstborn children to lonely and frightened elderly people in terminal cancer.

I was tired when I finally parked in front of the rectory, tired but content with having done a difficult job reasonably well. Maybe it was too early to retire after all.

Mike was waiting for me in the rectory office.

"Bad news, I'm afraid, Lar." His fingers were trembling. "Very bad news. A girl killed herself this afternoon."

"Coady Anne Condon?" I sank into a chair.

"Right." He nodded sadly. "An overdose of her mother's phenobarbital. Call for help that they didn't hear in time."

I felt horrible guilt. Why hadn't I insisted more sternly on therapy?

"Dear God!"

"Apparently she phoned another girl, a kind of mentor, and said she wanted to talk. The other kid was delayed, then came over to pick her up. There was no answer, so the other girl went away. Then she became uneasy and returned. She climbed up a window, saw the little tyke's body, broke the window, and called the fire department. It was much too late."

"Patti O'Hara," I muttered automatically.

"She called me, too. I went right over. Got there after the dead girl's parents. The father was hysterical. The mother seems to be a cold bitch. Maybe it's her way of dealing with grief."

"Maybe."

"The other child is most distraught. Blames herself. If-she'd-been-there-earlier sort of thing."

"Probably true, but irrelevant."

"She seems to be a healthy young woman. I'm sure she will be all right. Kids outgrow these tragedies. To make matters worse, I've just had a call from a distraught father of yet another child. Apparently some of the elderly nuns over at Mother Mary High School have been telling the young women that the tyke has gone straight to hell."

"Glory be to God!"

"The parents are worried about a suicide epidemic, like the ones they see discussed on TV. I assume that we will want to preach on this tomorrow."

"Sure, indirectly. God's mercy and love. The best way to launch an epidemic is to warn people about it."

"Sorry I couldn't do more, Lar."

"More? You did everything I could have done and probably better because you didn't lose your temper."

"She seemed such a sweet little thing, so pathetic, dressed up in some kind of prom dress."

"Dear God!" I had held that pathetic little frame in my arms a few weeks ago and assured her that God loved her.

Did He really?

Of course He did!

Then why?

To that question there were never any answers.

"The Forest Springs police chief was especially difficult, I fear. Gave the young O'Hara woman a hard time for not calling him and for illegal entry to the house."

"He would," I said grimly.

"Shall we call the young priest? I know your rule on vacations and I agree with it. Still . . ."

"There's nothing he can do now, Mike. If the situation deteriorates, I might change my mind. Had Patti O'Hara gone home when you left?"

"Just. The police chief seemed to want to hold her for questioning; her mother, who is a nurse, I believe, appeared and suitably routed him."

My first stop would be the O'Hara house. Let the dead bury their dead. First we must minister to live cupcakes.

She was sitting on the couch crying softly, her brother Desmond on one side and the ever-present Patrick McNally on the other, both holding her hands. Her mother and her father, Nick (a razor-sharp accountant) were watching carefully from nearby chairs. Mother and younger sister promptly departed when I arrived, "to make the priest a cup of tea."

"Now you listen to me, Patti O'Hara." I captured one hand

from her brother and the other from Patrick. "Don't blame yourself."

"If I had come on time," she continued to cry, "I was hung up in a conversation at Dunkin Donuts. It was sooo unimportant."

"It's not your fault."

"Or if I had climbed the window the first time—she was probably still alive then."

Both these statements were undoubtedly true, and irrelevant.

"Patti O'Hara, I said listen to your parish priest. Understand?"

"Yes, Father Lar." She stopped crying and looked up at me.

"What did I tell you when I asked you to keep an eye on Coady Anne?"

"You said I shouldn't blame myself if I couldn't help her, but, FATHER, I could have helped her!"

"I can blame myself for not telling you that Coady Anne had tried this two weeks ago. If I had told you that, you would have gone to her house on time, right? So I'm more to blame than you are, right?"

She considered that carefully. "No, Father, of course not."

I heard Peg O'Hara, back with cookies and waiting for the tea to come, sigh with relief.

"I was pretty sure she would try it again, but I didn't think it would be this soon. So I'm more to blame than you because I was so dumb."

"You're not dumb, Father Lar." She began to dry her eyes.

"We all could have done more for her. We did the best we knew. Coady Anne needed help, she wanted help, her mom and dad really didn't understand, she asked for help again and took too big a chance. None of us put the pills in her mouth, Patti O'Hara, and none of us decided that she didn't need a psychiatrist."

I heard a gasp behind me. Peg O'Hara, astonished at the Condons.

The story would spread through the parish like a prairie fire in days of old. I felt sorry for the Condons. Yet the truth must be told to protect Coady Anne's reputation and to lift the fear and the guilt and the potential for more self-destruction from the rest of the young people.

"Father Lar is right." Patrick McNally put his arm around her. "He always is."

Patti buried her head against her equerry's chest. "You're just saying that because you're going to be a priest, too."

Relieved laughter from all. The tea was brought on, and I drank a cup.

Ate five cookies, too.

Our High Club president was truly a cupcake. She did not, however, have strong guilt needs. She'd live with the pain for a while and then recover. As long as she lived, however, she would pray for Coady Anne.

Her parents escorted me to the door. "You came here first, didn't you, Father?" Nick asked with a quick smile.

"The living need help more than the dead."

"Was the first suicide try a phenobarbital overdose too?" Peg was examining my face closely.

"Yes, Peg, it was."

"So the bottle was left in the house, easily available for a second try?"

"I assume so."

"Father, that's murder!"

"Not legally."

"But morally!"

I hesitated.

"It's not up to us to judge, Peg."

"But, Father—"

"We can't prove anything. I'm sure the police will wonder, too. They'll also know that they can't do anything. It won't help at all if our suspicions spread around the parish."

"Most people will think it odd, Father. Probably deep down they'll be suspicious. They won't say anything."

"You're right, Peg. Most of the kids won't suspect."

The shrewder ones probably would, but they too would remain silent.

My next stop was at the Condons. It was a waste of time. Joe clung to my hand and wept continuously. Through his tears he muttered repeatedly, "Why? Why? Why?"

The answer was that he, damn fool, hadn't insisted on therapy for the poor kid.

Coady Anne's older brothers and sisters were dashing back and forth, answering the phone, tending to their mother, ignoring their father. The young women were crying. The faces of the young men were twisted in grief. Martina was sitting upright, lips tight, face drawn, eyes hard and dry.

"Oh, thank you so much for coming, Father. It's good of you. Father Quinlan was simply wonderful."

"My deepest sympathies, Martina."

"We all saw it coming, didn't we, Father? I suppose that there's often problems like this with the youngest. We don't mean to but we spoil them. They must have everything their way, and when they don't, they act out, isn't that true?"

"Yes, it is."

Although I wanted to ask her why her prescription pills were left so accessible, I choked off the words in my throat. God should judge, not the parish priest.

"She was such a willful, stubborn child. In a way this may be a blessing in disguise. She would have never learned to be unselfish, don't you agree, Father?"

"I loved her," I said hoarsely.

"We loved her, too, poor little thing. You were so nice to her over at the hospital that day. She was determined to do what she did, and she finally punished us all, didn't she?"

"We'll miss her," I said and bowed myself away from Martina.

I talked a bit to the rest of them, trying to make reassuring noises.

"Why, Padre? Why?" Joe asked once more, as I shook his hand in farewell. "Why did she do it?"

"She was looking for help, Joe. She really didn't mean to kill herself."

"We gave her all the help any two parents could give, Padre."

"I'm sure."

I got the hell out of that house of death.

Would Joe live the rest of his life in the self-deception that they had done all they could?

How else could he live?

Back at the rectory I made phone calls: to Sister Connery at Mother Mary to tell her to shut up the elderly nuns and their talk of hellfire; to Brother Mark at Saint Ed's to tell him to make sure that the young man who had invited Coady Anne to the school dance was watched and consoled; to Linda to ask that she and Brendan visit the teen hangouts that night— Dunkin Donuts, White Castle, Taco Bell—and check the state of morale; to Jeanne to keep the networks open to all her religious education students.

I put down the phone from the last call and discovered Jackie standing at the doorway.

"She's not in hell, is she, Father?"

"Certainly not, Jackie. God loves us all."

"Why did he take her then?"

"I don't know, Jackie."

"Her mother really hated her. You could tell."

"That's not up to us to judge, Jackie."

"Is it true that it happened before?"

News traveled rapidly didn't it.

"Yes, Jackie. I saw her over at the hospital."

"Maybe she wouldn't have had a happy life, would she, Father? I mean with that geeky mother?"

"We'd better leave those questions to God, young lady."

"Yes, Father."

Still frowning thoughtfully, Jackie went back to her office.

If we could keep all the kids alive through another week, the worst would be over.

Should I call Jamie?

Instead, I called Jeanne again. No answer. I waited a half hour and called the number at her apartment.

"Jeanne? Lar. I need an opinion. Call the young priest back?"

She hesitated. Was Don there?

So what if he was. None of my damn business.

"We don't need him yet, Lar."

"Let's stay in touch on it."

"I'll work out a Liturgy for your approval."

"I'm sure I'll make all kinds of changes."

We both laughed.

Don was there all right, perhaps in bed with her. No, certainly in bed with her. On Saturday afternoon. Well, more power to both of them.

The "straight to hell" interpretation rampaged around the parish Saturday night and all day Sunday, despite our homilies, and despite the best efforts of the high school authorities.

There were, thank God, no more deaths.

Turk volunteered to hear confessions Saturday night, such as they are in these days of birth control and no confessions (as opposed to the old days of no birth control and lots of confessions). Mike and I were free to deal with the processions of worried parents and kids.

By themselves the kids were easy. They talked out their guilt and circled around the frightful reality of death, which until that afternoon seemed so distant in the future. It would be distant again for most of them in a few more days.

The parents who dragged their kids in, however, were terrified that suicide might strike in their home next. They wanted me to condemn Coady and tell their kids that what she had done was a heinous sin. Unable to scare their kids, they wanted their clergy to do the scaring for them.

What good is it having priests around if they can't put the fear of God or the fear of hellfire in the hearts of your kids when you want them to?

"Tell Sandi that if she does what that little Condon girl did, she'll go right to hell."

"Sandi, do you believe Coady Anne went straight to hell?"

"I don't know, Father Lar. She was a nice girl. I'm sure God loves her."

"What she did was sinful, wasn't it, Father? Tell Sandi that."

"What do you think, Sandi?"

"I think she was scared and was looking for help. It was pretty geeky, you know, Father. We'll miss her, and I feel sorry for her."

"Do you feel it's wrong to kill yourself, Sandi?"

Long pause while the sophomore girl pondered.

"Not if you don't think it is. You can't commit a sin if you don't think it a sin, can you?"

"Tell her it's a sin, Father."

Bottom-line question:

Parish Priest: "Would you ever do what Coady Anne did?"

Sandi: "ME, Father? Barf city! FERSURE!"

So it went; some parents were more satisfied with my response than others. All of them worried—most of them needlessly (like Sandi's parents), some of them foolishly.

And a few of them not without reason. Like Martina Condon, these last were not ready to take the right steps.

The wake began on Sunday afternoon after Mass. It was a disaster area—baffled parents, grief-stricken kids, anxious nuns and priests. I stationed myself at Collins Funeral Home (the Catholic funeral home in Forest Springs) all day, both Sunday and Monday. Mike and Turk were there most of the time, too. So were Jeanne and Linda (with her Brendan in tow). And Patti O'Hara and her Patrick.

"Young man, we should put you on the payroll."

"I'd like that, Father. Oh, by the way, I guess my father had a lawyer write a letter to you. I hope you didn't worry about it."

"It was a harmless letter, Patrick."

"Poor Dad." He shook his head sympathetically. "It's just like him. He comes home from the hospital, shouts about something, makes silly threats that he'll never carry out, and then goes back to his patients. Forget the letter, Father."

"You're still going to Niles next year."

"You bet your life I am. After the way I saw you turn Her Ladyship around yesterday, I KNOW I want to be a priest."

"She's a cupcake, Patrick!"

"YOU BET!"

I hope God is as forgiving of my faults as Patrick McNally.

We managed to control most of the guilt and the panic on Sunday. There were, as Jackie would have said, "tons of tearful parents," not so much mourning Coady Anne as frightened that they would be the next target.

In Monday morning's newspaper there was a long article headlined:

SUICIDE IN PARADISE

The self-destruction of a young woman in the affluent suburb of Forest Springs over the weekend proves once again that you cannot buy immunity from the human condition. Nor does affluence prevent your children from acting out their hostilities.

The article, heavy with flights of purple prose to call attention to the author's literary excellence, was an attack on suburban life, on teenagers, and on Forest Springs. Pretending to be a defense of parents against their children, it also ridiculed parental ignorance, greed, and psychological naïveté. Coady Anne was depicted as a selfish little monster.

The author, a sometime priest turned sociologist, had, as far as I know, never visited Forest Springs and certainly had never met Coady Anne.

He had never been known, however, to miss a chance for self-promotion.

Martina believed it was a wonderful article. "Isn't it amazing, Father, how well that priest understood everything?"

Predictably no one else liked it. The fears and the guilts were rekindled and to them were added rage.

In midafternoon when the young people were filing in after school, I noted that Cook, in a dark gray business suit, hair swept up on her head, had joined the damage-control team to keep the crisis from getting worse. Repaying her debts to the crowd that had exercised its constitutional right to free assembly in her behalf, she was chatting forcefully and yet quietly with a group of teens. She looked every inch the professional. I wondered if she was still trying to disguise her brogue, an effort I had caught her making lately and had strictly forbidden.

I hurried back to the rectory for a quick supper on Monday. Cook had beaten me back.

"So you were helping out this afternoon?"

"Ah, sure, don't I owe those young people something in return?"

"You're not trying to talk like a yank, now are you?"

"Would it be after doing any good at all?"

While I was wolfing down a roast beef sandwich (à la Lake Kilarney, she told me), Cook swept into the dining room and cried, "The young priest is on the phone, Your Reverence!"

"Boss? Jamie. Sorry to interrupt your supper. Cook gave me hell."

"You're imitating my phone style."

"Highest form of flattery. . . . Is there something wrong in the parish?"

"What would be wrong?"

Long hesitation.

"Is Coady Anne dead?"

"I guess someone got to you. Yes, she did another overdose."

"When?" His voice was flat, dull.

"Saturday afternoon. I saw no reason to ruin your vacation."

"No problem. You did the right thing. If you don't mind, I'll catch an early plane, come to the funeral, and then fly back here. Is that OK?"

What the hell was happening?

"Certainly. Give my best to your clan."

"I will, Father. Thanks. . . . Are the other kids all right?"

"Patti O'Hara found the body. She was badly shaken, she's bounded back reasonably well."

"I see. Thanks much, Father."

When I returned from the funeral home that night, dead tired and profoundly discouraged about life, priesthood, and God, the parish parking lot was filled with cars. Lights in all the windows of the school, the hall, and the parish center glistened on the dusting of new snow, which glowed like a casual scattering of diamonds.

What was happening? Had I missed something special? A Confirmation that had slipped my mind?

Then I realized that the parking lot was crowded and illumined by lights from the buildings that ringed it every night of the week. No matter who had died, the committees, programs, projects, organizations, classes, and planning groups that constitute the complete suburban parish went on. Doubtless many of those who were to be found in the various assemblies had come from the wake.

It could have been my wake, and the meetings would continue.

The parish was an inertial force. Only Armageddon would stop the meetings.

Thus had we reconstituted by free contract the immigrant parishes of the old neighborhood.

In God's name, why?

What did such frantic activity contribute to the salvation of a single life? What good did it do Coady Anne Condon?

I knew the answer, but somehow it didn't seem quite enough: The parish community, bound together by whatever means we could find, provided patterns of meaning, directions, and goals for human lives. It existed so we could all of us together practice the skills of offering ourselves in service to others.

How many times had I said that?

How many times had I wondered after saying it whether the means were becoming ends as the ends were being forgotten?

I was too worn-out to worry about the answers.

Inside, on the bulletin board, I found a message Lisa had left: "Father Santini called. Please call him. IMPORTANT!"

Dolph Santini, the archdiocesan director of music and Liturgy, was, as I have said, a cipher. I had a hunch I knew what he wanted. So I didn't call back.

He called again at 11:30, waking me and Norah up from deep and troubling sleep.

"This is Dolph Santini, Father."

Norah sighed noisily, rearranged herself and promptly went back to sleep.

"What time is it?"

"Eleven-thirty."

"P.M.?"

"That's right. I'm sorry, Father. The Cardinal and Father Simon said that it was important."

"You gotta be kidding!"

"We've had some questions, Father"—he was reading from a text—"about the funeral of the young woman who killed herself."

"Christian burial is a matter for pastoral discretion, Dolph. Don't you people trust me to have any discretion?"

"In most cases, Father, we leave such matters to the pastor, but there's been a lot of media attention and we were wondering—"

"The Mass is tomorrow at eleven. Do you want me to walk out on the altar and tell the congregation that the Cardinal has forbidden Christian burial to this poor child? Is that what you and the other fucking sickies downtown want?"

"There is no need to be abusive, Father."

"Look, moron, you wake me out of a sound sleep in the middle of the night after two days of hell trying to prevent other young people from hurting themselves, and you have the guts to talk to me about my being abusive?"

"But, Father—"

"Don't 'But, Father' me, asshole. A wonderful little girl's life has been tragically cut short, and all you can worry about is media coverage and a handful of complaints. What kind of a priest are you?"

"The Cardinal told Father Simon—"

"Fuck the Cardinal and Father Simon, too!"

So saying, I slammed the receiver down. The Church had freaked out on complaints.

After an hour of tossing and turning, I slipped away into sleep again.

Then the phone rang.

"I said fuck off!"

"Is that you, good buddy?"

My friend the drunk.

"Who else would it be?"

"I thought it might be that nice young priest I've talked to a couple of times."

"You leave him alone."

"Not nice language to hear from a priest, good buddy."

"You wake someone up at night, you take your risks."

"Yeah, well, I wanted to ask what time your AA group meets."

The son of a bitch was sober.

"Wednesday in the ministry center, that's the north end of the school building, at seven-thirty."

"You stay away, you hear. I don't want you to know who I am."

"I don't want to know, either. . . . Good luck."

"Yeah, I'll need it. Pray for me."

"I will. God bless."

I didn't sleep for the rest of the night.

The next morning WFMT informed the world that Sister Faith, the Cardinal's press spokesperson, had responded to questions about the burial of teenage suicide by saying that the pastor had not asked for permission for Christian burial services. When pressed, Sister Faith had admitted that such decisions were normally left to the local pastor.

Always, always covering themselves.

Jamie arrived the next morning as the procession with the casket was winding down the aisle of our church. We had no time to talk. His face was tanned, but he seemed tired and tense. Not quite your Mary Poppins of a New Priest today.

The church was packed—kids, parents, nuns, brothers, priests.

I'd better be good.

"We are broken by sadness," I began. "We woke up this morning, not yet able to believe that this isn't a nightmare. We're not burying Coady Anne today. We can't be burying her today! Only last week she was at High Club, as alive as any of us! She can't be gone!

"Then we realize she is really gone. Sadness overwhelms us. Why have we lost her?

"Let us be clear: we are not sad for her. We are sad for our loss. She was a young woman who needed our help. Somehow none of us who loved her were able to give her that help in time. Now she is home with One who loves her even more than we do, and can and will help her.

"Why God called her home so early, we don't know. That she is safely home, we cannot and must not doubt. If we all loved her, how can we possibly feel that God does not love her? We must banish any hint of such doubts forever!"

Thus for the hellfire nuns.

"We are sad for ourselves because we could not love her enough and because we have lost her and because we cannot understand why we have lost her."

I talked mostly about God's love and our own hope. All the young women in church seemed to be crying. Many of the young men were, too. The Condons were weeping—except the stony-faced Martina.

"If love means anything," I wound up, "it means that we wish the other person to live forever. With our weak human love, we cannot make that will come true. But it is our faith that God can and somehow does make His wishes come true. We will all meet again. We will all be young again. We will all laugh again.

"At High Club last week, I said to Coady Anne as she left, 'See you next week.'

"And she smiled back at me and said, 'See you, Father Lar.'

"All I can do this morning is repeat what I said then: 'See you next week, Coady Anne, whenever next week is.'"

Now even I was crying.

The New Priest, gaunt and haggard, stared ahead grimly. What was eating him?

In back of church he shook hands with the Condons. His eyes bored a hole into Martina's. He did not smile. She turned away.

What does he know? I wondered.

Norah lay on the front steps of the rectory, head between her paws, sensing human grief. Although she was a clumsy, stupid mutt, she was sensitive enough to stay away from us.

"Will you drive me to the cemetery, Father? Mom has arranged for a limo to pick me up there and take me to the airport."

"Sure."

Naturally, a limo for the golden son.

"She died about three-thirty, Chicago time, Father?" he asked as we pulled away in the funeral procession—it was a short ride to Mount Golgotha Cemetery.

"As best as they can figure out. She was cutting it close. Even if Patti O'Hara had been punctual it would have been a near thing."

"I'll see Patti at the cemetery. She seemed OK at Communion."

"She's a survivor."

"Phenobarbital again?"

"Yes."

"Left readily available?"

"On her mother's bedstand."

"Murder, Father. That's the proper word to describe it."

"I agree. If she couldn't dominate the child, she would as soon lose her. Maternal love turned twisted and sick. Maybe she's destroyed all the other kids, too, with her rigid controls. Maybe Coady is fortunate."

"She is."

Silence.

"Control is sin, Father. It's an attempt by us humans to become God for other humans. Like Father Louis. He has a secret—the way the Church really is. So he controls people. That's not just a sin. It's sin."

"You're right," I agreed. What the hell had happened to my New Priest? "Poor Coady Anne was a victim."

"She's all right. We don't have to worry about her. She forgives her mother, so we must forgive her, too, even though it's hard. We must try to free her from sin, though that will be even harder."

"They'll surely move away now."

"So all we can do is pray for her. We have to do that."

"You talk like you—are sure about Coady Anne? Is that a theological conclusion?"

"No, Father, it isn't."

"No?"

"You remember Mom and Dad in the community conference room, looking for spooks. That wasn't just a joke. If there were psychic vibrations in the house, they would have picked them up. That part of Dad's novel *War in Heaven* isn't fiction."

"Oh." My skin began to crawl.

"I inherited it from both sides. Don't worry. It doesn't usually work, and sometimes it's wildly inaccurate, and sometimes it doesn't make any kind of sense until afterward. And then sometimes it's different."

"You knew about her death because Coady Anne checked in with you?" I glanced at him.

He nodded. "She's fine, happy, forgiving. I don't fully understand why it made me so sad. Reflecting afterward on what she said they had done to her, I guess. The experience itself was benign."

My hands on the wheel were clammy.

"Do you believe in it, Jamie?"

"Believe? No, I don't believe it. I *know* it. I can't prove it"—
he laughed, the New Priest once more—"especially not to
someone a generation removed from the West of Ireland with
the mix of superstition and skepticism that comes with that
background. But I *know.*"

"Did you talk to your parents?"

"Not yet. I will when I see them in Steamboat. I guess this
depression is normal. It happened the other times, too, not so
strongly. The other experiences weren't so vivid."

"Others check in?"

"Yes, it's strange. When my brother died in Vietnam, none
of us knew till the telegram came. Yet distant relatives, ones I
never met, still drop by."

"Oh."

He nudged my arm playfully. "Don't worry, Boss, it doesn't
show, and the Chancery will never find out."

I told him about Dolph Santini's phone call.

"Eleven-thirty the night before the funeral? Did he really
want you to call it off?"

"He didn't want to do anything except keep Joe Simon
pleased with him. Joe's afraid to call himself now."

"But, Father, why call in the first place?"

"There's no point in having power, Jamie, unless you use it."

"Why use it on *us*? There are many teenage suicides every
year."

I told him Mike Quinlan's theory that I threatened Joe
Simon.

Jamie was not as amused as I was. "You'd make a fine Vicar
General, Father. What would happen to Saint Finian's?"

"I'm not about to become VG, Jamie. And when I leave,
Saint Finian's will do nicely."

"No, it won't."

He was more gentle with Martina at the graveside. She still
refused to cry.

And Patti O'Hara smiled and laughed while he talked to her.

I was glad to see him leave in the limo for the airport. Not only Mary Poppins but a psychic Mary Poppins. Michael Jordan with ESP.

What next?

According to Mike Quinlan, the next move would be an attack on me through Jamie by the power structure.

Did they know what kind of a man they would take on? One that, I shivered, talks with young women on their way to heaven?

CHAPTER

46

Jeanne disappeared while I was on my vacation in Barbados. I should have known by then that I was asking for trouble every time I stepped outside of the rectory.

The week after the funeral we continued to struggle with young people and their parents—and the aftereffects of the sociologist's article.

Kids swarmed into the rectory, some alone, more of them in large groups. They complained that their parents were acting geeky about that "you know, like, totally gross article. They chill us out. Really barf city."

They wanted to talk about death. It was, as Jeanne was quick to comment, a rare chance for religious education which we ought not overlook.

Even Cook held court in her kitchen—sessions mostly for boys and characterized by much loud laughter.

"Do you think she's telling them dirty jokes?" Jeanne asked.

"All Irish humor is obscene," Mike Quinlan observed, "laughing at death. In the old days, they used to screw in the fields outside the wake and thus assert the primacy of life over death. Fuck you, Death! Not a bad thought."

"I hope Cook isn't telling them that."

"Cook," Mike insisted, "is, despite her vocabulary, too pious even to suggest it."

Finally, about the time Jamie came home from Steamboat Springs, the furor abruptly stopped. Both young people and their parents had turned away from the frightening challenge of death and turned back to the more mundane obligations of life.

The Condons departed for a long vacation to California from which I was sure they'd never return.

My cold, in abeyance during the suicide crisis, came back; sleep, troubled and deep during the crisis, deserted me.

Dolph Santini wrote me a note:

Dear Father McAuliffe,

I'm sorry that I disturbed your well-earned sleep the other night.

However, I believe that priests should display courtesy to other priests no matter what the time of day or night.

Prayerfully in the Lord Jesus and Holy Spirit,
Dolph

The Cardinal sent short, handwritten letters on occasion, an attempt at the personal touch which was frustrated by two facts: (a) he was quite incapable of saying anything in a letter because of fear that he would be quoted, and (b) we quickly learned that his notes were a ploy he used to "contain" people.

So members of his curia imitated him, often even to the use of clichés like "well-earned sleep."

I regret to confess that I replied in kind:

Dear Dolph,

Thank you for your note.

I also believe that priests, even Joe Simon's stooges, should display common sense no matter what time of day or night.

Lar

When Jamie returned, I was a wreck—angry, tired, sick. I pleaded that there was too much work, with Lent almost upon us, for me to fly off to Barbados.

"The reservations are already made and you paid for them, Father!" he insisted.

"You made them at your travel agent, and I've paid for them," I grumbled. "We have the Lenten series, the Sunday afternoon lectures, the Lenten Liturgies, the RCIA preparations, and nine weddings."

"I can cope."

"That's just the problem."

Cook arrived at the dining table at that moment. "Ah, sure, Your Reverence, I thought you were already gone and the young priest back from his vacation looking like a movie star!"

"Barbados"—Mike Quinlan glanced up at Cook—"is a corrupted form of Saint Brendan's Island. Did you know that, Cook?"

"Och, didn't they stay there to recover from the voyage, such as your man would if he had any sense at all at all."

"You're not the pastor yet, young woman."

"And if I were, wouldn't I be on the airplane already?"

"The kid is getting too pushy," I said—after she was out of hearing.

"That really settles it, Father. She won't feed you if you stay around. Mama Maggie will pick up the reservations at the travel agent—down the corridor from her office—and give them to me Sunday. Monday morning you'll be on your way."

"We'll see."

Before I could escape to the office for the evening's wedding instructions, he cornered me. "Why don't you phone that fabulous and legendary adviser of yours and ask her whether you should take time off?"

"I never should have told you about her."

I did phone her that night, however, after the office calls.

She was not pleased with me.

"You're afraid that they'll do very well without you at Saint Finian's, and then you'll know you're not indispensable."

"I *know* they'll do well without me."

"Then get thee gone. And remember, no heavy thinking or worrying or decisions—you read, play golf, swim, and bask in the sun and watch the pretty women in bikinis."

"I wish you were one of them."

"You know better than that," she spoke kindly.

"I can fantasize, can't I?"

"No law against that."

So Monday noon I found myself at O'Hare, at the right terminal this time.

"First class, yes, sir, you have seat 3-A reserved for you. Is that acceptable?"

"Are you sure?"

"Yes, sir. Here it is on the ticket: the 'F' means first class."

I would have downgraded the ticket if there wasn't a long line behind me.

I looked inside the ticket jacket and found a handwritten note—neat, clear, precise script:

Lar,

    Have a good rest.

    Thanks for being so good to our punk.

                                       Maggie

It would be worth my life to try to reject such a gift. As I fastened my seat belt, I mentally penned the note I would send from Saint Brendan's Isle.

Mag,

> Jamie has often said I needed an upgrading.
> I'm afraid I'll take First Class for granted.
> The punk is a pleasure to have around.

> > Thanks much,
> > Lar

I should have been ready for the two-room suite they had reserved for me at the Crane Beach Club.

I had always resented attempted patronage from wealthy people. The Keenans, however, were different.

So I did as I was instructed. I played golf, walked the beaches, bounced around the rocky roads on that breathtaking island, read, swam, and stretched out on the beach—much, as I told myself, Saint Brendan and his men had, if not in the comfort of the Crane Beach Club.

I did not, however, admire any pretty girls in bikinis. I assumed that such pleasures were not available for the Brendanites and hence I should not enjoy them, either.

As Cook would have said, I do lie a little.

My cold vanished and I slept soundly every night.

For two weeks I forgot Saint Finian's. Well, more or less.

As soon as I boarded the BWIA flight at Grantly Adams International Airport, the parish and all its problems blustered their way like a winter storm back into my mind. I could hardly wait to return and discover what disasters had happened in my absence.

God must have been displeased with my sun-baked luxury. A blizzard awaited us at O'Hare. We were three hours late in landing. The cold virus seemed to have been lurking for me on the plane.

By the time I finally pulled into the snow-covered lot at Saint Finian's, I was sure the fever had returned, too. It was like I never left.

Jackie was in her cubbyhole, poring over a trigonometry problem.

"Remember me, Jackie? I used to work here."

"Oh, hi, Father Lar." She didn't seem happy to see me. "You've got an awesome tan. Radical."

Norah, sleeping peacefully at Jackie's feet, opened one eye, considered me, and went back to sleep. Out of sight, out of mind. Faithless bitch.

"How's the parish?"

"Dr. Flavin is gone." She didn't look up from the trig book.

"Gone?"

"Disappeared." She sighed. "She'll never come back. It's too gross. . . . Mr. Lyons is up in your suite with Father Jamie."

I scaled the steps two at a time. Lyons was slumped in the sofa, Jamie outlined against the windows and the gray, snow-laden skies—a tableau of frustration.

"What happened?" I was gasping for breath.

"She's gone," Jamie said glumly, "vanished without a trace. Didn't show up for class a week ago Monday. I called her apartment. No answer. I called Don. He hadn't seen her since Friday. We went over to the apartment. Empty. A cleaned-out monastic cell. Money gone from her checking account and savings deposit. No trace. We called the police. Don hired a private detective. We talked to everyone. I thought about calling you, but we figured every day she'd turn up. Then it was only a day or two anyway."

I sat automatically behind my desk, coat still on. "Any warning?"

"We had a bit of a fight on Friday night." Don looked like a widower at a wake—his second experience with loss, too much for any man. "I wanted to talk about marriage. She had refused to discuss it. I guess I'm not the playboy type. Or maybe I pushed too much because I was afraid I'd lose her. I didn't think it was a serious fight. We, uh, kissed and made up."

And made love.

Then she was afraid that she'd ruin your life so she ran away.

I knew it wouldn't work.

"Then"—Jamie bit his lip—"there was the dumb letter in *The Bells*. My fault."

"What letter?"

Silently he handed me the last issue of *The Bells*.

To the Editor,

We wish to exercise our solemn obligation to render prophetic judgment against the exploitation of women which is condoned in this parish and everywhere in the capitalist world.

As professional theologians, we assert that it is un-Christian for men to lust after the bodies of women. It is un-Christian to permit genital attraction to degrade the relationship between the sexes. Men sin when they indulge themselves in such attractions. Women sin when they encourage such attractions. Women humiliate and degrade themselves when they try to enhance their attractiveness to gain the attention of men. Permanent commitment between a man and a woman ought never to begin with genital appeal and cannot be sustained by it.

The ephemeral beauty of women is a trick that men have used to enslave women. It is not just or fair that one woman be deemed more appealing than another woman. Judgments about physical beauty may have a place in the world of *Playboy* but not among Christians. That men should enjoy women who are more beautiful than others is a crime against elementary justice.

Pagan women and public sinners like Jezebel in the Scripture paint themselves and anoint themselves with scent. Christian women do not because they know that physical attraction is degrading. The enormous amount of money spent in this community on cosmetics, expensive clothes, and the frivolous physical fitness craze would support for a whole year many African villages. Shoppers at the mall and early morning joggers should ask themselves whether it be better to degrade and humiliate themselves to appeal to men, or to feed the hungry.

Sheila Ferrigan-McKittrick, M.A.
Blaise Ferrigan-McKittrick, M.A.

"What crap!" I threw the newsletter into the waste basket. "Unmitigated crap!"

"Just what she didn't need at this time in her life. I should have had more sense"—Jamie shook his head sadly—"than to publish it."

"She should have had more sense than to take it seriously. It's not your fault. . . . Are there replies?"

"Tons of them." Jamie smiled sheepishly and handed me another sheet. "I had to add another page, both sides, for next Sunday."

Nothing like an attack on cosmetics and clothes to stir up interest in the parish bulletin.

Twelve letters, all from women, attacked the Ferrigan-McKittrick jeremiad with varying degrees of literacy and intelligence. The most pungent said simply, "If God did not intend men and women to be physically attractive to one another, He should have made them differently than She did."

There was a long letter from one (Ms.) Patricia Anne O'Hara which detailed the falsehoods for which the Ferrigan-McKittricks had been responsible in the *NCO* article and demanded a retraction and an apology. Hardly to the point of "genital attraction," the letter was nonetheless politely devastating.

"Patti Cupcake reads the *NCO*?"

"Patrick McNally does."

"For such a sweet young man, he has a nice instinct for the jugular."

Unless I completely misunderstood the culture of Forest Springs, the Ferrigan-McKittricks had now sowed their own wind. The whirlwind would shortly be upon them.

"It doesn't help Jeanne. Too late for her."

Don Lyons leaned forward on the couch, hands clasped thoughtfully in front of him. "Don't blame yourself, Father. Those ideas abound in our world. She would have read them somewhere else eventually."

Yeah, but in fact, she had read the shit in the parish bulletin—and when I was away.

The little idiot. She knew what the Ferrigan-McKittricks were. Why take them seriously?

Because she was losing her nerve, that's why!

"She thinks she's not good enough, the usual shit." The New Priest was pacing like an angry, imprisoned animal, once more the quarterback kept on the sidelines by a failing defensive team.

"Jamie," I exclaimed.

"I don't care, Father. The language is appropriate in this case."

"That's what I always say."

He permitted himself a faint smile.

"God help me." Don spread his hands. "I love her so much that I can hardly think about anything else. She was . . . is an astonishingly lovable woman, despite all the things that have happened to her. Sensitive, generous, responsive, vulnerable—everything I could want in a lover and a wife. . . . I guess maybe I should have waited."

"The crisis would have had to come," I said heavily. "Don't worry, Don. We'll find her. She's still alive or she wouldn't have taken her money. Perhaps she'll come back on her own. Otherwise, we'll hunt her down. Maybe that's what she wants us to do. See if we really love her enough to drag her back, even after she's pulled such a damn-fool stunt."

I had now made myself an active part of the conspiracy. No, I was kidding myself: I had been a silent partner all along.

Jamie stopped his pacing long enough to turn an approving grin toward me. "By the hair of her head?"

"That would be in Mr. Lyons's area of attention. I'd argue the wording of her contract to serve as DRE for this parish. It is immoral to violate a contract."

For some crazy reason we all laughed.

My approach wasn't ridiculous, however. If love and passion failed with Jeanne, then legalism might work. Not for nothing had she been a nun.

"I guess you were right, Boss," my New Priest said after Don Lyons left. "It was too long a shot. Now we may have destroyed the poor woman completely. Youthful imprudence."

An excellent opportunity to sit on him, to put him in his place, to cut him down to size, to reef his sails, to contain his enthusiasm?

Right.

So what did I say?

"If it's any consolation to you, Jamie, I would have taken the same long shot. She was too important not to run the risk, particularly since she herself wanted to. The difference between you and me is that you thought of it first."

"Really?" The young man began to recover his normal verve.

"Fersure."

"Really fersure?"

I hope so.

CHAPTER

47

We worried about Jeanne all week. Jamie and I took her classes. Linda nervously assumed responsibility for the Lenten and Easter Liturgies. The young people fretted. Norah paced. Patti O'Hara called every day with a new idea.

Don Lyons hired another private detective.

Nothing.

Jeanne was a woman without near family, without roots, and save in Saint Finian's, without friends. She could easily disappear without a trace.

Maybe eventually her social security number would turn up somewhere.

We began to accept the fact that she was gone for good.

Late Monday afternoon, Lisa buzzed me. "Father Lar, there's a man on the phone who is crying. He won't tell me who he is, but he wants to talk to you."

"Father McAuliffe."

"Call off your Fascist thugs," a frail, broken voice pleaded.

"I beg pardon? Who is this?"

"You goddamn well know who it is, McAuliffe. Poor Sheila is hysterical."

So. The whirlwind had arrived.

"What's happened?"

"You know what happened. They booed us at school today! They're picketing our house! This is an outrage! It's all your doing!"

"How many pickets?"

"Four. . . . They're Fascists attacking our freedom of speech."

"I think rather they are exercising their own right of freedom of peaceful assembly."

"Sheila is hysterical! Please call them off!"

"Call the police."

Jamie had just returned from the skating pond in our local park, Norah bounding after him, his fair complexion glowing from the cold.

"I hear that the Ferrigan-McKittricks are entertaining some pickets."

"Really?" He looked quite innocent.

"You didn't organize them?"

"Purely spontaneous."

"You did tell them to keep it small so that they could not be accused of disorderly conduct?"

"Naturally. They have the same right of freedom—"

"—of speech as anyone else."

"Precisely." He shook his head sadly. "It doesn't bring Jeanne back, but it does restore some balance. They can't lie about people and not pay a price."

"An eye for an eye?"

"Mama Maggie would call it defining reality."

The pickets dutifully went home when the police requested that they leave. They did not reappear the next day because they had learned that the Ferrigan-McKittricks had fled the parish. The Catholic Left had wilted before the pale fires of a gentle revolution. I expected another McPhaul piece in the *NCO* but it never appeared.

The New Priest told me that he felt sorry for them and would, later in the year, try to search them out and effect a reconciliation.

"Deal me out," I told him.

"You don't mean that, Father," he assured me. "After all, you did make them lector and eucharistic minister."

"No good deed goes unpunished."

Don came to the rectory every evening, looking more like a ghost each night. He was the victim. I became furious at everyone, Jeanne, chiefly.

She had discovered intimacy and reveled in it. Then, confronted with the terrors, the sweet and awful terrors of belonging to another and of having that other belong to you, she had bolted. Having tasted intimacy, could she do without it?

Some women could easily give up intimacy once they had enjoyed it. They had not, however, drunk as deeply of its pleasures as Jeanne had—to judge by her self-revelation on our ride to O'Hare. Yet Jeanne had a strong and grimly determined will. As she had systematically gone about the task of seducing Don once he was offered to her, so she would with equal system and enthusiasm, go about the task of rooting out of her life the passions inside her that they had activated together.

She was not the kind of woman who would drift back in six months or a year and ask that we forgive her.

Yet she must be excruciatingly lonely now. If we could find and reclaim her now, she would never run again.

So all we had to do was find her.

We spent the entire staff meeting on Friday worrying about her. No one had the slightest clue.

The parish lumbered toward Lent, now a mere three days away. My fever returned intermittently. Well, I had shown them all. The vacation had not helped a bit.

Anthony Wholey had made the second-string basketball team after private lessons from the New Priest. Patrick McNally had taken the entrance exam at Niles. The Condons' home was sold. Brendan and Linda were to be married the week after Easter. No sign of Maria or Ed Sullivan, though their younger daughter still appeared at High Club.

I was praying again, despite my weariness.

The violence of the year had shocked me: George Wholey, the scene at O'Hare, Coady Anne, and the verbal violence almost every time I opened my mouth. I was looking for a fight, waiting to knock someone down, verbally if not physically. One day the provocation would come, and I really would flatten an adversary.

Maybe kill him.

My adviser told me I needed another vacation.

The violence inside of me was the result of anger—anger at the hypocrites and the phonies in the parish, anger at the Church, anger at everyone, including myself. The frustrations of life were finally catching up.

George Wholey might be a loose cannon; so was I.

I was slumped in a chair in the first-floor office, feeling sorry for myself and wishing I could spend the rest of my life on Barbados, when I saw a way of finding Jeanne Flavin. It was a far-out idea that no one had thought of yet.

Which of the porter persons was on duty today?

CHAPTER

48

Jackie was working on a spreadsheet at the word processing screen. "High Club budget, Father Lar. I'm like, 'Why not use Lotus 1-2-3,' and the space cadets are like, 'What's that?' Isn't that gross?"

"We've got to find Jeanne."

"Suppose she doesn't want to be found?" Jackie made an entry on the spreadsheet.

"If she doesn't want to be found, we won't find her. Some people run away and want to be found."

"That would be gross."

"Like you did when you were six and ran away from home and wanted to live at the rectory."

"That was DIFFERENT."

She saved her spreadsheet and turned off the PC.

"Jeanne has had a hard life. It's understandable that she'd be afraid."

"Yucky."

"Maybe."

"I don't know where she is. Really!"

"Like you could find out. Maybe by talking to the kids who were in her CCD classes. Some hints about where she might go for a vacation or a weekend off. Some close friend that she mentioned often."

"Like a mystery?" Her spirits soared. "And I'm like Angela Lansbury? Right? Especially now that she's lost all that weight and looks so yummy?"

"Right!"

"You take the door and the phones." She bounded out of her chair. "I'll use the phone in the parlor. We grant impunity, right?"

"Immunity."

"Really!"

A half hour later she returned with much less vivacity.

"Peru is in South America, isn't it, Father Lar?"

"That's right."

"Is that where she went?"

"WELL, Liz Kelly goes, 'She has this friend that's a nun who teaches in Peru. She talks about her a lot.' And I'm like, 'A

REAL good friend?' and Liz goes, 'When she was talking about retreats last year, she goes that when she needs a retreat, she drives down to Peru because it's so quiet that it's like a century ago,' and I'm like, 'How can she drive to Peru' and Liz goes, 'How do I know,' and I'm like, 'What's the name of the city in Peru' and Liz goes, 'Something like . . . ,' but she can't remember."

Well, it was a nice try. If she was in South America and we didn't know the name of the city, we'd never find her.

"Try someone else?"

"Fersure. But Liz Kelly has this fantastic memory."

I went back to the other office and pulled out a stack of marriage files. It was nice to see Linda and Brendan in the stack. The latter insisted that he was already part of the parish and that he would certainly buy a home in the community as soon as they could, probably in another year or two. In the meantime, after the wedding he would move into her apartment.

She said it would be embarrassing to have her husband living in the parish where she worked. She wasn't insistent about it, however.

Jackie came over to my office. "Nothing, Father Lar, should I keep trying?"

"As long as you can think of people to call."

I opened another folder. No baptismal records for a marriage that was the following Saturday. Why is it such a big deal to find baptismal records? I'd have to call them.

I reached for the phone.

Then I muttered to myself, "*Drive* to Peru!"

I knew where she was.

"Jackie, call Liz Kelly and ask her if the name of the city in Peru is La Salle?"

"La Salle?"

"Call her."

Jackie punched in the numbers.

"Liz? Father Lar's like, 'Call Liz Kelly and ask her if the city in Peru is called La Salle,' and I'm like, 'La Salle?' and he's like, 'Call her. . . .' REALLY! OUTSTANDING! RADICAL! AWESOME!" Her dancing eyes widened in astonishment and respect as she hung up. "Father Lar, you're a genius. How did you know?"

"We have towns in Illinois"—I grabbed for the *Official Catholic Directory* and searched for the Diocese of Peoria—"with funny foreign names: Cairo, Pekin, Milan, Vienna . . ."—I pronounced them all the Illinois way—"and Peru. The town next to Peru is called LaSalle." Sure enough only two convents and one from her order. A piece of cake. "And people call them by the combined names like Minneapolis–St. Paul. La Salle–Peru. It's only two hours away."

"Gee! Awesome!"

"Elementary, my dear Jacqueline."

Now how could we make sure?

I went back to the office to ponder what we should do. If we warned her that we knew, she might run. Call the parish and ask the pastor? Call the convent?

The pastor might tip them off. The nuns would go along with her plan to hide.

Who might know?

Gingerly I dialed the rectory number. A woman's voice answered, no, a young woman's voice. They had their Jackie and Lisa and Sarah and Jennifer, too. Didn't everyone?

"I want to write a letter to the Sister in charge at the convent to thank her for a special favor. Only I'm not sure of the name. Who is Sister Superior?"

"Well, like they don't call them that anymore, but the principal is Sister Connie."

"Uh-huh. That doesn't quite sound like the name. There are two others, aren't there?"

ANDREW M. GREELEY

"Fersure. Sister Trudi and Sister Bobbie."

We had indeed come a long way from Sister Mary Saint Angela of the Child Jesus.

"I think it's Sister Bobbie. Those are the only ones at the convent?"

I was now counting on the busybody mentality of the teenage woman of the species.

"Well, like, you know, they're the only nuns. But there's this Dr. Flavin that's staying with them. She's kind of cute, but she's not a nun, so I don't suppose she's the one."

"No, I'm sure not. It must be Sister Bobbie. Thank you. You've been very helpful."

"No problem."

Cool, very cool. Maybe when you quit the parish you can set yourself up as a priest-detective—the Father Brown of Forest Springs.

"Jackie, is the New Priest upstairs?"

"Working on the Easter Liturgy, Father Lar. He goes, 'You always have to be prepared' and I—"

"Call Mr. Lyons and tell him to come over right away."

"FERSURE!"

"I found her," I told them when they were assembled in my office. She's at Saint Cuthbert's Convent in La Salle-Peru, Illinois. It's maybe an hour and a half beyond Joliet on I-80."

Both of them were appropriately astonished.

"How did you find her?" Don Lyons's eyes were bright with newfound hope.

I explained.

"Brilliant, Father!" my New Priest exclaimed.

"Elementary, my dear Jamie."

The three of us were silent.

"Now what?" Don finally asked. "Should I call her?"

"She'll run maybe. Disappear again."

"Someone ought to drive down there and bring her back," Jamie suggested.

"Delicate task," I replied.

"Yeah, but she might be able to resist a voice on the phone. She can't resist a person."

"You should go, Father Lar." Don pointed a finger at me. "She worships you."

"Jamie should go. He's been close to her these past few months."

And he's responsible for this mess, I did not add.

The New Priest targeted both his index fingers at Don Lyons. "You plan to marry her, don't you?"

"I do," he squirmed.

"And she's your woman, isn't she?"

"I can hardly deny that."

"Then *you* go!"

He paused, shrugged. "I can't argue with your logic, Father. Now?"

"The sooner the better."

"All right."

I found an unopened bottle of Napoleon in my liquor cabinet (which the New Priest now kept in balanced supply).

"You might want to take this along."

He looked at the bottle and grinned. "You know too much, Father."

He took the bottle, however. "Never can tell when it will be useful."

So he understood, I hoped, that Jeanne's Achilles' heel was intimacy. Or maybe *pleasure* would be a better name for it.

"Give us a ring on the way back," I said at the door.

"I sure will."

"I hope it works," Jamie said softly as Don's Olds 98 pulled away. "What are the odds now, Father?"

"A little less than even."

"Don't be GROSS," the ever-vigilant Jackie insisted hotly. "With all the men that love her, OF COURSE Jeanne will be all right. You both should have more faith in God. Right?"

Norah woofed as though she were expected to reply.

"Right," the New Priest and I agreed in unison.

"AND"—in confrontation with Jackie you never had the last word—"in yourselves."

Norah woofed again.

CHAPTER

49

The snow had begun to fall, first in little flurries, then in a steady dance of white, then in great, dense blankets. Jamie and I watched the Bulls beat Atlanta and marveled at the incomparable Michael Jordan. We also worried anxiously about Don's safety on the interstate.

"He's a cautious lawyer and a prudent man," I said reassuringly.

"He's a knight in love riding to recover his lady fair. Snow won't stop him. Anyway, he should be there by now."

"And back."

At nine o'clock we gave up. Jamie returned to the Easter Liturgy. I considered the stack of marriage files downstairs and opted instead for Mozart.

At nine-thirty the phone rang in my room—where I had told Jackie to direct the bells when she left.

"Saint Finian's."

"I know where you can hire a very embarrassed director of religious education. Cheap."

"Don! Thank God!"

I put my hand over the phone and bellowed, "Jamie!" And in my best pastoral tones, into the phone, "I'll think about it. Actually we have a fairly good one on the staff, but she's rather expensive."

He chuckled and repeated my comment. I thought I heard a muffled laugh in the distance.

To someone who was in bed with him?

Was the Pope Catholic?

"How is she?"

Jamie came thundering into my room like the Sioux at the Little Bighorn.

"Fine, just fine. More ashamed of herself than she ought to be. Happy and eager to come home."

He had bedded his prize before phoning us. Well, what else did I expect?

"I think she still has a job. We'll be eager to have her back."

Jamie was dancing a weird Irish reel. Exuberant young man.

"Should I tell her how we tracked her down?"

"By all means. So she knows she can't escape from us."

"She says she won't try, and I believe her."

"I do, too."

"Incidentally, the storm is dreadful down here. I'm not going to try to drive home until it lets up."

"Don't even think of it, Don. And enjoy."

He laughed. "I intend to."

I phoned Jackie. "Jackie? Father Lar. She's coming home."

"Radical! Didn't I tell you! Should I spread the word?"

"Forget the Angela Lansbury details, just tell them she's coming back."

At my prayers that night I told the Lord God that I frankly envied Don Lyons. A warm motel room with a blizzard outside and your recaptured woman in your bed.

And a bottle of brandy. My brandy.

Well, the New Priest's brandy.

Which the New Priest had paid for.

They came back the next afternoon, about two o'clock. Jeanne, in slacks and sweatshirt, was pale and shy. She embraced Jamie first. "I'm sorry, New Priest, I really am. I'm such a geek."

Then me, a furious hug. "Dear God, Lar, I love you so much. I'm sure you've already forgiven me, but I'm so sorry." She wept in my arms. Having enjoyed the embrace as long as I dared, I handed her back to Don.

He looked pleased with himself, as well he might. She was his now and forever.

"You can take this afternoon off." I searched for my official voice. "I expect you back at work tomorrow morning. The young priest has been sweating out the Easter Liturgy."

"I'll be there," she promised. "With bells on! Oh, Norah, you wonderful pup. Yes, I am back! Settle down. I'm not going away again. Yes, yes, I really do love you. You don't have to slobber all over my face."

Beneath the shyness, there were strong hints of gaiety, even wantonness. She was now a prisoner of intimacy, a willing prisoner.

"Otherwise, I'll obtain a court order."

"It was that darn letter from Blaise and Sheila." She bit her lip. "Hysterical nonsense, and I responded to it hysterically. Remembering about that makes me feel ashamed. . . . Were there replies in *The Bells*?"

Jamie handed her the most recent edition. "I'm afraid the Ferrigan-McKittricks have left the parish. For the time being anyway."

"Poor people." She shook her head sadly. "Oh, my . . . 'Ms. Patricia Anne O'Hara' . . . Patrick McNally is the ghostwriter I'm sure. He'll be a very dangerous priest." She looked up and glanced slyly at both Jamie and me. "New Priest and Old Priest kind of combined."

We all laughed, rejoicing in the breakout of her gaiety.

"We need a wedding date, Father Lar," Don said firmly, "don't we, Jeanne?"

She gulped, shut her eyes, and then forced out the words. "We sure do." She struggled to finish what she started. "It's time your DRE became an honest woman."

"It's already in the book," I said smoothly. "A week from Saturday. We'll dispense with the first two readings of the banns."

"That soon!" She stiffened in terror. "Can't we wait?"

"Absolutely not," her man said.

She gulped again. "All right. I guess I don't have any choice"—then she smiled the most wonderful, radiant smile that had ever illumined her face—"do I?"

"None whatever," Don said firmly.

"Jamie." She turned to my beaming New Priest, who had won another one, right when I was wrong. "Would your mother ever see me, professionally I mean?"

"Mama Maggie? Gee, she almost always does what I ask her!"

"One more thing." She drew a deep breath, squared her shoulders, and tilted her jaw. "Since I'm apparently about to become a more or less permanent resident in the neighborhood, I'm ready to accept that job as pastoral associate."

Don gulped, Jamie rolled his eyes.

"One feisty lady, uh, woman." I walked over to the file cabinet in my office, opened the drawer labeled "D to J," and removed a contract.

"Here it is and a pen. Just sign on the line."

"Not enough money." She smiled disarmingly at me. "After my work here for three years, I'm entitled to top-of-the-line pastoral associate's salary."

"The finance committee . . . ?"

"The frigging finance committee, to quote Cook . . . you can get it by them, I'm sure."

You bet. I merely wanted to see how feisty the new Jeanne was. Pretty damn feisty.

"Jamie?"

"She'll make a lot more than either of us, Father. However, since we can assume that she'll run the parish, that's not inappropriate."

I inked out the salary in the contract, entered one at the top of the archdiocese's guidelines, and handed her the pen.

She signed it with a flourish, then hugged me. "Thanks, Lar, you won't regret it."

"The hell I won't. You and the New Priest will eliminate all need for me."

Everyone laughed.

"Small chance," Jamie asserted.

"We'll save you for solving mysteries," Don said, grinning proudly at his woman's nerve.

So that was that.

I walked with the engaged couple downstairs to the rectory front door. "Thanks for the brandy, Lar," Don said. "It was very useful."

"Be my guest."

"Was it *his* brandy! Oh my! I'll never get over my embarrassment."

He pushed her rump gently out the door. "I hope not."

Later, when she had thanked me again for everything and reported that her first session with Doctor Keenan had been a good beginning, she said, "Marriage will be difficult for me, Lar. But I'm going to make it work."

"The therapy might be hard, Jeanne. It usually is. You might be surprised by how easy marriage will be."

That story seemed to be destined for a moderately happy ending. Saint Finian's and my New Priest, however, were not out of the woods yet.

50

They got Jamie when I was away at New Mellary Abbey on retreat.

I pretty much collapsed halfway through Lent. I should have gone back to Barbados or somewhere in the sun like Tucson. Instead, I went to a monastery, much to the dismay of my adviser when she found out about it afterward.

Not that it would have made any difference where I went. This was not a year for me to leave the rectory, no matter how good the reason.

We filled the church for Jeanne's wedding with an exuberant throng of young people and adults. Don's kids—Ken, Ria and Helen, patently delighted—were the wedding party. They treated their new stepmother like she was a sister, an adorable little sister.

The bride, in a long white gown, strapless under the modest mantle she wore over it, was the least exuberant person in church. She did not seem unhappy or frightened. Rather she was oblivious, distant, curiously passive. Unresistant, she was permitting herself to be drawn into this union.

Somewhere in the dark and dank subbasements of her soul, fear and doubt lurked.

At the homily I told a Cherokee Indian story which Jamie had played for me on tape by Gayle Ross—the story of why Earth Maker had made strawberries.

I told it with my fake county Kerry brogue.

"Once upon a time, long, long ago, First Man and First Woman were living happily together in their cottage on the edge of the bogs. Earth Maker was their good friend, and he visited them often. First Man and First Woman loved each other very much and were happy together. Occasionally they had little arguments, which First Woman always won, but the arguments were never serious.

"Then one day they had a monumental fight, a real rip-roaring donnybrook. They fought over who started the fight. Then they had another fight about what the first fight had been about.

"Finally, First Woman had enough. 'You're nothing but a flannel mouth idjit,' she shouted. 'I'm sick of you. You can cook your own supper tonight and for the rest of your life.'

"And she strode out of the house and across the field and down into the valley and over the hill beyond, without ever looking back once.

"Well, First Man sat back in his chair and breathed a sigh of relief. ''Tis the end of that, thank God,' he said. 'The woman was a terrible trial. Talk, talk, nothing but talk. At last I'll have some peace and quiet around here.'

"Well, when the sun set over the ocean, First Man decided it was time to have some supper. Only First Woman wasn't there to cook it. Now, as much as I hate to tell you this, First Man was a real chauvinist. He couldn't boil water without making a mess. All he had for supper was a cold pratie. By then he was so lonely he only ate a few bites of it.

" 'Well,' he says aloud trying to chase away his loneliness, 'I'd better get some sleep. It'll be a hard day tomorrow, and all the work I'll finally catch up now that I have some peace and quiet.'

"The bed was terrible cold, and First Man was terrible lonely, and he hardly slept at all.

"And there was no warm pot of tea for him when he woke up in the morning.

"Well, the first thing, who do you think comes bursting into the house?

"That's right: Earth Maker, filled with enthusiasm as She always is, fresh back from another planet where He was straightening things out a wee bit.

" 'Ah sure,' says Earth Maker, 'I was after making two of you, wasn't I? Male and female if I remember right—and I always do. Let me see, you're the male, so where's herself?'

" 'Ah, she's gone, Your Reverence. Gone altogether.'

" 'She never did!'

" 'Ah, she did, stormed out on me!'

" 'Why would she be after doing that?'

" ''Och, I hate to admit it, Your Reverence, but we had a wee dust-up, if you take my meaning.'

" 'Dust-up?'

" 'A fight, Your Reverence, a terrible fight. The woman is so mad at me she'll never come back.'

" 'A fight, is it? You're a pair of idjits. What was the fight about?'

" 'To tell the truth, Your Reverence, I can't remember. We had a fight about who started the fight and then another about what the fight was about.'

" 'Terrible idjits altogether,' exclaimed Earth Maker. 'Well, do you miss her?'

" 'Sure, Your Reverence, I miss her something terrible. I'm so lonely my heart will break.'

" 'Well then, man, on your way. Go chase her and ask her to come back.'

" 'Wasn't I thinking of doing that? But she walks so fast and has such a big head start that I'll never catch up with her, if you take me meaning.'

" 'On your way, man,' says Earth Maker, thinking real quick. 'I'll go ahead and slow her down for you.'

"So First Man rushes out the door and across the field and down the valley and up over the hill.

"Meantime, Earth Maker, who as you know moves at the

speed of thought, catches up with First Woman, still striding along at a frantic clip.

" 'She should be tired now,' says Earth Maker to Herself. 'Let's see if this forest I'm after making will slow her down.'

"So *zap!* there's a great forest in the way of First Woman.

"And do you know what she does? Why, she just goes through it like it wasn't there, a hot knife through soft butter.

" 'Serves me right,' thinks Earth Maker, 'for providing the woman with a mind of her own. Well, this lake will stop her.'

"*Zap.* And doesn't a big lake appear. You know what First Woman does?

"That's right, clothes and all, she swims right across that lake. Australian crawl at that.

" 'Serves me right, for making her an athlete,' says Earth Maker. 'Well, she's hungry by now. I bet these pear trees and orange trees and apricot trees and peach trees stop her.'

"*Zap* again! And doesn't the most marvelous orchard in the whole world appear. What does First Woman do? She picks the fruit on the fly and keeps right on walking while she's eating breakfast and lunch.

"I told you the woman was terrible angry, didn't I?

" 'Well,' thinks Earth Maker, 'this is a real challenge. I guess I'll have to fall back on me ultimate contingency. I'll make strawberries. Sure, now 'tis as good a time as any.'

"There's one more *zap.*

"First Woman notices a bush growing across the road with beautiful white flowers. She stops and looks at the bush. As she's watching, she sees the flowers turn into lovely red berries.

" 'Ah, will you look at them berries now,' she says. 'Aren't they the same shape and the same color as the human heart?'

"And she touches one, and isn't it after feeling just like the human heart, soft and yet firm.

"And then doesn't she pick one of the berries and taste it.

" 'Och,' says First Woman, 'isn't it the sweetest taste in all the world. Sure, the only thing sweeter is human love.'

"And as she's eating the berry and thinking of human love . . . Well, you know who comes to her mind, don't you now.

" 'Ah, the poor man,' she says. 'He's after trying to catch up with me and by the time he does, won't he be perishing with the hunger. I know what I'll do. I'll just pick some more of these strawberries, and we'll eat them when he catches up. Then we'll go home together.'

"And sure isn't that just what happened. He caught up and she gave him the strawberries and they ate them together and they went back to their cottage hand in hand with Earth-Maker trailing along behind them, kind of like Norah trails behind the New Priest.

" 'Tis said they all lived happily ever after.

"Now, I'm warning you all—and especially you, Jeanne and Don—from now on whenever you eat strawberries, you'll remember my story and know again that the only thing sweeter than the taste of strawberries is human love. And you ask yourself is there someone waiting now for me to catch up. Or should I wait for someone who is trying to catch up with me.

"Sure, isn't that what this sacrament we celebrate today is all about!"

They were all smiling at the end. I resolved that at the banquet I'd give Jamie and Gayle Ross full credit.

After the final blessing, the new husband and wife turned to walk down the aisle and out into a bright false-spring morning and the rest of their life. The congregation broke into spontaneous applause. My New Priest, Patti O'Hara, and the ever-faithful Patrick had engineered the applause, of that I was sure. Jeanne paused on the top step of the altar, surprised and shaken by the cheers.

Then, perhaps remembering Cook's victory sign at the airport, she smiled and raised her bridal bouquet over her head in a gesture of triumph. She held it there while they cheered again.

The kids chanted "Jeannie! Jeannie! Jeannie!"

She flushed and leaned on her husband's arm as she walked down the aisle. The trumpets Dr. Ronzini had provided blazed their own hymn of glory.

She was not passive after that. Abandoned might be a better description, particularly when, before the cutting of the cake, the waiters brought in the dishes of strawberries for which the New Priest had arranged.

She insisted on dancing with me after the cutting of the cake at the club.

"Wow!" I said, as she drew me close.

"You mean my dress."

"What else?"

Bare shoulders and more than a hint of firm breast.

"The kids insisted that I look really bitchin'."

"I could think of several other words."

"Like?" She looked up in challenge.

"Well what about an adverb and an adjective?"

"Like?" She teased me with her eyes.

"Like gloriously seductive!"

"LAR!"

"You asked."

"This day is really a proof of what the Church is, isn't it?"

"How so?"

Theology might distract me from her scent and her warmth and the smooth skin of her back beneath my fingers. Not very likely, though.

"I came here three years ago as a sick and frigid bitch who had never lasted at another parish for more than two years. Now, I'm a happy bride, with a touch of wanton in me. The parish did it all. You, you especially, and Jamie and the kids and everyone."

"Our privilege."

"That's the real Church, the people at the Wedding Mass and the wedding banquet, not those people downtown that you fight all the time."

"I guess."

With her breasts, maybe a quarter uncovered, pressed against my chest, I couldn't dispute her theology. It was perfectly correct theology, however, under any circumstances.

"You wouldn't be you, with your tremendous passion for fairness, unless you fought them, would you?"

"I guess not."

"You're the real revolutionary, Father Old Priest. I was only a second-rate imitation."

The dance was winding down.

"Would I offend you, Jeannie, if I said that I envy your husband his prize?"

For a moment I held her very close. She leaned against me. For a few seconds that were an eternity she was mine and I was hers.

Then she laughed merrily, "I'd be offended if you didn't." The music stopped, and she patted my arm. "Thanks for everything, Lar. Everything."

I was still holding my breath about the marriage we were celebrating. Nonetheless, if she worked hard with Margaret Ward Keenan, the marriage part of her rebirth might be relatively easy.

If Doctor Keenan's son, on whose head the principal credit or blame for this day must ultimately rest, had any of the bittersweet emotions that I felt, he certainly didn't show it.

"Congratulations, Boss!" he exulted as he shook my hand, after we had waved good-bye to the married couple on their way to somewhere where it was not merely false spring. "You really pulled this one off!"

I just laughed.

I picked up the new virus at the wedding banquet.

I was feeling woozy when I called my adviser that night.

"Poor Lar, did a mean old man steal one of your women away from you?"

"That's not it."

"Sure it is. Don't worry. She'll always be part of your harem. Like I am."

"Maybe."

By which I meant that I was too sick to argue.

"You go to bed and enjoy a good night's sleep. You sound like you're sick again."

"I'm fine."

So fine that I didn't hear the alarm the next morning. When Mike Quinlan came to haul me out with the news that the seven-thirty Mass crowd was waiting for me, I couldn't stir out of bed.

Mike took the Mass and told the congregation that the pastor had a fever. That brought Dr. LaFarge, the rectory M.D., to my room at 8:30.

"Flu, Lar. Bad. The bug—"

"—that's going around. . . ."

"Fever for four or five days. Another week of weakness. Three or four weeks after that to recover your full strength."

"It's Lent, Doc!"

"Tell that to God. He invented the virus, not I. Don't leave your room till the fever ends. Drink lots of liquids—"

"And get lots of sleep. Yeah, I know."

"You won't have much choice about the sleep."

He was right. I had glorious, if confused, dreams. About women, what else? Unfortunately, I was too sick to enjoy them.

They took care of me like I was a Renaissance prince, everything but the peeled grapes. Cook kept me supplied with tea and "biscuits" every hour. The New Priest appeared several times a day to recount parish stories to cheer me up. The porter persons sent up rock-hard chocolate chip cookies they had baked and flowers.

Sister Cunnegunda told the school children that they would pray for the pastor's "speedy recovery."

"Or the grace of a happy death?"

"That might have been implied."

I did not, however, feel much like laughing.

One day Brigid sailed in with green-colored biscuits to accompany her strong (very strong) brew of Bewley's tea.

"What's the green for, Biddy?"

"Sure, isn't Your Reverence a terrible sick man and himself not knowing that today is Paddy's day."

"Is it now?" I sipped the tea. Brigid felt that tea was too strong if the spoon bent when she put it in.

" 'Tis." Loud West-of-Ireland sigh. "And wasn't the parish after having a wonderful dance last night?"

"You never went, did you?"

"I did so and with ever so nice a young man and himself from the county Mayo at that."

"Did he bring his wolfhound?"

"Ah, isn't Your Reverence still delirious?"

If a man whose parents came from the county Kerry doesn't remember Paddy's day, he certainly is in a bad way.

Although I was sick, my mind kept churning; so much violence, so much anger, so much hatred. I'd been here too lo worked too hard, tried to do too much myself, didn't advantage of the relief a hardworking curate had offer summer vacations in five years. One winter vacation. A games in the summer. Running to stay in condition I enfun or relaxation in that. No fun at all. Work, wor modern joyed the work, but I'd had it with being a past Another suburban parish. I needed time off, a long ti early. If sabbatical. I was entitled to one next year. I'

they didn't give it to me, I'd take it anyho

In my present condition I wasn't any good to anyone, including myself.

When the fever finally gave up on me after a week and let me go, I was still weak and depressed, and firm in my resolve.

I needed time to think about my plan and pray over it. Still unsteady on my feet, I called the Trappist abbot at New Mellary Abbey out in Iowa. Was there room in his guest house for a priest on Passion Sunday weekend?

"We call it First Sunday in Passiontide, Father. The Sunday after is Second Sunday in Passiontide."

"Father Abbot, Palm Sunday is still Palm Sunday, no matter what the liturgists say."

He chuckled, the way only abbots can chuckle. "I quite agree, Father. We'll be glad to have you anytime."

I asked Jamie whether he could handle the second-to-last weekend in Lent without me.

"No problem." He waved his hand. "You're flying back to Barbados?"

"No."

"Arizona is wonderful in late March."

"No way. New Mellary."

"A monastery?"

"Don't you believe in them?"

"Not for a vacation after you've been sick."

"It's not a vacation, Jamie. It's a retreat. I have to put my ꭎl back in order."

ꞌI don't accept the distinction. Wouldn't it be better to re-ꞏ ꞏur battered body first?"

aw ꞏied that in Barbados, and it didn't work. Keep the world ꞏn't tell anyone where I am."

not ꞏtill in the depths of postinfluenza depression and I wa꜠ clearly. Nonetheless, I had convinced myself that I ꞏ

ꞏ my adviser about the weekend retreat with the

Trappists. She would no more approve than would the New Priest.

Although it wasn't quite spring in the barren fields of Iowa, winter was over. I fell quickly into the rhythm of the Benedictine Rule and settled down to peace.

This was what I wanted. Perhaps not a Trappist vocation, but surely peace and solitude. I would write a brief letter when I returned to apply for an early sabbatical. They would grant it eventually on the condition that I would turn the parish over to an administrator when I left. It wouldn't be Jamie. Too young, don't you know? Still a bit imprudent.

When the sabbatical was over, they would ask me to take another parish, since the administrator had done so well. By then I wouldn't want to be a pastor anywhere.

Hard on Saint Finian's? They would have to learn to do without me anyway. No one lived forever.

Hard on the New Priest? They had surely marked him for further studies and higher office anyway, had they not?

I wrote the letter out in longhand on Passion Sunday afternoon. The next morning, relaxed and at peace with myself and the world and satisfied with my decision, I drove back to Forest Springs from Iowa.

The sky turned cloudy on the drive back and the temperature dropped. The weather forecasts on the radio predicted snow flurries with accumulation. Winter was back, cruel old grandparent who refused to die.

The rectory was strangely silent when I drove up behind it. Somehow grim and cold.

Mrs. Clarke wasn't at her desk.

I walked up to my parlor. I no sooner was inside the door when the phone rang.

"They knew I was coming." I permitted myself more of the self-pity I had so lovingly developed at the monastery. "Never a moment's peace."

No one answered the phone, so I picked it up.

"Saint Finian's. Father McAuliffe."

"Joe Simon. Where the hell you been?"

"On retreat and what's it to you?"

Back so soon and already violent.

"We've been looking for you."

"I told Jamie not to tell anyone where I was."

"Yeah, well, Jamie is the problem right now. The big problem."

My stomach turned uneasily.

"What kind of problem?"

"Morals charge. Playing around with little boys. We have witnesses. Open-and-shut case. He's finished in the priesthood. And you're probably finished as a pastor."

CHAPTER

51

I could not speak.

"Are you sure?" I finally managed.

"Certainly we're sure. The Cardinal is terribly upset. We're in a bad enough financial bind as it is without something like this. The Cardinal wants to settle it quickly to avoid more scandal than that young punk has already given. He's having a meeting down here tomorrow afternoon at three. You'd better be there if you know what's good for you. You're already up shit creek without a paddle."

"Highly original metaphor, Joe."

I was beginning to recover my powers of expression.

I glanced at the headline in the morning paper, and continued reading:

PRIEST, JUDGE'S SON,
PLEADS NOT GUILTY
ON MORALS CHARGE

Reverend James Keenan, 25, son of retired federal judge Jeremiah Keenan, pleaded not guilty in Cook County Suburban Court in Yorkville Center to charges of sexually molesting an altar boy. The alleged victim is an altar boy at Saint Finian's parish in Forest Springs, where Reverend Keenan is stationed as a Roman Catholic priest.

Charges were brought by George Wholey of the parish, who has said that his son Anthony, 13, was sexually molested by Reverend Keenan during an altar boy picnic last week at Great America.

Reverend Keenan, whose mother is Doctor Margaret Ward Keenan, past president of the American Psychological Association, refused comment to the press. His father told reporters that he is confident of his son's innocence.

"They have no evidence," Judge Keenan said, "to present a case. We're already filing a twenty-million-dollar slander suit against Mr. Wholey. When the charges against my son are dismissed, we will also sue him and the Forest Springs police department for false arrest."

Reverend Keenan's uncle, Monsignor Patrick M. Keenan is pastor of Holy Angels parish in Lake Grove. Monsignor Keenan was unavailable for comment.

Sister Faith Schultz, spokesperson for the Chicago Chancery, said that the Cardinal cannot and will not tolerate such behavior by his priests.

"Father Keenan," Sister Schultz said, "is as liable to prosecution for a felony offense as anyone else."

There was a lot more background information about the Keenan clan.

A wonderfully juicy scandal for the Chicago media.

I looked up. Mike stood in the doorway.

"Dear God, I'm sorry, Lar. If you were here, you might have stopped them. . . . Jamie wouldn't tell me where you were."

"New Mellary," I said automatically. "I'm dazed, paralyzed."

"I don't blame you. They came just like the Gestapo, in the middle of the night. Wayne Rogers and a young flunky. They took him off to Saint Charles Borromeo on the north side of the city. They found him a lawyer and tried to talk him into leaving for the funny farm down in Baltimore. Then the Chicago police showed up on a warrant from the locals and arrested him. His parents took over then. He's home with them waiting trial."

"Did Jamie protest when they took him?"

"He went quietly, politely. You know what he's like."

"Billy Budd?"

"Billy Budd. I made videotapes of what was on TV. It's awful."

It was worse than awful: George Wholey attacking Jamie and the archdiocese; Jamie being dragged out of Saint Charles in shackles; Jamie being arraigned; Anthony Wholey saying, "He did bad things to me"; Maggie looking wretched; Jerry red-faced and furious as the TV journalists shoved microphones at him and Maggie; Mick Whealan, the lawyer the Keenans had hired for Jamie, suavely denying all charges.

"We certainly have slander and false arrests complaints to make. Probably conspiracy, too."

The Keenans would fight back to protect their own, no doubt about that.

So that was the tragic flaw of my Mary Poppins of a new priest? Dear God, I would never have dreamed it.

More television pictures: the parish church, kids coming out of school, reporters trying to trick them into saying something, fierce "no comment"s from the kids—they watched the news, too. Jill Wholey in tears. Several reporters asserting that Father Laurence McAuliffe (my ordination picture on screen), the pastor of Saint Finian's, was out of town and unavailable for comment.

The inference was that I had skipped to avoid the heat.

I carefully read the newspaper accounts that Mike had clipped for me. It was not clear that there was any testimony from the other ten boys on the picnic to Great America.

George Wholey again, "He's been chasing my poor little guy for months. Anthony didn't know what he wanted."

I stared out the window at the flat, dark sky for a long time. A long, long time. I shouldn't have gone off to the monastery without telling someone else.

What could I have done?

The house phone buzzed. "Lar? Jeanne. Would you come downstairs for a moment?"

"Sure."

She was wearing a flowery spring dress. Her skin was tan. She seemed happy, despite her irritation.

"Good honeymoon?"

"Wonderful. . . . Then I come home yesterday to this idiocy about Jamie."

"Idiocy?"

"He's innocent, Lar, as I'm sure you agree. There's nothing wrong with being gay, but on the face of it, the suggestion that Jamie might be gay is absurd."

"Joe Simon says they have witnesses."

"The only witness is Anthony Wholey. All the other mass servers say that he and Jamie were never alone."

"He should have brought the girl servers too."

"In these days, yes. Innocent that he is, Jamie didn't want to bring them without me or Linda along. I was on my honeymoon and Linda was shopping for her bridal gown. Poor dumb Jamie."

"The other kids say nothing happened?"

"More than that. . . . Jackie?"

Our porter person galloped into the office, a listless and dispirited Norah trailing behind. "Yes, Jeanne?"

"Tell Father what the kids tell you about Anthony Wholey?"

"WELL"—her eyes were round with excitement and outrage—"a lot of the kids my age have brothers in eighth grade and they say, 'What's wrong with this Wholey geek,' and the brothers say, 'His father made him do it,' and they say, 'He admitted that to us,' and they go, 'We go, "We'll beat it out of you," and he goes, "My mother won't let me go to school anymore."'" She paused for dramatic effect. "Father New Priest was framed, Father Lar!"

It began to look like it. God forgive me, I had assumed that he was guilty.

"Thanks, Jackie," I said automatically. Norah buried her head in my lap and looked up at me with sad eyes. Poor pooch was a member of the most intelligent breed of dogs in the world, but she couldn't figure out what we humans were doing to one another now.

Jackie bounded out to leave Jeanne and me to our plots and schemes.

"We should—"

I raised my hand. "My mind has been rotting in a monastery for four days, Jeanne. Give me a chance to screw it back on right."

I patted Norah's enormous head while I thought.

Why had I suspected him? Because Joe Simon had said "witnesses." He meant Anthony. *Witness*, singular. And unreliable. Likely to break down in court, too, in face of testimony from the other kids. It would be messy. No matter what happened, Jamie's reputation would be in tatters. There must be a better way.

I thought and thought. Oh, yes, there was a better way, all right. More anger and violence and hatred and pain. Right after I had forsworn all of that at the monastery.

Well, there was no help for it. They had started it. I would finish it. I would finish it in spades.

Three o'clock tomorrow afternoon? That should give us plenty of time.

I surfaced from my reverie and dismissed the hound of

heaven. "Call your husband, Jeannie. The three of us have a job to do tomorrow morning."

The wolfhound jumped enthusiastically. She knew that the action was about to begin. Dear God in heaven, was it!

"It'll save Jamie?" She looked so pretty when she was worried.

"You'd better believe. Now, excuse me, I want to talk to the Keenans."

"Dr. Keenan." Maggie seemed quite in control of her emotions.

"Mag? Lar. I've been away."

"That's what Jamie said. He wouldn't tell us where you were."

"Typical. How is he?"

"Jamie? Oh, he's fine. Nothing worries him much. I collected his computer yesterday, and he's working on the bulletin for next Sunday when he's not playing golf at Oak Park Country Club."

"What's the picture?"

"Well, as I hardly need tell you, Jamie is neither gay nor pederast. It's all in the Wholey kid's mind—and his father's. The criminal charges will collapse. The Assistant State's Attorney on the case has already talked to the other boys, and she admitted to Jerry that she has no case at all. She doubts that the alleged molestation ever happened. She's Jewish, thank God, and hence likely to be easier on a priest than one of our own. Jamie's done a lie detector test, and there's no support for the charges. Wholey refuses to let his son take a test. That'll be leaked on the five o'clock news tonight."

"The State's Attorney will drop the charges?"

"Almost certainly. Then we ask for a summary judgment on the civil charges, too. In the meantime, Mick Whealan says we have several strong civil complaints of our own."

"So it looks good?"

"We're worried about his reputation, Lar." Her smooth voice broke for a fraction of a second. "Naturally, he wants to remain a priest. Naturally, he doesn't want to fight. I told you we had raised an innocent."

"What did Simon tell you?"

"That because of the scandal it would be impossible for Jamie ever to be a priest in Chicago again, even if the charges were dropped. He adds that if we make a settlement now and pull the story out of the media, the Cardinal will make an arrangement for him somewhere else."

The bastards! Even if he is innocent, give him the heave-ho!

"Does Jamie want that?"

"He'd be happy to have it all go away, even if it's the end of him in Chicago. His only fear is letting you down."

Her voice cracked again.

"Letting me down?"

"The other side wants you replaced as pastor."

"So I heard. . . . Simon invited you and Jerry to this conference at the Chancery tomorrow afternoon?"

"Yes." She was crying now. "We wanted to bring Packy. Father Simon forbade it."

"He's afraid that Pack will throttle him."

"I guess." She laughed through her tears. "He might just do that."

How could Joe Simon be so stupid to risk letting me into their star chamber room again? Probably wanted to win a home game against me. Dummy!

"Now listen to me, Margaret Ward Keenan. We'll win tomorrow afternoon. I won't tell you yet why. You don't want to know. Believe me, we'll win. This I promise you: Jamie will be back with us at Saint Finian's for Palm Sunday."

We'll blow those blockbusters a mile high!

God forgive me for it—I was beginning to enjoy myself.

I ambled down to Mike Quinlan's room.

"This year"—I jabbed my finger at him—"they don't hang Billy Budd; they don't burn Joan of Arc; and they don't crucify Jesus of Nazareth."

CHAPTER

52

The job we did in the morning took longer than I had planned.

When we had finished, I called Packy.

"Pack? Lar. You coming to the auto-da-fé this afternoon?"

"You bet! Asshole Simon warned me off, so naturally I'm coming."

"Don't bother. We'll win."

"What makes you think that?"

I told him.

He was silent for a moment.

"I'm glad you're on my side, Lar," he murmured softly, "real glad."

"Per Omnia Saecula Saeculorum."

"Amen." He agreed fervently. "Don't get too close to the explosives when you push the plunger."

"I've learned one or two things in twenty-five years."

I was late at the Chancery.

The Keenans were waiting in the antechamber. Sure, the usual technique. Make people fret so they'll lose their cool.

Two of the finest Catholics in the archdiocese, and Joe Simon was treating them like shit.

Both Maggie and Jerry, however, were in full possession of

their anger. A lot more wit than fat Joe Simon possessed would be necessary to shake them.

She hugged me. He shook hands.

"Where's Mick Whealan?"

"Father Simon said not to bring him."

"I bet the other side has lawyers in there now."

"They're talking?" Maggie's eyes opened wide. "Without us?"

"Bet on it. . . . Don't worry, the day is ours!"

Before I could explain or show them the document in my inside suit pocket, John Price appeared from the conference room.

"Ah, Father McAuliffe, you're a bit late."

"No, John," I said, "I'm on time. I know all about the wait to shake up the victim."

He lowered his eyes. John still didn't like what was happening.

"Would you come in now, Mr. and Mrs. Keenan, Father?"

"Judge and Dr. Keenan, if you don't mind, John."

My retreat-born good intentions long since forgotten, I was just warming up.

"Of course, Father." He turned red. "I'm sorry, Judge and Doctor."

Maggie cocked an eyebrow at me and grinned. She now believed that I was indeed holding the ace of spades.

All the aces, in fact, and all the kings, too.

They were all inside waiting for us.

Joe Simon, fat, bald, and florid, was sitting in the middle of the conference table, in the Cardinal's usual place. On his left, a skinny and ashen layman—Bill Hanratty, the Chancery's legal counsel—slouched. On the other side, my old friend, Father Louis Almaviva was contentedly smoking a cigarette.

Joe Wholey, looking uncomfortable in a three-piece navy blue suit that didn't quite fit him, was kneading his hands back and forth and glowering ominously at one end of the table. One of his crowd, a third-rate lawyer from Yorkville, sat next to him, clutching a stack of legal documents.

At the other end were the Lord Inquisitors—Wayne Rogers, Dolph Santini, and the young Hispanic auxiliary who looked like he wanted to bolt.

As usual, John Price sat at the far end with his open note-book.

No need for a Sony this time.

"Come in, sit down, Father McAuliffe, Mr. and Mrs. Keenan," Joe said in a voice that pretended to be cordial.

"The correct titles, Joey"—I leaned back in my chair and relaxed—are "Dr. and Judge Keenan. Or Judge and Dr. Keenan."

They had carefully arranged the table so the three of us— the defendants—were outnumbered and almost surrounded.

Joe turned scarlet and gave me a look that said "you'll never learn, will you, bastard!"

"I'm sorry," he murmured ungraciously, "Judge and Mrs., ah, Dr. Keenan."

"One more thing, Joe." I smiled genially. "Would you ask Father Aquavelvet to put out his cigarette? It's not healthy for the rest of us."

"Almaviva!" Father Louis snapped as he extinguished his cigarette.

"Sorry," I said. "I confused it with the opera."

"We're here for serious discussions, Father," Joe said sternly.

"I understand, Joe."

At that point Joe should have suspected that I was arrogantly confident because I held the high cards. If he had called a recess to find out why, I would have shown him the document and saved him a lot of intense embarrassment.

He missed the cues. I sat back to listen till it became my turn.

I reflected that I was glad the archdiocese's legal officer was there. He'd see the implications that Joe might miss.

"Now." Joe rearranged the pile of papers in front of him and pulled on his French cuffs—they were all wearing French cuffs because the Cardinal does. "Let me make clear that this is an informal discussion. The Cardinal has asked me to convoke it to see if we can arrive at a solution that will satisfy all the parties and at the same time avoid scandal, which does incalculable harm to the Church and the poor simple faithful. I'm sure we all want to avoid that, don't we?"

He glanced around the table. I smiled pleasantly back at him when his eyes flicked across my face.

"The Cardinal wants me to emphasize to everyone the importance of avoiding scandal. The media are outside on Ontario Street waiting for us. Should we announce a settlement, one which was sensitive to the injuries done to the Wholey family as well as to our concerns about Father Keenan's future in the priesthood, it would put an end to scandal and make the Cardinal very happy."

Again he glanced around the room. I put on my solemn-high face, impassive and unreadable. I must contain my good spirits, lest I ruin it all.

"Very well, then. Mr. Wholey has asked Father Louis to speak for him because he himself is not an accomplished public speaker."

"Thank you very much, Father." He bowed at Joe and tugged on his French cuffs. "I speak for myself and for the Wholey family when I say that we are most desirous of avoiding the grave danger of even more scandal to devout souls than has already been caused by this most, most unfortunate incident."

I stared at him like I was Mike Ditka staring at Jim McMahon.

"We are prepared, for the good of the Church, to drop all

charges, criminal and civil. We ask the archdiocese to make a token payment of a hundred thousand dollars to the Wholey family to cover part of the cost of the medical treatment our poor little Anthony will need. Beyond that, we seek nothing for ourselves. However, we understand that Father McAuliffe will be relieved as pastor at Saint Finian's and Father Keenan, after suitable reflection in an appropriate house of prayer, will be translated to another diocese and given work where he will not be subject to this heinous temptation again."

That was the deal that Joe had already cut, a reasonable and sensible deal if Jamie were guilty. Joe had doubtless persuaded himself of that guilt. If you were charged, then you were guilty.

In the Catholic Church anyway.

"That seems to me, Father Louis"—Joe tugged on his cuffs again—"to be a very reasonable and generous offer. I think I may say that the Cardinal would find it quite acceptable."

"It would certainly contain the scandal," Wayne Rogers agreed piously. "And protect the faithful."

Contain was one of the Cardinal's favorite words.

"Mr. Keenan, ah, I mean Judge Keenan?"

The judge glanced at me and began. As usual with a skillful lawyer, he was slow and indirect at the beginning.

"Thank you, Monsignor," he promoted Joey, "I'm grateful for this opportunity to reason sensibly. In my many years on the bench I have often had occasion to say that there are few problems that litigants can't solve long before they come into a courtroom."

He waited for this cliché to sink in.

"I must note for the record that I see is being taken by Father Price that Dr. Keenan and I were told not to bring a lawyer to this conference. I observe, however, that both the archdiocese and Mr. Wholey are accompanied by counsel."

He paused again.

Joe Simon did not speak. Somehow he had persuaded himself that two of the most famous and distinguished Catholics in the archdiocese of Chicago were not all that important.

"In absence of response to that remark of mine, I shall continue.

"It is of no concern to us as parents what payment the Cardinal in his wisdom might want to make to the plantiff's family. As regular Sunday churchgoers and contributors, we might have a few questions about such an expenditure. However, I deem it inappropriate to raise such issues at the present time."

Joe Simon tugged at his cuffs again.

"I'm delighted to learn that plaintiff is prepared to drop his charges, criminal and civil." Jerry Keenan folded his big hands comfortably, hands which had once skillfully held the stick of a Grumman F6F Hellcat. "I might say that I think such a decision is prudent. Should a satisfactory solution to this troubling matter be concluded, I feel quite confident that we would withdraw the various complaints that we have filed already or are contemplating. It might be appropriate to remark here that I was assured only two hours ago by the Assistant State's Attorney in charge of this matter that she can find no grounds for not voiding the charges against Father Keenan. So his good name is already vindicated. I take it that other counsel here present understand that there is little chance under such circumstances that the civil action against him—or for that matter, against the Church or against Father Laurence McAuliffe— would prevail in the face of a motion for summary judgment. As I say, dropping the charges is, on the whole, a prudent decision for plaintiff."

He paused once more. Joe Simon was straining to understand. A faint smile crossed John Price's face. He *did* understand. Father Louis glowered ominously. He did not like Jerry Keenan's assumption of a judicial role. Bill Hanratty squirmed nervously. Unlike the Vicar General and Moderator of the

Curia (to give Joe Simon his full title), he knew that it was dangerous to underestimate Jerry Keenan.

"Nonetheless, we are, I think, very close to a happy solution. There is but one point of difference I see between the two sides. Well, perhaps there is a second one, but I cannot speak to that."

"What is that point?" Joe demanded impatiently, glancing at his wristwatch.

John Price rolled his eyes.

"That point is our son's reputation. Under no circumstances will we accept a settlement that implies in any way that he is anything but innocent of the charges. The second point—as I say, perhaps only indirectly our concern—we will put no pressure on Father McAuliffe to step down from his pastorate." He paused again, licked his lips for dramatic effect and continued. "As a point of fact, I should be afraid to do so. Having witnessed the intense loyalty that exists in that parish, I would be very much afraid that my house would be surrounded by chanting teenagers, some of whom are almost the size of defensive linemen for the Chicago Bears."

The F6F roared off the flight deck.

Maggie was grinning proudly. How many times in their years together had she seen her man pull that kind of stunt.

Not only John Price but the auxiliary Bishop did not bother to hide their smiles. The Bishop even laughed. He was promptly silenced by a glare from Joe Simon. Thus for the power of an auxiliary in Chicago "at the present time."

"They are both guilty," Father Louis responded venomously. "They both must be punished."

He probably believed it, too. No question about his good faith or Joe's. They were what we would have called in the seminary "culpably ignorant": they should have known better but they didn't.

"That's simply not possible, Mr. Keenan." Joe spread his

hands on the table just as the Boss did when he was trying to soothe things over. "The Cardinal has set his face against Father Keenan's continued presence in this archdiocese at the present time."

Always that little cop-out line at the end. What did it mean? They said it so often that it meant nothing.

Jerry Keenan considered Joe Simon very carefully.

"I would regret, Monsignor Simon, to find myself faced with the necessity of requesting a subpoena for the Cardinal to defend my son's reputation. Let me assure you, however—and I may flatter myself that your counsel will tell you I do not make threats lightly—that if it be necessary to call the Cardinal to a deposition or to a courtroom or even to name him as a defendant in a civil complaint to protect my son's reputation, I would not hesitate to do so, with however much regret."

Bared fangs, a naked sword.

Fifty-millimeter machine guns were raking the Zero with the Rising Sun on its wings.

"I can't believe you'd do that, Mr. Keenan," Wayne Rogers intervened. "Think of all the harm you'd do to the Church."

"I'm cognizant of that, Father. However, if I may, you don't have a son and I do. You don't understand the raw primal emotion in our species that requires of us that we protect our young. You say you do not believe me, Father. Let me reassure you on that matter: you had better believe me."

Joe squirmed again and tugged once more at his French cuffs. Then he glanced at his watch.

"We don't seem to be making much progress. I wonder, Mr. Keenan, if I might ask you to reconsider. Is there no give, no bend in your position?"

"None whatever."

I decided that the time had come to end the charade. Now was the appropriate hour for the cavalry to ride over the hill.

"I wonder," I said in my most humble and self-effacing

voice, "if I might say a word which might ease the dilemma in which we seem to find ourselves."

"We don't really need your input," Joe barked.

Power, raw naked power. Assumed and misused.

And dumb.

"I should think that as someone who is a defendant in the suit and whose pastorate is being bandied about—"

"*No!* I said *no!*"

"Well, there are always the reporters outside."

Bill Hanratty, the lean lawyer for the Church, whispered in Joe's ear. Joe frowned and shook his head. The lawyer whispered again.

I caught John Price watching me and winked. He turned away to hide his smile.

"Very well, Father McAuliffe," Joe said reluctantly. "We can give you a few minutes." He glanced at his watch. "Please make it brief."

"I shall try to do so, Father Simon. I should like to suggest a third alternative as a solution. I'm sure the various attorneys here can word it legally. It consists of the following points:

"One, all charges against Father Keenan are dropped.

"Two, Mr. Wholey reads a public apology to the mass media exonerating Father Keenan of all charges against him.

"Three, Mr. Wholey makes a payment of two hundred and fifty thousand dollars to the Inner City School Fund of the archdiocese in return for which the Keenans drop civil action against him.

"Four, Father Keenan is restored as a priest in good standing in the archdiocese.

"As to the question of my departure from Saint Finian's, I think under the circumstances that issue is rather beside the point. I will at least forsake all claim on Father Simon's job when the Cardinal finds out how badly he has bungled this matter."

Jerry Keenan laughed. His wife grinned broadly. John Price

stared at me in disbelief. Joe Simon's mouth hung open. Wayne Rogers and Dolph Santini frowned as they tried to figure out what was happening.

"This man is outrageous." Father Louis jumped to his feet. "Expel him from the chamber."

George was on his feet, too, face purple, hands clenched. "What the hell you trying to pull?" He advanced toward me.

"Careful, George, the last time you tried to slug me, Father Keenan was around to protect you. He's not here this time."

"Shut up, all of you!" Joe Simon bellowed.

His counsel, wiser than he, leaned toward me, "Might I ask, Father, why you believe this solution is likely to be embraced?"

"Sure, Mr. Hanratty. First, because it is just. You must understand, even if Father Simon does not—and incidentally, Judge, you anticipated the wishes of the Holy See by promoting him to the sacred purple of the Monsignorate—that the State's Attorney's decision not to seek a trial for Father Keenan is prima facie evidence of his innocence. No one in this room wants the reputation of an innocent man to be ruined, do they? Not even for the good of the Church?"

"Second?" Bill Hanratty was watching me intently. I might be even more dangerous than Jerry Keenan.

"Second, I have a deposition that was taken this morning which I think settles the issue conclusively. With your permission, I will read it."

"This is unnecessary," Father Louis was screeching like a wounded Chihuahua. "They are guilty! Punish them!"

"That's not the way we do it in this country, Father," I fired back at him, "not even in your country since the end of the Falange."

"Your behavior," Joe Simon was purple with rage, "is outrageous."

"Counselor, should I read it?"

The lawyer turned to Simon. "We'd better permit it, Father.

I won't be responsible for what happens if we don't. As I told you before this meeting, we are not dealing with fools."

"Thank you, Mr. Hanratty."—I smiled urbanely—"for the compliment."

"No!"

"I don't see why!" Wayne Rogers agreed.

"Perhaps—" the auxiliary Bishop began.

"I said *no!*"

"All right." I rose. "I'll stroll outside and read it to the media. You'd better activate Sister Faith, Joe, so she can recite her usual something that means nothing."

The word "media" cut through Joe's Teutonic blubber like a bolt from a crossbow.

"All right, all right. Sit down everyone. I suppose we have to listen."

He should have called for an adjournment to find out what was in the deposition. A smart lawyer would. Joe was neither a lawyer nor smart.

"This is a true copy of a deposition, given under oath and recorded in the presence of Ms. Mary Catherine Hughes, a notary public. The deposing lawyer is Mr. Donald Lyons, who is acting for me and for Saint Finian's parish. The deponent is Ms. Jill Wholey."

I fully expected George to come after me. There was no one in the room, with the possible exception of my New Priest's father, who would pull him off. It's bye-bye land for you, George, if you try it.

This was more fun than blowing up Mile Hi. The guilts would come later.

George did not come after me. Instead, he slumped down on the table, his head in his hands.

"Father Simon," Father Louis interjected, "stop this charade!"

"Let him make a fool out of himself." Joe stared at me with contempt.

"Incidentally, Bishop, Reverend Fathers, distinguished representatives of the bar, gentlepersons, I have a fifth condition: you get that sumbitch"—I gestured at Father Louis—"out of town and keep him out."

Joe Simon laughed sardonically.

"I'll now read the deposition.

" 'L. You understand the nature of an oath, Ms. Wholey?

" 'W. Yes, I do.

" 'L. You are testifying freely.

" 'W. Yes I am.

" 'L. May I ask why?

" 'W. My husband, poor man, is destroying our family. He has driven away my boy Sonny and my daughter Michele. Now he's ruining poor little Anthony.

" 'L. I see. Why is he doing this, Ms. Wholey?

" 'W. Because that demon of a priest is making him.

" 'L. What priest do you mean, Ms. Wholey?

" 'W. Father Louis.

" 'L. Is that his full name?

" 'W. Louis Almaviva is his full name. He belongs to some kind of foreign secret society.

" 'L. I see. He is close to your husband.

" 'W. He runs our lives. And ruins them, too. He is the one who urged George to beat poor Michele and me. We used to be happy before he came along and ruined everything.

" 'L. He urged your husband to beat you and your daughter.

" 'W. Yes. He said American women were too independent and should be kept in their place.

" 'L. I see. Now what can you tell us about the charges against Father James Keenan?

" 'W. There's not a word of truth in them. Poor George thinks so but only because he wants to think so. And Father Louis made him want to think so. The man is a demon.

" 'L. How do you know this to be true, Ms. Wholey?

" 'W. Poor little Anthony told me so. You see, Father Keenan, who is a wonderful young priest, has been going out of his way to be nice to Anthony because the other kids don't like him. Anthony bragged to George about how the kids were beginning to like him because of Father Keenan. He even made the basketball team. George told that horrid, horrid priest, and *he* planted the idea in George's head that Father Keenan was trying to sexually molest Anthony. George began to work on Anthony to admit it. I don't think the child knows what sexual molestation is.

" 'L. I see. Then what happened?

" 'W. Well, last week Anthony came home from an altar boy picnic up at Great America. He was terribly happy about how much fun they had and the way the other boys seemed to treat him like one of the crowd. Then George really began to work on him. He told him that if he was a real man, he'd tell the truth.

" 'L. That's all right, Ms. Wholey. Take your time. There's no law against weeping under oath.

" 'W. Well, there's nothing that Anthony wants more than for George to think he's a real man. So he finally admitted— George put the words on his lips—that Father Keenan had done "dirty things."

" 'L. Do you know as a fact, Mrs. Wholey, that this alleged assault never happened?

" 'W. Absolutely! Anthony told me that night after the police arrested poor Father Keenan. He's told me every day since. He's tried to tell George and so have I, but George won't listen. That demon priest won't let him.' "

At that point, George Wholey tried to leap across the table to drag the deposition out of my hands.

Instead, he collapsed, unconscious, on the table, a slab of meat stretched out for the butcher.

I thought of the wedding picture in which he looked like Marlon Brando and she looked like a high school homecoming queen.

"Look what you've done now!" Joe Simon bellowed. "You've killed the poor man."

The five-o'clock news showed ambulance attendants carrying George Wholey out of the Chancery office and then delivering him, still unconscious, to the emergency room of Northwestern Hospital, just down Ontario Street.

CHAPTER

53

"He fainted."

"What?"

"That's right," Jerry Keenan said softly. "Nothing wrong with him—heart, lungs, brain, assuming that there is a latter."

"You saw the five-o'clock news?"

"Not to worry, Lar. We won. . . . And am I glad you're a friend."

"But—"

"The ten-o'clock news will carry a report that the hospital says that all George Wholey's vital signs are normal. 'Sources' have suggested that the reason for his 'fainting spell' was that evidence was produced at the Chancery office conference which conclusively proved Father James Keenan's innocence."

"The woman is dangerous."

"Tell me about it. . . . He'll be released tomorrow afternoon and will read a statement that we've prepared for him. The lawyer for the archdiocese will see to that. We have Bill Hanratty scared stiff. Father Louis, you'll be happy to hear, has vanished from sight."

"The contribution money is still part of the settlement?"

"It has to be. That establishes beyond question Jamie's innocence."

"How's he doing?"

"Jamie? Oh, he's asleep now. He played tennis with his sister all afternoon. You've worked him so hard he's a little out of condition. I'll wake him up if you want to talk to him."

"No, let him sleep. He's entitled."

So am I, but not tonight. Or for a good many nights to come.

Dear God in heaven, what had I done to the Wholeys? They were pawns in another man's hands. I have destroyed them, as ruthlessly as if they were annoying bugs.

I called the key people in the parish and told them that we'd won and that they'd have to wait for tomorrow to learn the details.

"Father Jamie will be back, Father?" Patti O'Hara demanded anxiously.

"You bet he will," I assured her.

Then I pondered what I had said. Joe Simon wouldn't be that stupid, would he?

CHAPTER

54

I had underestimated Joe's stupidity.

He called the next day at 5:15, right after the news programs had shown George—looking confused and uncertain—reading through his apology. Jill was by his side holding his hand. George seemed quite contrite.

The anchorwoman concluded the story: "Sister Faith Schultz, spokesperson for the Roman Catholic archdiocese, said that despite the exoneration of Father James Keenan, no decision had been made about his reassignment."

"No decision!" I yelled.

"They're not through with him yet." Mike sighed. "They never give up."

Sure enough, an hour later Jackie buzzed me to say, distaste dripping from her alto voice, "Father Simon on the phone."

"Yeah?"

"Well, I guess that's taken care of, huh, Lar?"

I could hardly believe my ears.

"What's taken care of?"

"The Keenan case. You saw it all on TV?"

"Yes, I did."

"I wanted to talk to you about Jamie's next assignment. I assume you agree that he ought not to return to Saint Finian's?"

"Why ought he not?"

"Well, scandal . . . you know."

"I know of no scandal."

"All the media attention."

"I want him back."

"Can't you bend a little, Lar? You've taken everything. Can't you give us something?"

"No."

"You put us in a difficult position."

"If he doesn't come back, he's not exonerated."

"Sure he is."

"The Keenans won't think so."

"They are of no concern to us."

"They are to me. And, Joe, they could still go after you and the Boss. Look at the Judge's war record if you have any doubt about his courage."

"Well, the Boss has really set his face against Jamie's return. He thinks it will upset the people."

If the Boss had a tragic flaw, it was his desire to be liked by everyone, to keep everyone happy. So to avoid upsetting people, he offended almost everyone.

"Does he want five hundred teenagers milling around his house shouting 'Give us Jamie!'?"

"You wouldn't do that, Lar. Not to the Boss."

"I couldn't stop them if I wanted to."

"We'll cross that bridge when and if we come to it."

"You're a Bourbon, Joe." I sighed. One more fight. Always one more fight. And another night without sleep as my heart thumped and my blood raced and my guilts tormented me.

"Whadaya mean by that?"

"You never learn and you never forget. . . . Listen to what I say and listen very carefully. If you don't promise me that Jamie Keenan will be back here and stay as long as he wants, I will phone a friend at Channel Two News. I will tell them how you and the Cardinal tried to railroad out of the archdiocese a priest of whose innocence there was no reasonable doubt. I guarantee that it will be on the ten-o'clock news and in the morning's papers."

I didn't know anyone at channel 2.

I knew someone who did.

Did I ever.

Silence from Joe as he was trying to assess whether I really meant it.

"Well, I guess we can work it out. . . . Hey, what if he doesn't want to go back to your place?"

"Is the Pope a Mormon?"

55

His Holiness is not a member of the Church of Jesus Christ of the Latter Day Saints. Jamie came home to a hero's welcome—a parade with Norah puffed up as self-assigned grand marshal marching in front of the Saint Ed's drum and bugle corps.

"How was the retreat, Boss?" was his first question as we shook hands, while the kids chanted, "Fa-THER Ja-MIE! Fa-THER Ja-MIE!"

"Weren't you ever worried?"

"A little at first, when Father Rogers dragged me out of bed and when the police arrested me. Then I figured that I was innocent and I had a lot of good people on my side, so it would work out."

"Who on your side?"

"Oh, God, my parents, you. So I didn't have to worry, did I?"

Is Jamie Keenan a Billy Budd or not?

You figure it out.

The Cardinal had apparently apologized to him personally—though what I would consider an apology and what Jamie would consider an apology might be two very different things.

The Boss wrote me a personal, handwritten letter, the usual overworked and now-ineffective ploy. He said nothing in it, as usual: a hope for a reconciliation after an unfortunate breakdown of communications.

I threw it away.

A phone message awaited me when I came back from the Palm Sunday services. "The Cardinal called. Please call him back." On the pink slip was the supposedly private number at his house.

Should I call him and "end the breakdown in communications"?

He was better than most of them and a lot smarter than the nitwits they were making bishops these days.

Moreover, he really did want me to like him. He wanted to be friends with me. He was, in his own way, as sweet and vulnerable as Ron Lane had been. He was a genuinely nice man caught in an unfortunate era when it was necessary sometimes to do bad things for "the good of the Church."

I pondered the pink slip with his number.

What harm was there in responding to his openhanded offer of "reconciliation"?

I tapped the message against my fingers. About what had we fought?

He would have deported Brigid to Ireland when there were legal grounds for her to stay. He would have shipped Jamie out of the archdiocese with a cloud over him that would have lasted all his life.

He would have done both these ugly deeds "for the good of the Church." He would have ruined two lives "to avoid more public scandal"—by which he meant media reports that would attract the attention of his masters in Rome and diminish his clout.

Moreover, if he were to encounter similar situations in the future, he would try to do exactly what he had tried to do to Brigid and Jamie.

Sure, he wanted to be friends. He also wanted a personal relationship with me that would "contain" me—put a little more "bend" in my reactions, to use Joe Simon's creative expression.

I crumpled the pink slip with the phone message and threw it away, too.

The next day, troubled by what was left of my conscience, I sent him a handwritten note, taking a leaf from his own book:

Steve,

I like you; I don't trust you. I wish I could. Maybe someday the Church will change so I can.

Best regards,
Lar

I also threw away, under orders, my letter asking for an early sabbatical.

The orders came from my adviser. She demanded that she buy me lunch, an exceedingly rare event.

"Now," she said over the table at a Thai restaurant just off Michigan Avenue, "I want to talk to your splendid young priest."

"You can't meet him."

"I don't want to *meet* him. I want to talk to him. He knows about me, doesn't he? You couldn't keep me a secret."

All right.

Then she laid down the law—regular medical checkup, exercise every day and not just jogging, three weeks' vacation every summer and every winter, a full day off every week, no more bad language because it simply upset me, golf at least twice a week in the summer, no more drinking—

"Hey, I'm not an alcoholic!"

It did not matter. It was not good for me right now. Maybe later. If I needed medication to sleep, I should ask Dr. LaFarge for a prescription.

I was also to play tennis again. I was good at it, and I could play it inside during the winter.

"Who will I play with?"

"Me. Once a week."

"You?"

"I'll beat you most of the time; that will be good for your humility. I'll be able to check up on you. We'll put you back in good health before we even begin to think of a sabbatical, much less a resignation."

I imagined her long white legs beneath tennis shorts and decided that a weekly look at them was probably worth keeping all the other rules.

Jamie was trying to help the Wholeys "restructure" their marriage.

Figures, doesn't it?

On Holy Saturday morning, before he left to visit them, he stopped by my study, Norah in tow.

"Boss, Marty Regan might show up before I get back. He's made a Grumman F6F he wants to show me."

"Marty Regan?"

"Good kid. Grown a couple of inches in the last few months. I told him my dad flew an F6F and he made one for me."

"Helldiver?"

"Those were dive-bombers. Wings tended to fall off. The F6F was called the Hellcat."

"Ah."

"No, Norah, you stay here with the Boss and keep an eye on him for me."

Obediently the hound of heaven curled up at my feet.

Marty Regan, huh?

One of the reasons I so obediently followed my adviser's orders was that after one year of my New Priest, I wanted to see what he'd do next year for an encore.

There was another encore I wanted to check out, too.

Later Holy Saturday morning, Jennifer rang from the office to tell me that Mrs. Sullivan wanted to see me "if you have time."

"I guess I have time."

Maria was standing in the office, flushed and uncertain. She was wearing a white spring suit and light-blue, turtleneck blouse—perfect for the sunny April day it was. She also seemed even more slender, the muscular leanness of the addicted long-distance runner.

"Hi, Maria, you look more gorgeous than ever."

Her face turned a more dusky red.

"Thank you, Father."

"Sit down, why don't you?"

"At the coffee table instead of the desk? I don't deserve the promotion. I don't deserve even to be in the rectory."

"Don't be silly, Maria. Now sit down."

"Yes, Father."

"What's on your mind?"

She paused, looked away as she searched for words, and then fixed her aquamarine eyes on my face.

"I want to begin by saying how sorry I am. . . . Can this count as a confession, Father? I really need to be reconciled this Holy Saturday."

"Sure."

She lowered her eyes and knelt on the floor—not necessary in the new Church, but it was what she wanted. She had slipped to her knees, gracefully, as she did everything. "Bless me, Father, for I have sinned." Sign of the Cross. "Well, it's been about nine months, and I haven't been to Mass much in the last few months. . . . What I was about to say is that first I am very sorry for insulting you. That was disgraceful. I really am sorry."

"I believe you, Maria."

"And I am so deeply, deeply sorry for what I have done to my husband and children. I hope they forgive me as gently as you do."

"Never a doubt."

"I'm having lunch with him today. My invitation. I will let him tell me what he's been wanting to tell me all these months—if he still cares."

"I'm sure he does."

"I'll understand everything he says, and that will close the last escape hatch. Then I'll try to win back my children. That won't be easy. They're so hostile and with so much reason."

"I'll bet on it."

"Then I'll be my own person, someone I always was but never knew. And maybe start living again. Or—I don't know—maybe living for the first time."

"Wonderful, Maria. I'm so happy for you."

She looked up at me, her eyes glistening.

"Do you want to know what happened?"

"I sure do."

She remained on her knees, this abject but happy penitent.

"We had an awful fight with the divorce lawyers yesterday. Again. On Good Friday. I was a bitch on wheels. I knew it, and I was ashamed of myself. I didn't want to try a reconciliation or anything like that, but I was disgusted with the person I had become. It shows what a snob I am, Father, but I was not only a bitch, but a bitch without class!"

She laughed at herself.

"Anyway, I drove by church. I hadn't been inside it since I was so rude to you. It was Good Friday, so for a reason I can't explain, I went in.

"There were a few elderly people praying—saying the stations. I haven't done that since high school. I still don't know why, but automatically, I guess, I began to say them, too. At first it was an empty gesture. It meant nothing. I kept saying that this one would be the last, but I went on to the next. At the station where Jesus speaks to the women of Jerusalem . . . the sixth, I think it is?"

"I think so, too. . . . No, maybe it's the eighth."

"Anyway, it happened. I don't know *what* happened. Whatever it was, it really happened. I started to cry. The tears poured out. All the grief of my life. I didn't understand why I was grieving, I couldn't help myself. I sobbed and sobbed and sobbed."

I listened and watched, fascinated by the radiant glow on her face.

"The peculiar thing, Father . . . I can't explain it at all . . . is that my grief was joy. I was sobbing with joy. Pain and ecstasy all mixed up, grief and gladness confused, so I couldn't sort anything out. What do you call that, Father Lar?"

"Grace, Maria."

She considered my answer. "As good a name as any. So"—she dabbed at her eyes with a tissue—"here I am on Holy Saturday asking for forgiveness from God and from you, Father."

I gave her absolution, assigned the Our Father for a penance, and helped her to her feet.

"Wish me luck this afternoon, Father." She clung to my hand. "I pray it's not too late. I hope they all come to the Vigil Mass with me this evening."

"They'll be there, Maria, never a doubt."

"Nice doggie"—she patted Norah on the way out—"I was rude to you the last time. I still want one of your puppies."

I decided that her name went to the head of the list for the bitch's first litter.

"Is there sex in heaven, Father?" Maria asked as she turned from Norah to walk to her car.

"There had better be," I replied. "Or something like it that's even better."

Right. And say nothing more.

Just before the Vigil service began, as the church was plunged into darkness, the New Priest whispered in my ear, "The Ferrigan-McKittricks are here. They told me that they've decided to forgive the parish and reconcile themselves with it."

"Do we have a choice?"

"They're sending a letter for *The Bells*."

"Alleluia!"

"I told them that I'd publish it if it was a response to the questions raised by Cupcake Patti."

"And?"

"They said they'd forgive even that demand."

When the lights went on and the New Priest sang the Exultet—the hymn heralding the Resurrection, I noticed the Ferrigan-McKittricks in the first row of the congregation, puffed with virtue as they forgave us everything.

No sign of Ed and Maria Sullivan.

Was my prediction wrong?

I preached about the symbolism of the fire and the water—the story of a God who, despite all good taste and right reason and plain sanity, had fallen in love with his creatures. God's passion for us, I said, first sensed by the Hebrew prophets, is like that of a man and woman falling head over heels in love with one another. The only difference is that God's passion is more violent and more reckless than the strongest of human passions. Easter is an invitation to renew that romance between God and us and to simultaneously renew our romances with one another.

The New Priest nodded in agreement.

I saw Ed and Maria as I swung through the church with a bucket of Easter water and doused everyone with the liquid that had been impregnated with the sacred fire of the Risen Lord.

I made sure to soak all the giggling kids—part of the ritual that everyone, especially the Pastor of Saint Finian's, enjoyed. I was also careful not to miss Norah, who had curled up in the back of church to keep a careful eye on the unusual nighttime ceremonies. She turned her huge head away in disgust.

I favored the Sullivans with a large torrent. Maria and Ed giggled like five-year-olds.

As I had predicted, her family did attend the Vigil, the feast of fire and water, the feast of the union of the male and female in God. At Communion Maria and Ed held each other's hands tightly. The kids beamed contentedly.

Naturally. You don't pull a stunt like that Eighth Station one for nothing—a tidal wave of grace to a woman who wants it, needs it, and is ready for it even if she doesn't realize it. You engulf her with the flaming passion of a lover whose desire for her exceeds anything she can imagine.

All we poor priests do is prepare the way for You. Which is why You employ us.

While You were possessing her—for which I envy You as I envy Don Lyons—You sent an irresistible sign to one of those priests, one who has been wallowing in a hot flood tide of grace since the day his New Priest arrived, and didn't have the sense to comprehend that he had been swept up in the surging current.

It's not only Jamie's encore for which I'm waiting around Saint Finian's.

I want to see Your encore too.